THE GIRL OF ASH AND SNOW

C.M. QUINN

The Girl of Ash and Snow
C.M. Quinn

Editor Kerry Murphy
Cover design by Miblart
Interior design by Breakout Designs

ISBN 978-0-6453153-0-1

To the fighters and the dreamers, never give up, never surrender and take to the skies. The future is yours to claim.

THE GIRL
OF ASH AND
SNOW

Table of Contents

Part 1 ASH

Part 2 SHADOW AND FIRE

Part 3   The City

FENWARE
THE GRAY ARMY
THE TEMPLE
DANOMIR
MIDARAN
TARTH
THE FOREST OF SILENCE
CITY OF SLAVES
GRISK
MIDLAN
KALDEN
THE SEA OF ALOMIRAN
THE MITHRA ARCHIPELAGO
TORANELLE
DESIRELLE

Part 1

ASH

Chapter 1

They soared through the clouds, an obscure mass blackening the sky, yet they triggered no fear. When the people looked up, they rejoiced, for salvation had come

—Excerpt from The Dragonir Chronicles.

THE VILLAGE WAS going to starve, Wren realized as she eyed the bare shelves of the storeroom.

The four boxes of dried and crushed red powder were stacked on the otherwise empty shelves. Years ago, the room had been stocked with crates bursting at the seams. Now, the space seemed wasted, the dwindling haul mocking her failure.

Lost in thought, she didn't notice the door had opened until a figure appeared beside her. Glancing over, caution tightened every muscle.

"Figured I'd find you in here," said Vaughn, his gaze alighting on the sparsely stocked shelves. "I didn't realize how low our supplies were."

"There's less each year," she replied, folding her arms across her chest. After a lengthy silence, she turned to him. "Everyone ready?"

Shadows flickered in his eyes and he paused before saying, "They're ready, but I need to talk to you... and you've not exactly made it easy these past few weeks."

Oh. So that's why he'd come.

Turning around, she headed for the door. "Can we talk about this after the climb?"

His hand shot out, seizing her wrist. "Wren, please—"

"What more is there to discuss?"

"Perhaps *why?*" he pushed. "You gave no reason—"

Weeks of burning feelings and unsaid words swelled up, spilling out.

"And you provided me with every reason," she snapped. "Gods, Vaughn, you didn't even argue with your family when they asked if I would retire after we married. You know how much those cliffs mean to me. Better than anyone else. I told you I wouldn't be grounded after marriage, or did you think I would change my mind once you had a ring on my finger?"

His mouth opened and shut, saying nothing.

All the words that lay between them carved a gulf of silence. Wren couldn't muster another one to her lips. Instead, she pulled her hand free and headed out. This time, he followed without argument.

There was work to be done.

The mountains were determined to kill her.

The wintry wind howled, pinching her cheeks red as she hauled herself up the cliff face. She kept moving, reaching high to grasp familiar holds fastened to the coarse stone. Every shift of her hands and driving push from her legs propelled her up.

Though the sun beat down from a cloudless sky, it gave little warmth. It was too high for that.

The climb today offered scant shelter from the harsh wind. It was not the kind she usually trusted a new team member with. However, these were desperate times. They had already exhausted all their other climbs, and this was the last one they could try before winter hit the village.

All they needed was a decent harvest, or...

Shaking off her grim thoughts, she reached up again as a gust of wind slammed into her side. Her hand slipped.

Shit!

Swallowing the lump in her throat, Wren tightened her grip with her other hand and thrust herself back onto the cliff.

If you freeze, you die. The snarling voice of her teacher shot through her mind.

There was no stopping until Wren reached the top and hauled herself over. Ragged breaths burned as she rolled onto her side. Seizing the moment to breathe with eyes shut, her body slowly calmed down.

You're alive. Get it together, she scolded herself as her eyes flickered open and she sat up.

Wren's gaze drifted to the cliff's edge. A pale hand reached up to grip, followed by another, and she watched as Vaughn hauled himself up. His pale skin was flushed and shimmered faintly from sweat, yet somehow, he was as frustratingly handsome as always.

His tawny eyes regarded her for a moment, worry tightening his face. He dusted the flecks of snow off his furs as he said, "Wren?"

"I'm okay. I merely lost my hold for a moment."

His lips tightened into a thin line. Before he could say more, the huffing breaths of the rest of the team announced their arrival.

First, Flynn, a red-haired, long-limbed climber with a sharp, rigid face that glowed as he hauled himself over. Only his smile and jewel-green eyes softened the hardened planes. As he stepped away from the edge, another climber appeared.

Mira, the smallest, newest, and most unlikely climber of the group stood up. She dusted off her climbing furs, peering about with a doll-like face.

"Is it much further?" she asked.

Wren pushed herself to her feet. "It's close. Are you okay? We can rest here."

Mira shook her head. "No, I'll be fine." A gust of wind surged against them and the youthful climber shivered. "*Gods*, why is it so much colder here? The other harvest points aren't nearly this icy!"

"The higher you climb, the colder it gets," explained Wren. "Hence why we needed to wear thicker uniforms today."

Flynn stepped beside Mira, slinging his arm over her shoulder. He dwarfed her tiny frame, the size difference making Wren smile.

"We're at the bottom of the old country; we're in dragon territory now."

Mira rolled her eyes. "Wyverns, you mean? No one has seen a dragon for hundreds of years. I doubt there's any left."

"Still," persisted Flynn. "You grew up with the stories, just like us. These mountains are the true home of the dragons, just like they're ours. Nothing will change that."

Those green eyes that knew too much looked at Wren, quiet assurance in his gaze. It gave her hope that they'd find a way out of the death sentence facing their home.

"Flynn is right. No matter what, this place is our home," agreed Wren. "Now, that's enough chatter. We have a lot of work to finish before we return."

Turning around, she set off down a narrow path, faintly dusted with snow. The others fell in behind her. The sheer cliff on either side, worn smooth from years of wind and rain, rose so high that light turned gloomy.

Wren could see enough and pushed on, straight up the steps, cut into the rock. At the top, the stone walls on either side fell away, revealing a clearing. It resembled a bowl carved into the mountain itself. Several paths veered off to clearings that led to the remnants of the ancient city far above.

The clearing was divided into fields of dark earth, one of which still held a struggling crop of red flowers. At the far end stood a stone well. Flynn strode over, water skins in hand, and filled them, one by one.

Wren went to the plants and with the other two, plucked the flowers, carefully wrapping and packing them away in their bags. Vaughn hovered by Mira, instructing her on the best way to harvest the flowers without damaging them. When everyone had finished, they sprinkled some dried seaweed, imported from the coast, plus some crumbled chicken manure over the plants, and then gave them a carefully measured amount of water from the filled pouches.

As she stood up, Wren yawned and glanced skywards, holding a hand to her face as the sun slanted down, glinting sharply off the ice that clung to the cliff high above. The cloud obscured the kingdom up there that Wren knew existed, just out of reach, beyond the ability of any climbers. Even hers.

"You've got that look in your eye," remarked Vaughn.

She lowered her gaze to his and smiled. "What look?"

"Wren, if there was anything, it'd only be ruins."

"We might be their descendants."

"And now we're humble farmers. We may not have riches, but we have all we need."

What she knew he was really asking was, *why wasn't I enough for you?*

"That's not what I meant," she said.

Please don't start another argument, Vaughn, she entreated silently.

The thought of repeating this morning's talk left knives in her guts. She didn't want to admit that she'd realized months ago she didn't love him enough to marry him and that it was her cowardice that kept them together until he offered her a ring. That was when she knew she couldn't be silent anymore, and she'd never hated herself more for her weakness.

Vaughn sighed.

She cut him off with a warning look. "We talked this morning, Vaughn. If you want to continue this, we can do it later but don't expect me to change my mind."

He looked away. "It's just—"

"We were never suited to marry. That won't change."

He stilled, shifting restlessly on his feet. "It doesn't need to, Wren. I'm engaged."

She was silent for a moment. *Then why are you so determined to rehash the past?* Curiosity finally got the best of her.

"Oh. Who?"

"Lilly Farthing."

Lilly, a pleasant, graceful girl with raven locks and dark eyes, appeared in her mind. A blacksmith's daughter, shy by nature. She was as far from Wren as anyone could be.

She nodded approvingly. Lilly was the girl for him. She was everything he desired in a wife. Wren had seen the longing looks Lilly threw at Vaughn. She only hoped that he might express the same ardent love he'd felt for Wren to his prospective wife.

"I'm sure she's thrilled about that. The girl's been in love with you for years," said Wren.

His eyes widened. "What?"

"You didn't know?"

Vaughn blushed. "The marriage was... arranged. I mean, I asked, as was proper but..."

Naturally, it was arranged. Your parents never wanted you to marry me; they were relieved they had to carry out no work for me to say no. She wasn't in the mood to remind him of all the uncomfortable dinners she'd endured – all of which he recalled in a considerably different light.

"But what? You don't love her because of your feelings for me?" she finished, her anger bleeding away, leaving her emotions strung out.

His silence said everything.

They'd scarcely been friends before she became a climber. She could count on one hand how many times they'd spoken prior to that. They had entered the school in the village a year apart, though in the end, she had surpassed him in skill. So far as to catch the eye of the old leader of the climbers and he'd appointed *her* as his replacement. She wondered idly if Vaughn had ever been jealous of that. It was not something they'd ever discussed.

"Wren! Vaughn! Are you both ready?" Flynn called from the path. Mira stood behind him, arms folded, shivering.

He sighed—Wren could see the fight flee from him—and set off after the others.

Wren stood her ground for a moment then followed, but before she had taken two steps, a shriek split the air from behind.

She froze. Vaughn spun around, his gaze snapping up to a point on high on the cliff. A look of horror on his face. Behind him, Mira and Flynn rushed to his side, shock turning their faces white.

With dread pounding in her chest, she turned. Silently crouched on the rocky outcrop above was a wyvern. Its claws clenched tightly around the edge of the cliff as it watched her with a predatory gaze. Its nostrils flared, drawing in the scent of her fear, devouring it.

This one, it seemed, had its focus on her. She dropped her hand, flicking a signal for Vaughn to run.

"I'm not leaving you," he whispered.

"Be the hero, Vaughn, *save them*," she said, a glint of urgency in her eyes.

Before he could react, she bolted straight to one of the nearby pathways leading upwards, and the wyvern leaped off the outcrop in pursuit. Focusing ahead, she felt the shadow rush over her and she dropped—too late. Claws sank into flesh, grabbing her.

A scream tore out of her throat. The ground slipped away, her bag falling from her. Frantically, she struggled to free herself, but the claws sank deeper. Pain exploded, tearing through her shoulder and arm in throbbing waves. Higher and higher she rose. Glancing back down, she met Vaughn's terrified gaze as Flynn dragged him back. Gritting her teeth, she forced any trace of pain and fear from her face. No way in hell would their last memory be of her afraid.

A thousand emotions flashed between them.

Wren tore her gaze away as she was lifted higher, piercing the thin veil of cloud. The air grew brutally cold, biting through her thick furs. Below her, jagged rock gave way to ancient walkways carved into the mountain way. Bridges emerged from the cloud and connected to other cliffs and pathways forming a labyrinth. As the wyvern drew her up with the beat of its enormous wings, she saw the first hints of the old empire.

Holding her breath, she glimpsed the first houses carved into the mountains, empty shelves, lifeless. Some jutted out, impossibly perched with large outcrops, polished smooth.

The wyvern banked sharply, cutting through a narrow pass and into a large clearing–a small lake in the center, its pale blue water glittering against the frost-touched ground.

It dropped her and she hit the ground, hard. Something crunched beneath her. Dazed, she rolled to her feet and looked down. Bones. With a scream, she scrambled away and barely had time to react before the wyvern landed, snarling at her. It had brought her to its nest to feed.

Lifting her gaze, she stared it down. Where fear had knotted in her gut, something else kindled. At first, little more than a smoldering spark, flickering up.

There's no way in the hell I'm dying here, she thought, yanking out her two climbing daggers.

The beast prowled forward, circling closer. It snarled softly, teeth glinting viciously in the sun. A quiet promise of death.

The wyvern lunged. Wren rolled to the side, barely missing the slash of its claws. In a blur, she rushed at the wyvern as it spun and launched herself onto its back, thrusting the blades into the scales. To her surprise, they sank in—deep. Warm blood gushed down her hands, soaking through her gloves.

The beast roared, thrashing furiously to throw her off. She held on, desperation tightening her grip. With a cry, she pulled out one blade and stabbed again. As it thrashed, she scrambled up its neck and slammed the dagger into its throat. Hot blood sprayed her skin.

Howling, the wyvern jerked to the side, hurling her off its back. She flew through the air, hitting the ground with a sharp burst of pain. A metallic taste filled her mouth, agony burning through her.

Scrambling to her feet, legs shaking, she spat blood, staring down the wyvern as it spun. The beast's silvery scales were streaked with dark red. It glared at her with feral eyes.

"*Come at me!*" she yelled.

It launched at her, and she hurled both daggers before spinning away. Scales flashed inches away from her face.

Then it crashed onto the ground. She sprinted past the piles of bones. Other climbers rotted away in their tattered furs. A glint of silver caught her eye.

A shriek split the air. Cursing, she spun around and saw the wyvern staggering to its feet. One dagger embedded in an eye and the other in its shoulder. A bloodied wing hanging limply at its side.

Silver flashed beside her, catching the sunlight. It was a sword.

The wyvern screamed again and launched. Without thinking, she reached down and grabbed the weapon. A feeling of warmth burst through her limbs instantly. Wren raised the blade as a wall of gray slammed into her.

Darkness overwhelmed her as it threw her to the ground.

This is it, I'm dead.

Chapter 2

*I have been born anew, my bones reformed and as I stretch
out my wings I feel as though I am free.*

—Excerpt from Princess Yelena's diary

I CAN BREATHE, was the first dim thought that flickered in Wren's
mind as she woke. A thin sliver of light pierced the veil of darkness
around her.

Sunlight.

She reached out, flailing in the dark for a moment until her fingers
sank into the ground. She dug as deep as she could and pulled. The

weight pressing down on her back made every breath a battle, her lungs screaming to expand. Her pulse raced desperately, fighting to keep her from collapsing. She just had to keep pulling, dragging herself forward. Inch by inch, clawing along the softened earth. Dirt smeared across her cheeks and lips.

With a final burst of strength, the weight shifted off her. At once, the air rushed into her chest, filling it. The darkness retreated from the fringe of her vision and she rolled onto her back, breathing hard. Blood pounded in her ears. She lay there until her heart slowed and she turned her head slightly.

The wyvern lay dead beside her.

As the pain dimmed, she sat up slowly. Her clothes were stiff with dried blood, crinkling. Her nose wrinkled at the smell. With a shudder, she dragged herself to her feet, swaying a little as the world lurched.

She was alive.

Her shoulders throbbed from where the wyvern had held her. Reaching up, she probed the joints. The claws had cut into the furs but, mercifully, they hadn't broken all the way through to her skin.

Small miracles, she supposed.

Her gaze fell back to the wyvern, unable to look away. It was the size of three or four carts and had to weigh twice as much. She couldn't fathom how she hadn't been crushed under its weight.

I ought to be dead.

A shudder rippled through her.

Glancing around the clearing, Wren realized how exposed she was. Her hands twitched, remembering the sword in her hands, how right and familiar it had felt.

She walked over to the wyvern and kneeled, pressing her hands against it. The carcass rolled over as if it weighed nothing at all. Embedded in its side, she saw the sword sunk right down to the top of the hilt. Her hand curled around the hilt, and she pulled, yanking it free.

Steadying herself, she straightened up and turned her attention to the sword. She eyed it curiously. It was impossible to see any marks on it because of the layers of blood and grime. Still in pain, she took a deep breath and walked over to the pool, where she set the sword aside. Exhaling slowly, she tugged her gloves off, finger by finger. The crystal-clear water turned red as she immersed them. Once they were clean, she wrung them out and set them on the grass beside her to dry.

The sword was next to be cleaned. She plunged it into the clear water, watching as the blood dissolved away, producing a pale red cloud around it. Drawing up the strange blade, she carefully placed it on the grass, marveling at it for a moment.

It had appeared right when she needed a miracle. Wren had never believed too seriously in religion or fate, yet as she sat there, close to the dead beast, she wondered.

Was someone or something watching over her?

Ridiculous.

Wren shook her head and gingerly stood up. Her clothes were stiff and heavy with the wyvern's blood. Not one to be shy, especially with no one around, she shed her clothes and waded into the water, groaning as the cold soaked into her bones. After washing and scrubbing herself raw, she ran her hands over her braided hair, trying to rinse out the blood without undoing it. Her hair gradually retook its muddy brown tones.

Once dry, she pulled on her inner fur layers first, which were mostly free of blood, aside from a few splatters. The outer layers were a mess, however, so she tried to remove the blood as best she could. Glancing skywards she guessed she had a little time before the sun fell. She wrung out her clothes, then used her coat as a makeshift bag to carry them in.

Tomorrow, she'd have to figure out how to get down, given this part of the cliff was unfamiliar. It was likely there had once been wooden stairs that connected it to the ground below, but they'd probably long rotted away. Still, there had to be a way down, even if it wasn't easy. There had to be something she could use to climb. Luckily for her, the wyvern could be eaten and with the cooler nights, the meat would last.

As much as Wren wanted to explore to satisfy her curiosity, she knew she had to get down before she was starving or too exhausted to climb. And of course, she needed to show everyone she was very much alive. Vaughn would, no doubt, spin tales about how she bravely drew the wyvern's attention, saving them all. And that, faced with such tragedy, it was he who held the team together and led them back down safely, proving he was a capable leader.

Shaking off the thought, she set off. Through the narrow pass, she emerged into a valley carved out between the rocky land, looking as though it had been scooped out from the middle of the mountains. Houses were built into the stone cliffs, with a few narrow streets parting them, but less than Wren would have expected. What made up for the lack of streets were the outcrops that jutted out from most of the homes, some of them almost the size of the house itself.

She walked on. Darkened doorways sat beneath the houses, which, upon closer inspection, held steep sets of steps winding upwards – leading into the house as a secondary entrance.

It suited the strange way the houses sat in the middle of the cliffs. She studied the rock around each of the houses. Many were too high and too far away, but she saw what looked to be parts worn by indents possibly from where bridges once hung.

It was eerily silent, as though nothing alive dared disturb the realm of the dead. A place where ghosts watched from the shadows and guarded their past. What secrets, she wondered, lurked here? Wild stories abounded over how the empire fell. People said one day they were thriving, the next they were no more and the mountains were silent. What monstrous thing brought this seemingly indestructible empire to its knees?

Unease knotted within Wren.

At one of the houses, she finally stopped and stared into the dark steps. After a pause, she made her way inside and placed one hand on the wall, using it to guide her way up. Nearer to the top, light pierced the darkness, and she could see a rectangular shape above her. A doorway. She made her way into a short hall, which opened into a living area. Tall ceilings, wide spaces, and sparsely arranged furniture greeted her. At the far end, the tattered remains of a large door with shadowy scraps of fabric hanging from the frame guarded the threshold to the outcrop.

A door led off the main room, into what looked like a sleeping area. The bed frame had mostly rotted away, looking like a mangled clutter of wood and remnants of fabric. Next to it was a chest, which seemed in fairly good condition. She eyed the room with interest. There was the palest hint of a painting across the walls, a mural of sorts. Much of it had flaked it away but the unmistakable shape of a golden dragon stretched over the back wall, majestic and eternal.

Her father used to tell her stories about the dragons. *The golden dragons, Wren, were the most powerful of the dragons. They ruled their kin, fiercely and with a fire within that could burn an entire kingdom.*

Wren hadn't thought about her father's stories for some time but now, walking amongst the remains of this ancient world, she wondered whether they were true.

She reached out and touched the mural, running her fingers over the picture, drawing it with her hand. She tried to picture the dragon for real, to imagine it soaring above her, landing and then greeting her. She remembered the old stories that said the dragons could talk, that they were extremely intelligent, and that their human counterparts, the Dragonirs, who lived just as long, could take the form of the dragon. Was the mural, she wondered, that of a dragon or a Dragonir?

Withdrawing her hand, she returned to the living area and set her wet items on the outcrop, stretching them out to dry. Then she set about searching the house for supplies.

It was unlikely, of course, to assume there would be anything useful left but she had to be sure. In what might have been a kitchen area, she found jars of spices, long rotted and only their faint scent lingering. There were also some jars of wine, which she tasted, but quickly spat out. After wiping her mouth, she continued searching through the rest of the house.

What little was left wasn't much use. A few scraps of clothing, some blunt tools, and broken pieces of jewelry made of what might've been precious stones. All of it seemed to speak of someone leaving in a hurry.

Hells, she wondered if all the houses were the same. Where had everyone gone?

A cold feeling stole through her, as though a ghost brushed a kiss against her neck.

She returned to the living area and checked her coat, but it was still a little damp, so she headed back outside and off to the wyvern.

The beast lay where it had fallen. It wasn't her first choice for food but, given the circumstances, there was little alternative.

Her daggers were sharp, so cutting into the leathery skin was easy and she peeled it back, exposing the still-warm flesh beneath. She made quick work, carving out just enough to fill her and wrapped it up with a roll of cloth she had packed for emergencies.

She took the parcel with her to the pool, where kneeling she scooped several large handfuls of water down her throat, drinking greedily until her stomach hurt.

Her thirst satisfied, she grabbed the parcel of meat and headed back to the house.

The air had chilled from the cool wind that blew in through the open windows. Using what little materials that she found, plus some flint stones she discovered in the kitchen, she started a small fire in the living room. Her stomach growled, so she carefully unwrapped the meat and speared it with her cleaned daggers, holding it over the fire until all sides had browned and the meat was firm. Wren wrinkled her nose at the pungent smell that came off the roasting meat. Deciding that even if it tasted foul, she was hungry enough to eat anything, she tugged it off her daggers and bit into it. The meat was chewy and left a muddy taste in her mouth, but it was enough to fill her.

By the time the sun dipped below the mountain peaks, she had set up a small bed and covered it with her now dry furs. Not yet ready to sleep, Wren sat on the outcrop, her legs dangling over the edge. From her vantage point, she could appreciate the number of homes, plus the dozens more at greater heights were far more than she'd initially realized. Advancing her gaze upward, she spied the thin layer of cloud, had dissolved, and there she saw it – a *castle*. It dominated the peak, a pale white structure that seemed to be a part of the mountain itself. Outcrops dotted its sheer walls. Several enormous towers rose impossibly high, like the outstretched fingers of a hand, grasping for something out of reach.

Her grandmother had told her tales of the rulers of this land. Queen Evanya, and her two children – Adrian and Yelena – and those who ruled before. Wren's favorite story was of the enchantress Dragonir Litania, who had won the heart of a prince. Yet, for all the stories, the sight of the ruined kingdom abandoned tempered her excitement.

She wanted to tell the villagers what she saw but knew they wouldn't believe her. They would call her mad and say her mind was addled from the cold.

In time, her memories would blur and this place would retreat further into the darkness, forgotten.

With that sobering thought, she returned inside and sat by the fire until it was little more than a smoldering pile of ash. There, she curled up and let the dreams of dragons carry her away into a long sleep.

It was the fierce cry of a wyvern that shocked her awake. She scrambled to her feet, dashing to the bedroom to peer out of the small window. At first, there appeared to be nothing, but then a flash of gray shot straight to the ground below, hitting the stone, hard. Her eyes widened.

First, the wyvern she'd heard, with its mottled scales and wings bent down, acting as its front legs. Its claws dug into the earth as it snarled at the creature before it.

Her body pulsed with shock. *That creature is no wyvern.*

Not with those four distinct legs and glistening black scales.

The wyvern had two thick muscled rear legs and talons at the tip of their wings, acting as forelegs, and their scales were pale brown. It was dwarfed by its counterpart. It was several feet taller than the wyvern and had a wingspan far greater. With a row of spikes running from its snout to the tip of the tail, she knew exactly what it was. As though it had been summoned straight from her mother's stories.

A dragon...

The wyvern exploded forward, and all hell broke loose.

Chapter 3

The loss of a climber is never easy for the village of Fenware; and those that brave the cliffs, the grief of losing their team-mate, is all-consuming.

—Excerpt from Alaric Fenley, head Climber.

THE RETURN TO the village was something Flynn would never forget. The sound of the howling wind, of footsteps crunching on newly fallen snow, and the rapid beating of his own anxious heart, would mark that walk in his memory forever.

He hated the feeling.

Mira trudged beside him with her arms wrapped tightly around her waist. Dried tears stained her red cheeks, and she kept her gaze firmly on the ground. He wanted to reassure her, but was at a loss for words himself. All he kept seeing was Wren's face with the look of fear followed by one of conviction. And as quickly as it had happened, she was gone.

He looked at Vaughn, who was marching down the track several feet in front. Since the attack, he hadn't said a word beyond the growling commands for them to head back down the cliff. After that, he'd fallen silent.

When the wooden arch of the village came into view, faintly dusted with snow, he hesitated. *Gods, her family...* Vaughn came to a stop in front of the arch, then turned back to them.

"I'll go tell her parents," he murmured, his voice hollow.

"Vaughn..." Flynn took a step to him. "Do you—"

"I'll go alone," he finished and strode off into the village without another word.

Flynn looked at Mira. "Do you want to go home? I'll take the flowers and gear back if you do?"

The flowers felt meaningless after what happened, but he was just at a loss for what else to do. He couldn't think, couldn't focus on anything but one breath at a time.

Mira shook her head. "I'll go with you."

They set off into the village, heading straight for the Climbing Hall. Once word got out that they'd lost Wren, everyone would flock to the hall. Gifts and well-wishes would flood in. Which meant they'd have to find a...

Hells, a replacement and a new leader. He supposed that'd be Vaughn. No way in hell would Flynn take it on.

"Flynn?"

"Hmm?" He pushed the door into the hall and walked inside, keeping it open for Mira to follow.

"Do you think it was quick?" she whispered.

It took him a moment to understand what she was asking. He swallowed the lump that had knotted in his throat. "Yes."

Her sharp eyes examined him. "How are you so sure?"

He didn't want to tell her he'd seen a climber taken before. His brother. Common knowledge was that his brother had fallen during a climb. Only those present at the time knew the truth. Few would want to join their ranks if they knew the true number of climbers snatched by wyverns.

Vaughn would ensure Wren went down as one of them if only to ensure she was remembered for her sacrifice.

"Wyverns don't play with their food," he replied as he shut the door behind her.

When the sun fell, all the jobs had been finished. Flynn had cleaned every bit of kit, whilst Mira stowed it and wrote the defects he noted. One line was frayed, so that was set aside to be repaired. He finished up by placing the harvested flowers into the baskets, which he'd drop by the harvesting hut in the morning.

When he moved back, rubbing the back of his neck to ease a knot that had tightened there, the door opened. Vaughn walked in and took a seat by the cold fireplace. His shoulders slumped, the weight of the visit finally taking its toll.

"They know," he announced.

Flynn drew closer and set a hand on Vaughn's shoulder, squeezing it before he drew away and took the seat across from him. "I'll have my father send a basket of supplies over tomorrow with whatever money Wren had stashed away. She'd want them to have it."

Vaughn nodded, his gaze drifting to the cold fireplace. "Would you consider stepping up to be a leader?"

"You don't want it?" Flynn tried to sound surprised, but he knew Vaughn had little interest in taking Wren's position.

With a deep breath, Vaughn stood and looked at Flynn. "Wren wanted you to be her successor."

"Me? Why? You're the senior out of the four of us."

"Wren knew I'd retire once I married, which was why I had intended to look over the young climbers and see which ones would be ready for the next season." Vaughn fell silent, his gaze impossible to read as Flynn studied him. "She preferred you over me."

And I'd hoped you'd once prefer me to her.

31

Flynn didn't miss the bitterness in Vaughn's voice or the silent accusation. He resisted the urge to mention once again that nothing had ever happened between Wren and himself. Primarily because he didn't like the company of women.

A secret only Wren knew.

"I see," replied Flynn softly. "You know I don't want this, but Wren did. That's the only reason I'll agree."

Vaughn nodded tightly in silence.

The candle sputtered out on the table, plunging the climbers' hut into near-total darkness. A thin band of moonlight cut in from one window, cleaving the shadows around Flynn in two. He pushed back his chair, rising with a groan. The last of the record diaries were updated, detailing the harvest and the state of the plants. The only thing he hadn't been able to bring himself to write was Wren's death.

It was too soon, his chest hollowed out from the loss. Her face kept appearing in his mind and the pain choked his throat.

Another day, he told himself as he pushed the chair in, then set the diaries on the bookshelves.

The fire had long since died, leaving a biting chill. White clouds swirled with every breath as he grabbed his satchel hung up by the door, then headed out. The door clicked shut behind him. He slid an external latch, ensuring that if the wind whipped up, the door wouldn't open and let the snow in.

Satisfied, he turned around. Snow fell softly from darkened clouds, gathering on the thin layer that dusted the road. The row of working huts was shuttered up, the lanterns by the doors snuffed out. Only the howling wind that stole through the village broke the silence, as though the mountains, too, were mourning their loss.

He stopped and looked at the long shadow from the looming mountains. Somewhere up there was Wren. He hoped it had been quick, the pain little more than the flash of a star across the night sky.

Sighing, he set off, pulling his fur coat tighter around his body. The air grew sharper, the white of his breath leaving swirling trails behind him. Winter wasn't due for a while longer. This chill was the calm before the storm, the herald of blizzards that would assault them for weeks on end. It would leave a heavy layer of white over everything. People would remain inside or gather in the huts for communal meals, sharing heat and food.

Normally, he liked that time. The slower pace, the quiet conversation over blazing fires. The scent of spiced ale filled the air, mingling with the aroma of sweet bread and hearty stews. There would be games, laughter, kisses stolen in the shadowy alcoves, and when spring would finally emerge, new life would come with it. By summer, the cries of babies would wail out across the village and Flynn would once again enjoy the refuge the cliffs offered.

But as winter approached, the additional responsibility thrust upon him twisted like a knife in his gut. He was glad that the streets were quiet that night as he made his way home. As he rounded the final corner to his street, he stopped. A single lantern was lit at the front of his house. He smiled. Of course, his mother had left the lantern glowing. She always did.

He drew closer, a moth to the flame, and a figure stepped away from the front door. The amber glow lit their face.

Alaric. Wren's father.

Flynn frowned. The man had always been the quiet sort, laboring for hours by himself in his workshop. He fixed broken wagons, tools, cooking utensils, even the few weapons they possessed. To him, nothing was beyond saving. But that was all Flynn knew of the man. Alaric seldom attended communal meals and, when he did, he barely spoke. He would keep close to his wife, his eyes on her and only her.

So, what brought him out in the middle of the night?

As Flynn came nearer, Alaric stepped onto the street. The tall man with his muscled limbs and trimmed beard cut a striking figure, a man who commanded every room he entered. His dark blue eyes caught the torchlight, and Flynn was struck by how much Ellie looked like her father... and how little Wren did.

"Mr. Dumare, what brings you here tonight?" asked Flynn, glancing briefly at the front door. "My parents should be home."

Alaric's gaze studied him closely for a moment, piercing in its intensity.

After a beat, he spoke. "I came to see you. My daughter commissioned something to be given to you if anything ever happened to her."

"Me?"

He nodded and lifted a small wrapped parcel from the bag slung over his chest, then held it out. Flynn stared at it for a moment. The weight of what the gift meant didn't escape him. A lump lodged in his throat as he gently took the package, then unfurled it with trembling hands.

A set of simple but well-made climbing daggers lay in his palms. Their sharpened edges glinted in the torchlight; the tanned leather hilts soft to the touch. He took them in hand, testing their weight. Perfectly balanced and snug. Custom made for him.

Tears burned his eyes as he carefully wrapped the daggers, then slid them into his bag. He wiped his eyes before he looked up. "They're beautiful."

To his surprise, there didn't seem to be any trace of sadness in Alaric's eyes. Only that steadiness he'd seen from afar, as though the man were a mountain himself, unmovable. Alaric nodded. "They'll serve you well."

A long pause stretched between them as if Alaric wanted to say more or was waiting for Flynn to speak. He wasn't sure what to say or why the man didn't move to leave. *What is he waiting for?*

Flynn cleared his throat. "Uh, I should head inside."

Alaric blinked, then nodded and held out his hand. "Of course. Goodnight, then."

Flynn took the offered hand, squeezing it back when a shock jolted through his chest. Alaric pulled his hand away before Flynn could process what happened. He nodded once more, then strode off into the dark. His footsteps made no sound in the snow, and when he disappeared from view, it was as though he'd never been there at all.

Flynn went inside, but he couldn't shake the jolt that had shot through him when he'd shaken Alaric's hand and the chill that had lingered in his chest afterward.

Chapter 4

May I be forgiven for what I must do. Regardless, my soul is damned to that monster.

— Excerpt from Litania's diary

WREN WAS RUNNING before she knew it, flying down the steps two at a time, sword in hand. She sprinted out, releasing a feral cry that pierced the air.

The wyvern stopped dead, turning its head to look at her. Then, with a savage cry, it rushed forward, heading straight for her. At that moment, the black dragon was forgotten.

She held firm, her heart thumping painfully; then at the last second, she dived out of the way. As she jumped to her feet and spun around, it was on her again. She swung the sword, slicing through the beast's chest.

Blood sprayed, warm and thick on her skin. The foul stench filled every breath. The wyvern screamed, recoiling back and turning, slamming its tail straight into her. White flashed across her vision, followed by the sense of flying, and of pain hitting her everywhere at once. She slammed into the ground. The unconscious world reached out, hooking its talons into her mind.

Get up, you fool! Her inner voice howled as she tried to blink the darkness away.

Groggily, she pressed her palms into the dirt and forced herself up. A wall of scale and teeth rammed into her again, pinning her down. Claws pierced flesh and bone. She screamed, throwing her hands up as she caught the side of its jaws, stopping them inches from her neck.

The force of it bearing down was shredding her strength to ribbons. She tried to hold on, determined to return to her people. Her hands slipped up its neck, the gnashing teeth coming closer.

Her grip slipped.

The wyvern's mouth descended—

A force slammed into it, tearing it off her. She rolled to her side, her head spinning. Gasping for air, she could only watch—her body unable to do anything more at that moment—as the dragon and wyvern clashed.

They wrestled, jaws snapping, claws tearing. Blood painted everything red, a trail of carnage as they fought.

She staggered to her feet, clinging to the front of the house for support. It was all she could do *not* to fall flat on her face.

The dragon suddenly rolled the wyvern onto its stomach, clambering on top. The sheer size difference pinned the smaller wyvern to the ground. It let out a squalling cry as it tried to wrestle the dragon off. Deaf to its pleas, the dragon clamped on the wyvern's neck and twisted sharply.

The sickening crunch of bone heralded the end of the fight.

She froze as the dragon leaped off the wyvern. It unfurled its wings, stretching them wide and tall, letting out a roar that echoed like a clap of thunder among the mountains. As it closed its powerful jaw and folded its wings, its attention turned to her. Jewel-green eyes narrowed.

Wren tried to speak, to move, but what strength she had was slipping quickly through her fingers. Her legs collapsed beneath her, sending her tumbling to the ground and into unrelenting darkness.

Acrid smoke and the salted smell of roasting meat wound through her mind, through dreamy, half-conceived thoughts, bringing with them a faint crackling sound.

A fire. It had to be. That, or her mother's warnings, had turned out true, and she was in the demon realm, burning.

An eternity seemed to pass before she could force her lids to part. A slit of light cut in—dim, burnished red. It softened, warmed, and bled to an amber glow on gray stone. Her eyes refused to open wider, so she turned her focus to what else was around her.

As she lay there, she willed her fingers to move, and lifted a hand to her shoulders, finding only smooth, undamaged skin.

Relief flooded her. She'd always been quick to heal since a small child and never fell ill—a truth that had been hard to hide from those she called friends and kin.

Drawing in a deep breath, and opening her eyes wider, she was at last able to see a smooth brown stone ceiling with several hairline cracks splintering across its near–perfect surface.

Frowning, she sat up, feeling thick furs fall to her side, and looked around, warily. Immediately, her gaze fell to the loose shirt that swallowed her form. All traces of the fight little more than memory except for the nudging approach of a headache.

Looking around, she took in her surroundings. She was in a living area, much like the one she'd found, though twice the size, with a burning fire close by. Beyond it was a table covered with weapons—her sword included—and books, piled high, and messily arranged. A tapestry hung on the wall, tattered at the edges, depicting a woman with long brown hair and strangely sad eyes. A golden, thorny crown sat on her head.

Tearing her gaze away, she spied a bedroll nearby, and a trunk at the foot of it, which was fastened with a heavy lock. She peered around the room, saw the entrance, then opposite it, the doorway that led to an outcrop that looked twice the size of the one she'd found.

A man stood there, framed by gloomy gray daylight.

From behind, all she saw were broad shoulders that tapered to a narrow waist. His attire was black and simple, though too nice for a commoner. Wild and curly brown hair hung short as if it had been hacked in haste by a blade.

As if sensing her stare, he turned.

Pale olive skin, a strong face with a stern expression, and harsh features greeted her. Jewel green eyes met hers. For a breath, he stared at her before he strode over.

Instinctively, she braced herself and backed up against the pillows. He stopped.

"Who the hell are you?" she blurted out.

He tilted his head to the side as if her question amused him.

"The dragon brought you to me, told me you saved him. When you're ready, I'll escort you back down, and then any debt will be considered paid."

"A lone man up in the mountains is best friends with a dragon?"

His nostrils flared. "Yes."

"Are there any more, or is it just you two?"

"My friend is the last," he replied tightly.

She flinched at the pain on his face and looked away. "I guess I can say that part of the stories were true."

His expression hardened. "Speak nothing of what you saw today."

She narrowed her eyes. "Who would believe me, anyway?"

Gods, no one in my village, she thought wryly.

The answer appeared to satisfy him. He nodded stiffly.

"Good. I will take you down in the morning," he said stiffly and turned to walk back to the outcrop. "You shouldn't have come here. This place isn't for your kind."

"I didn't come here by choice. A wyvern grabbed me."

He froze, turned slowly, curiosity flickering in his green eyes. "You were *taken?* What happened to the beast?"

"I... I killed it."

"You killed a wyvern?" Skepticism dripped from every word.

Fire heated her cheeks, her hands clutching the furs tightly. She thought about the sword, how it felt in her hands. It was an instinct she never knew she had... and the realization was *unnerving*. "Yes."

His expression was unreadable as he nodded. "Well, I suppose that accounts for the other wyvern's fury at you. They don't like climbers and they're protective of their kind. It must've smelled the blood on you." He paused, then looked at her again. "That was your kill by the lake?" She nodded, and he continued. "You returned and cut it up?"

"I am from the village below this place. There, we waste nothing. I had no food, and the beast was dead," she said.

"A wise decision. There isn't much to eat here if you do not know these parts well."

She lowered her gaze and saw her bandages again. "You undressed me."

"Your clothes were badly torn and there was a lot of blood. I thought you had injured yourself, but I found no wound," he stated, staring at her to explain. "After that, I dressed you in clean attire but I kept on what was not damaged."

Which explained her pants.

Her breath hitched. "I heal quickly."

"I see," he murmured.

"You're not surprised by that?"

"Not the strangest thing I have seen."

He turned from her and walked back to the outcrop.

Wren rose with a stiff groan and walked over. At the threshold, she leaned against the doorway, studying him for a moment. Questions burned her tongue.

"Yes?" he asked softly, glancing at her over his shoulder.

"I never asked your name."

There was silence for a moment, then his reply: "Lorca."

"Wren Dumare."

For a moment she wondered if he'd provide his family name; when he didn't, she fell silent. She looked at the ruins, her mood darkening. The longer she looked, the more something inside her twisted into knots, tightening until a flicker of rage burned within her. She blinked, looking down. Her hands were curled into fists, nails biting into her palms almost to the point of blood. Exhaling, she looked at him again.

"How did you come to live here?"

He stood abruptly, turned, and pinned his inscrutable gaze on her. "You need to rest for the journey tomorrow."

The story would not be hers that night. She held her ground, deliberating, pushing him, but she sensed it was unwelcome territory. With a sigh, she retreated inside and lay down, curling toward the fire, drawn by its warmth. Her mind drifted away to all the events that had occurred and she wondered how she'd return, having seen what she had and knowing what she did.

A door had opened, and she wasn't sure how to close it, let alone if she even wanted to.

The soft footsteps of Lorca stirred through her ear as she woke up. The dappled light of morning sun spilled into the living area, brushing over her. She rose and found a plain shirt, black pants, and a matching coat with a faded golden dragon embroidered on it laid out for her. The clothes were finer than anything she'd ever owned before.

Lorca walked in from the outcrop, his jacket banished, revealing a sleeveless shirt that clung to his well-muscled frame. Swallowing hard, she lifted her gaze to his and frowned.

"What do I tell my people? They're going to notice the different clothes and well, the fact I'm *alive* after a wyvern took me."

He stared at her, silent for a moment. "Tell them the truth or as much as you can. They will accept it."

"You're awfully sure about people you've never met."

"If they care about you, they will be blind to faults in your story. The alternative will be too uncomfortable to consider." He waited a few moments before continuing. "I only ask that you don't speak of my friend. For his safety, he likes to be left alone, and only tolerates me on occasion."

She barely had time to nod before he strode into a nearby room. When he came back, he had a bag in one hand and a sheathed sword in the other. It was the blade she had fought the wyverns with.

"My friend said you used it well. Consider the belt an extra gift," he said.

Somewhat shyly, she took the belt and fastened it on her back, and sheathed the sword. Then she took the bag he offered, which she found contained her climbing daggers, her water skin, plus some supplies.

She looked up. "This is generous, thank you."

He studied her closely for a moment. "You're surprised?"

"A little. Doesn't mean I'm any less grateful, however."

At the compliment, he shifted awkwardly, as if unsure how to respond. After a beat, he cleared his throat. "I will depart your company before we arrive."

She nodded. "Oh, okay."

A distant cry split the air—a wyvern's call. A shadow darkened his face and he sighed, then grabbed his bag and slung it over his back. Curiously, she noticed, he held no weapons. Not even a staff. He brushed past her on the way to the exit, lingering only to usher her out.

"We best be off. It is a hard journey down," he said as he turned and strode out the door.

She stared at his back, wondering just who this man was. Living in the ruins of a dead empire with only a dragon for company, and not to mention being constantly dogged by ravenous wyverns. What kind of life was that?

What kind of person would choose that?

Chapter 5

Trust? I trusted Adrian, but he will stop me if he knows the truth. So, I lie, and I pray that one day, he will know all and forgive me. For now, however, I gather my things, my courage, my heart, and step into the night. Fate awaits me, her hand outstretched—I take it.

—Excerpt from Litania's diary

THE SNOW WAS falling gently as they marched down a path cut into the mountains, dusting her clothes and leaving a thin layer on the ground before them. Within hours their tracks would be no more.

He hadn't spoken since their departure, preferring to walk at a hard pace, always two steps ahead. Enough so she couldn't see his face, and couldn't read those dark eyes that betrayed so little. It was maddening.

Once he'd seen she could move with her injuries, he seemed eager to be rid of her.

After several short climbs down smaller cliffs and ledges, they reached another narrow path and a small cliff to descend. He scrambled down over the edge, vanishing from view. She followed after but he was already at the bottom by the time she looked down. He didn't even wait at the bottom before he was striding away. She dropped down as fast she could and jogged after him.

It was the silence that frustrated her, mainly because her thoughts kept drifting to the sword and the ruins and everything else that she'd seen. She was twisting herself up until there was a sharp throbbing behind her eye.

Wren gave up trying to get his attention and instead focused on the narrow path that sloped down the side of the mountain. On one side, a sheer cliff that stretched high into the cloud, and on the other, a drop that went down further than she cared to look. Heights didn't terrify her like some; still, it didn't mean she looked down when she was climbing.

The low, mournful howl of the wind that cut through the mountains was all that she heard above the crunch of their boots in the shallow snow. It was a sound she normally loved when she climbed. It made her feel as though she were a lone soul on the mountain, free of the worry below, unbound. But now it was truly depressing.

When the path cut between a slim gap in the cliff beside them, darkness closed in. Wren closed the distance between herself and Lorca. Something was unsettling about the dark. Sometimes she swore a presence was watching her from it.

The darkness was short-lived as the path they were following opened onto a small valley nestled between twin peaks. Snow sloped down sharply on smooth sections of rock, then slipped between the bare trees that jutted up like mangled hands, defiantly reaching for the sun. The sun was low, slipping quietly behind the furthest peak, with shadows rapidly advancing across the valley.

Lorca stopped and turned to her. "This is where we part ways. Follow this path until you come to a low cliff. Climb down it and continue to follow the path below. You will come alongside a frozen waterfall. The river running off it will be your guide. From there, a small trail will lead you back to the northern edge where your village is."

With a curt nod, he stepped past her, as if that was to be his goodbye. A tangle of words cluttered in her mouth. She spun around and tried to summon *any* of them. But he was gone, vanishing into the darkness.

Somehow, she felt if she followed, she would see nothing, as if he were a specter that had dissolved once gone from her. With a sigh, she turned back and set off. Perhaps she would see him again one day, however unlikely that might be.

Darkness had descended on the village of Fenware and the plumes of smoke were already rising from the houses, thick coils that twisted up into the blackening, angry sky. A storm was coming.

The wind whipped around her as she walked down the path to the village. Thanks to her furs, she felt no cold, only irritation as the wind tried to snatch her cloak away. When she reached the threshold, still shrouded in darkness, unbroken by haphazardly lit lanterns, she paused.

The second she entered, she'd have to forget about the empire of legends, the man, the *dragon,* even about the sword strapped to her back.

With a deep breath, she stepped forward.

"Who goes there?" a stranger called from the dark.

She squinted into the dark as the figure came closer, holding a lantern.

"Vaughn?"

He froze, staring at her as though she were a ghost, risen from the dead to haunt him. "Wren, you're... you're *alive*."

She pushed back her hood and smiled. "Yes."

With a soft curse, he hauled her into his arms, squeezing her as if his life depended on it. Despite all their history, she eased into his hug and savored it. He smelled faintly of ash and earthy notes, which at that moment, never smelled so good. She was home, safe and sound. Tension bled from her shoulders, vanishing into the air.

He pulled away first, one hand still lingering on her arm. "But I saw the wyvern take you! How did you survive?"

"Another wyvern came and they fought, dropping me. Luckily, I didn't fall far and I managed to sneak away. After that, I found some ruins, some old clothes, even a sword. Once I had rested, I made my way down," she explained, the lies coming easily as she glanced over his shoulder. "My family?"

Her breath hitched. She wanted to see them again. Did they think she was dead?

"Spirits above, you're one lucky climber," he blurted out, snapping her focus back to him.

She shifted restlessly on her feet. Vaughn might be ecstatic she was alive, but he wasn't the easiest to fool. If anyone might see through her lies, it was him.

"Vaughn, my family..."

"Your family. I... I told them you died. We all thought you died."

Her mind froze. "Oh gods, I have to see them. C-can you let the team know I'm back?"

"Of course," he said and stepped back. "You don't know how good it is to know you're alive. I...I thought I'd never see you again."

A lump lodged in her throat. Her heart fluttered in her chest. Their time together was over but that didn't mean she was immune to him. He was always too damn good at saying the right thing sometimes. If only they had been better suited...

"I'm not going anywhere, Vaughn." She flashed him another smile and moved around him, breaking into a jog.

The streets were quiet, the lanterns extinguished for the night, save for the rare one that glowed amongst the gloomy night. A heavy silence permeated the air, broken only by the distant howling wind and the soft voices from within the homes. Plumes of smoke billowed up from chimneys, coiling high into the star-lit sky.

No one crossed her path as she navigated the familiar route back home. She sprinted harder, the cold air nipping at her cheeks, but she didn't care. She flung herself around the last corner and dashed up to her home. But out the front, she stopped dead for a second, white clouds of breath swirling around her lips. Her stomach gave a nervous flip before she strode up the steps. She grabbed the handle and flung the door open, striding inside.

A wave of warm air washed over her. The smell of stew invaded the first gulp of air inside. Her stomach gave a loud grumble...and her gaze fell on the two figures seated by the fire. Her parents jumped up in alarm, their faces turned ashen. For a second, they didn't seem to know her; then, her mother let out a strangled cry, slapping a hand to her mouth.

Her father, to his credit, looked pale and shocked but stood firm. "Wren?"

"Yes, Papa, it's me," uttered Wren, her voice trembling. "I'm okay."

With the words said, her mother rushed forward, pulling Wren into her arms, sobbing on her daughter's shoulder. Awkwardly, Wren wrapped her arms around her mother, while keeping her gaze on her father, wondering what he might say or do.

Their relationship had always been distant. There was not quite the same affection in his eyes when he looked at her, compared to when he looked at her sister, Ellie. Still, she knew he cared for her in his way. He eventually strode forward, squeezing her shoulder, and offered a small smile.

Finally, her mother pulled back, teary-eyed. "How? Vaughn told us a wyvern got you." Wren started to answer, but her mother held up a hand. "Oh gods, you've come so far, come sit! I'll get some food, yes, some food. You must be hungry and cold, too!"

Wren was hungry, but she was by no means cold after running home. Still, she removed her sheathed sword, then sat, pretending to warm herself by the fire, watching idly as her mother hurried about, gathering up some cheese and salted meat, before setting a small pot of stew left-over from the evening meal on the stove. As it warmed, her father sat down in front of her.

"What happened?" Those piercing blue eyes seemed to regard her more closely than they ever had.

It took her a moment to find her voice. She told him her lies. Whether or not he believed her words, he gave little indication. Only when his gaze flickered to the sword resting by the fire did his eyes betray something, widening slightly.

Recognition.

She summoned the question to her mouth but, thinking better of it, pressed her lips together. It wasn't the right time for an interrogation.

The door to her bedroom opened.

Ellie emerged, rubbing her eyes tiredly. Her long blonde tresses were unbound around her heart-shaped face, and she was wearing one of her thinner night dresses. Seeing Wren, however, her sister's hand fell and her jaw dropped.

"Sister?"

Ellie was across the room in a flash and Wren was on her feet, embracing her. As she did, she peered over Ellie's shoulder, the faint smell of perfume touching Wren's nose, and saw her father staring at her with a stony, unreadable expression.

Wren couldn't tear her gaze away.

Before dawn spilled between the mountain peaks and over the village, almost everyone knew of Wren's miraculous survival. Well-wishers came in droves, knocking on the door, curious to see her. The entire time she remained cloistered in her room, secure from their prying eyes. In time, she'd venture out. Their curiosity was only natural. She was the only climber who had returned after being snatched by a wyvern.

Who could blame them for their excitement?

Nothing ever happened in their sleepy village aside from the regular sale of the red flowers, which were dried and ground, made into a fine powder, and sold in small vials. A single trader came every year, paid handsomely, and then left without staying a night, let alone conversing with anyone he didn't have to. It was a trade agreement that had been in place as long as the village had existed.

By midday the attention had waned, giving time for Wren to slip out. She wore her thick furs for climbing and had her cloak set about her shoulders, with its hood down. Most of the villagers had started work. The women were in the main hut, grinding down the dried flowers. Most of the men were working in the few fields that skirted the village, on the side of the hill, where they grew what few things were able to survive the cold.

The few who were out smiled and waved at her. A couple came over and touched her reverently, murmuring how wonderful it was to have her back. She only wished she felt that way, instead of the strange sensation gnawing at her mind. Deep down, she was so happy to be back but she couldn't help but feel changed. She just wished she knew why.

Wren made her way to the climbing hut where her team was rigging up harnesses and studying maps of the mountains. Safe passages were always changing as avalanches happened or thick ice clung to cliff faces, making ascents impossible. New ones had to be found and marked. Then they had to carve indents for climbing tools in the cliff face.

None of her squad seemed to notice her standing at the edge of the room, warm in her furs, until Vaughn stood upright, stretching out his lean body with a long yawn.

"Wren, what are you doing here?"

Across the room, Mira and Flynn looked up from their seats by the fire. Shock flooded their faces, followed by relief.

"Where else would I be?"

"Your family..."

She glanced around the hut, taking stock of the gear hung on the wall, and the maps strewn across the main table. "I just wanted to stretch my legs for a bit and see what I'd missed here."

Vaughn nodded. "Yes, well, there's a bit for you to catch up on. You'll probably want to talk to Flynn. He took over with your orders after you..."

"Died?" she offered, trying to sound teasing, to which he flinched. Cursing internally, the smile fell from her lips. "Sorry."

Vaughn ushered her to the main table, where Flynn and Mira joined them. She embraced them both, but as she drew back from Flynn, he punched her softly in the arm. A ghost of a smile tugged his mouth upwards, easing a little knot of worry in her gut.

"What was that for?" she asked.

"Scaring us and putting me as your replacement. I didn't even know you'd considered me," he said, but there was no heat in his words, only relief.

She went to explain that she'd been intending to talk to him about it, but Mira strode forward again, hugging her.

"I, for one, am glad you're back," she announced. "I was getting worried being the only girl on the team, especially after Flynn selected two new climbers to join—both boys."

Before recent events, Wren had put little time into looking for new team members. It had been something she had been planning to do *after* the season. As tricky as it was to work with only four members, it was doable.

She looked at Flynn in surprise. "To work this season?"

"Without you, we were short, and the boys had shown promise since last year. Tane and Orson."

It was the two boys she'd had her eye on. "Good students. Teacher spoke well of them but I don't want them climbing with us till next season. If they pass their final assessments, then they can join us."

Flynn was silent for a moment. "We were..."

"It's okay," she assured. "I get it." She turned her attention to the maps sprawled across the table. "Mira, did you end up getting the seed count?"

Mira lifted out a list buried among the maps. "Seven bags. Unfortunately, even with whatever we get from this season's small yield, we will still be under last year's count."

Wren ran her hand over the map, tracing the routes and considering their options. "We need to figure out how to boost our yield. Now more than ever with our final product less and less each year."

"What happens if we can't figure out a way to increase our crop or stop our seed stocks dwindling?" asked Mira.

The future of their home appeared grim and uncertain in Wren's mind. Her job as their leader was to have successful harvests, which thus far hadn't been great. When she had taken on the role, she had such hopes to find a way to increase their yield. The old leader, Roland, had expressed those thoughts as well...and at that moment, she couldn't help but feel like she was failing them.

This was her home and she'd be damned if she let it die without a fight.

Chapter 6

From the ashes of an empire, we will rise again—in one form or another. Our time is far from over. We are Dragonirs. We are eternal.

—Queen Evanya's diary, final entry

WREN DREAMED SHE was flying; golden wings outstretched, shimmering faintly as the wind burst up through the turbulent clouds below. High above her the sun beat down a steady heat, tempered only by a bitter breeze.

She angled her wings, snapping them to her sides, as she shot downward, piercing the clouds. The wind cut like a blade, droplets of rain slashing her face as she burst through the cloud bank. Ominous, billowing plumes of smoke rose from the peaks of snow-capped mountains. They stretched out for as far as the eye could see, and swaths of fire rained down from the very clouds she'd descended from.

A savage cry tore through the air, anguished and soul screaming.

Wren sat up in her bed with a gasp, clutching her chest. She stayed there until her heart slowed, thoughts cleared, and her mind focused. Her gaze flew to the door, half expecting someone to enter. When no one did, she closed her eyes for a moment, sitting there in the darkness. Her throat burned, scraped raw.

With a sigh, she opened her eyes and dragged herself out of bed, stumbling over to her chest. Lifting it open, she dressed in her furs and then laced her boots on. She left her cloak hanging from the wall.

There would be no climbing today, so she omitted the strapping she usually wore on her back. Standing, she glanced at her sword, tucked quietly beneath the bed. For all her father's strange expression of recognition, he hadn't said anything. In fact, no one had. Despite their concerns of her being missing, presumed killed, and the story she'd told them, they ignored the topic and asked no questions about the sword.

In the four days since she'd gotten back, and still felt it was as though they were walking on eggshells around her. She was restless, itching for a climb. Aside from the short expeditionary one, which wasn't very high and involved more hiking than she liked, there was nothing available. The fields left to tend didn't need to be touched for several more days. Given the wyvern attack, it was standard practice to withdraw from climbing for a while.

She kept herself busy helping her mother to prepare food in the central hut, ensuring that those working on the drying and grinding of the flowers had food to eat.

On her way there, she saw Flynn by the well, drawing up a pitcher of water. He waved her over with a broad grin, his white teeth flashing. Smiling, she wandered over.

"Morning Flynn!"

"We didn't get to talk much when you came over," he complained, feigning hurt.

"I... I needed to get out. I was tired," she replied awkwardly. "Sorry."

He shrugged. "Hey, it's fine. We're all just glad you're alive. Not every day does someone survive a wyvern attack, you know?"

"By the grace of the spirits," she murmured.

He snorted. "You believe in them as much as I do."

The ghost of a smile tugged at her mouth. "Maybe, but you can't be spouting heretical stuff. How's the expedition going? Any new routes?"

A shadow clouded his face as his brow furrowed, making him seem older, wearier. "I found one but it's a hard climb," he said. "Why don't I get all the information for you?"

Wren nodded. "Good."

The prospect of a hard climb excited her and filled her body with energy. The mountains called to Wren, singing to her soul. The village might be her home, the place she cherished deeply, but those cliffs called to something else within her. It always had, though some days growing up, it really felt like she was alone in that sentiment.

"I'll come over to the hall later to see the maps. A climb would be the best thing for me right now. I need the ice and wind and sky. It'll put things back in perspective," she said.

The long look Flynn gave her said he wanted more of an explanation. The mood of talking passed, and she lied, saying that she was late and her mother would be angry. Then she promised to return later that day, to see what he had. That seemed to ease him, so he smiled and let her go.

She strode toward the hut, ready to sink her hands into some dough and forget everything else.

A few hours later, Wren could barely stand on her own two feet. Not one accustomed to tiring easily, she was forced to sit in the corner of the kitchen on the stool. Her mother came over and handed her a mug of steaming hot tea.

"You look exhausted. Go home and rest," she urged.

"That's *all* I've been doing," snapped Wren. Regretting her words immediately, she bowed her head. "Sorry, Mother."

Her mother gently touched her shoulder, which somehow made Wren like a fragile doll.

"I'm just glad my baby came home. I worry every time you climb. It scares me half to death but now, well I'm glad you've stopped."

Wren looked up. "Stopped?"

"Given up climbing, of course."

Her brow furrowed. "I haven't."

Her mother stared blankly. "I thought..."

Who told my mother I was quitting?

"I'm here because there are only minor climbs and hikes for new routes. I just spoke to Flynn, though, and he's got a good climb ready for me," said Wren quietly, then looked at the fire. "In a few days, I'll be back on the cliffs."

When she looked back, her mother was at the table, aggressively slicing vegetables, her lips a thin line.

Silence reigned heavily in the room.

Wren walked over to her mother, kissed her cheek, then murmured goodbye, and that she was heading back to sleep. Her mother said nothing as Wren retreated, though her slicing slowed.

The walk home was uneventful, and she found the house empty with the fire cold. She changed into her sleeping furs and climbed under the thick blankets. Wrapped up in their comforting warmth, she fell into a deep sleep, drawn by the dull ache in her body and a weariness that she couldn't explain.

In the evening, she woke up again. Ellie had returned and was sitting by the fire. Needle in hand, her sister mended one of her dresses, humming softly. Bathed in the amber glow, she appeared ethereal to Wren, a kind of spirit in the flesh. Sometimes, she'd had that thought growing up. Her sister, the quieter one, always had that air about her.

The strange daughter, some had said, then looked at Wren with a pitying look, *and the wild one.*

Even when they'd both been in the school to become climbers, there had been those whispers about them both. She'd never let it bother her but, after a time, Ellie stopped coming. It had been a sore point between them for a little while.

Her sister glanced up. "You're up."

"When did you get back?" asked Wren.

"Not long. I had a little mending that I wanted to finish. How are you?" Ellie held up the dress, eyeing it for a moment before draping it over her lap.

"Tired more than I like," confessed Wren. "I'll be okay soon enough, though. I have to be."

Ellie scrunched up her face. "Honestly, I don't think I could return to climbing after being snatched away by a wyvern. It wanted to eat you, Wren! How does that not scare you?"

Because I stared it down... and won.

Wren shrugged. "What happened to the girl that used to follow me everywhere? I remembered you also wanted to be a climber. You were good, too. I always thought we'd be up there together."

Ellie set her needlework down in her lap. "I grew up, Wren. I decided I wanted different things."

"You've said that but you never really explained it further, though."

Ellie rolled her eyes. "I want adventure, Wren. A life beyond this village. I want to live in a place where I'm...well, more. I don't know how to explain it."

Her breath hitched. Growing up she'd known her sister had struggled with feeling different, just like she had. Whilst Wren had never sickened and healed quickly, Ellie always seemed to find herself around death. From discovering dead animals in the woods, being close by when the elderly or sick passed, or when fatal accidents occurred. It was never directly Ellie's fault...but that shadow never seemed to be far away.

"Where will you go?" she asked.

"Who knows? Danomir is a large kingdom and who says I must stay there. There is a whole world to explore," said Ellie wistfully.

The thought of her sister leaving twisted through her. She knew that look in Ellie's eyes though. This wouldn't be something she could get her sister to abandon. One way or another, Ellie was destined to leave Fenware. She just wished she didn't feel so tethered to the mountains, that she could go with her.

"Do our parents know?"

Ellie snorted. "What do you think?"

"They deserve to, Ellie," replied Wren, her voice low. "You can't blindside them with this. They deserve the truth."

When she looked at her sister, there was hesitation and fear in Ellie's eyes. "They'll stop me."

"You won't face them alone."

Surprise flickered across Ellie's face, which hurt more. It made Wren ashamed that her sister needed to lie, to act alone. As if that were the only option.

"But you could risk your position as leader of the climbers. Papa has a lot of sway with them. He could make things difficult for you," argued Ellie. "I didn't want you to lose your position because of me."

Wren closed the distance to her sister and kneeled, setting her hands on Ellie's. When her sister finally lifted her gaze, Wren smiled.

"Climber numbers are so low they won't risk taking me off the squad. So, don't you worry about me, okay? I'm your big sister and it's my job to be there for you."

When Ellie left for her work at the stables, Wren headed off to the climber's hut. Mira was inside, packing her gear by the warm glow of the fire. Behind her Flynn sat at the table, reading, pausing only as Wren approached and, seeing her, he set the book aside.

"Hey, Wren."

"Flynn, Mira. How are things here?"

"I've finished sorting the gear," called Mira from where she sat. "I've checked over yours and Flynn's, but left it out for you to pack when you're ready."

Walking over to the table Wren eyed the sprawled-out map, running her finger over one of the trails. Flynn stood and pointed to one of the closer peaks, less than an hour's walk, followed by what looked to be a decent climb.

Wren nodded, then glanced back at the map. "That's the new track?"

"It's the one I mentioned before. If the weather holds, it might give us a new place to prepare for cultivation," ventured Flynn.

No black dots on the map, which meant no handholds in place. It wasn't a problem for her—she'd climbed without them before. She would just have to take more care.

"I'll look for places where the holds can be placed and mark them as I go. When I reach the top, I'll find a rigging point for you to put the holds in."

It was far from wyvern territory, so there wouldn't be any worry of her going alone. And at that moment, she needed some time away, if only to get her thoughts in order. Everything was changing too fast and she was at a loss on how to proceed.

She traced her hand over the map, then stepped back and massaged the base of her spine.

"Want to take a seat?" asked Flynn, gesturing to the seats by the fire.

Nodding, she sat down, closing her eyes for a moment as she soaked in the warmth.

"Here's a drink."

When she opened her eyes, Flynn was holding out a mug of spiced ale. Taking it gratefully, she took a small sip and enjoyed the warmth that settled in her gut. Her gaze drifted to the flames dimly aware Flynn was watching her.

"Can I ask you something?"

She nodded. "Sure."

"Why did you choose me? Is it because of what I am? That I won't marry a woman and be distracted?" The doubt in his voice cleaved a hole in her heart.

How can you believe that I think so little of you? "You were the best choice. Vaughn has no interest in being a climber long-term and Mira is too inexperienced. You have the skills, the calm temperament, and the head for the hard choices."

It seemed to satisfy him. The tension bled from his shoulders and he fell back into his chair, somber, lost in his thoughts. Whatever was going on in his head, she had no idea but hoped he would talk to her soon. If he didn't, she push him.

"There are rumors of abandoning the village," he murmured.

It wasn't the first time she'd heard that but the tone in his voice made her pause. She leaned back into her chair. "We had a decent harvest this year. I admit it wasn't as much as the year before, but we just need to find some new spots. There's still a chance. We can't just give up."

"And we won't, but even you have to admit we're running on borrowed time," he replied.

As much as she hated to admit it, he was right. It was fast becoming a matter of when their mysterious buyer, whomever the merchant sold directly to, stopped buying. Unless she found them new spots to harvest and their yield dramatically increased, there wouldn't be any other option but to leave. They were all living on borrowed time.

She sank deeper into her chair, mulling over their options. There had to be something they could do. "Call me stubborn, but we're not dead yet. Spirits above, I just wish the elders weren't so damn afraid of going elsewhere to sell the flowers or branching out."

Flynn scowled into the flames. "I asked my father about that. He said the elders were bound by a trade agreement. I tried to push, but he said there had been serious consequences before when the village tried to change things."

Surprise flickered through her. "He actually gave you an answer?"

The scowl fell from his face, the corners of his mouth twitching as he glanced at her. "We were enjoying some of his favorite spiced ale and he started talking. There's nothing wrong with that."

She smiled, the burden resting on her shoulders, feeling for the moment, a little lighter. "Nothing at all. Wish that ale would solve our harvest problems though or find us some new fields."

He held out his empty mug, grinning in the firelight at her. "Who knows what tomorrow will hold?"

Chapter 7

Dragonir and Dragon are far more alike than we might like to believe. Perhaps that is what scares us? One is human, granted the ability to become a dragon, though at no small price. The other, though possessing numerous abilities, is rarely able to take a human form. It seems our form challenges or repulses them. Perhaps both.

—Excerpt from the Dragonir Chronicles Vol 6

THE CLOUDS PARTED, revealing a bright, jewel-blue sky and a warmth from the sun that wasn't chilled by icy winds. The perfect time to climb.

With the rest of the climbers helping to dry and prepare the ground flowers, Wren had some time to spare. She'd told Flynn she'd inspect the route he was curious about and see if it was a viable climb. He'd agreed, making her promise to return before dusk.

One never climbed alone, but Wren had been doing it for years. Often sneaking out as a child, it had carried on, even as she grew more experienced and knew what dangers the cliffs held. She'd once tried to explain the burning desire but they didn't understand. Sometimes, she had to be alone, that even amongst her own team or within her village, she felt *different*. Being on the cliffs made her feel centered in a way she couldn't make them understand.

A day like one that shone outside with calm skies and little wind.

Wren double-checked her gear, then reached up and grasped the first hold. She dug her feet in, propelling herself up. The ground rapidly vanished beneath her as she scrambled up the cliff.

For one moment, the worries about her village's future were quiet.

As she came to the first outcrop of a cliff, she hauled herself onto it. Twisting around, she sat up, letting her legs dangle over the side. The long slope of the mountain cut down into a sprawling valley that advanced to the horizon. Small tendrils of smoke wound up through the thick forest, showing signs of the other villages within it.

It was easy to look out, to miss that smoke, and to think perhaps you were all alone in the world.

She took a sip from her waterskin, then replaced it in her back holster before she rose and set off again. She climbed swiftly, avoiding any unnecessary pauses but being careful not to tire herself. When her hand finally curled over the edge, she scrambled onto the safe ground and flopped onto her back.

After she was fully rested, she sat up and looked around. The ground sprawled out before her, resembling a fair-sized clearing. It was enclosed by steep cliffs on all sides that rose high into the clouds.

They resembled a white veil separating her world from the ghostly one that existed above. It shouldn't have drawn her, but after catching a glimpse of the ruins, she wanted to return. It was like an itch that she couldn't scratch.

With time to spare, she surveyed the clearing from end to end. In the middle, she kneeled on and dug her fingers through the grass, squeezing the near-black soil. It was slightly damp to the touch, which was a good sign and as she brought it to her nose, the rich earthy scent filled her lungs.

Her heart squeezed painfully.

Each time she reached a new spot and inspected the soil, a sharp pain burned in her chest. More than once, she was almost brought to tears, though she could never pin why.

Sighing, she pushed herself to her feet. Moving on, she walked to the edge of the clearing, inspecting the rock face for any places to climb up. At first glance, it looked like there were places they could fix holds.

As she neared the end of her survey, she found the cliff wall folded inwards, revealing the small mouth of a narrow cave, scarcely more than a slit in the rock. If she hadn't been walking so close to it, she probably would've missed it completely.

Inching nearer, she peered into the thick darkness, hearing a faint trickle in the distance.

Water.

Her heart leaped. It was rare to find a clearing with a water source they could access. Before her time, the climbers used to have one, but it was lost after a terrible storm. Now, they had to bring the water up with them.

But if there was water through that crack, then there was hope for her village. With a deep breath, she slipped in, plunging into the darkness and using her hand as a guide.

Moving along, the sound of water grew louder and the darkness softened before her, parting slowly to reveal the dull glow of daylight. She crept closer until she passed across the threshold of light.

For a moment, she was blind before her eyes adjusted. A sprawling cave stretched out in front. The stone walls curved up, meeting in the middle at an opening, revealing a bright blue sky. From the opening, a thin bubble of water trickled down. It dripped into the pond below, mirroring the sky.

And growing around the edge were the red flowers she'd spent her life cultivating. The tricky plants that required so much care, were growing wild in this cave. She smiled as she crouched over them. Yet when her fingers brushed over the flowers, her heart squeezed painfully.

She drew back her fingers as an icy chill brushed against the nape of her neck.

A low growl sounded behind her.

Startled, she jumped to her feet, spinning around. Her heart slammed against her ribs.

From where she'd entered the cave stood a huge wolf-like creature with glowing red eyes. Its lips pulled back as it growled at her.

Her legs buckled as she struggled to understand how the hell this creature was on the mountain. The only sign of life she'd ever seen before was the occasional bird or wyvern. It made no sense.

The creature inched forward, one enormous shadowy paw after another.

She yanked out her daggers, breathing sharply. "Get back!"

It ignored her, growling louder as it came closer, ears flattened. Her shouting appeared to only anger it.

She'd confronted a wyvern and won. Bracing up, she lifted up her daggers, praying to any deity that would listen, that her blades would pierce its skin. If they didn't, she'd be dead.

The beast's burning eyes moved to the flowers, then back to her. It growled again.

Surely it isn't protecting the flowers? She frowned, wondering why no climber had ever encountered this before. Or perhaps they had and never lived to tell the story?

Finally releasing the breath she'd been holding, she stepped to the side and began moving away from the pond. Strangely, the beast crept to the flowers, keeping its eyes on her before it sank to its stomach.

Her heart slammed sharply against her ribs as she backed out of the cave, keeping her gaze on the creature. When she finally made it back out into the clearing, she didn't stop moving until she reached the edge of the cliff.

Wasting no time, she slid herself over the edge and began her descent. She scrambled down, trying to ignore her tangling thoughts of the wolf and the flowers. All she wanted to do was to get as far as possible from the creature, and the cave that stirred feelings she didn't understand.

Lost in her thoughts, a piercing shriek broke her focus. Her hand slipped. Gasping, she held firm with the other hand and reached up to grab the rock face again. A shadow flashed overhead. Seconds later, talons sank into her shoulder. A fiery pain flared, bone-crunching and muscle shredded, as she was ripped from the cliff.

No! Not again!

Air rushed from her lungs, devouring the scream that burst to her lips. Her chest squeezed tightly, as she tried desperately to breathe. Talons sank into her shoulder, shattering bone and piercing flesh. Molten fire roared through her limbs. She tried to fight it but the abyss consumed her, body and soul.

And from deep within the void came a thundering roar.

Chapter 8

It is by no decree that the Dragonirs do not venture beyond their own territory or by the fact we permit no human within; it is only by their reclusive nature they seek the isolation and safety of the mountains. They are watched by those below, who hunger for the lands beyond their reach.

—Excerpt from the Dragonir Chronicles

THE WARM CRACKLE of a fire-filled her ears as she slowly stirred awake. The smell of smoke, and of meat roasting on the fire, filled her lungs with every deep breath she took. Her stomach growled, rousing her further into the waking world. She opened her eyes, perceiving everything in a hazy blur before it cleared, bringing into focus darkness spotted with glittering jewels.

Stars, she realized, as she took in the sprawling night sky above her. Groaning, she rolled over, and there *he* was, stoking the fire idly. His eyes were unfocused and fixed on the flames.

As if he sensed her staring, Lorca looked up and regarded her with a cautious expression. She felt exposed in his gaze but held it anyway, defiance keeping her eyes steady.

"Your clothes were, um, shredded in your fall," he said.

Glancing down, she took stock of her new state of dress beneath the thin blanket draped over her. A fresh shirt and pants, with boots that felt a size too small on her feet.

"How am I alive?" she asked, recalling the moment the wyvern ripped her off the cliff and feeling the pain in her chest. "Why didn't the wyvern kill me?"

He set the stick he'd poking the fire with to one side, quiet for a moment. "The dragon saved you."

"He just happened to be in the area?" she ventured dubiously.

Wren studied that dark and handsome face, wondering once again what secrets he kept buried within, and his curious connection to the dragon.

"He knew you were on your own, so he wanted to make sure you were safe. Especially since the wyverns don't seem to like you," he replied, the corner of his mouth twitching. "You like to climb alone, don't you?"

"You say that like you've watched me."

He shook his head but there was a faint smile tugging at his mouth. "No, but my friend has seen your climbers take to the cliffs. He tried to keep the wyverns away, to keep your people safe, but their hunger made them more aggressive. He is sorry you were attacked twice."

Wren had never seen a dragon watching over her people. But for all her reluctance, she couldn't figure out what malicious intent Lorca might have. What could he hope to gain by lying to her when she had nothing to give him?

"Is this to be a thing for us? Wyverns attacking me, the dragon saving me, you patching me up? It makes me seem quite helpless," remarked Wren, smiling.

He snorted. "You killed a wyvern by yourself. I'd say you're not help-less."

She tried to sit up, but a wave of dizziness rushed over her. Abruptly, she turned and emptied the contents of her stomach by the fire. Red-faced, she wiped her mouth and looked up, horrified. "I'm sorry."

Then, slowly, she glanced down and froze.

Among the reddish contents were shards of bone.

Snow crunched beneath her boots, puncturing the surrounding si-lence. Wren tried to focus on it. She wanted to keep her mind away from all that had happened and the look in Lorca's eyes as he led her back down the mountain.

It had been a look that she'd been trying to forget since he left her to continue the rest of the way.

Shaking her head, she pushed on down the path. She kept her eyes on the snow, which must've fallen in the night she'd been asleep, and tried to brace herself for the fight she knew was coming.

By the time Wren glimpsed the village up ahead, she was on edge, her mind tugging in several directions. The creature, the meeting with Lorca, the shards of bone she'd thrown up. All of it twisted in her thoughts, leaving her confused and uneasy, half terrified of herself.

What happened after the wyvern ripped me off the cliff?

When she approached the edge of the village, she saw no one. It was quiet, *too* quiet.

She slowed, lingering for a moment, wondering where everyone was. A sense of unease slithered down her spine.

As she came to the climber's hut, the entrance opened, and Vaughn and Mira stepped outside. Their heads were close together as they spoke in low voices.

"Vaughn? Mira?"

The pair of them looked up, eyes widening. Vaughn moved first, clos-ing the distance with a look of relief. He pulled her into his arms, squeezing her tightly. She didn't fight him, but when he relaxed, she un-tangled herself from his embrace.

Mira approached from behind him, studying Wren. "You're okay. When the snowstorm hit last evening, we were worried. Flynn said you'd probably hunkered down somewhere and would come back safe."

"I was lucky and found a cave," replied Wren. "I hid there until the weather eased."

Vaughn nodded, a look of hope flickering on his face. "You were fortunate indeed. Storm aside, was there anywhere good to plant?"

She shook her head. "No. All stone and no water source."

The hope in his eyes spluttered out. "Damn. Guess it doesn't matter right now. We've got bigger problems."

"Bigger problems?"

"The merchant came early," he explained, then glanced around, as if someone might overhear him. "We should go inside."

Mira cleared her throat. "I have to head home. Let me know if you need anything?"

With a nod from Wren, Mira hurried off, leaving Vaughn and her alone. She wondered if he saw the lie on her face.

She followed him into the hall, where Flynn sat by the fireplace. He glanced up at her, relief on his face as he gave her a small smile.

Vaughn sat down across from Flynn, leaving her to take the spare seat beside him. She glanced between the two men, uneasy at the grim looks on their faces.

"What's happened?"

"The merchant came early," said Flynn softly. "He took what little powder was left and gave us the standard delivery of supplies."

"But we haven't finished harvesting. Why would he come now?" asked Wren, confused.

There were still at least two weeks of work left to be done. Two more fields had to be harvested. After that, the plants would die and go to seed with the final approach of winter. Which would give her team only a brief window to gather the last of the seeds.

She glanced between them before settling on Vaughn, leveling a searching look at him.

"There's more," he began. "The merchant said there's a lot of unrest near us. Empress Alexandria's men have been sighted in nearby villages, rounding up people of the accused."

"Well, we should be fine," she replied. "We have no business with any of that kind of thing. We keep to ourselves."

Flynn sat forward in his chair. "Perhaps, but I can't help but wonder why he came so early? Every year, when he took his leave, he would say he looked forward to returning next year. He didn't say that this time. I wonder if it was a warning?"

A chill passed through Wren. "So, are the elders saying we must abandon the village? Or praying this unrest doesn't touch us?"

Shadows darkened Vaughn's eyes, a look of contempt on his face. "The elders are discussing what to do."

"Which means they'll be talking about it for days and I guess we may not have that much time."

Vaughn and Flynn shared a look, which she couldn't read. Vaughn sighed, worry darkening his face.

"The merchant told us what happened to those captured. He said they were sold into slavery."

Silence hung heavily between them.

The elders remained in discussion well into the night, much to Wren's dismay. The hall was barred, ensuring no one intruded on the meeting. She wanted to know what ideas they were considering.

She had to act, do something. It wasn't in her nature to just sit and wait for disaster to hit.

Reluctantly, she retreated to her home, where her mother watched her enter from her seat by the fire. She said nothing as Wren continued into the room she shared with her sister, who lay fast asleep, curled up beneath the furs.

Wren stripped off her clothes, wincing as she surveyed her bandaged wounds. She carefully lifted the wrappings to inspect the damage. What had once been red and ugly was mostly healed. Lorca must have cleaned the wounds and changed her bandages before dressing her.

Gods, how many times will he undress me?

Once she changed into her night shift, she crawled under the blankets and wrapped herself up, closing her eyes in an effort to sleep.

After an hour or so, sleep refused to even nudge at her mind. She kicked away the furs, staring up at the moonlit ceiling. Dozens of wild ideas swirled around in her head, leaving her to consider what to do.

The mountains *were* the best option. And there was one person who might know of somewhere safe the villagers could go. A place that could offer them shelter, even from wyverns.

Perhaps she could ask the dragon himself if he would consider aiding them. If a dragon was nearby, anyone attempting to attack her people would think twice.

Now, knowing what she had to do, she got up and donned her furs, and strapped on her sword. If she were to encounter a wyvern again, she'd best be ready. Before she left, she kissed her sister's forehead, vowing to return with a way to keep the village safe.

She closed the door behind her and taking a deep breath, headed out.

The village was quiet and lit only by a few low burning torches. Near the entrance, she glimpsed a figure striding up from the path below. Even without seeing his face, Wren knew who it was and without a chance to hide, he saw her, too. Vaughn pushed back his hood and peered at her in the dim light.

"Wren, is that you? Where are you going?"

"I can't stand idly by and wait for the elders to make a decision. Not when I might have a way to help our village," she said softly. "I'm heading out but I'll be back by dusk."

He touched her arm, leaning in a little. "It's dangerous out there, especially at night."

"It'll be dawn soon enough."

"The village is a mess of worry right now. You're needed here," he argued.

She stepped closer to him. "You need to convince the elders to stay until dusk. I'll be back by then."

"Why can't you do it?" he insisted.

A rueful smile lifted her mouth. "The elders *tolerate* me. They like you. If anyone can convince them, it's you. Besides, you know I climb quicker than you, so I'm faster on my own. Which is what I need right now."

He didn't seem sure and, as he glanced back at the village, then at her, he sighed. "What could be out there that could save us?"

"I met a man up in the mountains. He is friends with a dragon."

There, I said it. She watched his eyes widen, the shock parting his mouth.

"What?"

"I'll explain everything when I get back, but time is of the essence. Please, just *trust me*," she urged, grabbing his arm.

He looked like he wanted to argue with her and push for more answers. Then he sighed and the fight fled out of him. Relief filled her as he reached out, gently cupping her cheek.

"You come back to us, okay?"

She nodded, not trusting herself to speak as she turned away and set off into the dark.

Chapter 9

And so, it was, the Avalon dragon, Vaska, stepped forward and set a wreath of fire upon Evanya, crowning her queen. The room sang out in praise, two voices louder than all—her two children, Adrian and Yelena.

—Excerpt from the Dragonir Chronicles.

AS WREN RETRACED the hard path through the forest, she kept a brisk pace. When she hit the cliff face, she steeled herself. She wasn't coming back down without a solution.

The jagged cliff was an easy climb. Reaching up, she grabbed the rock and hauled herself up. The ground fell away, and as she powered up the cliff face, muscles burning, she spied the top. Pulling herself over, she stood.

What little snow had fallen a few days ago was now mostly melted away. It was a familiar pattern around this time of the year. It'd be another month, at least before the heavy snow set in which would remain for the winter.

A narrow path stretched before her, winding up into the mountains. There were a few sections where the path rose steeply, forcing her to climb.

With each hold that she grabbed, Wren found rising confidence in her sense of direction. Somehow, she *knew* where to go. It was as if something was calling her. She didn't want to think about where this feeling came from, or how she'd convince Lorca to help her.

As the sun spilled over the mountains, Wren emerged from the path, the sunlight warm against her cheeks. She pushed back her fur-lined hood and peered out, half expecting Lorca to be there, waiting for her.

Yet only the bones of a dead empire stared back at her, unseen ghosts stirring. A strange prickle of sadness rose in her chest, thickening in her throat. Swallowing it back, she pushed on, setting off down the middle of the valley where the houses rose on the cliffs on either side.

"Lorca!" she called out, her voice echoing.

No reply came. She reached the end and peered up along the cliff face, squinting at the thin layer of cloud that swirled above. Something tightened in her chest. A thought whispering through her mind in a voice that wasn't hers.

Climb.

The cliff loomed before her, the end nowhere in sight, lost among the clouds. With a deep breath, she reached up to the first hold she spied and pulled herself up, climbing with care for what felt like an eternity. Her limbs burned, and a thin layer of sweat gathered on her brow. The ground beneath her fell away and soon the cloud consumed her completely, icy moisture gathering against her skin. She pushed herself to keep climbing. Finally, she broke through the clouds, and the end was in sight. With a last burst of energy, she surged up until she was able to drag herself over the edge and onto the flat ground. With several steadying breaths, she stood, dusted off the snow, and looked around.

The ruins of an ancient city stared back at her. A long, wide street was flanked by homes and what might once have been shops. It was as though the whole city was carved into the rock itself.

Advancing her gaze over the ruins, she glimpsed what seemed to be a long path snaking up an otherwise untouched section of rock. It curled right up to a set of ornate golden gates, guarding the entrance to the largest structure she'd ever seen. A thousand houses blended into one, with a hundred or more platforms jutting out. Two vast spires flanked it, rising from the rock. At the top of it, where the cliff ended, she spied a large dome-like building—the kind she'd seen in books.

The palace of Dragonirs.

She'd never seen a real palace before, only exaggerated drawings in books which didn't do this one justice. Though smaller than some of those pictured, it was still colossal, even from a distance. In her foolish dreams, she'd imagined finding a city full of legends, of dragons and life. But instead, she saw only ruins, a city abandoned—dead.

She stared, an odd thumping sensation filled in her chest. Instinct pulled her again, one step at a time, in the direction of the palace.

Was Lorca there? Was he drawing her to him, or was it perhaps some other force?

She hoped he was, though she wondered why he'd choose to live there. It was, of course, the largest building in the city and possibly still furnished, but it was also so desolate and quiet. It seemed such a lonely choice, full of ghosts and empty, whispering halls.

Shaking her head, she set off across the dead city, calling out his name, pausing only to listen as her voice echoed against the ruins. A lone voice with no reply but hers.

The path she was following, wound up and snaked back and forth along the cliff, rising to a large clearing, dominated by the golden gates. They still shone, as if someone polished them every day. She reached out, but as her hand nearly touched them, they opened, soundlessly and smoothly, admitting her to an opulent courtyard set before the entrance.

"Lorca?" she called out, but there was still no answer.

Tentatively, she crossed the courtyard and approached two huge golden doors, which were engraved with the images of two dragons. Their eyes gleamed a vivid amber.

Gems. A shiver snaked down her spine. It was as though the dragons themselves were staring at her...

She felt like an intruder as she walked into a grand foyer, thick with shadows, pierced only with light that spilled in from behind. As her eyes adjusted to the gloom, she saw a grand staircase, with a pair of ornate stone dragons perched at the ends, as if standing guard.

Her feet carried her over, her hands tracing the details of the dragons. Their long, angular heads were bowed, their eyes downcast to the floor. They were carved of blackened stone, polished smooth.

Turning from the staircase, she continued down a nearby hall, the darkness thickening around her. Just as it consumed her completely, a light erupted on either side, followed by another and then another, bursting to life in a long line before her. Lit torches guided her way. She froze, wondering what magic conjured them to life. Forcing herself to continue walking, they remained lit until she passed across a section with windows on one side, sunlight washing over her. She paused, peering out across the city, imagining what it might've looked like when it was alive and vibrant.

A flash of her village, abandoned, just like the city, forgotten to time, burst in her mind. She hurried on.

The palace passed by in a labyrinth of rooms and halls. On many of the walls hung tapestries that spun stories she'd never heard of. Statues of men and women stood guard at doors and in rooms. There were even some in what might have once been private gardens. Their lifeless eyes kept watch, and Wren could have sworn their gaze followed her as she moved on.

In a room full of paintings, she paused. A myriad of faces adorned the wall, most of which were wearing finery bearing the same symbol of a dragon circling fire. At the end of the room was a painting of a dark-haired woman, barely thirty and eternally beautiful. Her jewel-green eyes glowed against her olive skin, and the sharp slope of her nose was distinct above the proud jut of her chin. The bearing of a queen. Wren's gaze fell to the inscription beneath and though she couldn't read it she felt the name whisper through her mind, almost as if she *recognized* her.

Evanya.

The last Queen of the Dragonirs.

What must it have been like for her to stand in her palace, watching as her empire crumbled?

Was she helpless, or did she fight to the tragic end?

As she turned to leave, another torch illuminated the room, revealing a picture of a man and woman. Their shared eyes, nose, mouth, complexion, and noble expression spoke of shared blood. But it wasn't *that* which held her still. She couldn't tear her eyes away from *his* gaze, for she recognized exactly who they were.

Prince Adrian and Princess Yelena.

The youthful prince bore a dead reckoning to Lorca.

"What are you doing here?" thundered a voice from behind her.

She spun around with a curse, a hand on her racing heart. Before her, cast in the glow of a torch, was Lorca. His dark jewel-green eyes, the eyes of a *prince*, stared back at her, unflinching.

"You..." The words died in her throat, swallowed by shock.

All the pleas she had in her mind to implore him for aid shattered as she tried to connect the man she barely knew with the prince from the stories. The prince who had loved the Queen's sorceress, Litania, and whose love had not been returned. Who, before he could run, had wandered into a dragon cave full of nests and slept a whole night in the dead of winter, curled at the side of a wild dragon. The prince who had taken his dragon form on his fourteenth birthday, the youngest of any Dragonir.

"What are you doing here?" he repeated, striding to her.

When he stopped before her, she couldn't tear her gaze away. Finally, the words came to her as the shock ebbed away. "I need your help. My village is in danger."

Those immortal eyes searched hers, but for what, she didn't know. She felt them burrow into her soul, tearing back walls, hunting. When he withdrew, his face betrayed nothing. Her breath stayed caught in her chest, her heart frozen.

"You shouldn't be here." He spun away, but she seized his arm instinctively.

With a deep breath, he jerked his arm out of her grasp and strode away. Wren ran after him.

"*Please*, I'll-"

He stopped and looked at her intently. "You'll *what?*"

"If you help me hide my villagers from slavers. I'll pay any price I must."

Those emerald eyes burned, searching for something in her. "Any price?"

She thought of what would happen to her sister and her village, and turned away, saying, "I'll do anything you ask, give my life even... but if you truly refuse, I'll go. I don't have time to wait for a decision." She held her breath, anticipating his refusal.

He cleared his throat, speaking after a tense silence. "How did you get into the palace? The gates don't open for just anyone."

"They did for me."

His eyes widened, betraying a look of surprise. It was hastily concealed beneath an unreadable mask.

"You seek sanctuary for your people. You want nothing more?"

Wren frowned. Was she meant to be seeking more? Had she done anything to give that idea? What bothered her was that he seemed *disappointed*.

"Just that." Her frown deepened. "I told you I would pay any price for their safety."

He nodded again, as if the price was, for the moment, irrelevant. "Very well. Come with me."

Chapter 10

Idris and Vaska believe the end beckons at the hand of betrayal. They say the spirits whisper to them in their dreams—beware the broken Dragonir. I now must turn my gaze inwards on who will betray us all.

—Excerpt from Queen Evanya's diary.

FLYNN STARED UP at the ceiling, Vaughn's words playing over in his mind. *She's gone.* Those two words had ripped the air out of his lungs. The look in Vaughn's eyes had been enough to prove he wasn't lying. Wren had run off on some wild scheme to save the village.

Alone.

He cursed her foolishness and sat up, throwing the covers aside. He knew how deeply she loved the village and understood that determination in her eyes. She was a storm unto herself and he pitied anyone who stood between her and whatever she set her mind to.

He swung his legs over the side of the bed, wincing as his feet hit the cold floor. Accepting that sleep wasn't happening, he padded his way out into the living area. There he found his mother rolling out dough. The warm, yeast smell filled the air, touched faintly with sweet notes. Realizing what she was making, he grinned. She glanced up at him, her weathered face crinkling into a smile. She pushed away from the table and limped over to him.

An injury from her years as a climber had never healed right. He knew it pained her, but she never liked to show it.

"What's wrong?" she asked, looking him over from head to toe.

Even when he was smiling, he knew she saw right through it. Little escaped his mother's shrewd gaze.

"It's nothing." The lie tasted like ash in his mouth, but he worried if he said Wren was gone, that something might happen to her.

She frowned and caressed his cheek. "You're too young to carry so much on your shoulders."

"I'm okay, Mother." He looked at the dough left on the bench. "Sweet bread again this month? You're spoiling father and I."

His mother chuckled softly. "I thought since you've been working so hard, we could have some sweet bread. Your father got me some sugar, so it seemed a fitting way to—"

A thunderous bang swallowed whatever she was going to say next. Flynn spun to the front door as more explosions sounded outside. Then screams filled the air.

"Flynn! What's going on?" his mother asked, grabbing his arm.

"Stay inside," he ordered, taking one of his daggers from his belt. "Whatever is happening, you stay inside, okay?"

"Flynn..."

He threw open the door, shock gutting his chest as chaos greeted him. He turned back to his mother. The sight of her trembling and the ashen look on her face made him hesitate. But he knew he had to find his father and figure out what was happening.

He strode forward, quickly kissed her brow, and returned to the door, pausing as he glanced back. "Hide, Mother. I'll find Father."

Then he was out, slamming the door shut behind him and racing down the road. Strange glowing and large spheres materialized in the air everywhere he looked. As each one appeared, armored men came running out with swords aloft. Their savage cries filled the air as they descended on the defenseless village.

Blood pounded in his ears, his mouth filling with ash. Dread filled his gut.

It was as though the demon realm itself had descended upon Fenware.

Flynn ducked behind a wagon as a portal burst to life a few feet away. Heart racing, he pressed himself against the wheel, watching as a dozen men surged. They went straight to his neighbor's home, crashing through the front door. Screams resounded from within, and then the men spilled out, dragging the occupants out. Kids squirmed to break free, adults thrashing and clawing to escape. Mothers screamed as infants were ripped from their arms. The soldiers ignored the pleas and tears, moving with brutal efficiency.

The mother, Reena, broke free and jumped to her feet. One man spun back, driving his sword through her chest. Hal screamed for his wife as the blade was yanked out and Reena crumpled lifelessly to the ground. Blood glistened on the blade, lit by the glow of the firelight. A dark stain darkened on Reena's back.

"Get them back to the portals—*now!*" one man snarled as he spun off, striding into the village.

Flynn waited until their backs were turned and dashed across the road, slipping in behind a row of houses. Screams, pleas for mercy, and terrified cries for help encircled him as he hurried along, heart thumping. The blood roared in his ears.

The crackling of flames soon reached him. He rounded the corner, and smoke flooded his lungs. His chest burned, and coughing, he squinted through the haze.

The long road stretching out before him burned. A wave of heat slammed into him.

Flames licked the houses, with smoke billowing thick and black into the sky, blocking out the sunlight. It looked like one of the seven hells had descended on Fenware. Shouts came from behind him, growing closer. He peered down the burning street, trying to decide where to go next. Only one option lay open to him. He darted to his right, running down the middle of the road.

A portal materialized in a burst of white light. He ran harder, right past it, as more men rushed out. Someone shouted. He'd been seen.

He didn't stop running, darting down behind the dining hut. Sweat beaded his face as he spied the village square, with the meeting hall in the middle. His heart was slamming viciously against his ribs, nearly ripping itself out of his chest. The blood drained from his face as he looked at the building, knowing with dread his father had last been working there.

Flames devoured it.

He stopped dead, grief roaring through his mind like a storm unleashed. A scream welled up from his soil, barely contained by dwindling self-control. In the middle of the street were armed men hauling people through an open portal. Behind them lay a row of bodies, their throats opened to bloodied smiles. One man with red hair caught his eye.

Father!

His knees wobbled, threatening to give out when a man looked up. Their eyes met across the smoky air. The world slowed to a crawl. He tried to tell himself to move, to run. He had to get back to his mother, get her out. But fear pinned him down, choking the scream of fury that was trapped in his throat.

More men spotted him, their shouts erupting around him. Several men came running toward him, swords drawn.

Finally, his body moved. He spun around, taking off down the road. There was only one way forward. He'd have to circle back to his house and get his mother out. Heat burned through his legs as he sprinted through the back streets.

If they haven't already got her too, a voice threatened.

Shuddering, tears burning his cheeks, he raced to the tree line. If he could just make it there, then he could hide among the trees. Heat burned his lungs with every breath, singing his lips and skin. Ash clung to his sweat-soaked face, the gray rivulets running down his face, brushing his lips. The fetid taste filled his mouth but he didn't care.

Just keep moving!

He burst past the last house, the tree line within reach.

"Flynn, this way!" screamed Mira, emerging from the shadows up ahead.

She waved him down. Blood streamed from a gash on her head, ash and soot dirtying her face. But she looked otherwise okay. Her eyes widened suddenly, catching sight of something to his right. His gaze darted over, his heart freezing for a moment. A soldier.

"*Run!*" he screamed. She hesitated and he pinned a pleading look at her. "*Run, Mira, run!*"

He turned, drawing his dagger and hurling it at the closest man. It hissed through the air and slammed into his eye. The man screamed, staggering back, clutching his face as blood bloomed and spilled down his face.

The rest didn't stop for him.

Flynn drew his last dagger and sprinted at them. He had to buy time for Mira. Screaming, he hurled himself at the first man, ducking low as a blade swung, missing his head by inches. He spun back around, driving the dagger. The man dodged.

In a blink, a force slammed into him. Pain exploded in his chest. Hands grabbed at him; the dagger ripped from his hand. Another force hit his back, driving him to the ground and pushing his face into the dirt.

"It's over, you fool. Keep fighting and we'll slit her throat," a man sneered, his breath hot on Flynn's ear.

He twisted his head to the side, watching in horror as two men restrained Mira, her gaze on him. She was white as death and tears glistened in her eyes. He didn't struggle as they dragged him to his feet, tying his hands behind his back. All hope crushed.

"That's better," said the man. "The more you fight, the more that die and there's been enough of that."

A young man, barely older than Flynn, jogged over. His face was slick with sweat and blood. Cold gray eyes flicked over the two prisoners, then back to the one who had been ordering Flynn only moments before.

"Sir, we've found some women holed up with screaming infants. The men can't get inside but orders were to take everyone," he asked, then added with a note of uncertainty. "Should we burn it?"

The leader hesitated for a moment. "Burn it."

"*No!*" The cry burst from Flynn's mouth as he surged forward.

A force dragged him back, and a blow struck him from behind, knocking the air out. Wheezing, pain burning down his back, the other men closed in. Their hands rested on swords; the threat was clear.

"You want this girl to die, don't you?" sneered the leader.

Flynn paled, dropped his head. "I..."

But the lack of words was enough. The leader stared at him with his cold eyes, daring Flynn to fight. To give him any reason to slay Mira. But Flynn's heart wasn't in it. The fight was shattered. As they led him and Mira into a portal, Fenware vanished behind them in smoke and flames, and the darkness took hold.

Chapter 11

Stories were told that the dragons chose their home because an ancient spirit offered them sanctuary. When that spirit died, the dragons left the mountains, abandoning the Dragonirs to their doom. These were the stories told but I know the truth, which was far more tragic, though I am sworn to secrecy.

—Excerpt from Litania's diary

THE PALACE WAS a labyrinth full of ghosts. As they ascended higher, passing through rooms that looked as though no time had passed within, Wren felt as if those ghosts were watching her. The palace had been holding its breath for three hundred years and now its anticipation rippled over her skin, lifting the hairs. Every so often she'd glance at Lorca, who seemed unaffected. Maybe he was used to it, the watching.

The silence.

When they came to another large room, adorned with more portraits, something felt different. An icy presence brushed against her, stopping her dead in her tracks. She turned slowly, lifting her gaze past the myriad of faces of people long gone, to one of the largest paintings on the wall.

A woman, perhaps Wren's age, with unbound brown hair that fell around her bare shoulders. She stood on a clifftop, wearing a simple white dress with a deep neckline and a golden crown resembling thorns and leaves. Her piercing blue gaze stared back at Wren, as if to say, *I belong to no one.*

She didn't realize Lorca was beside her until his arm brushed hers. "It's the only painting ever made of her – the Spirit of the Mountain. My sister saw her sometimes, though they never spoke."

"That's her real name?"

Lorca shrugged. "It was all we ever knew her by and she never deigned to correct us. I don't think she was concerned about things like that."

A pang of loneliness tugged at Wren. In her mind, the spirit stood alone among the mountains. She didn't seem like this godly, ethereal figure, too lofty for mortal concerns.

"She looks lonely," murmured Wren. "Was she the only spirit?"

"She was the only one who kept us safe."

Lorca studied the painting, as if he was seeing her for the first time, and looked uneasy. Abruptly, he turned away, striding to the door, forcing Wren to hurry after him. At the doorway, she cast a backward glance at the painting, those blue eyes still fixed on Wren. It felt as though the painting was speaking to her, a ghostly presence stretching out, filling her mind.

Hello, Wren.

A chill rushed down her spine and she hurried after Lorca, falling into step beside him as they headed down a wide hallway, guarded by statues of men and women, each carved from polished stone.

They watched her, those silent guards of stories that were hidden from her.

What might they say if they were able to speak?

At the end of the hallway, a large set of golden doors swung open as they approached, admitting them into an enormous room flanked by polished white pillars that stretched up to an arched roof high above. The floor was a dizzying pattern of colored titles, far more than Wren had ever seen before. For a moment, she stood staring in awe.

"This way," murmured Lorca.

When she looked up, he was watching her again with that piercing gaze. She stared back until a flickering, warm light caught her attention. Her feet carried her closer, diminishing the distance until she stood before a fire pit, forged of iron with a design of twisted and thorny vines. A steady flame burned within it, emitting less heat than she would have expected. Wren's gaze sharpened onto the two iron hands that stretched up from within the fire, cradled together where, once, they might have held something.

"In the last weeks, Vaska bore an egg. When the empire fell and the dragons left, it was too young to be moved. I was tasked with safeguarding it until it hatched," Lorca explained quietly, as though he was back in the palace the day the empire fell, watching as his world burned.

"What happened to the egg?"

He was silent for a moment, so she glanced at him. Those green eyes darkened to near-black, anger marring his face. "It was taken."

"How could someone take an egg from here?"

He spun on her, nostrils flaring. "I do not know who took it or why. This palace has a mind and magic all its own. It let the intruder in and leave with the egg, though it has never let me know *who*."

She flinched at his rage, shrinking away. "I'm sorry."

His eyes softened. He sighed and looked back to the fire, lost in the past. On his face, an expression of pain, raw and unflinching.

"Will you help me?" she asked softly.

He stepped up to the pit and paused. "If you can reach into this fire and touch the stone hands, then I swear by the Spirit of the Mountain, I will do whatever I must, to help you save your village. I will hide them and protect them with my life." He paused, then went on saying, "if you pass, we will become linked, our minds tethered. This will remain until the deal is fulfilled."

"As in you will be able to read my mind?"

He shook his head. "Not quite but we will be able to speak without words. It will also mean I can find you if we're separated. It will mean my dragon and I can help keep you safe."

"The dragon will help?"

To her surprise, he turned and nodded. "Yes."

A dragon would scare off slavers. After all, who would defy a beast of fang and scale and fire? Still, what he asked... A climber was nothing without their hands, and she'd seen what severe burns could do. She would never climb again.

"If I burn my hands, I can't get back down to the village," she said, turning her gaze to the fire.

"The dragon will carry you down," he replied.

So in order to save the people she loved, she'd have to give up climbing. It was a simple choice. Wren stepped up to the pit, the fire bright on her skin. She drew in a deep breath, steadied her nerves, and shoved her hand into the flames.

She squeezed her eyes shut, expecting the agony of the fire, and readied her mouth to scream.

The scream never came.

She opened her eyes slowly, afraid she might see a hand so badly burned she didn't have a chance to feel the pain.

"Spirits above..."

The fire danced on her skin, tickling softly, warm to the touch.

"It seems you have yourself a dragon, Wren," Lorca declared and spun around, striding to the door.

She tore her gaze from her hand and hurried after him.

"That's it? You'll help?"

The door opened before them and, as they went through, he slanted her a bemused look. "You did as I asked, therefore I am yours."

I've done it. I've found a way to save the village, she thought with a burst of jubilation. His words echoed in her mind, loud as thunder.

I am yours.

Unlike before, the way out was easy and they hurried through the city. At the cliff edge, Wren went to lower herself down to climb, but Lorca put a hand to her arm and gestured for her to step back from the edge. Then he walked a little away from her and stopped. She opened her mouth to ask what he was doing when a flash of white, so blinding she had to cover her face, exploded before her. As it dimmed, she moved her hands from her eyes and gasped.

An ebony-scaled dragon stood before her, staring at her with *jewel-green* eyes.

"You... *You're* the dragon?"

The dragon bowed his head, a low rumbling noise resonating from his chest. He walked over to her and then dropped to his belly. With a deep breath, Wren carefully climbed onto his back, crouching down low and grasping the spines, which mercifully stopped at the base of his neck.

She pressed her lips together to stop herself from making a sound as he moved, rising slowly to his feet and walking over to the edge. Her heart seized as he unfurled his colossal wings, stretching them wide, as though easing a stiffness from them.

Then he leaned forward—and jumped.

For a moment they plummeted toward the ground before the wind caught his wings and he steadied. Wren locked on his back, too uneasy to move, keeping her eyes firmly sealed shut.

Open your eyes, Wren. Lorca's soft voice brushed through her mind, strangely calming.

When she steeled herself to look, she gasped. They were soaring through the mountains above vast peaks capped with snow, a wild world unto itself, an ancient land that would not—*could not*—be conquered by mere men. It was easy to imagine a thousand dragons soaring the skies, the Dragonirs leaping to the air with them, a mirage of color and scale and fire. She imagined younger dragons taking to the skies clumsily for the first time, shooting down the sides of steep cliffs, waiting at the last moment to snap open their wings, catching the gusts of winds that propelled them up to where their elders circled protectively.

As the last wall of mountains sloped down, giving way to the expanse of land below where, somewhere, her village was. She couldn't lift her gaze, however, from the horizon. Though the land was flatter, it rose and fell in waves, smoothed over, as if by the winds. Vast tracts of crisp green, dark lines cut through them like the veins of the earth itself. A land she hadn't thought about before because her eyes had always been on the mountains, not on what might lie beyond them.

For the first time, Wren saw the beauty Ellie did.

Hold on, said Lorca, giving her little warning as he dipped downwards, flapping every so often as gusts of wind whipped up. Wren closed her eyes as he descended, her stomach churning as she gripped even tighter.

Moments later, he shifted his wings and gave two hard flaps, slowing hard and stretching out his limbs. They hit the ground with a thump. Wren jumped off his back before she could even let herself think—and screamed.

Her village was burning.

Part 2

SHADOW AND FIRE

Chapter 12

The dragon Orvana raised her head to the full moon and let out a cry that made the mountains tremble, the winds howl mournfully and the sky weep. Her soul broke in two as the girl at her feet, who still wore her broken crown, took her last breath—the first queen of the Dragonirs had died.

—Excerpt from The Legend of Inara, Vol 6

WREN SPRINTED TO her home. Stricken, she desperately scanned the raging inferno. Her legs trembled and quaked, threatening to give out. The flames consumed her vision, the air thick with smoke and ash that fell like gray snow. She raised her hand, shielding her eyes, as she stared at what was left of her house.

Blood roared in her ears and every thump of her heart was like a knife to the chest. She gasped for breath, unable to think of anything except that she had failed them and they were all gone. Her legs buckled, a tortured scream coming from deep within her.

"No, no, no, no..."

A hand fell on her shoulder. She reacted, hauling the figure over her shoulder, pinning them down. Realizing who it was, she froze, her grip firm around Lorca's throat.

"*Wren*," he wheezed.

Shock pulsed through her. She scrambled back and jumped to her feet. Ragged breaths shuddered through her chest as the reality of what had happened slammed into her, tearing at her mind, shredding her soul to ribbons.

"They can't be gone," she cried, shaking. "They were just *here*. I promised them..."

Her voice trailed off, hoarse, her emotions twisting inside of her like a storm. The inferno raged on and grew hotter, rising into the sky until black smoke blocked out the stars. "Lorca, I—"

He cupped her cheek, forcing her to look up and meet those green eyes full of sympathy. "Wren. I saw drag marks all over the roads, which cut off abruptly. That means some people were captured."

Some.

One word cut like a knife. Yet it also offered a tiny shred of hope. A slight flicker of hope kindled within her.

"Do you sense anything?" she asked him suddenly.

She'd heard stories that some Dragonirs could heal, create portals, even resurrect the dead.

Lorca turned from her and leveled his gaze on the burning village. He raised a hand to the flames as if they could reveal some truth to him. She watched on, anxiously, until his hand fell and he turned to her.

"Portals were used here a few hours ago if I'd hazard a guess," he announced. "I can't tell where they went. That was my sister's specialty, not mine, I'm afraid. I can merely read the lingering magic left in the air."

Her heart fluttered as she took a step toward him. "Then they're alive somewhere. I have to find them. I need to go to the nearest settlement and find out what happens to those they capture."

He frowned. "That's a lot of land to cover. You would have to venture far from here."

She returned her gaze to the flames consuming her home. These mountains were all she'd ever known. But now, as her world was devoured, she knew there was only one path before her. "I understand our deal was to find a new home for my people, but... well, as you said, there's a lot of land to cover. I could use an ally."

"We will conclude our deal when your people are safe. Right now, that isn't the case," he replied simply.

Shock wrenched her gaze back to him. *He was agreeing?* While she'd hoped he might come, part of her wondered why he was willing to leave the mountains. Something had kept him there, isolated from the world. "You're going to help me?"

"Unless you don't want me to?"

"I do!" she blurted out. "I mean, of course, I'm not going to turn your offer down."

Something flashed in his eyes, vanishing before she could get a read on it. "I swore an oath. Until it is satisfied, I'm yours."

Her heart thumped loudly, unable to form a reply, bound only to his magnetic gaze.

"We should go. Say your goodbyes." He broke away first and moved away from her. When he stopped, white light erupted from his skin. It dimmed as quickly as it had appeared, revealing his sleek, black form, wings tucked at his side. He lowered himself to the ground.

The moment to leave the village had come. She looked once more at the burning ruins of her home, a quiet fury stirring deep within her soul. For the first time in her life, she whispered a prayer to the Goddess of Death, Lyria, and then went to Lorca, climbing onto his back. As she got comfortable, she fed that fury, kindling a small and steady flame.

She would bring her people home.

They flew until the sun had set beyond the horizon, plunging the sweeping farmland into darkness. Lorca flew above the clouds for most of the flight, hiding behind them. He dipped down as the sun fell, land-ing in a small clearing in the middle of a thick forest. On the descent, Wren spied a nearby road, well-worn but otherwise empty.

When Lorca landed, she scrambled off and stretched out her legs with a groan. Hours crouched on his back had left her sore and stiff, and she grumbled quietly as she tried to ease the knots out. To her sur-prise Lorca didn't shift back; instead, he curled up on the ground, tuck-ing his wings at his side. He opened his enormous jaw, flashing sharp teeth in a long, howling yawn.

"I'll gather some firewood," she announced.

Hunger clawed at her stomach as she walked away. Heat flushed her cheeks, hurrying her on. She wasted no time in gathering armfuls of twigs and small branches, then returned, setting them up for a fire. As she stepped back, Lorca flicked open his eyes lazily, then spat a small bolt of flame onto the pile. With some careful tending, the fire slowly crackled to life. Wren sat back on her haunches, then remembered that her pack she'd made for the mountain still had some dried meat, plus a bread roll. It wasn't much, but she ate it hungrily. It didn't fill her, but she was no longer starving, which was something.

Lorca didn't eat, but she didn't know how often he needed food and figured he'd hunt if he got hungry. Though, the thought of him leaving made her restless, glancing uneasily over her shoulder. She'd rather face the perils of the cliffs and stare down wyverns with her sword than have to deal with strangers. She would, though, for her village.

We will find them, said Lorca.

In less than a day, a Dragonir had gone from aiding her in moving her village to a safer location, to joining her in rescuing her people. He hadn't explained why just acted as if it had been his intention the whole time. She decided to ask him.

"You didn't have to come with me. You agreed to help me find a new home, not take on an empire to rescue some strangers," she asked softly. "Why?"

He fastened those darkened eyes on her as if choosing his words care-fully. *You did as I asked. In truth, when this settles, I have a favor to ask, but not now. It's not time.*

He elaborated no further and closed his eyes as if drifting off to sleep.

The conversation, it seemed, was over. It left Wren with more questions than before, as well as an ally she barely knew.

She dreamed she stood in the middle of a clearing on the side of a mountain. A wild storm raged, cracks of thunder splitting the air. Rain swept down, thick droplets thudding against the ground. The wind roared around her, biting and mournful.

Wren's gaze fell to her feet.

Nestled in the dirt, defiant to the tempest, was a small plant blooming with red flowers. Wren knew from experience the tiny plant could endure foul weather, its roots a spiderweb deep beneath the ground.

As she raised a hand to her eyes, shielding them from the rain, she turned slowly. A cliff rose in front of her, stretching high into the dark clouds, and almost completely encircling the clearing. To her right, the smooth rock became jagged.

A flash of movement caught her attention, and she watched in shock as a woman stepped out from within the rock. Her shimmering form solidified with each step she took away from the stone.

Wren stared at the woman's face. It was the same one she had seen in a portrait only a day before, hanging in the gallery of the Dragonir palace.

The Spirit of the Mountain.

Only there was no defiance on this woman's face. She rushed past Wren as if she didn't register her presence and kneeled in front of the flower. The spirit gently brushed the plant, relief washing over her face. It was such a strangely tender moment. A sharp pain surged through Wren, making her stagger back with a cry.

The woman's head snapped up and rage flashed in her eyes.

"You're not welcome here. This is mine," she hissed. Her hand snapped up, a bolt of dark energy shooting from her fingertips.

It slammed into Wren's chest, plunging into her heart. Darkness erupted around her, then exploded once more into light as she woke up. She jolted up with a gasp, her hand clutching at her heart, instinctively probing for the wound. When she found none, her hand rose to her face, slick with sweat.

Wren?

When her hand fell away, she glanced at Lorca. He'd lifted his head from his front paws and was watching her, unblinking and unreadable.

"I'm okay. Bad dream, I guess," she mumbled, rubbing her eyes to dispel the look of fury she'd seen on the spirit's face. "Did I wake you?"

You were talking to yourself. Do your people speak a second tongue? He lowered his head as if it was too heavy for the moment.

"No, why?" Her heart pounded painfully in her chest, a sharp reminder that the dream wasn't real and that her heart had not been pierced.

He glanced at the fire, which was reduced to glowing embers in the quiet night air. *You were speaking in a tongue I had not heard before.*

Chapter 13

Among dragons, there is a distinct hierarchy. Different species enact certain roles within their society and, at the head of this, are the Avalon dragons. Golden creatures with an unparalleled affinity with magic, whose wisdom guides us, select our rulers. I wonder, though, what we will do given that our esteemed queen's bonded pair has produced not a single egg?

— Memoirs of Videnskaya, Lady Advisor to Queen Evanya

THEY'D FLOWN FOR a day before Lorca informed her that he needed a rest. After landing in a small open area within an ancient forest, they proceeded on foot. That worked fine for Wren, who was relieved to have her feet back on solid ground.

The sun was edging closer toward the horizon, shadows closing in around them. It grew harder to see ahead, so she kept close to Lorca as they walked along. More than once they had to snake through the trees because of his size. He'd explained staying too long in his natural human form was difficult.

"I don't understand, though. You were born a man so why does your original form pain you?"

He didn't respond, and she began to think he didn't want to answer her question.

Spend too much time in dragon form, you lose sight of yourself. Soon enough, spending time in your original form hurts until the pain forces you back into your dragon form.

She mulled this over before another question tugged at her mouth. "What's the longest you were in this form?"

Two hundred years.

She tripped over a rock, catching herself on his front leg. "That's so long!"

He stopped sharply, his head snapping up, nostrils flaring. As she straightened, she squinted through the thick forest, wondering what had caught his attention.

"What is it?"

Death.

She steeled her spine, peering ahead. "Should we divert?"

No point. I don't sense anyone alive. His nostrils flared. *The sooner we understand this land, the better.*

He glanced down at her before setting off again. The leaf litter crunched underfoot as they moved forward, the only sound to cut through the silence.

When the surrounding trees thinned and the land sloped downwards, the first hint of smoke touched her nose. By the time they reached the bottom, the stench filled her lungs. A warm breeze stirred with it, faint wisps of ash floating in the air, hinting at the aftermath of something truly terrible.

With a deep breath, she pushed on, Lorca close at her side.

The last of the trees fell away, revealing the remnants of a small village. The bones of dwellings, charred black, denoted where people might have once lived. Broken and blackened fencing edged empty fields, cluttered with the remains of dozens of farm animals. Many appeared in piles together, as if they'd tried to stampede their way out and failed—or perhaps they'd never even had that chance.

A knife twisted in Wren's gut as she crept forward, unease trickling down her spine. Why had this village met its end? What had they done to deserve such a fate? Perhaps, like hers, they had done nothing.

Her hand curled into a fist, nails biting into flesh. As she stepped out of the tree line, she realized Lorca hadn't moved. His dark gaze remained locked on the village.

Wren frowned. "What's wrong?"

He blinked. *Nothing.*

Biting her lip, she sensed something was bothering him and wanted to uncover it. Her mouth opened when he stepped back, white light flashing blindly around him. As it dimmed, he stood before her.

The bag strapped to his back had fallen during his shift from dragon to man. Lorca bent down, bundling up the excess straps and tucking them away. Then he looped the bag over his back, straightening up to look at her.

Her heart gave a nervous flip. Wrenching her attention from him, she walked into the village.

Lorca fell into step beside her, his gaze scanning their surroundings, his face unreadable

The first house they passed was little more than a pile of charred wood and stone with the remains of a fireplace. Among the wreckage, she spied cracked plates, bowls, thin scraps of material, and a doll blackened by the smoke.

She kneeled and picked it up. It was carefully stitched together with poor materials and stuffed with wool. A well-loved toy. A knife twisted in her gut. Had the child been killed? Or taken like her village?

Her mother had told her many stories about the people from beyond their village. The fighting, the lawless towns, the unrest throughout the empire. *Stray too far, Wren and the monsters in the lowlands will devour you,* she'd warned her. *They are cruel and terrible creatures.*

In the end, the monsters had found them anyway.

With a deep breath, she brushed off her knees and set the doll down.

Perhaps one day that child would return, somehow, and pick up that very doll. Her family would rebuild, and it would be like nothing had ever happened.

Perhaps.

Lorca kept quiet beside her, his gaze sweeping over the carnage, his mouth a tight line. She gently touched his arm. Flinching, he wrenched his gaze away, finding hers.

"Are you okay?" he asked quietly. The quiet note of tenderness caught her off guard.

She nodded, heat flaring across her cheeks. "Yourself?"

His gaze strayed to the destruction again. "We used to trade with the lowlands until my father and his team were ambushed. They were slaughtered. After that, my mother forbade us from coming to the lowlands." He sighed deeply. "Nothing changes, I suppose."

Both of them had looked down from the mountains, yet with such vastly different fantasies. To him, the world below must've seemed new and exciting, enticing him from his ivory tower. For Wren, there was an appreciation of beauty, but only from a distance.

Blinking away that train of thought, they moved on. They passed a few more homes, each in a similar state of destruction when something caught her eye. A symbol, she realized, had been painted onto a door. A yellow bird with a red line through it and a circle around it. What did it mean? She stared at it, the questions mounting before she reluctantly pulled away and ventured on.

It wasn't long before they sighted the first body and then many more that littered the road. The elderly, women and children, and a few men. Their bodies were badly beaten, made blue by the weather and time, and beginning to rot. Others were lying among the smoldering wreckage, blackened by the fire. Some houses still crackled away, with flames devouring the last of the wood and sending plumes of smoke into the air.

As they rounded a corner into what might've once been the village square, Wren's foot caught, sending her stumbling forward. Lorca's hand shot out, catching her upper arm. She steadied and turned around, feeling the ghost of his touch through her furs. Her gaze slid down to what she'd tripped over.

An outstretched arm hacked off from the shoulder.

"*Gods!*" She stepped back into Lorca's chest and sidestepped around him, putting distance between her and the arm.

"Are you okay?" he asked.

"Let's go. There's no one living here to help us."

They walked for several more hours until the sun had retreated beyond the horizon, plunging the world into darkness. Both of them were exhausted. No sooner had they picked a spot that Lorca dropped the bag onto the ground. He dug out a blanket, a water pouch, some dried meat, and crusty bread. Once he handed it all to her, he stepped back and flashed white, growing larger to take his dragon form.

He sank down, folding his wings in close as his head rested on the ground.

"You okay?" Wren asked as she unrolled her blanket, setting it down next to him.

He turned his head to her, still on the ground. *I'm tired.*

Nodding, she turned away from him. "I'm just going to grab some wood for a fire. I'll be right back."

Watch yourself and stay close, he warned.

"Okay," she replied and set off into the forest.

She didn't have to venture far. The approaching winter had already stripped the trees of their leaves, cluttering the grounds in piles of burned orange and red. She found several fallen sticks, bundling them up in her arms until she had enough. Then she headed back, finding Lorca watching her as she entered the clearing.

There was something about his gaze, especially at that moment. It was as if he was studying her, piercing through all her defenses.

With a deep breath, she set the sticks up for the fire. When she finished, she stepped back. Without needing to be asked, Lorca opened his mouth and breathed flames onto the bundle. The fire took hold and soon burned steadily, chasing away the lingering chill that hung in the air.

She sat down by it, enjoying the warmth, and began to eat. Once she finished the bread and washed it down with some water, she glanced at

Lorca.

"Are you sure you don't want to have some?" she offered, holding out the meat and fruit, which she hadn't yet touched.

I'll hunt later. In this form, I do not need to eat often. He was quiet for a moment, and she thought he might be sleeping. *Wren, can I ask you something?*

"Yes, of course." She smiled. "I've asked you so many questions. It must be my turn."

Why did you become a climber?

"It seemed the natural choice for me. I was always drawn to the cliffs and took to the work easily." She pulled her knees up to her chest. "Can I ask you something? I saw your clothes aren't ruined when you change—how is that even possible?"

I'm not sure exactly. My sister explained it like this dragon form, for Dragonirs anyway, is more like an illusion we wear. So, our clothes remain when we change in and out of the forms. It might not be true, though. I wasn't exactly the best student, not like my sister. His voice was quiet in her mind, heavy with a deep, aching sadness.

"That's something we have in common then," she mused, flashing him a quiet smile. "I loved the mountains. I learned to read and write, and when I was old enough, I begged to be taken on as a trainee climber. Let's just say I was persistent."

Now that I can believe. How old were you when you became a full climber?

"I started practicing when I was nine, began formal training at eleven, and finished it by fifteen. So, I've been on the cliffs for three years now as a climber, with the past year as team leader." Her gaze fell to her scarred and calloused hand, remembering her first official climb.

You became a leader quite young. Is that common?

"At seventeen? No. I was a bit of an exception. In one season, we lost three of our team and our leader was badly hurt. Honestly, I was surprised when he gave me the job over Vaughn or Flynn. He said I had good instincts and could read for storms, so the choice for him was easy to make."

Lorca fell silent for a moment. When she glanced back at him, his head was down. He was staring into the crackling flames, the amber glow reflected in his eyes, seemingly lost in thought.

The conversation over, she finished her food and stretched out on the ground next to Lorca. She lay on her back, staring up at the starlit sky through the spiderweb of tree branches above.

Wren? His voice was soft against her mind, tentatively nudging.

"Yeah?"

It's been three hundred years since I last saw this settlement. It might be gone. I mean, I was breaking the law by venturing that far south, so I only visited once.

She rolled over onto her stomach, propping herself up on her arms. "I know the chances aren't exactly favoring us but I'm too damn stubborn to give up when things get hard."

Warmth hummed through their bond, pooling in her chest. *You have the heart of a dragon, Wren.*

With a smile, she shifted onto her back, closing her eyes.

Chapter 14

I seek a way to save my people, but I sometimes wonder if I am fighting the inevitable. I refuse to yield to the dark future that is approaching.

—Excerpt from Queen Evanya's diary.

SORCHA EMERDINE RACED through the caravan, her hair billowing wildly behind her and a grin stretching her lips. People sitting around cold fireplaces, breaking their fast in the icy morning, glanced up in curiosity as she dashed past. A few called out, but she couldn't stop. There was too much to do.

She slowed as she approached her destination, Madam Kara's tent. She stopped, steadying her nerves, as she reminded herself of all that was at stake. The fire flickered defiantly in her, adding to the resolution that had guided her in all that she had done since she was ten years old.

Summoning her courage, she slipped inside.

The scent of spices washed over her, providing a momentary sense of comfort. She'd spent so much time in this tent after suffering from her visions and nightmares. Closing off the memory, she glanced around. "Madam Kara?"

At the back was a partitioned section, hiding where Kara slept. Something rustled from behind, and after a moment, a woman swept into view. Tall and strikingly graceful, Kara wore a simple blue gown. She was barefoot, moving silently as she approached Sorcha. With her long onyx black hair spilling unbound down her back, she gave the ethereal air of a woman who had guarded their people for nearly one hundred years.

By rights, she ought to have been dead or, at least, a wrinkled old woman. Ancient magic flowed through her veins, keeping her young.

And she was the only one who knew who Sorcha really was.

"You're looking better," drawled Kara. "How're the headaches? The sickness?"

"I'm managing, but that's not why I'm here. It's them! They're on their way, just like I said they would be." She tried, and failed, to sound calm, if Kara's doubtful look was anything to go by. "They'll be at Tarth within the next day."

Kara lowered herself into the chair by the large table that dominated the room. Her gaze remained on Sorcha, betraying nothing but a calm expression. It was maddening to Sorcha and had more than once gnawed away at her confidence.

"Tarth has the interest of the capital right now. That is the last place you should be. What if anyone were to figure out—"

"No one will know," cut in Sorcha. "Besides, the time to act is fast approaching, and I need these two. With them, there is hope and frankly, with everything that is happening, that's what we need. That's what this empire needs."

And I also require some other items in that city...

A long beat passed before Kara spoke again. "You are soon going to reach a point where there will be no return."

"And you could have thrown me to the wolves years ago and left me to do this on my own," countered Sorcha. "But you didn't. You let me sow the seeds for what must be done. If you don't believe in what I'm doing, why not stop me? Why not abandon me?"

Sorcha stared at Kara, her heart slamming in her chest, the rush of blood in her ears. The weight of years of hard work was bearing down on her shoulders. She *had* to convince Kara, or her plan was doomed before it even got off the ground.

She reached out to the chair in front of her and, keeping her gaze on Kara, she sat down.

Kara's hand settled on the table, two fingers tapping the wood. Her hand flattened out as she sighed. "You are one of my people. How could I abandon you, even as reckless as you are?"

The hard mask that Sorcha wore on her face cracked. She leaned forward. "The Northern region is in turmoil. Remote villages are being destroyed or enslaved, supposedly for hiding rebels. The rest of the empire is nearly tearing itself apart in debt. People are starving and most of the strong men are being forcibly drafted into the army. Hell, the islands in the Mithra Archipelago are in turmoil. The time for being idle is over."

Kara tilted her head to the side. "Is that what you think I am doing? Being idle? This caravan is safe and that remains so because we do not get involved in the affairs of this land, as much as we are able."

"This empire is *dying*," snapped Sorcha. "You see it everywhere we go. We have fewer places to trade every year. Hell, we're lucky we even got the ones we did this year. I'm not a fool. I know we're running low on funds and that's risky as winter approaches."

Her heart drummed away in her chest, each beat a clap of thunder that quivered through her soul. It felt like an eternity as she watched Kara's hard, granite-like expression. For all the years she'd spent studying the woman and preparing for these kinds of chats, Sorcha still felt woefully underprepared.

Kara's hand lifted to her chin, rubbing it for a moment before lowering it back to the table. The action was a familiar one. A tiny flicker of hope lit inside of Sorcha, too shy to reveal itself on her face.

"You are pushing yourself too hard with your visions, Sorcha. The full-blooded fae who possessed that ability would only use it once every few years. I've seen the price of those who use it frequently. It killed them, and I know you have been forcing visions every week for the past two months," said Kara, her voice full of warning.

Sorcha released the breath she'd been holding. "I know, but now more than ever, I need the information they give me. I can take it. We have to intercept these two before we lose them."

And if that is the price I must pay, then so be it.

"How can you be so sure you need them?"

"One of them is a Dragonir prince."

The calm mask Kara wore shattered. Her eyes widened, parting her lips slightly. Sorcha pushed back from the table, straightening up in her chair. She had the advantage.

"I have the right blood in my veins, but that's it. So, I've spent years spreading the rumors of my survival. I've prepared and schemed. Yes, there are people who are readying things for my arrival. But I must still do my part."

"But those people you approached with rumors did not know who you were. If they did, you'd be dead," finished Kara.

Sorcha nodded. "Everything is in place, but if the first part of this is to work, then I need them. Not just the prince, but the girl too. There is ancient magic in her veins. A power that is waiting to be released. I can *feel* it. And to secure their help, we need to go to the city of Tarth."

In icy twilight air, Sorcha groomed her horse to distract herself. The conversation with Madam Kara was done and all that she could do now was to wait, which wasn't something she was overly good at.

What she hadn't told Madam Kara was the other reason she needed to go to Tarth. There might be a plethora of loyal families in the city who were eager for her return. But hearts could be changed, bought, or broken by loss. They might sing their loyalty now, but she had to be sure. There was too much at risk.

She knew she was playing a dangerous game but what choice did she have? The time for standing idly by as people were butchered in the name of false accusations was over. She had the power, and the blood, to do something. By the spirits, she would become whatever she had to in order to achieve her goals.

Thinking of this, he combed the mane of her mare, humming softly. She was almost lost in thought when she heard the sound of soft footfalls on the grass coming from behind her. It was a stride she knew well. The only person who kept trying to sneak up on her since she was a kid.

"I know you're there, Jed," she declared as she turned around.

With a small smile, Jed held up his hands in defeat. His moon-pale skin glowed in the night air, making his harsh features seem softer, gentler. It was nice when he didn't look so angry all the time, more like the boy she'd grown up with.

"I heard you were talking with Madam Kara for hours," he drawled. "I think that's the longest you have ever sat still for."

She laughed. "I can sit still!"

"And I can carry a horse on my back." He folded his arms across his chest. "So, what'd you talk about?"

"A lot of it was private, but I can tell you we're heading to Tarth. There are some things we need to pick up before we make the trip to the coast," she declared, turning to gather up her grooming tools.

There would be no more productive work with Jed around. He was always far too good at needling her for answers.

He pinned her with a searching look. "Pick up *what* exactly?"

"Some scrolls and a few other supplies," she said cryptically. "We're going to need them, given we will travel through the Forest of Silence."

The smile on his face vanished. "Why the hell would we go through there? It's full of demons."

"It's faster than taking the capital road. Besides, with everything going on, I don't think Madam Kara wants us anywhere near Miradan," explained Sorcha.

Half a lie, really. There was danger near the capital, but that wasn't why they were going to divert through a forest rumored to be full of demons. It had taken a lot of convincing with the right pieces of information to get Kara to agree.

Jed sighed deeply. "I don't like it but Madam Kara has never steered us wrong before." He uncrossed his arms and looked at Sorcha. "Anyway, I came to ask if you wanted to join us sparring tomorrow."

She smiled, despite all the worries gnawing at her mind. "That sounds perfect."

Chapter 15

*Vaska is in mourning for another failed clutch. The depar-
ture of her sister, Inakara, only deepens her grief. I cannot
help but wonder why now, of all times, did Inakara decide to
leave the mountains?*

—Excerpt, Queen Evanya's diary.

AS WREN AND Lorca crested a hill, a city rose from the morning
mist. Its glittering stone spires resembled jeweled hands reaching for
the heavens. The sun inched a little higher, sweeping its light over the
lower towers, then down onto the other buildings erected from the
same pale stone. From every window, door, and tower they saw re-
splendent gold and red flags fluttering in the wind. Lowering her gaze

to the wall that rimmed the city, then down to the large gate that marked the entrance to the city, Wren felt a shiver of excitement pass through her.

A city, she thought with wonder.

Beside her, Lorca knelt down in human form. He'd changed back some hours ago, conversing a little as they trekked.

Kneeling on the ground beside him, she studied the sprawling settlement. It was more than she could have ever imagined and, unlike the ruins in the mountains, it didn't stand silent, forever waiting for a future that wasn't going to come.

It was alive.

"When I last saw this place, it was little more than a large town," reflected Lorca, a hint of unease in his voice. "I honestly expected it would be long gone by now."

The truth of how long it had been since he'd left the mountains seemed to weigh heavily on him. She followed his gaze to the road leading to the entrance.

A long line of wagons and horses stretched from the gate and down a gently sloping hill. Never had she seen such buildings, nor so many people. She wondered if this was how the Dragonir's empire might have looked. Full of life and splendor, of magic and energy.

"I've never seen so many people before in my life," she mused.

Lorca stood up. "We need to gather more supplies before we head in. Right now, we look suspicious."

"Stealing, I assume?" she inquired, glancing up at him, framed by an outline of sunshine.

The corner of his mouth twitched. "Why do you sound so interested in the idea?"

"If it means getting in there and getting the information we need, then I'll do whatever needs to be done."

She got to her feet and set off down the hill. Lorca followed her through the thin forest, the dappled light spilling across them in lazy bands of pale gold. At the bottom of the hill, the tree line ended, running alongside a well-worn road. It led in the city's direction and with the amount of traffic they saw heading that way, Wren hoped that meant someone would soon come along this road.

Wren crouched behind a thorny bush, studying the road.

"What about a damsel situation?" she proposed.

Lorca glanced at her, one brow lifting. His mouth twitched. "Can you play that part?"

His skeptical tone left her fighting a smile. "We'll find out soon enough, won't we?"

The reply was the ghost of a smile on his face, her heart responding with only a tiny flutter. Heat flooded her cheeks.

His head pricked up. "I hear someone approaching."

Two riders dressed in fine leathers, with polished swords at their hips, and laden saddlebags came into view. Wren drew her sword and yanked her palm across the blade, slicing it. Blood blossomed immediately, then trickled down her wrist, dribbling on the grass.

With a curse, she hurried out and began to cry.

Spirits above, please let me sound convincing, she prayed.

She stumbled out onto the road, wailing as loudly as she could. Forcing terror into her voice, she ran to the men who pulled their horses to a stop. One of them jumped down, rushing over to her. Concern brightened his naïve, youthful face. She almost felt guilty about robbing them.

Almost.

"Miss, you're hurt! What happened?"

"Oh!" she wailed. "A beast! It attacked our camp. I—"

She threw herself into the young man's embrace, sobbing. As she burrowed her face into his chest, the other dismounted and began walking toward her.

Lorca crept from the trees, low at first, then with a burst of speed, he swept forward, placing one hand on the back of the advancing man's head. In seconds, he was out cold.

The man whose arms were around her let go and turned, hearing his companion fall. Confusion flashed across his face, but Wren was fast. She pulled out her dagger and held it to his throat as Lorca strode forward. His hands glowing with ribbons of energy.

"Sorry, but don't take this personally. You have something we need."

Lorca strode forward and slammed his flattened palm onto the stranger. He crumbled like a doll to her feet, still as death.

"Did you kill him?"

"No, he's just unconscious. I didn't think you'd want them dead."

She glanced down at the men, hoping they'd take some time to wake.

"Let's tie them up in the shade but close enough to the road so when they come to, they can call for help. That should buy us enough time to slip into the city."

She took the first one by the collar and dragged him into the trees. Lorca grabbed the other man and followed. Then, taking some rope from the horses, she tied up both men, using climbing knots she knew wouldn't come undone.

They returned to the horses, which shifted nervously and neighed softly. Lorca held out a hand, murmuring beneath his breath, calming them.

The bags had food inside, sleeping rolls, a blanket, an old pot, and a metal box. There was also a cloak in each, which they donned. Lorca's cloak was a little short on him, which looked comical. When he looked up from fastening his cloak, she smiled.

"What is it?"

She forced the smile away, though the edges still twitched. "Nothing."

A long silence stretched between them before he turned to his horse, muttering under his breath.

She mounted her horse, then seeing his jaw clench nudged her horse over and asked, "What's the matter?"

"I dislike riding," he confessed.

There was something endearing about him at that moment. Her heart gave a quick flutter as she fought the urge to smile wider. "Come on. The sooner we're in the city, the better."

He nodded and awkwardly climbed on, grabbing the reins, mirroring her.

"How is it that a climber is good at horse riding?" he asked as they set off.

She held the reins with one hand. "We don't climb all year. There's time to kill when we finish all our maintenance and planning. I learned to ride from a young age. I'm not as good as my sister but I can manage well enough."

He nodded, accepting it without judgment.

On their way to the city, they discussed what to say if the guards asked what their business was. They ran over it several times before falling into a long silence, broken only by the sound of their horses.

In the corner of her eye, she saw Lorca's hands tighten to near white on the reins. He looked like a young climber about to do his first real ascent. She edged her horse closer so that their thighs nearly touched.

"We can do this," she murmured.

He frowned for a moment, then nodded. She held his gaze until the lines softened. A practiced look of calm settled instead. Aware she was staring, Wren cleared her throat and turned her attention back to the city and the diminishing line.

"Remember our story again? We're married bounty hunters, seeking criminals and runaway slaves," she recited quietly, knowing Lorca's sharp hearing would get every word.

He nodded and at the gate, he repeated their story to the guards, who only half-heartedly inquired. The larger of the two, a balding man with a ruddy complexion and squinting eyes, glanced at Wren's sword at Lorca's side.

"Pretty sword for a bounty hunter," he remarked.

"My bride price," corrected Wren. "Works well enough for our job."

The guard stared at her as if scarcely impressed by what he saw. "And what job is that?"

"Running it through ignorant men," she said.

The man blinked and, opening his mouth to speak, was cut off when someone behind them shouted impatiently. His mouth shut.

Lorca reached out and set his hand on Wren's, like an adoring husband might, or one scolding her for insolence. Then he glanced at the guard, all warmth gone, replaced by impatience.

"Our travels have been long. Might we continue inside?"

The guard nodded. "Welcome to the City of Tarth."

He waved them through and once they passed inside, Wren released the breath she'd been holding, as well as the tension in her shoulders. She studied the busy road ahead of them.

"Dismount?" she asked, turning to Lorca.

He was already off his saddle, stretching out his legs. Rolling her eyes, she did the same and looked at him for direction.

"We need to find an inn to stay in, with stables for the horses, if possible.

If we're lucky, we'll be able to get some information at the bar," he said with a small smile. "Drunk folk talk loose and sing truths, as my mother used to say. That was how she met my father."

They set off down the busy street, walking side by side. The city was thick with people, smelling sour and fetid, and the cacophony of noise was dizzying.

"Why aren't there any stories about your father?"

A shadow fell across his face. "He died when I was young. It nearly broke my mother's heart. She said even the dragons cried. He was a quiet man who loved books. He did nothing to warrant a story I suppose."

"I'm sorry." She cursed her stupid questions, her gaze falling to the ground.

He shrugged, his gaze clouding over. "It was a long time ago... and everyone I used to know is gone."

There was no right answer. Nothing that would ease his grief at that moment. All she could do was lure his mind away from the memory.

"Come on, let's keep going," she murmured, a hand gingerly touching his arm.

When it seemed like they'd walked for an eternity, and Wren felt frustratingly lost in the labyrinth of streets that she swore all looked the same, Lorca stopped and pointed to a nearby building. She saw the sign showing it was an inn, and looked at him, relieved.

"Finally."

They approached and found a boy out the front, who led them down a narrow alley to the back where the stables were. Lorca fished out the required coin and instructed him to feed and water the horses.

They gathered their bags and headed toward the directed door. Inside they continued along a long hallway to the front area, full of patrons, where they found the innkeeper.

Lorca organized a room, giving time for Wren to hang back and study the customers sitting at the tables. A few glanced her way, looking her up and down, lingering. She met their gaze, returning a cold, steely look.

She would not be intimidated by them.

A hand gently nudged her arm. She glanced at Lorca, who had moved to her side. There was a key in his hand, dull and rusty.

"Let's go. We have a room."

'Room' was a generous term. It had a bed, though scarcely big enough for two people, and nothing else.

Wren turned to Lorca, relief flooding through her. It was one step closer to her people.

"We made it inside."

"You seem surprised," he remarked.

"A little, to be honest. I'm trying to be hopeful but how are we meant to find my people in such a vast empire?"

Chapter 16

Inakara returned today under the cover of darkness. She swears me to silence and entrusts me with her most precious treasure—the crown of her former partner, Queen Estreleya, my great grandmother. A cursed crown that was said to mark the end of our empire. May the gods have mercy on us all.

—Excerpt from Queen Evanya's diary.

"WE DO IT the only way we can. One step at a time," said Lorca. "While we're here, we get as much information as we can."

She walked over and slumped down onto the bed. "We need to figure out the most likely place they would've been sold. We must get a map of the city."

The long list of a plan formed in her head. It comforted her as much as anything could. The cold tug of shame and failure gnawed at her mind. If she'd only been faster to find Lorca or hadn't wasted so much time in the palace...Her heart squeezed painfully. She'd failed her people when they needed her most.

Closing her eyes, exhaustion tugged at her body. The bed shifted as Lorca sat down beside her.

"You haven't been sleeping much since we left," he remarked.

Releasing a heavy breath, she opened her eyes, peering at him from beneath her lashes. "I keep seeing my village. The flames, the smell of smoke...If only I'd been faster, then maybe—"

"You don't know that. Not for certain and you can't torture yourself over what might've been. Trust me, you will only drive yourself mad." The shadows of ancient grief darkened his face.

"Lorca, do you—"

"Don't finish that question," he said tightly. His hand returned to his side. "I can't talk about that...not yet."

She sat up, itching to touch him, to offer some bit of comfort. As he pulled off the bed, she realized he didn't want that. He needed some space. She got up and went to the door, pausing for a moment.

"I'll be downstairs but...when you're ready to talk, I'm here."

With a deep breath, she shut the door behind her and strode downstairs. Only once she reached the last step did she exhale. The stench of sour beer and sweat filled her nose as she entered the main area. Tables were crammed with people playing games of cards or drinking, half-shouting at each over the cacophony of noise. She side-stepped the chaos and sat down at the bar.

She ordered some ale from the bartender as he passed and slid over a coin. The man returned a moment later, shoving over the frothy mug in front of her. He snapped up the coin and moved on to the other patrons. Her hand curled around the mug and she lifted it, downing the drink in a single go.

With a sigh, she set the wooden mug down, closing her eyes for a moment. Drawing in a long breath of the fetid air, she forced her eyes open.

"Hell of a day, ay?" a girl teased as she slid onto the stool beside Wren.

Wren opened her eyes, taking in the young girl with ash brown hair and amber eyes. "More like a hell of a week."

The bartender drifted back, wordlessly refilling her mug. With a nod, Wren slid over another coin and he refilled her mug.

The girl turned to her Wren, holding out a slender, pale hand. Her amber eyes glittered brightly. "The name's Sorcha."

"Wren."

"So, what brings you to this fine city?"

"Slaves. My husband and I are in the market for some." Wren sipped at the ale. "Recommendations for some good markets for that?"

Sorcha's brow lifted. "You must not be from around here if you're looking for Tarth for slaves."

"What do you mean?"

Sorcha shrugged and gestured to the bartender for another drink. Only when she had the next one in hand did she turn to Wren.

"As a rule, all slaves must be branded and processed via the City of Slaves. Markets outside of that city are practically unheard of. Hell, I can think of only one other and that's the small one in the city of Midlan. It's a market that the Empress strictly controls. So, are you looking to buy, or are you trying to find someone?"

She set the mug back down and glanced around, wondering if anyone had heard Sorcha's question. But no one seemed to even care that someone might be seeking someone sold into slavery.

"What do you mean?"

"There's not a lot of love for the Empress in this city, certainly not in these parts." Sorcha raised her hand, ordering two more drinks. She slid across the coins for the drinks, then pushed one over to Wren. "When were your people taken?"

Wren answered before she could stop herself. "Two days ago." She stared at her mug of ale for a moment before she spoke again. "You say that like I'm not the first person to come here looking for people?"

Sorcha's fingers drummed idly on the side of her mug. "You're not." Her hands curled around the mug. "The northern territories are on the cusp of an all-out war with our beloved Empress. She has ordered the sacking of many villages as a result."

There was a quiet fury in the young woman's eyes. The rage felt real, hardening every word she spoke. Wren's gut instinct told her the girl was being honest, at least as far as her feelings on the village attacks. But beyond that, caution stayed any eagerness on Wren's side.

Can I trust her?

As she fell into an uneasy silence, the door to the inn slammed open. A gust of stale air rushed in, whipping up strands of her hair. She blinked, looking up.

A bear of a man stood in the doorway, surveying the interior of the inn for a few minutes. Then he stalked inside with two other soldiers in tow. Their uniforms, crisp and sharp, were out of place amongst the roughly dressed drinkers. The newcomers scanned the densely packed room, hands resting on the hilts of their swords.

The threat was obvious.

This is not good. Fear froze her in the chair.

Beside her, Sorcha stiffened but didn't look at the men. Her grip tightened on the mug. Those golden eyes shot to Wren, *my life is in your hands.*

Resisting the urge to panic, Wren turned slowly on her stool. She, too, had a reason to avoid trouble and hoped it had nothing to do with the two men they'd left tied up outside the city. Her heart slammed painfully against her ribs.

The first man, tall as a tree, with thick limbs and a ruddy face, swept his gaze across the room. They lingered briefly on Wren, then flickered to Sorcha.

"You!" he yelled, pointing at the girl.

If being a climber had taught her anything, it was to be opportunistic—even in the face of fear.

Wren thought fast and leaned over, placing a tender hand on Sorcha's. "My dear, they're looking at you."

Sorcha turned on her chair and looked at the man.

"Is something wrong?"

The man glanced at Wren. "You know this girl?"

"Yes, of course," answered Wren. "She's family."

"She looks nothing like you."

It was true. Sorcha's olive skin was a far cry from Wren's paleness. Years hidden beneath climbing furs and cloaks kept skin protected from the sun—whenever it deigned to appear above their village.

"Distant relative on my husband's side."

Wren saw his gaze shift just to her right. A warm hand fell on her shoulder, squeezing softly. Even without looking, she knew who it was, and the tension eased from her body.

"Causing trouble, my lovely wife?" Lorca's voice brushed over her like a lover's touch, sending shivers rippling down her spine.

The man eyed Lorca with a look of disdain before he turned to his men. "She's not the one we're after. Keep searching!"

No one moved in the bar until the men were gone. Lorca lowered himself on the stool beside her, casting a curious look over Sorcha, lingering for a moment. Sorcha returned that interest briefly before looking away. She said nothing until she finished the drink, then leaned over it, staring at the bench.

"You didn't have to do that," Sorcha murmured.

Perhaps, but Wren wasn't about to dismiss an opportunity when it arose.

The good-humored girl from before had slipped away, revealing a harder look in her amber eyes. She didn't seem so child-like anymore to Wren.

"I need information, and now you owe me," stated Wren pointedly.

Sorcha lifted her hand, ordering three more drinks. "Well, better order a drink for us all and get comfortable. I'll tell you everything I know."

Chapter 17

Our crops have failed. The dragons are hunting further and further afield, causing tension with the neighboring lowland kingdom of Danomir. We are running out of food, water—even time. I refuse to yield to this damned prophecy but with each day, I feel hope slipping like grains of sand through my fingers.

—Excerpt from Queen Evanya's diary.

WREN WATCHED SORCHA down the last of her drink before pushing the mug away. The bartender moved to refill, but she shook her head. With a curt nod, he moved on.

Sorcha twisted in her chair, blinking slowly, appearing to study Wren and Lorca. A beat of silence followed, broken only by the intermittent murmur of the patrons nearby. As the girl started to speak, the door behind her opened. Sorcha's mouth slammed shut, tension shooting into her body, and she turned in her chair to look at the new arrival.

"Dammit," cursed Sorcha.

Wren followed her gaze. In the doorway stood a woman, tall and well-built, wearing a red blouse, leather pants, and a long cloak that hung off her broad shoulders. Her gaze latched immediately on Sorcha, thin lips compressing into a tight line.

"Sorcha!" fumed the woman.

Sorcha held up her hand, her eyes crinkling with humor. "You found me."

"Come." The command made Wren feel like a little girl again, somehow at fault with her mother.

Sorcha gestured to Wren and Lorca. "But I made friends, Omi!"

Omi considered Wren and Lorca for a moment as if picking apart every aspect of them. Her gaze returned to Sorcha. "We must go. Madam Kara wishes to leave."

"I haven't got what we came here for yet," she argued.

Wren didn't miss the way Omi's eyes flickered to her, lingering for just a moment before darting back to Sorcha.

"Madam Kara wants you back and that is the end of the conversation."

Sorcha's jaw tightened and she looked like she wanted to argue, but then, seeming to think better of it, released a heavy sigh, her shoulders dropping. *"Fine."*

With a final apologetic glance at them, she slunk over to Omi, murmuring something into her ear. Surprise flashed for a brief second over Omi's face. A whispered conversation played out between the two of them, a war of personalities. A fight that Sorcha must have lost because her head dropped and she stayed put as Omi approached.

"Say nothing of her. Understood?" The threat in the older woman's voice rang with a chilling tone.

Wren barely nodded before the woman spun around, striding out of the bar, dragging Sorcha along with her. There was not even so much as a backward glance before the door slammed shut behind them.

"Well, that was strange," drawled Lorca.

"Yeah it—" She was cut off as Lorca suddenly gasped.

He doubled over, pain twisting his face.

"Lorca, what's wrong?"

Another wave of pain marred his face. He stood up, gripping the edge of the bar. Nails gouged the wood as he wrenched his hands back, shoving off the bar shakily. A thin band of sweat glistened on his brow.

"I-I have to go."

"*Go?*" Panic sharpened her voice. "Go where?"

He leaned in close to her ear, his breath fanning her cheek. She swore she heard the rapid thump of his heartbeat.

"I have to fly. *Now.*"

Pushing past her, he hurried out the door, Wren quick on his heels. Out onto the street, she nearly lost sight of him as he darted down a nearby alleyway. He tripped, catching himself on a wall. Another tremor of pain tore through his body, sending him staggering onwards. Wren hurried after him. At the end of the alley, he stopped, and she reached out to touch him, but he spun around, eyes dragon-like, claws drawn. He held up a taloned hand, stopping her from getting closer.

"I can't fight this," he rasped out. "Go, I'll find you."

She didn't think the alley was big enough for him to shift, let alone enough to take off. He turned away from her and dug his claws into the wall, heaving himself up. With agility exceeding any climber, he scrambled up the side of the building and vanished over the top. Seconds later, she heard the rush of wind and glimpsed a flash of black shooting up into the sky.

With a deep breath, she slumped against the wall.

What in the hell?

Wren waited until midnight for Lorca to give for any sign he was okay. None came. When the sheer weight of all that had occurred finally hit her, sleep dragged her into its mindless oblivion.

When she woke the next morning, sunlight was peering through the top of the window. The light danced over her sword beside the cot. She pushed back the scratchy blanket and stared up at the ceiling, her mind a mess of tangled thoughts.

Where the hell have you gone, Lorca? Hoping that he was okay was all she could do for the moment.

Groaning, she dragged herself from bed and dressed, strapping her sword to her back. She slid each of her climbing daggers into the sheaths on her thighs, then slung her bag over her shoulder.

In it, she'd stuffed her cloak, blanket, some dried meat, and cheese. As for the horses, she'd grab them in the evening and then head out of the city.

With a deep breath, she went downstairs, where she ordered a small meal. She waited at the bar for a few minutes before a cold pie was delivered to her. It was bland and stale, leaving her to chew slowly and force every bite down. The man returned to collect her plate when she was done.

"Some of my maps were damaged in our travels. Do you know where I can go to buy some replacements?"

He stared at her, then shrugged before rattling off a series of directions. She repeated them back twice, much to his obvious irritation, before heading out.

The street stank of something festering in unseen cracks, fermenting in the morning warmth, where no cool breeze could dispel it. Crowds moved feverishly, seemingly oblivious to the stench. People pushed past Wren, their heads bent down, an atmosphere of suspicion and fear thick in the air.

Even as she ventured deeper into the city, where folk dressed in finer attire and the buildings were cleaner, the tension remained.

It was as though the city itself was holding its breath. Was it that way in every city? How anyone could live like that, she had no idea.

She kept her head low, like everyone else, and hurried on without pause. Cutting across a sprawling city square, edged by low stone buildings, she continued through a stone archway.

It led onto another busy street. She paused, her gaze alighting on a mural. Two people stood before it. One of them was crying softly in the arms of the other. It was a woman, her face twisting in rage as she looked at the mural. The man held her in a protective embrace.

"I *hate* her," snarled the woman.

"*Hush,* Mirella!"

"She enslaves her own people and no one does *anything*. Then she puts her face everywhere as if we might love her more," sneered the woman, then tore herself from the man's embrace, looking at him as if he were a demon. "They killed my *sister,* Ulrich! Your *wife.*"

"Orvana was a traitor. You best remember that and where we are," he pointed out; his gaze looked up, catching Wren's stare. "Eyes are everywhere, even in this city."

"This city will be one of the first to fight back," hissed the woman. "And I'll be there, with or without you."

Wren hurried on, rattled by the man's cold words. As she advanced through the city, she kept hearing snatches of conversation, whispers of slavery. The city was on edge, awaiting something. But what?

Shaking her head, she continued down a wide stone set of steps into a courtyard edged with two-story buildings, the bottom of which served as stores. Signs hung out the front with faded, cracked lettering. She searched for the one she was after and found it at the very end, nestled with one side against the city wall.

Gingerly, she knocked, and without waiting for an invitation, pushed the front door open and stepped into the dimly lit store. A wave of dust billowed up around her, sending her into a sneezing fit. Her lungs choked on the thick dust and her eyes burned.

"You're not from here," commented a rumbling voice.

She squinted through watery eyes and wiped them clear, standing up as her lungs finally drew in clear air. Frowning at her from behind a counter, stacked high with piles of books, was a small, stocky-looking man, with a pair of spectacles slipping down his nose.

"No. I've come for a map before my partner and I head off again," she said carefully. "I need one that shows the way to the coast."

He stared at her for a moment longer, then nodded slowly. "I might have one but it won't be cheap. Let me see?"

She waited as he stepped into a back room and rummaged around noisily. When he returned, he held a rolled-up map in his hands. He set it on the counter, beckoning her closer.

"That'll be a hundred gold for the small one."

She had no idea if that was expensive or if she was being cheated, so she dug out the pouch and began to count the coins. Quickly, she realized she didn't have enough. The man's eyes narrowed, his palm resting on the bench, fingers twitching.

Gods, now what?

She pretended to rummage out more coins when his hand snapped out, grabbing her wrist. He snatched his hand back with a hiss.

"You have dark magic in your blood," he muttered.

"Dark magic? What the hell are you talking about?"

He stepped back sharply. "Get out! Get out you monster! I don't want any trouble!"

Wren's gaze snapped to the map, then lifted back up. "The map?"

"Just get out!"

Confused, Wren snatched up the map before he could stop her and darted out. She didn't stop moving until she'd gone an entire block. Ducking into a narrow alley, she quickly stashed the map into her bag and slung it over her shoulder. Harsh breaths fell rapidly over her lips. Her body burned, a thin sheen of sweat on her skin.

After waiting for a few minutes to calm her breathing, she stepped back out onto the road, backtracking her way to the square. As she rounded the corner nearest the archway, she froze. An enormous crowd was heading in the same direction.

Wren spun around, about to hunt for an alternative path when the crowd surged toward her. Before she could react, she was swept into the chaos.

It ferried her along, helpless as she was pushed through the archway and into the square. Everywhere she looked people were pressing up against her.

Anxiety crawled into her gut, twisting like a knife. Darkness edged her vision. Her heart slammed against her ribs. In a panic, she shoved forward, sending people staggering out of the way, making a gap. Several snarled at her. A hand reached to grab her, but she slipped from their grasp and found a narrow path at the rear of the crowd.

When she finally glimpsed an opening, she leaped through it and staggered into an alleyway. There, she slumped against the wall, breathing raggedly. The crowds, all those bodies crushing against her, had left her shaky and weak. Her heart beat a panicked rhythm against her ribs, pain lancing through her chest. She pressed her hand to her heart as she dragged in gulps of air, willing herself to calm.

Finally, she opened her eyes and gasped. Standing in front of her, smiling, was Sorcha.

Her eyes glowed gold.

Chapter 18

Our hatcheries are empty and the skies no longer sing with the songs of new fledglings. The youngest of our dragons join their elders in hunts further afield. They do not say it, nor do they have to. I know. The dragons are seeking a new home, one without Dragonirs. They do not believe we will survive what comes to us.

—Excerpt from Queen Evanya's diary

WREN WATCHED IN shock as Sorcha blinked, her eyes bleeding back to warm amber. She glanced to the street, the humor fading from her face as a small patrol of city guards stalked past. No one paid any attention to them. Once they were gone, she sunk against the wall, her eyes closing for a moment.

It looked as though some heavy weight pressed down on her shoulders, briefly diminishing the energy that she had exuded.

"Well, today has been interesting," Sorcha said dryly, opening her eyes. "How's yours been?"

Wren thought about what the map seller had said, and she looked down at her hands. *Magic?* She looked up to find Sorcha studying her.

A heavy breath fell from her lips. "It's been a long and strange day."

"Wren—"

"I'm sorry. I have to go." Wrenching her gaze back to the street, she pushed away from the wall.

Sorcha's hand clamped down with an iron grip on her wrist. Instinct kicked in. Wren spun around, yanking her hand free. Sorcha winced.

"Sorry. Just hear me out, please?"

Wren started to feel cornered, trapped by more than just the city's walls.

"Why?"

Sorcha bit her lip as if hunting for the right words. "I need your help."

Wren turned. "I don't have time for this."

"*Please.*"

A single word, dripping with a plea so damnably familiar, stopped Wren dead in her tracks. Her jaw tightened.

At that moment, Sorcha sounded like Wren's sister, begging to be released as a climber. That shame at having to beg, at being brought so low, had warred in Ellie's eyes.

With a deep breath, Wren turned, refusing to yield emotion to her face—to even hint at the memories stirring in her mind. "With what?"

Sorcha glanced again at the street, then ushered Wren to follow her, as if in fear of being heard. Reluctantly, Wren walked deeper into the alley, out of earshot of anyone passing. Another silence followed until Sorcha began speaking in a hurried tone.

"I know who you are, where you're from—I saw what happened to your village."

Wren stepped forward, anger flashing. "*You were there?*"

"Not that like," blurted out Sorcha quickly. "I foresaw what would happen in a vision. That's how I found you. Look, I need you to get an item for me. It wouldn't be for nothing. I can help you in return."

"A *vision?*" She didn't hide the skepticism that dripped from her voice.

Sorcha straightened up, her gaze steady. "I've been able to summon them since I was young. That's how I know you're a climber and right now, I need someone with your skills to retrieve something for me."

"This item really that valuable?" Wren's voice was low, wary.

Sorcha nodded. "More than you know. If you do this, I will get you and your partner to the City of Slaves. Hell, I can get your entry and all the contacts you need to find your people."

The help she so desperately needed was being dangled before her. But she didn't like it when things were offered so easily. The problem was she had so few options. Her stomach flipped as she mulled it over.

"You'll take me to the City of Slaves?" asked Wren.

"Yes. We're due to join in on a festival in a nearby town, but it's a straightforward journey from there to the city. Besides, it's best not to travel without protection in this land. You'll be safer with us," rationalized Sorcha.

Wren stepped up to her, squaring off, just like she had against the wyvern. To her credit, Sorcha didn't so much as flinch beneath that stare.

"You better hold up your end," warned Wren.

Sorcha held her gaze for a moment before she stepped aside, gesturing to follow. Wren fell into step beside her as they exited the alley. As they did, Sorcha's face changed mid-stride, a seamless shift to a girl with green eyes and long black hair. Catching Wren's stare, she winked conspiratorially but said nothing. It took control not to ask. The use of magic in front of her was still jarring.

More so that *no one* in the crowd seemed to notice the transformation.

She kept quiet as she followed Sorcha through the streets. There were fewer people than before. The stale breeze brushing over her skin offered some relief from the heat. It was nothing compared to the crisp wind of the mountains, but it was better than no breeze at all.

As the outer city wall loomed closer, the shadow stretching out over the already gloomy streets, Sorcha quickened her pace. Without warning, the girl ducked down a narrow road. Wren hurried after her, nearly crashing into Sorcha's back as she halted.

Those delicate features shifted seamlessly again, returning to her original face. Wren kept a few paces back as Sorcha knocked on an old wooden door. A moment later, the door clicked open, and a hooded figure peered out at them. Pale hands slid back the hood, revealing a young man, a little older than Wren, with cold, harsh features. His stone-gray eyes looked at her, then back to Sorcha, before he stepped aside to let them pass.

"Omi is going to be pissed," he said, frowning.

Sorcha snorted, waving a hand dismissively. "She already left the city. By the time she even realizes I'm *not* in the caravan heading back to camp, it'll be too late." She paused in the narrow hallway and looked at him for a second. "I'm glad you're here, though. Who else came with you?"

"Who else was dumb enough to defy Omi on a few scattered words from you? Just Lida and myself."

A shadow passed over her face. "Eda didn't come?"

The man shook his head. "She's trying to win Omi's favor to approve her match with Marceline. You can't blame her for that."

The look on Sorcha's face said otherwise, though she remained silent. She seemed disappointed that only two people had answered her call. With a nod, she stepped ahead of him and he fell in behind her, with Wren following.

They entered a small room, lit by two lamps burning at either end. A wooden table dominated the small space, and a young girl sat on a chair beside it. She watched them as they entered, her gaze lingering on Wren.

"Who is she?" Suspicion laced the girl's silken voice.

Wren opened her mouth to speak, but Sorcha beat her to it.

"This is Wren. She's a climber, Lida."

Recognition lit Lida's sharp face. "One of those mountain people? They never come down this low. How can *she* be one of them?"

Wren touched Sorcha's shoulder, silencing her, and stepped forward. "Slavers took my people. Otherwise, I wouldn't be here." She glanced at Sorcha. "What do you need me to do?"

Sorcha nodded and turned back to the others. "We need your help to retrieve some scrolls from the top of a tower. It's not one that we can just walk into, unfortunately."

Lida looked Wren up and down. "You don't look like you could do the climb."

"*Enough* Lida," snapped Sorcha. "I need your help, not your attitude."

The girl flushed angrily and looked down at the table, scowling. Her delicate hands curled into fists, scrunching up the folds of the cloak wrapped around her. Sorcha closed the distance and set a gentle hand on her shoulder. There was a tenderness in her actions, even a kind of intimacy. Lida dragged her gaze upwards, and the fire burning on her face dimmed. She relaxed her grip on her cloak, flattening her palms on her thighs.

"With her, we can get the scrolls back. It's why I convinced Omi to talk to Madam Kara, to bring our people to this city. I told you, timing is everything."

Wren stepped forward. "You moved a whole caravan to come here, just for me?"

Sorcha looked at Wren cautiously. "Well, for the scrolls *and* you. Does this change anything?"

Ice slipped down her spine. The whole plan reeked of deception but even if there was a small chance it might help her get her people back, then she had to take it.

"If you keep your end of the deal, then no," affirmed Wren.

Jed clasped his hands together, drawing everyone's attention to him. "Great, now we've sorted this, can we get down to business?"

There was no moon that night and thick clouds gathered above the city, the air heavy with the promise of rain. A kind of weather made Wren anxious. Climbing in the rain was tricky, and she preferred to avoid it as holds became slippery and could loosen up rocks.

As she strapped up her wrists in a nearby alley, she knew there was no turning back. Sorcha stood beside her, a heavy cloak covering her narrow frame, still as death. Her glowing golden eyes fixed on Wren.

"Please don't fail," said Sorcha, the vulnerability clear on her face. Her eyes faded to normal once more, no longer illuminated in the shadows.

Wren cracked a dry smile. "If I fail, it means I'm dead. I don't plan on dying tonight."

Sorcha nodded, satisfied. Wren reached out and touched her shoulder the way she did with new climbers, worried about seeing their first wyvern.

"I'll be back soon."

She withdrew her hand, giving her complete focus to the task at hand. A low wall, a little taller than a one-story home. It was nearly polished smooth, but Wren had scoped out a rougher section an hour earlier. She dug out two small daggers and stepped up to the wall. Reaching up as high as she could, she stabbed a blade in between the seam of two old bricks. Using her daggers to create holds, she rapidly scrambled up and quietly slid onto the top, then vaulted over, landing softly on the ground below. There was a narrow gap between the wall and the tower and a small bush nearby.

Footsteps sounded close by. She saw a shadow coming from around the corner and slid behind the bush. With bated breath, she waited as the guard marched past her, oblivious to her presence. His soft footfalls retreated into silence. Once he'd passed, she exhaled and crept out, stepping up to the tower. The wall looked easy enough to climb, made of rough stone bricks. The weather had worn away some places and left the seams in between the brickwork exposed.

Without wasting time, she dug her foot into the first seam she found, then reached up and sunk her fingers into another. She dug the soft point of her boot in, then the next, and started her ascent.

The ground dropped away from beneath her, and a cool breeze brushed softly against her face. The imperfections in the walls forced her to shift sideways several times, coiling up along the tower. As the window in question neared, she slowed her climb, then paused briefly.

Her ears strained for any sign of life within the room.

When silence greeted her, she positioned herself next to the window, clinging to the wooden frame with one hand. With her free hand, she slid a dagger out from the sheath on her thigh.

She'd never broken into a room before, but Jed had shown her how to use her dagger to do it. With care, she slid the dagger between the frame and the window and flicked the latch up. Holding her breath, she slowly opened it and swung inside, landing softly on both feet. Her heart thudded in her chest, the faintest gleam of sweat on her brow, and she paused, half expecting the door to burst open.

When no soldiers rushed in to arrest her, Wren breathed again. She took a moment to examine the room, seeing chests stacked high and a large bookshelf stuffed with scrolls, almost bursting at the seams against one of the walls.

The room was just as Sorcha had described. Right down to the quill left out on a desk, right next to an open pot of ink.

Well, that's creepy.

She went straight for the scrolls, her gaze scanning the mess, hunting for one that bore the wax symbol detailed to her. Seeing it, she picked it up, eyeing it for a moment. What was on this scroll that was so damn valuable?

Behind her, she heard footsteps rapidly approaching. She rushed for the open window and swung out onto the side of the tower, dragging the window shut behind her. As she dropped out of view, she heard the door inside open. Deciding not to linger, she made a rapid descent, almost to the point of carelessness.

Halfway down she heard someone shouting from above. She looked up, but the window was still closed. Whoever it was must've realized that someone had been in the room but didn't yet know how they'd entered.

Several feet from the bottom, she dropped to the ground and raced to the other wall. Scrambling up, she vaulted over and landed with a roll on the other side. She jumped to her feet and took off down the alley.

Sorcha was waiting for her at the end, astride a horse. In her hands, she held the reins of another. Jed and Lida were beside her, keeping watch.

"We need to go—*now*," said Wren.

Sorcha handed her the reins, and Wren pulled herself up into the saddle.

"Did you get the scroll?" Lida asked impatiently.

Wren gestured to her bag. "Yes, but we have to go."

Lida opened her mouth to speak, but shouts resounded from the tower. Her impatience shifted to sharp focus as she nudged her steed and took off into the dark, followed swiftly by Jed. With a firm kick, Wren galloped after them, Sorcha racing alongside her.

"What the hell did I just steal?" Wren hissed at Sorcha.

"The future," Sorcha answered.

They charged off into the darkness as shouts rang out through the city.

The trouble wasn't over yet.

Chapter 19

*I wonder what the ruling monarchs of the lowland kingdoms
would think of how we select our rulers. That is not by blood,
nor collective decision, that we choose. Rather, the two ruling
dragons, Idris and Vaska, choose one whom they believe is of
substantial merit and honor. In our nearly three hundred and
fifty years, this has not once betrayed us.*

—Excerpt from Queen Evanya's diary.

THE SUN BEAT down on the two hundred or so people that had
gathered in the marshaling yard to be processed into slavery. At the far
end of the stone enclosure was the blacksmith's hut, where the brands
were being prepared for the future slaves. Standing along the perimeter

of the yard were dozens of guards, each of them armed.

Aziah, known only to outsiders as the Empress's assassin, watched the processing, trying not to let herself think too much. If her mind wandered, if she let that dangerous little voice rise, her heart would soften.

A death sentence for someone like her.

Beside her, the lord managing the affair stood with his muscular arms folded over his broad chest. Those cold, dark eyes watched the processing without a hint of remorse. For him, this was simply a matter of business. A basic trade of flesh for coin.

Though from his frequent glances at her, he didn't much like her company. Her reputation probably kept his tongue silent. Which was just as well. She was hardly in the mood to talk, let alone to the waste of air that he was.

At least, that was her belief until he drew in a deep breath, then turned to her. A shadow passed over his face as his brow furrowed. "Why the insistence on these prisoners being sold together? I don't like it. This is only going to bring the Empress trouble."

Aziah drew in a deep breath, the sea air sharp on her lips as she spoke. "It isn't your place to understand the mind of our esteemed ruler."

It took a great deal of self-control to keep any sarcasm from her voice. After all, she was the loyal right hand, the blade of the empress. Death was her business and the only friend she had left.

He glanced at her but held his tongue, remembering exactly *who* he was talking to. It was enough for Aziah as she looked back to the people, a chill coiling tightly around her heart. He was right. It wasn't normal practice for slaves to be kept together. It was a recipe for disaster, or would be, had Aziah been ignorant to the plans of her Empress.

She pitied them, but that was all she permitted herself to feel. If she let her heart soften, it would break, and all she had done would be lost. So, she kept silent, watching the procession. All she could do was be a witness, so that perhaps one day, once the ashes settled of what was about to happen, she might tell their story.

That someone would know of the terrible fate that befell a remote mountain village called Fenware.

"Will you stay long?"

Spirits above, he was still talking to her?

She reached up and slid her hood back, savoring the air that flowed over her face, slick with sweat. The effect was cooling, and she nearly groaned with pleasure. Schooling her features, she turned to him.

She pushed back from the railing and turned to leave. "Send word to the Empress once the matter is concluded."

He gave a curt nod, perhaps seeing no need to delve further—or simply understanding the consequence of being too inquisitive.

Before she returned to the capital, she took an offered room at the city guards' barracks. She had been given a private chamber courtesy of her position. It overlooked the training courtyard, where soldiers were sparring with wooden swords. She watched this for a moment, studying their training before she retreated inside and shed her cloak.

In the room's privacy, she could take off her outer tunic, until she stood barefoot in her leather trousers and undershirt. She wouldn't be leaving until dawn when she'd be required to return for her meeting with the Empress.

With the past few days finally catching up on her, she retreated to the bed. The second she crawled onto the hard mattress, the nightmares sunk their claws into her and held on.

She surrendered to sleep, letting them devour her whole.

Chapter 20

Litania has returned from her pilgrimage north. A journey that was meant to bring clarity to her magic. Only, now there is a troubling look in her eyes. It is as though she is fighting a battle with a demon in her mind—and losing.

—Excerpt from Princess Yelena's diary.

WREN CLUNG TO the back of the horse, hunched low, as the four of them raced through the streets. Hooves thumped against the cobbles, echoing softly against the cries that came from behind them. The alarm stretched across the city, through the labyrinth of buildings and narrow streets. Sleepy locals stirred in their beds. The promise of a hunt woke them, their shouts ringing out from the houses and buildings as the riders passed.

Ahead, a cart partially blocked the road, leaving only a pinched gap free Sorcha's horse jumped over, followed by Jed and Lida. Wren's heart seized in her chest. She'd never done that before. Her hands tightened on the reins, every inch of her screaming to yank on them, stopping the horse.

The horse jumped. A stifled scream tore from her mouth as the horse landed.

Lida twisted in her saddle. "Shut it or you'll give away our position."

Wren scowled, saying nothing.

They rounded a corner, out onto a wider street. She crouched down, urging her mare on. Sucking in deep breaths, she continued after the others as they raced toward the exit. The city wall loomed ahead in the distance, casting a dominant shadow.

As they came to the last stretch of road meeting the main gate, a dozen guards barred the way, four of them with arrows nocked and aimed. The clank of a wheel and chattering chains filled the air as the gate descended.

Sorcha slowed her horse, trotting for several moments before she swung down out of her saddle. Lida and Jed glanced at each other. Wren nudged her horse to stand beside Jed.

"Now what?" she asked.

Jed put a finger to his mouth, then pointed to Sorcha. The girl approached the guards, her hands spread wide, as if in peace. When she was several feet away, she stopped.

"You will not let us pass freely, will you?" mused Sorcha, hands on her hips.

"No one is permitted to leave the city," barked the middle guard, a gold symbol emblazoned on his chest.

Sorcha sighed. "Not even if I say please and smile prettily?"

He snorted. "Not even for a pretty thing like you. Now, why don't you and your friends hand over your weapons and come with us for questioning."

Sorcha straightened up, squaring her shoulders. The girlish air melted away, someone confident taking her place. Wren watched, entranced, as she raised one hand to the men. In the palm of her outstretched hand, an orb of light started to glow—small at first, then growing rapidly.

"I apologize, but this is going to hurt," she declared, not sounding at all sorry.

Sorcha flicked her wrist, the orb bursting out from her hand. Just before it hit the middle guard, it exploded, the shock wave sending the rest of the men flying. The gate let out a grinding shriek as the metal twisted, stopping it halfway down.

Gods above, who is this girl?

Sorcha dropped her hand and staggered forward. Jed jumped down from his horse, racing toward her. Just as Sorcha's legs buckled, he grabbed her and draped her arm over his shoulder so that he could help her stand.

Wren dismounted and helped Jed get the half-conscious girl onto his saddle. Sorcha's horse, who had lingered off behind, trotted over and nuzzled her leg. Lida rode up and grabbed its reins casting a look of disdain at Wren.

Jed swung up behind Sorcha, one arm encircling her waist. He drew her close protectively, a look of worry wrinkling his brow.

"You don't have to stick around," said Lida, throwing Wren a pointed look, as if to say, *you're not wanted.*

Wren lifted her chin. She'd be damned if she let some girl bully her out. "Sorcha and I have an agreement."

Lida pressed her lips together but didn't argue the point. Jed clicked his tongue and, with a kick of his heel, the horse surged forward. Wren and Lida quickly followed, no one saying a word as they raced out of the city.

As the forest grew thicker around them, Wren watched as Sorcha finally stirred, pushing Jed's arm away.

"I'm okay now," she said, a faint sheen of sweat glistening on her brow.

She didn't look right to ride by herself, but Wren kept quiet. Jed slid down from the saddle, then held out a hand, helping Sorcha down onto the ground. As he helped her back onto her horse, Wren didn't miss how his hand lingered. Nor the way his gaze remained on her until she gave him a curt nod.

Seemingly reluctant, he climbed back onto his horse.

Sorcha twisted in her saddle to face Wren, a wry smile twisting her lips. "Hell of an exit, wouldn't you say?"

Wren's brow lifted. "You're just full of surprises. Is this a common occurrence for you?"

"Would it scare you off if that were the case?"

"No."

Sorcha nodded approvingly. "The main camp is just over the next hill."

Worry gnawed at Wren. The further she traveled from the city, the more she wondered how Lorca would find her. Sharp talons sank into her mind, reminding her she also had no way to find him, not without revealing what he was.

"Gods, the scroll better be worth it. Omi's going to kill us all if Madam Kara doesn't," muttered Lida. "I don't know how you're so calm, Sorcha."

Sorcha froze in her saddle, her eyes glazing over. A moment later she blinked and said, "We need to go. *Now.*"

Wren couldn't hear anything at first, aside from the quiet stir of the wind rustling the leaves.

Then it came.

The approaching sound of horses' hooves beating an ominous drum, a death song closing in. Sorcha opened one hand again, summoning ribbons of light. The light spluttered out. A frown tugged at her face, dismissed in the next breath, fixing into a steely look. The glow in her eyes spluttered out, too. A candle snuffed out by a gust of wind.

She kicked her horse and shot off into the dark, the rest quick to follow.

As they thundered through the forest, Jed reached down to the bags on his saddle, fishing out a quiver of arrows, which he slung over his back before he bent down again. This time he untied a bow strapped to one of the bags and brought it up. Letting go of the reins, the horse followed behind Sorcha's, while Jed nocked an arrow.

With more skill than Wren had seen anyone show astride a horse, he twisted in his saddle, drawing up his bow. Without missing a beat, he released the arrow. It hissed through the air, landing with a muted thump.

She returned her attention to Sorcha's back. The girl rode with a fierce focus, racing uphill. Underfoot, the ground grew loose, the horses struggling to keep their pace. Wren tightened her grip on the reins, praying the horse wouldn't lose its footing.

The sound of the guards faded. A glance behind showed their horses were struggling to keep up.

Three men remained in view. Wren wrenched her focus back, her heart racing.

Where had the fourth gone?

The hill finally flattened out. Their pursuers started closing the distance and Jed released two more arrows. Two successive thumps, followed by a clattering crash and the reducing rush of hooves, indicated his shots were successful. He released another arrow. No thump came and their last pursuer remained, closing fast.

She considered—momentarily, anyway—trying to twist in her saddle, to fling her climbing daggers, and quickly dismissed the thought. It was unlikely they would find their target, and her daggers were precious. The last physical tie to home.

The trees thinned around them as they raced along a flat stretch through the forest. As they burst into a clearing, Sorcha turned sharply again, circling back, stopping dead. Wren followed Lida as they wheeled around, facing the approaching rider.

Jed twisted again in his saddle and fired off an arrow. It whistled through the air. This time, his mark didn't miss, and the rider tumbled from his saddle with a heavy thump. His horse bolted off into the trees. Jed swung down off his saddle and strode over to the rider, who rolled onto his back with a groan. The arrow was buried deep into his side. Jed cursed and crouched over the man. He glanced at Sorcha.

"He'll live."

Sorcha's mouth tightened to a thin line. A single nod. Whatever that meant, or what was going on in that head, Wren had no idea.

Jed turned from her and pulled out the dagger from his hip. Without flinching, he ripped it across the man's throat. Blood sprayed. Wren froze. The sudden visceral act sent shock waves rippling through her.

Wren spotted Lida smiling at her but it didn't quite reach her eyes.

The victory was short-lived as an arrow shot out of the trees. Sorcha threw up her hands as if to stop it, but she failed and it slammed into her side, sinking deep. A cry tore from her. Jed was up in an instant, releasing an arrow into the trees. A thump resounded close by, and a man staggered out of the trees. He fell to the ground, blood pooling from the arrow sticking out of his neck.

"Sorcha!" Lida cried, jumping down from her saddle.

Sorcha clutched at her side, wincing as blood trickled through her fingers. "Dammit. I'm in so much trouble."

Jed rushed over, slinging his bow over his back. "You're seriously concerned over what Omi might say? You have an arrow in you."

She narrowed her gaze. "Oh really? I hadn't noticed."

"Now isn't the time to joke around," scolded Jed.

"Just pull it out," snapped Sorcha.

"That'll make it worse!" Jed argued. "I'm not carrying your *corpse* back! Omi would *gut* me—*slowly, very slowly.*"

Sorcha snorted. "No, she wouldn't. She *likes* you. I'm the problem child, remember."

"And yet you insist on throwing your magic around so carelessly—which gets us into this mess," he bit back.

"For our *future,* if we ever hope to have one!" Sorcha's cheeks were flushed, eyes glowing like twin suns.

Silence fell, as though the world held its breath at this declaration. She wondered once more just who the girl was, what the fire was that pushed her. It made her feel like she was rapidly falling out of her depth. She shifted restlessly in her saddle. Amongst these three, she was the stranger, uncertain of what to say.

Involuntarily, Wren glanced down at her hands. Once more, she wondered how there could be any magic in her at all. She dismissed the thought for the moment.

Wren glanced again at Sorcha. She looked unafraid but in some discomfort from the pain.

Dawn beckoned over the horizon, bathing everything in shades of gold. It might've been a pretty sight, were it not for the bodies and the stench of blood.

"Come, let us get this over and done with before I bleed out everywhere," Sorcha declared. "The camp isn't far."

The concern lingered on Jed's blood-splattered face as got up onto his horse. He pinned a hard look at Lida. Lines of worry etched his face.

Sorcha nudged her horse to a slow canter, leaving everyone to hurry after her.

At the bottom of the hill, they slowed to a brisk walk. Sorcha swayed every so often in her saddle. Jed made a move to her, but she straightened up at the last moment. Once her hand snapped out, and she cast a warning look at Jed.

He drew back. His gaze shuttered as he dropped his head, yielding to that silent command.

The trees momentarily thickened around them again, branches above intertwining to block out the emerging day. Darkness stayed on, stubborn, broken occasionally by bands of sunlight.

Sorcha stopped again, looked about a moment, and then went on.

She and her horse vanished into thin air. Wren opened her mouth in alarm, but Jed and Lida followed suit, disappearing as well. Wren hurried after them. A wave of cold washed over her and then receded. With a shuddering breath, Wren saw she had arrived at the caravan. It unfurled before her, as though a curtain had been peeled back.

Makeshift stables were erected off to the side, housing the horses. A couple of youths tended to them. At first, they smiled at the arrivals. Then one frowned, looking at Sorcha. His gaze snagged on the arrow. He darted off, calling out. His shrill voice carried around the encampment, followed swiftly by others.

More people emerged from tents and around corners, drawing closer. All wearing colorful robes, their hair long and braided. Several were armed with swords and other weapons.

Five, Wren counted, had arrows knocked on their bows. Loose, though, and pointed at the ground. The reaction, Wren assumed, was for her. Her hand instinctively moved to the dagger on her thigh.

The crowd parted without warning and the familiar figure of Omi appeared, striding alongside a tall, regal woman with long, flowing black hair. She had a striking face and a pair of eyes like the blue sky on a clear climbing day. She looked at the group and her gaze pierced through them, like a freezing wind.

Omi saw Sorcha as she dismounted and hurried forward, shouting at others to come. Several came as requested, and Sorcha was ferried off.

Lida and Jed dismounted and stood nearby as if awaiting punishment. The regal woman stopped and cast her gaze over Wren, appraising her.

"And just what has my dear Sorcha brought into my camp?" she asked, looking at Wren for an answer.

Wren considered staying in her saddle because it was easier to get away. But at the end of the day, there was a deal. She had to hope – no, *trust*– that it would be honored. She dismounted and moved in front of her horse, which was quickly led away. Exposed and feeling alone, Jed and Lida offered no comment. Their eyes were downcast, and Wren could see a smile tugging faintly at Lida's mouth, smug as ever.

"My name is Wren. In exchange for aiding your granddaughter and her friends, she promised me passage."

"Indeed," drawled the woman. "And what did you do for her that was so valuable?"

"I retrieved a scroll. Sorcha seemed pretty intent on having it."

The woman's brow lifted, silent for a moment before she turned to the gathered crowd. "Relax. All is well. Return to your work. Make all preparations. We depart at first light. Jed and Lida, you may leave too. I will talk to you both... later."

The people, roused from their curiosity over Wren, dispersed. Mutterings trailed behind them, swirling rumors. Sorcha's friends cast her a lingering look, then wandered off, whispering to each other. Once everyone was gone, the woman turned back to her.

"Come with me, Wren. It seems we have much to discuss." She gestured for her to follow. "You may call me Madam Kara."

Chapter 21

There was no mistaking it. Dragons held grudges. Vaska especially.

—Excerpt from Queen Evanya's diary.

MADAM KARA'S TENT stood in stark contrast to her cool, reserved air. From the brightly colored exterior and warm, luxurious touches within, it hinted at an almost whimsical nature.

The main area boasted high walls that met in the center, supported by a post draped with ribbons of vibrant cloth. At the rear was a single cream sheet that partitioned off a private section. In the middle of the room was a large table covered with an assortment of maps, scrolls, and books haphazardly scattered atop it. Four chairs were tucked in, arranged around the edge. There were several wooden stands with lanterns hanging off them around the tent, throwing a warm, buttery glow over the furnishings.

It was eerily quiet, as though the tent itself held its breath. Wren watched Kara glide around the table but remained standing, unsure of protocol, as the woman lowered herself gracefully onto one of the chairs. Those jewel-blue eyes looked Wren up and down with her brow furrowing slightly.

"Where did Sorcha promise to take you?" she asked, resting one jeweled hand on the table.

"To your destination on the coast. From there I will travel to the City of Slaves."

Kara nodded. "And what do you seek there?"

"My village was attacked. I wish to find my people and return them to the mountains." Wren straightened her spine, squaring her shoulders. Even as her heart raced nervously, she tried to appear confident and determined.

Surprise flashed across Kara's face. The woman stood up and pushed away a pile of books on the table to reveal a sprawling map of the empire, much like the one that Wren had bought from Tarth. Only this one was far more detailed and had notes scribbled around cities and towns.

She leaned forward staring intently at Wren. "Show me."

Wren's gaze was drawn to the expanse of mountains on the top end of the map. She drew closer to the table and pointed to where the remains of her village stood.

"There."

When she glanced up, she glimpsed a flicker of something unreadable in Madam Kara's eyes. "That's quite remote. Why would anyone bother such a village?"

"I don't know," confessed Wren. "I was meeting with a friend who was helping me organize a safe place to move everyone to. When we returned to start the move, the villagers were gone."

"Gone?"

"We had heard rumors of village attacks and the survivors being enslaved. My friend sensed the use of magic in the village to summon portals so we assumed my people were likely taken away to be sold as slaves."

Kara nodded thoughtfully, rubbing her chin as she took in all the information. "And what if they were sentenced to death, rather than sold? If your people were taken because of some offense, then they may have been executed."

A long silence hung between them. Finally, Wren answered, "Perhaps but if death was the goal why use portals to ferry them away? They left the bodies of those they butchered."

Kara's eyes pierced through her. "And what of your friend?"

She hesitated, a multitude of lies poised on her lips. Her heart gave a nervous flutter before she found her voice. "We were separated."

"But you believe you will be reunited before we leave?" inquired Kara.

Wren was silent for a moment, considering this conundrum. Lorca had sworn an oath to her and stayed by her side, faithful and helpful. It felt wrong to leave when something might've happened to him—or worse? And yet, the longer she waited, the further her people were from her. She was torn in both directions, either choice yielding pain.

"I don't know," murmured Wren. "I need to find my people but my friend has saved my neck, so I owe him."

Madam Kara dipped her chin in acknowledgment. She returned her gaze to Wren. "How old are you?"

"Eighteen."

"So young. Is this your first time in the lowlands?"

She felt the woman study her closely, as though she could see right into Wren's soul. It peeled back her defenses, stripped her bare. She didn't know why she was so interested in her. Did she see her as a kind of threat to the caravan?

Wren shifted on the balls of her feet. "That's why I agreed to get the scroll for Sorcha. I am a stranger in this land. I need help and information."

Kara's mouth opened. "I will have to consider a few—"

The entrance to the tent burst open. Lida rushed in, red-faced.

"The barrier is weakening. Something is pushing it," she said in a rush. "Madam Kara, you best come look."

Madam Kara nodded, rising from the chair and striding around the table. She was out the door, following Lida in a flash. Wren hurried after them as they took off through the maze of tents to the edge of the camp.

Another group of people had gathered, several with weapons in hand. Suspicious looks fell on Wren as she strode past them, falling in behind Madam Kara and pausing at the front of the group.

The caravan leader approached the barrier and pressed her flattened palm against it causing it to shimmer and pulsate, patches fading in and out. She pulled back, moved back, then slammed both hands together. A deafening *bang* exploded from her.

The barrier vanished.

Screams spilled into the air as a shadowy creature swooped down. Glossy black wings flared wide just above the treeline. Her breath hitched at the black dragon that landed, relief bleeding the tension from her shoulders.

Lorca.

As he tucked in his wings, he craned his head over the crowds, searching until their eyes met across the clearing. She'd broken into a run and was halfway to him by the time she'd realized she'd moved. A weight lifted off her chest. No sooner had his head lowered to greet her had she thrown her arms around his snout, and she pressed her forehead to his. His warm breath flared around her and she felt him ease into her arms.

"You're okay." A shaky breath shuddered through her chest.

You have made friends without me, he grumbled.

She snorted. "I had to make do. Why didn't you come to me before? Where did you go? What happened?"

I underestimated the effect of spending so much time in human form. It forced my change back to this...The weather made it impossible to stay too close to the city, so I had to wait until you left. He lifted his head from her embrace to look at the gathering crowd. *Well, I'd best introduce myself.*

She felt his body stiffen; then, after a beat, he burst into light, dimming quickly to reveal his familiar human form standing before her. The transformation stole her breath for a moment. He offered her a small, reassuring smile that did little for her racing heart. She went to return it but his gaze snapped to something behind her. As she turned, he was pulling away and striding to Madam Kara.

He dropped to one knee, bowing his head. "Great Dragon Inakara."

Kara's eyes widened. "Prince Adrian, you're alive...*how?*"

Wren hurried to his side. *Inakara?* As in the sister of Vaska, the leader of the dragons that once lived in the mountains? From the shock that plastered his face, it was her, someone from his past.

Lorca pushed himself back up to his feet, half turning back to Wren. "It's a long story, as I imagine yours is but, please, call me Lorca. It's been a long time since I was called Adrian."

Kara tilted her head at the name, then nodded. "Lorca then. You may call me Kara"

"As you wish," replied Lorca.

The whispers from the crowd grew louder. Kara turned around. "All is well. Please, rest now. We have a long journey ahead of us."

The crowd trickled away until it was only the three of them. Lorca and Kara regarded each other, a silent conversation playing out, leaving her standing there awkwardly. She could feel Lorca's happiness flow through their bond and though she was glad for him, she couldn't deny the stab of jealousy. It was an ugly knife that twisted in her gut, prickling her cheeks with shame.

Neither seemed aware of her darkening mood.

Lorca broke the silence first. "You're *alive* and *here*. Why not—"

"Why am I not with the rest of my kin?" One thin eyebrow lifted, a ghost of a smile playing on her lips, touched with a quiet sadness. "My sister, remember. She does not forgive so easily."

"But what happened wasn't your fault," he argued. "How can she blame you for that?"

"She doesn't. There are other sins which I am guilty of but enough of the past. I presume you wish to stay with Wren." When he nodded, Kara continued on, "then so be it. I must think about this deal Sorcha has struck with your friend here but you will know my answer soon. I'll have one of my people find a tent for you to join tonight. For now, explore." With a curt nod, she strode off, leaving them alone.

Lorca returned to Wren's side. "A dragon's oath is binding. If she agrees, then she will never break her word."

Wren glanced at the camp, uneasy. "And if she says no?"

"Then we'll come up with another plan."

After asking around, they found Sorcha's tent. She was recovering from the arrow and sitting up in a chair, wrapped up in a cloak. A smile stretched her mouth as Wren entered, followed by Lorca. Delight lit her eyes.

"So, now we have *two* dragons here. How wonderful," declared Sorcha.

Lorca shifted. "I am only a Dragonir. Inakara is the dragon."

Sorcha waved a dismissive hand. "Details, details."

Wren smiled. "You're looking well for someone who had an arrow in them."

"What can I say? I'm very hard to kill. It's not the first time someone has tried. Omi found me on the side of the road as a baby, cradled in a dead woman's arms. She had an arrow in her too."

Questions bubbled up as Wren pictured the blood-soaked babe. Had that origin lit the flame that burned in those amber eyes? She leaned forward. "Did you ever find out where you are from?"

Shadows shuttered Sorcha's gaze. "No."

A heavy silence consumed the small space.

An hour or so later a woman came from them, informing them that accommodation had been found. Lorca said that he would be sleeping outside in his dragon form. Accepting this, the woman led Wren to her tent, where Lorca shifted and curled up outside of it.

The interior was simple with a row of bedrolls on one side and several boxes on the other. She was given one to sleep in, along with a change of clothes and a night shift. They were a little tight on her, especially around her arms and hips. She made do as best as she could, changing quickly, and crawled underneath the blanket. Sleep claimed her quickly, dragging her into oblivion.

Chapter 22

The death of my husband has left a gaping hole in my court. My two young children have not spoken in days, and whispers follow in my wake. Yet this all seems small compared to the final words of my husband—that the Spirit of the Mountain isn't who we believed her to be.

—Excerpt from Queen Evanya's diary.

IN THE BLISTERING sun, the sea air sharp on his skin, Flynn surveyed the large pen the guards had marched them into. The thin and scratchy clothing still clung to his sweat-soaked skin. It was as though something was crawling through them. It seemed likely as he tugged it off his chest again, trying to get some relief.

Yet even as a lazy breeze spilled in over the stone wall guarding them, it provided little relief. Waves of heat rippled over the mass of people, all huddled together, but not quite touching. The rancid stench of sweat and burned flesh swirled around the trembling masses.

In that place, the spirits had forsaken them.

A few tried praying around him but even those furtive pleas faded away. What was the point? Hopelessness filled Flynn as he stared out across at what was left of his people.

There's so few of us left...

Friends, family, neighbors—gone.

Grief hollowed out his chest, threatening to devour the last shreds of hope that he'd had when they'd arrived in the city. Fighting the urge to touch the brand blistering on his upper arm, he looked around in search of Mira. She'd been one of the most recent to be branded. He'd heard her screams from the branding hut all the way across the yard.

He saw Vaughn by the wall, standing protectively by Lily, and headed over. As he neared closer, Vaughn glanced up, exhaustion in his dark eyes.

"Flynn, what is it?"

"Have you seen Mira?" he asked.

"Alaric and Sarah were with her by the main gate." Vaughn pointed with a shaky hand, quickly dropping it.

Nodding, Flynn left the couple and waded through the crowd. Wren's parents beckoned him over and stepped aside from Mira. Ellie stood close by, a look of concern on her face.

The young climber sat with her back to the wall, cradling her arm. The brand had already blistered, and the arm was swollen. She glanced up, fighting back tears and failing. A pang of worry tightened in his gut. Mira was the closest thing he had left to family. They weren't blood but they'd grown up next to each other, family in all the ways that mattered.

He dropped, kneeling before her. "How's it feeling?"

"Like shit," she replied, wincing.

"Good to see you've still got some fire left in you," he murmured, glancing up as a shadow passed over them. "Hold on, okay?"

She grunted a response, and her gaze lifted to the guard, unreadable.

A guard was walking along the wall above them, a bow strapped to his back. Sensing Flynn's gaze, he stopped and stared for a moment, his lip curling. It took all Flynn had left not to spit at the ground and scowl. Internally cursing, he wrenched his gaze away and looked back to Mira.

Dark shadows lingered beneath her eyes. Her shoulders dropped, what little fight she had bled away. Mira released a shaky breath. "What's going to happen to us?"

He sucked in a deep breath, then exhaled slowly. "I don't know Mira, I really don't."

"We're going to be sold as slaves, that's what," muttered Ellie, shuffling closer.

Wren's sister slumped down next to Mira, scowling at the stones. Flynn shot her a warning look. Everyone knew what the brands meant. That didn't mean that was to be their fate forever. He wasn't accepting that. Somehow, he'd find a way to break them free. He just had to be patient, find an opportunity, and exploit it.

He cleared his throat. "That may be so—"

"And we'll be split up soon. One guard taunted me about it last night. He told me they spirit away all the kids for private sales, anyone deemed pretty to be sold to the brothels, and the rest probably to the mines." Ellie's gaze moved to her hands—which Flynn noted uneasily were shaking—and she exhaled.

He reached out for her hand, squeezing it reassuringly. "We will stay together."

Ellie's gaze flickered up, hardening. "Don't make promises you can't keep."

Wren... he opened his mouth to argue on Wren's behalf, but Ellie stood. She dusted off her dress and stalked off. Flynn watched her melt away into the crowd, his chest heavy. That same shadow of darkness he'd glimpsed on Ellie growing up returned, their people shrinking away from her as she walked.

Loathe as he was to admit it, Ellie was right. He shouldn't make promises he couldn't keep.

At night everyone was forced into large warehouses, which contained rows of enormous cages, each housing at least thirty or forty people. They were crammed in and huddled together, desperately clinging to what little heat they could create together. The bitter night air had swept in, clouds of white breath swirling amongst their shuddering bodies.

Flynn sat close to Mira, whose arm had grown hot to the touch. Sweat glistened on her trembling body. He didn't have to be a healer to know what he'd see if he looked at her wound.

Spirits, don't take her too, he prayed reverently, glancing through one of the tiny windows high on the wall where moonlight spilled in.

"Flynn?" Mira's voice came through dangerously soft.

"What's wrong, Mira?"

A shudder rippled through her body before she mustered a reply. "I wish I could see the mountains again."

"You will, I promise," he replied fiercely.

Dread filled his gut as he brushed the hair from Mira's brow. Beneath his touch, she shuddered, moaning softly. His own hand was jittery, tingling along the skin. He pressed it into his leg, forcing it still. Most of the time he wasn't sure whether he wanted to breathe or scream.

Since their capture, he'd become an unintentional leader of sorts among the village. He hated it, loathed watching the few that had died already. He was terrified of how many people he was about to lose, and the thought devoured him whole.

"I know Ellie doesn't like you making those promises, but I do. We need hope," she whispered.

Her rambling continued off into incoherency, doing little to ease the fear in Flynn's heart. He held on as if that might tether her to the mortal coil. Deep down, he wondered if she'd even make it to dawn.

With his mind twisting into knots over the future, he scarcely heard the main doors screech open to the warehouse. The hushed whispers from everyone else broke his reverie. Carefully, he released Mira and sat up, squinting through the darkness.

Moonlight streamed across the narrow path that ran from the doors through the middle of the warehouse. Several men stood in it, hooded and featureless. One held a lantern, spreading an amber glow among the swaths of blue and silver.

The man in the middle turned and murmured something to another before he strode off down the warehouse. The others followed close behind.

Every so often they paused at a cell, shining the lantern across the terrified faces. Flynn's heart slammed loudly in his chest, a death march that chilled his soul as they drew closer. Their footfalls thudded too loudly against the stone, each a tolling sound, echoing eerily. It grew louder, inching in his direction. Every so often they paused, whispered among themselves, one would shake their head, and they moved on.

Just two cells away they stopped again. The men muttered among each other, but Flynn was close enough to catch snippets of their conversation.

"That's the one Lauri wanted," he announced.

"Are we sure about this?" another replied. "The empress gave strict orders about this lot."

He turned to the one that spoke, a warning burning in his dark, soulless eyes. "The empress isn't here. Besides, slaves die in transit all the time? What is the loss of one? Now, shut your damn mouth and do what I'm paying you for."

The other man's head dropped. He murmured a reply, then stepped back. The argument was over.

Flynn's stomach dropped as he realized what was about to happen and that he was helpless to stop it.

The one that spoke first fished out a key from his cloak and unlocked the cage, while the ones that flanked him drew their weapons. A man holding the lantern stood in the doorway and raised it, pointing to the middle of the cell. The burnished lantern light danced over the muddied tips of his fingers.

Frozen with fear, no one dared move a muscle.

Flynn strained to see who he was pointing to but he couldn't make it out.

"You. Come with us," he ordered his voice echoing through the warehouse and rousing anyone who hadn't yet fallen asleep.

His heart froze in his chest as Ellie rose shakily to her feet.

"Me?" she asked.

"Yes, you. *Move.*"

Ellie glanced around as if someone might stand and fight the men, but no one stirred, not with the exit to the cell guarded by heavily armed men. Then she looked at him, and his heart thudded hard against his ribs. He tried to rise but his legs buckled and he sank back down. The muscles in his legs quivered from the effort. If he tried to stand again, he reckoned he'd fall flat on his face. But he couldn't just stand by and do nothing. He couldn't fail her...

Defeat emptied whatever hope she still had left. Her shoulders slumped as she took a step forward.

No!

Two of the men turned around. Flynn realized he'd said that out loud and that he'd stood up, staring them dead in the eye.

"What did you say?" The question dripped with venom in the man's voice.

Silence seized his tongue. *Speak you fool! Do something!* But his body refused to move and the words didn't rise to his lips. He licked his dry lips, trying to find his voice again. Silence choked him. His heart sunk as the men grinned cruelly at him, their satisfaction at his silence palpable.

They turned away, dragging Ellie with them. He watched a stray tear slide down her cheek and her body shake as if she were holding back the tears. Just like her sister, refusing to show fear. At the last second, she flashed him a brittle smile.

Like she was thankful someone had tried to save her.

"NO!" Another voice roared through the dark.

Alaric.

"You can't take her!" he bellowed, fists slamming on the metal, echoing like claps of thunder.

Power flooded Flynn as he strode to the edge of his cell, slamming his fists against the bars. It was all he could do but, then, he saw Ellie was unchained and they weren't holding her.

"*Run, Ellie, Run!*" The words ruptured from his mouth like a crack of lightning.

Ellie's eyes widened, then snapped to the gaping door. The silver light of freedom. She burst forward, sprinting for the escape. Stunned, the men didn't move for a second, startled by her boldness.

Run, Ellie, run!

Then they ran after Ellie. The last Flynn saw was her long blonde hair shining in the moonlight as she ran like her life depended on it.

Flynn's heart pounded in his chest. *Please, let her get away!*

Chapter 23

Yelena does not believe I found clarity on my journey deep into the mountains. What she doesn't know, what I can never utter to anyone, is that I found the truth I needed. I found my future.

—Excerpt from Litania's diary.

AZIAH HAD BEEN summoned. The unexpected call from the empress twisted in her gut as she emerged from the portal. She didn't dare to lift her head, lest she betrayed her unease and worry. Eighteen years of careful planning and scheming had ensured her cover would not be blown. That didn't mean, however, the threat of being exposed at any moment ever left her. It followed her clinging like a second skin.

She cast her gaze over the war room, devoid of the usual array of Empress Alexandria's inner circle. More importantly, the spymaster was absent. That human had eyes like a hawk, far too perceptive for her liking. And his loathing of her was no secret, mostly in part to her fae heritage.

A traitor to her kind, he'd whispered more than once, knowing that she could hear him.

Turning from the war table that dominated the room, she moved over to the bookshelf, eyeing the contents. She was familiar with every book there, her fingers itching to take one of them and read, but that quiet pleasure would have to wait for the moment.

The door swung open, the click of heels against stone drawing her focus from the shelf.

The Empress had arrived. Dressed in a flowing golden gown, the woman was striking with her obsidian curls, woven with glittering jewels. No part of her was unkempt. Magic kept her face youthful, her cheekbones sharp, her lips rosy.

Aziah had heard people whisper stories that the Empress had sold her soul to a demon in order to remain youthful and in power. It had all seemed absurd long ago. However, eighteen years at the Empress's side had given Aziah reason to believe there might be some merit to the rumors. Yet all of her quietpryings revealed only unsettling clues that weren't solid enough to prove the stories true.

It was maddening.

She bowed, then rose gracefully, pushing back her hood with practiced calm. "Empress, how may I serve you?"

Alexandria stared for a moment, then swept in silence over to the table, sitting down. "I have received troubling rumors pertaining to the City of Slaves."

"Who do you wish killed?" She clasped her hands behind her back.

"No one."

Surprise snapped like a whip in Aziah's chest. She refused to let it show as she picked her words with care. Was she being tested? Her loyalty examined? It wasn't the first time, but the last had been, what, ten years ago? Aziah had gone to even greater pains since then to cover her tracks, to ensure her loyalty was never in question.

No family, no friends, no one close enough to know the truth.

Alexandria sighed. "It seems the stories of the supposed survival of my niece have surfaced once more. My spymaster has intercepted letters suggesting that she may still be alive."

A chill rushed down Aziah's spine. "I will discover if there is merit to them."

"See that you do. It goes without question that if you discover my niece, I want her head," said Alexandria coolly. "And if you discover who aided her escape, I want their heads, too. I will not stand for traitors in my court."

Aziah dipped her head. "Consider it done."

Alexandria was silent for a moment, her sharp blue eyes narrowed. It was as though that gaze was hunting for a crack in Aziah's mask, ready to slip in and discover the secrets she hid from the world. It was a look she hadn't seen for some time, but the effect was no less chilling. This was not the woman often exposed to the court. Alexandria had played the part of politician carefully, taking pains to control every aspect of her image. She left nothing to chance.

This was why Alexandria was revealing the monster beneath, the one who had brought the fae to their knees and seemingly had no enemies in her court.

The look was a warning.

"Go," said Alexandria, her voice soft like a knife, cutting, deadly.

Aziah bowed and spun, striding out to the balcony that jutted off the room. She snapped her fingers, summoning a portal, and, without looking back, strode through. The world tumbled away and darkness took hold.

Chapter 24

It is with a heavy heart I write that Ellory, my oldest friend and the court's head sorceress, passed away. Her daughter, Litania, now inherits the title, though she lacks her mother's gift. Time was never on Ellory's side, unfortunately, especially given her foresight abilities—such is the fate of all who bear that burden. Her final vision has sent shock waves through my court—our empire will fall in my lifetime.

—Excerpt from Queen Evanya's diary, first entry of her final diary.

SORCHA HEADED TO Kara's tent before the sun nudged the horizon. The sky was still starlit, clear, and the air crisp against her skin. The chill melted away at the earthy warmth that washed over her as she made her way inside. As expected, Kara was awake, already dressed in her riding gear.

Kara had cast the dress aside for a pair of traveling slacks and a loose shirt that was tucked in. The boots were by the table, ready to be donned at a moment's notice, and the well-worn leather jacket was draped over the chair behind Kara. It was all a mirror to what Sorcha wore and, at that moment, she realized how much of her style echoed Kara's.

Even after all these years, she mused.

Kara glanced up, shadows under her eyes hinting at a sleepless night. The thought made Sorcha relieved she wasn't the only one who hadn't gotten a decent sleep.

"That fae has lost his mind. How are you so sure he'll do as you ask?" asked Kara as she dropped to the map. "You're risking quite a lot on him."

Sorcha smiled. "Because I offered him Wren."

"So, you are planning on double-crossing him?" said Kara, lifting her gaze.

"I have a plan to manage him. He will serve an end to me and that's all. And besides, you sensed the magic in her; both fire *and* darkness, bound by a spell. That is the kind of magic we need." She hoped Kara would understand. Strong magic would be needed for what was to come and that meant Sorcha couldn't waste an opportunity like Wren walking away.

Kara's lips tightened a thin line. "I do sense that magic about her but that's what worries me. Her fire magic feels strong, and I have my own theories about that. What worries me is the darkness lurking inside her. It feels ancient, powerful. Are you sure about all of this?"

Sorcha had been plagued by that question for years. For so long, it had been without an answer...but that time had passed.

"Yes."

Chapter 25

I fear what I must do, but I cannot fight her anymore. Soon, she will devour my soul completely. Forgive me, Adrian, forgive me.

—Excerpt from Litania's diary.

THE ENTIRE CAMP was packed up and on the move by the first stroke of amber across the dawning sky. People stripped tents apart and bundled them up onto carts. Horses were saddled and hooked up to their carts as they neighed restlessly in the cool morning air. Platters of small cold pies, dried fruit, salted meat were passed among the chaos.

Wren had taken part in stripping the tent she'd been in, as well as packing supplies. When the last of it was heaped up onto the assigned cart, she headed off and collected her horse. She was to join Madam Kara at the front of the caravan for the trip.

With that, she hurried off to the mounting yard. She noticed that there was only one horse left in the yard, so she guessed Lorca had already collected the one assigned to him. Once she saddled up, she led it out onto the road near the caravan where carts were being lined up.

The frenetic activity mixed with a strangely sharp sounding chatter and cautious exchanges stirred a flicker of curiosity and unease in Wren. She could sense the mood had shifted since her arrival, with the morning bringing a nervous air.

Something is amiss, she realized as she swung up onto her saddle.

Her horse pawed nervously at the ground, snorting softly as if it too sensed trouble in the air. With a little coaxing, she headed over to Lorca, who swung up onto his saddle several feet away. As he settled, taking hold of the reins, he shifted uncomfortably.

"I will never get used to this," he grumbled.

"Kara wouldn't let you fly?" Wren stopped so that her horse was alongside his. She glanced skywards at the smattering of clouds that swept south, stirred only by the soft wind that stirred lazily through. She went on to ask, "Or walk alongside in dragon form?"

"There are a few small villages close by and, given the weather, she doesn't want to risk me being seen." He sounded less than thrilled by the order.

She didn't miss the way his grip tightened on the reins, his knuckles turning white. Nor the way he shifted in his saddle and the tension in his body.

"Is there anything I can do to help?" she asked.

He shook his head. "There isn't much that can be done except for me to make it until sunset. I spoke to Kara before. She said there is a deep forest where I might have some room to shift there."

She nodded. "If you need a rest, let me know. I'll make sure she stops."

At that, he smiled faintly, and her worry eased.

With a flick of her heel, she nudged the horse forward. Lorca fell into step beside her as they rode up to the front of the caravan where Kara waited.

The caravan leader dipped her head as they approached. "We're about to head off soon."

They waited until one by one, men and women approached on foot, declaring they were ready. When the last one had set off back to their cart, Kara wheeled her horse around.

The time to move had come.

Soft conversation rippled over the long caravan, along with the quiet clatter of hooves and wheels over the hardened earthy road.

It was difficult not to think about her family, and about what they might be enduring. Her climbers would survive. They had faced danger before, and their bodies and minds were hardened. But the rest? The families and their children? She shuddered.

She nudged her mare forward, trotting up beside Sorcha. The young woman started to sing in a language Wren had never heard before. As her voice lifted, crisp and sweet, Omi joined in with huskier notes. More voices joined in as the song traveled down the long caravan. It swelled, with others banging pots, whistling, and even some clapping further back. She tried to join in but realizing she sounded like a dying beast, fell silent.

To her surprise, a familiar deep voice swept in. Lorca.

The song seemed to come easily to him, his face lighting up with every word that tumbled from his lips. The confidence with which he sang spoke of a connection to his past. She wondered if it was a song he'd sung in his youth.

Catching herself staring at him, she wrenched her gaze back. In the corner of her gaze, she caught Sorcha grinning.

Kara's hand snapped up, a closed fist, and choked the song into silence. The caravan jolted to a stop. Her hand dropped as she twisted in her saddle. Wren stilled, the hairs lifting along her neck. Something was amiss. She waited for Kara to speak, though the urge to ask what was wrong burned at her lips.

"Wren and Lorca, you're with me. Omi, you have the caravan. Sorcha, move to the front," she ordered, then wheeled around and set off.

Wren and Lorca took off after Inakara.

Ahead, the ancient forest rose to meet them, looming ominously. Long shadows stretched out like the hungry grasp of some old, ravenous demon. It seemed ready to devour the willing caravan, whispering this deadly promise with a mournful wind.

This icy breeze that flowed out smelled much like any forest; yet after a moment, Wren sensed there was something else that lurked within it. A sour tang. The stench of death.

She tightened her grip on the reins, her knuckles turning white. "Something isn't right."

Lorca nodded tightly. "I feel it too."

"What is it?" she whispered.

His brow furrowed, silent as he appeared to consider this. "I...It can't be. Why would she take us through a place like this?"

Like what? Wren nearly asked but was cut off as Kara jumped down off her horse. She watched the woman stride forward as if she might repel any darkness by herself.

Wren slid down from her saddle. With one glance at Lorca, he did the same and joined her as they approached Kara.

"Do you sense it?" she asked them, though Wren felt as though the question was directed more to Lorca.

He nodded. "Yes. Do you still plan to go through?"

Her gaze slid back to the forest, narrowing. "Time is of the essence, and our usual route is far too dangerous to take."

"What awaits us in there?" asked Lorca quietly.

"Nothing that cannot be handled," Kara murmured. Finally, she turned to them, uncrossing her arms. "Are you both ready?"

It was a strangely weighted question. There was meaning in it, but Wren couldn't pin down exactly what it was. A tightness twisted in Wren's chest. She buried her trepidation. They had to push on. The city was so close she could practically see it in her mind. Her people were within reach.

Lorca held out a hand, snapping his fingers; tendrils of fire dancing through his fingertips. "I know a few tricks."

"Good."

Sorcha rode up to them. She leaned down in the saddle, her ear to Kara. A tense moment passed between the two, then Sorcha straightened up and wheeled her mare around, trotting off back down the caravan.

The girl stopped at each cart, talking to the riders and the drivers. The effect of this was immediate. Those astride their horses drew their weapons and readied their bows. Once she reached the end of the caravan, Sorcha turned back and returned to the front.

Kara raised her hand upwards, then dropped it. With the signal given, the caravan advanced at a cautious pace as it entered the forest. The heavy air pressed down on them. It stank of rot and damp leaves, clinging to their skin.

Wren shifted uneasily on her saddle. An icy feeling cloyed at her insides, stirring through her mind, a gentle whisper. Something in the forest was watching her. Almost like the darkness was waiting for her. One hand released the reins, drumming her fingers against her leg.

She glanced at Lorca. "After we get out of here, can you teach me to use this sword?"

"I'll teach what I can, but I'm afraid I'm a little rusty." The corner of his mouth tipped upwards. "It will be a lesson for both of us."

Wren bit back a smile, her cheeks warm. "Okay."

He glanced away quickly and trotted up to Sorcha. She tried not to frown, wondering what she'd said was wrong. They talked, glancing occasionally at each other, there was an intimacy between them. Jealousy prickled along her skin.

She was an outsider, exposed. It didn't help that Lorca kept looking at her like she was something she wasn't.

The caravan trundled onwards, deeper into the forest until all sunlight seemed to disappear almost entirely. Only narrow bands of gold pierced the scant gaps in the canopy above, illuminating their narrow but well-worn path. Soft chatter drifted down the caravan, yet it seemed no one dared to speak louder with even the horses moving slowly, hooves soft against the forest floor. A thin mist swirled in, suddenly; as though one minute absent, the next it moved among the horse's legs.

"This mist stinks of demons," murmured Sorcha, her nose wrinkling. *Demons? Is that what Lorca sensed?*

Wren hadn't realized Sorcha was there. When she looked over, the girl's eyes glowed gold. Threads of light wove between her hands that clasped the reins, with several snaking up her arm.

"Are demons normally here?"

Sorcha glanced over, uneasy. "No." She glanced around, then back to

Wren. "Stay sharp. Trouble is coming."

Without warning, she trotted forward to Inakara. Several moments passed, then Sorcha was back off; she was halfway down the line, the start of a warning coming out of her mouth when a shadow leaped from the trees. It slammed into her, dragging her off the horse and disappearing into the thicket.

Someone screamed. Wren started to turn, but a shadow caught her eye and she wheeled back just as something launched at Lorca. He was off his saddle, crashing into the thicket. She, too, surged forward, but something slammed into her, sending her flying off her horse—pain exploded through her... and darkness dragged her under.

Chapter 26

I try and try to speak to Litania...but with every attempt, she retreats further from us all.

—Excerpt from Prince Adrian's diary.

THE AIR WAS freezing, and icy needles pierced her skin. She jerked awake with a soundless scream that scraped her throat raw. Bindings pinned her down. Groaning, she sunk back onto the cold wooden board as she stared up at the stone ceiling. The air was heavy with moisture, stinking of rot and decay.

She strained against the binds and twisted her head, seeing nothing but a plain room. With a curse, she slumped back.

It seemed an eternity before the sound of footsteps broke the silence.

Her heart seized. She turned her head, watching as a cloaked figure walked into the room. They crossed the threshold and two gloved hands pushed back the hood, revealing the sharp face of a man.

No, not a man. She corrected herself.

With pointed ears, skin like the moon, and eyes that glowed gold, there was no mistaking the man for what he was.

"You're a fae," whispered Wren. Unease stole through her. "What do you want with me?"

A cold, conspiratorial smile lifted the corner of his mouth. Wren steeled herself, but a trickle of unease slithered down her spine. She strained again, but he was at her side in an instant, his cold hand pressing against hers. She froze. Her gaze slid to his, which was full of hunger and amusement. Like she was something precious or something to be devoured.

It was unclear which was right—perhaps both.

"Such *power* within you and yet so trapped. What foolishness to bind such a creature? It's cruel, really." He leaned in close so that Wren could smell the rancid stench of his breath brush her cheek.

Fire lit within her. With just those words, she was back with Lorca, seeing *that* look in his eyes. The one that said Wren was something more than a climber.

"I don't have any bloody magic! Why is everyone so convinced I'm something I'm not?"

First the man in Tarth, next the fae. Even Lorca looked at her like she was something *more.*

He smiled condescendingly at her outburst as if she were nothing more than an insolent child to be corrected. His hand drifted up her arm, along her neck, lingering at her cheek. It might've been a kind action, were it not for the shivers that rushed into her skin as his thumb brushed her cheek.

"Now, now, your magic calls to me. The beauty of its song, so bright and golden...and yet so dark as well. I had a vision of your arrival in the forest and the demon attack, so I had to come, I had to save you." His touch lingered and he leaned closer as if her eyes were the most enchanting thing in the world. "After seeing the chains that bind you, well I rather think it's time we free the magic within, don't you? It deserves to be free."

His hand fell from her cheek as he moved around the table so that he stood behind her. Then he set his hands on her head and he leaned down, murmuring something softly under his breath, so gentle she couldn't hear it clearly. Then he stepped away from her and walked back into view, regarding her solemnly. Panic surged through Wren as she struggled against the binds, trying with every inch of strength she had to break free.

Nothing budged.

Tears burned her eyes. She didn't say a word though, because of the look in his eyes. She knew that nothing she said would stop whatever he had planned, so she steeled herself and bit back the rising fear that threatened to consume her completely.

He held up a hand and snapped his fingers, flames erupting to life within his grasp. His gaze slid to hers. Then, without hesitation, he slammed his hand down onto her torso, and fire exploded across her skin.

Wren screamed, not from pain, but from something within her that was wrenched tight once more—and shattered.

Chapter 27

I sensed another crack in our world today, demon energy trickling out, infecting the lands. Is it tainting our people, too? I seek the guidance of the Spirit of the Mountain but, as usual, she seems deaf to my pleas.

— Excerpt from Queen Evanya's diary.

HER BODY THROBBED in pain as one by one, her senses returned to her. Cold air nipped at her skin, tore through her clothes, and sunk deep into her bones, leaving an agonizing ache rippling in every limb. A stale stench passed over her lips, smelling faintly of blood and something rotting. It twisted in her gut and clawed its way up her throat, making her gag as her eyes sluggishly flickered open.

At first, all she saw was darkness. She squinted into the gloom until the details sharpened around her. A stone room, strewn with muddied straw remnants, and dark stains splashed across the floor with a single door opposite her at the far end. Flickering above it was a lantern emitting a faint glow.

Minutes passed before her mind cleared, and memories of the attack flooded back in. Panic erupted from deep in her gut.

Oh, gods, where am I? Where's Lorca? The others?

Her mouth filled with ash as she tried to move and something hard rattled above her head. Her gaze snapped up, locking on the iron chains that were holding her by her wrists, suspending her from the ceiling.

Like a slaughtered animal, ready to be carved. She wrenched her gaze back down, scanning the room. Even as waves of fear tore through her, she clung to her training. It was by no means a cliff, but fear was her old friend. She'd conquered it before.

Breathe.

She had to slow her breaths, trying to clear her thoughts. Wren forced the air over her lips with agonizing control, fighting back the panic that threatened. It hurt, but she pushed on, a thin band of sweat gathering on her brow.

When her heart ceased to slam against her ribs, a flicker of calm filled her, briefly keeping the panic at bay.

Then the door swung open.

Her breath hitched.

The fae man swept in, clad in black silk robes, his white hair flowing long around his youthful face. Golden eyes stared at her, a small smirk twisting his cruel, thin mouth. There was no warmth in that face and as he glided forward, the smile took on a predatory gleam.

"Oh, good, you're awake," he crooned, stopping in front of her.

She flinched as he brushed her hair away from her brow, tucking it gently behind her ear. His fingers were like icy daggers gliding over her skin, pain lancing into her face. A gasp of relief tumbled from her lips as his hand fell away and he reached up, tapping her chains.

She dropped suddenly, crumpling like a broken doll to the ground. *Move, you fool! Run!* But her body refused as she lay limp on the ground.

Tears pricked her eyes as his hand grasped her shoulder and he leaned in close. Icy breath fanned her cheeks. "Follow me."

Somehow, she stood, even as pain roared through and darkness threatened the fringes of her vision. His hand slipped to the small of her back, pushing gently. Her feet moved, each step like walking on broken glass. Even if she wanted to cry, she couldn't—it was like she was a prisoner to his command.

By a miracle—or perhaps a curse—she stayed conscious as he guided her out of the room. It was impossible to keep track of where they were going through the labyrinth of tunnels, lit by evenly spaced lanterns that flickered to life as they passed and then died behind them. Twice she swore she lost consciousness, the pain tearing her mind to ribbons, but somehow, when she came around, she was still walking.

As they turned a corner, they stopped before a plain wooden door. The fae slid in front of her and pushed it open. Then he propelled her forward to the middle of another room, this one at least twice the size of the last.

And she wasn't alone.

The blood cooled in her veins as her gaze latched onto the two bloodied figures hunched over in chairs. Sorcha was out cold, her face bloodied and bruised. Beside her, Lorca was stirring awake, lifting his head groggily. Those bright green eyes found hers, widening instantly.

Wren... His hoarse voice brushed her own, like even the effort of talking that way was nearly too much.

She wanted to speak, to run toward him and free them. But her body refused, holding her there like a prisoner.

The man moved to her side; his hands clasped behind his back. A pensive expression settled on his face. "None of these fools spoke to me. Couldn't explain why someone wanted you hurt."

She tried to mouth a reply, but her body once again refused. The man blinked, sensing this, and turned, touching her cheek.

"Why are you doing this?"

He cocked his head to the side. "I just told you that? Gods, the woman didn't say you were an idiot." With a wave of his hand, he silenced her once more. He swept over to Lorca, grabbing him by the hair, yanking his gaze up. Half turning back, that cruel gaze found hers. "I was told there was something different about you, but I don't see it. There is *nothing* powerful about you but I am nothing if not a man of my word. So, let's see if we can break you, shall we?"

Wren was helpless as he snapped his fingers, summoning ribbons of light to his fingers, then slammed it down onto Lorca's chest. His head snapped back; a cry ripped from his lips. Red flooded his cheeks as spasms shook his entire frame, the chair rattling.

Make it stop!

But the man struck Lorca again.

And again.

And again.

Wren screamed in her mind, trying to shred the control that bound her, but it was no use. No matter how much she thrashed against his control, it was useless. No, *she* was useless.

He paused and stepped back. "These two are truly pathetic." Then he turned to her. "Since you aren't even strong enough to save them, now it's clear I should focus my attention on you."

Ice flooded her veins.

"*G-get away from her,*" snarled Lorca.

Her gaze met his, the green of his eyes shifting in and out of the dragon's slit gaze. *Shut up you fool,* she wanted to say, *do you want to die?* She would do something, buy them time. She just had to find this man's weakness. Everyone had one.

The man spun around, snorting. "And what do you plan to do about it? I have you chained."

The corner of Lorca's mouth twitched, the weary expression falling away as if were little more than an act. "Watch me."

The man stepped forward. Lorca exploded forward out of his chair, surging forward into the man. Fire erupted from his hands. The man dodged, summoning ribbons of light to his own hands. They came together in a series of blows and dodges. In a flash, Lorca was slammed up against the wall, pinned for a moment.

His mouth snapped open, fire bursting out, slamming into the side of the man's face. He staggered back, screaming, as the flames blistered his flesh. Taking his chance, Lorca burst forward—

The man's hand snapped up.

Energy exploded out, slamming into Lorca's chest, sending him crashing into the wall with a sickening crunch. He fell like a broken doll, groaning as he struggled to stand. Fire flickered precariously in his fingers, then sputtered out.

Get up! She shouted down their bond, begging him to move, to be okay.

He was the last connection she had to the mountains, her friend, a hope that she might find her people. Beyond that, she had wrenched him from his home, bound him to her in a desperate mission. It was her fault he was here. She couldn't fail another person, not again.

The man stalked over to Lorca, clutching a glowing white hand to his burned face. Already, the skin was healing. Her hope disintegrated, joining the ash of her life.

"What *are* you?" asked the man. "You don't have the stink of a fae brat?"

Lorca pressed his palms into the ground and forced himself to his knees, his gaze burning in defiance. "I am a Dragonir."

Interest sparked in his eyes. "Dragonir, you say? Your parts will fetch a decent price. Your unconscious friend here, too. Not too many half-blooded fae with her level of power. Not that I can say the same for *her*."

"Don't you fucking touch her," snarled Lorca, surging up to his feet.

The man's hand snapped up, a bolt of energy crashing into Lorca's chest, sending him crumpling to the ground. This time, he didn't move.

Lorca!

She couldn't lose him, not now. They'd only just begun. His stories, his quiet presence that steadied her, his strength that couldn't be extinguished.

Hells, his last act couldn't be trying to save her.

Tears pricked her gaze as the man stood over Lorca, light blazing in his hand. He raised his hand.

Wren screamed, her body thrashing against his control, desperately trying to break free. Her chest tightened. A single word surged up from the depths of her soul... and it slammed into something within her.

In her mind's eye, she saw a towering clear wall and a writhing mass of black energy twist beyond it. Tendrils of red glowed faintly within, barely perceptible.

That single word roared through her, as though it were calling on whatever was trapped behind the wall.

She saw herself standing in front of it and let that single word rise to her lips.

No.

And she slammed her fist into the wall.

A crack splintered up, a tiny fissure opening up. Darkness exploded through, surging into her. Power roared through her limbs, infusing every inch of her until she burned with it. Whatever she had unleashed, it was ancient and hungry and angry.

Her eyes snapped open.

One hand snapped up as energy burst from her fingers, slamming into the man, sending him crashing into the wall with a sickening thud. As he crumpled to the ground, his control shattered away. The weight of his power lifted.

Wren gasped, breathing hard as she pushed herself to her feet, wincing as the pain threatened to drag her under. She stumbled forward, falling to her knees as she grasped the chains, yanking hard. The metal shattered in her hands, freeing Lorca.

The ribbons of energy retreated into her fingers.

Her hand shot up to his cheek. "Lorca! Lorca! Can you hear me?"

His skin was hot and clammy to the touch. A groan broke through his lips as he forced his head up. "Wren?"

She hurriedly wiped the tears from her face, forcing herself to breathe slower and steady her heartbeat. He was okay, as was Sorcha. That was what mattered. "I'm here. I'm right here."

His gaze slid to the man who lay still on the ground. "He's still alive..."

A chill passed through her. He was out cold. Killing him would be easy. Hells, he'd been about to kill them all. She bit her lip, unsure what to do when a strange yearning whispered through her mind.

Kill him.

"No." The single word came out, resolute. She wouldn't kill him, even if the darkness raging within her howled for it, demanding blood. Whatever she'd awakened, it was...vicious and cold.

"Wren, we have to get out of her here," said Lorca hoarsely, his gaze sliding to Sorcha. "Can you help me grab her?"

It took all she had left to wrench her gaze back, nodding. He stood, teetering awkwardly for a moment before he went over to Sorcha.

Wren moved to her, kneeling down and gently lifting Sorcha's head. The girl whimpered, her eyes flickering open, unfocused for a moment as they stared back. Flashes of gold burst across her amber eyes, dimming as quickly as they appeared, as though her power was trying to peek through.

Sorcha groaned again as Wren broke the chains, freeing her. "W-where are we?"

"No idea, but we're getting out. Reckon you could stand?" asked Wren, carefully looping her arms around Sorcha's waist.

To her surprise, the girl stood, cursing softly under her breath. It was the last complaint Wren heard as the three of them staggered out of the room, bloodied and bruised. She was changed, a part of her cracked open and as the darkness yawned open within her, she shivered with unease.

They crept through a maze of hallways and stairs that were devoid of any other signs of life. The thick shadows that enveloped every inch of their gloomy prison were broken only by lanterns that, like before, lit as they neared, then sputtered out in their wake. Wren peered into rooms they passed but saw no windows and no furniture. Only the silence followed them, as though this place devoured any noise they made.

Every so often, Wren swore something brushed against her. A presence that followed them, watching her, waiting. For what, she didn't know, and that only deepened her unease.

Eventually, they reached a large, open room with a set of wooden double doors. Wren glanced around and saw there were no furnishings or windows. The only other door was the one they'd exited from.

Lorca gingerly untangled his arm from Sorcha, leaving her to Wren, and limped to the doors. Wren watched with bated breath as he pushed them open and moonlight washed over him. It bathed the room in swaths of silver, chasing back the shadows that surrounded them.

Something behind her hissed.

Wren let go of Sorcha and spun, freezing. From the door that they'd come from, stood a single wolf-like beast. Its molten red eyes stared her down, sending shivers down her spine. Night-black fur rippled with shadows as if it wasn't quite solid. It was just like the one she'd seen in the mountains.

There were no red flowers this time.

"Wren!" Lorca hissed. "Walk to me!"

But she couldn't. She was ensnared by those red eyes, an icy presence slipping into her mind. The darkness inside of her stirred, as though summoned by the demon. It stepped forward slowly, its head dipping as a low snarl tumbled over its lips.

Her heart raced.

Lorca was calling her again, but she still couldn't respond. A few feet away, the demon stopped, and something in its demeanor shifted as it cocked its head to the side. It stared at her silently. She swore she *felt* its recognition, a prickle of awareness that lifted the hairs on her neck.

I know you, it seemed to say before it bowed its head and retreated into the shadowy woods.

A long breath escaped her, the tension bleeding from her shoulders. Sensing eyes on her, she turned. Sorcha and Lorca looked at her warily. Wren shifted uneasily beneath their gazes and stepped past them, through the double doors and out into the moonlit clearing.

She heard them behind her, but her focus was on the ancient forest. It seemed outwardly the same as before. It loomed above her, swelling with power, leaving bumps along her arms. Yet something else tugged at her gut as she stood there, as though something was reaching out to her. It whispered her name like a lover's caress, luring her into the shadows. Her feet itched to move, to answer the call when a hand gently brushed her own.

She turned and saw Lorca's worried gaze. "What happened back there, Wren?"

Behind him, she looked at what they'd left—a large dilapidated house, with its tiled roof missing sections, and an ancient beard of ivy consuming one side. It seemed so innocuous from outside that it was almost impossible to believe what evil lurked beneath the earth.

A place that had nearly become their grave.

"I..." The words fell away as she looked at her hands, then back up at him. "I don't know." And that was the terrifying truth. She had *no* idea what she'd done or what to think of the power she felt humming in her veins. Just past him, she spied Sorcha leaning heavily against a tree, fighting to stay awake. "We have to get her back to the others."

His mouth opened, then shut, his gaze shuttering as he spoke again. "I'll change."

Wren turned to him, ready to argue he was far too weak to shift, let alone carry both Sorcha and herself. But before she could say anything, his form flashed with its blinding light, then dimmed quickly. In his dragon form, he looked free of any wounds, though as he moved to Sorcha, she didn't miss the stiffness in his gait.

"Lorca, we—"

She's in no condition to walk anywhere, he replied.

"And you are?"

I'll heal faster in this form. Now, can you help Sorcha onto my back?

Sensing the futility of arguing, she nodded and walked to Sorcha, who looked up as she neared. Curiosity flickered in her eyes. "I sensed power in you but I didn't expect, well, *that.*"

Wren could only nod as she looped her arm around Sorcha's waist and helped her up onto Lorca's back. As she climbed up behind her, she remembered the way Sorcha had looked at her in the house. Whatever she was thinking, she didn't want to know. All she wanted was to get out of that forest and focus on finding her people.

Ready?

She wasn't. Not really, but she bent down, placing one hand on Lorca's side, not trusting herself to speak. He twisted his head back, eyeing her until she nodded; then, turning back, he spread his wings and launched into the sky.

Yet even as they flew from that place and she closed her eyes, she saw that wall within her once more, barely containing the raging darkness on the other side. Darkness trickled through the crack that she'd created... and as a deep breath passed over her lips, the crack grew.

Chapter 28

Litania tells me she plans to leave with her human lover. This will break my brother's heart. Worst of all, though, is that I heard Litania talking to herself at night. Something haunts her and now, whenever I see her, I see shadows clinging to her skin.

—Excerpt of Princess Yelena's diary

THEY FLEW FOR the better part of several hours before they reached the end of the forest. As the tree line fell away and the rolling hills of sprawling meadows, broken by the occasional cluster of trees, Wren caught sight of the caravan.

It was between some small hills, guarded on one side by a tumble of rocks and thick bushes. The faint shimmer of Kara's shield stretched over the camp like a dome, glinting in the sunlight.

Lorca slowed and glided lower, his mind brushing hers. *Finally.*

His exhaustion throbbed through their bond, bone-deep and touched with pain.

As he landed softly, Sorcha stirred and cursed under her breath. "Spirits above, home has never looked so good."

Home.

A pang of longing lanced through Wren's heart. She was so damn far from her home, or what little was left of it anyway. Mainly, she wanted to have her people home, safe and sound. Another part of her, however, wanted something more. Revenge. To tear apart those who hurt her people, to make them bleed and beg for mercy.

It was that part of herself, though, that scared her. A monster had been awakened deep in her soul and it was out for blood.

The ground met them swiftly as Lorca landed with a graceful trot. Crowds of people spilled out from the caravan, corralling around them with worried eyes and shouts for aid. Lorca stopped, tucked his wings at his side, and dropped to his belly. Wren slid off him, taking care as she helped Sorcha down.

He glanced at Wren. *I need to rest in this form.*

She nodded and placed her arm around Sorcha's waist, turning toward the gathering crowd.

Kara emerged from the crowd, shadowed closely by Omi, who took one look at Sorcha and rushed forward. She took hold of the girl and pulled her away, guiding her toward the waiting hands of more people.

Left alone, Wren swayed, meeting Kara's gaze... and something erupted from within her chest. She threw her head back, crying out soundlessly as she sank to her knees.

Someone called her name. Lorca, maybe? Or Kara? It didn't matter as the darkness dragged her under and she could hear no more.

She dreamed she was standing in the middle of an open field, a wild storm raging around her. A feral wind howled, biting into her skin, broken only by the crack and boom of thunder. Rain lashed the field without mercy, soaking the earth. Every droplet belted her skin, stinging her cheeks red.

Several feet away, a woman stood with her back facing Wren. The wind whipped at her tattered blue dress and her wild brown hair, yet she remained still as a statue. Wren reached out, willing her feet to move. But nothing happened. She opened her mouth to call out, a sense of panic rushing up from within.

The woman walked forward with slow, wandering steps. Wren tried to call out again, but her voice remained choked in silence. Her heart pounded, every thump a crack of thunder in her chest. She tried to close the distance but even as she screamed at her own body, trying to make it yield to her command, she was frozen.

She didn't know this woman, but she had to reach her.

I'm right here!

Finally, the woman stopped again. Lightning split the sky in an explosive flash of white and splintered a web of light across the ground. She realized it wasn't just rain that soaked the ground.

Blood.

Her gaze snapped back at the woman. With a scream, Wren staggered back. There was no distance between them anymore. The stranger had no face, like a blank doll, with one hand stretched out.

Remember who you are.

The woman's hand shot out, closing around Wren's throat, yanking her forward, so that mere inches separated them.

Remember.

A savage scream tore from her throat as Wren's hand snapped up, grabbing at the arm.

"Who am I?" she howled.

The woman vanished in a plume of smoke, dropping Wren unceremoniously to the ground. Pain burst up through her knees. She sank forward, sinking her hands into the bloodied earth. Squeezing her eyes shut, she dropped her forehead to the dirt and screamed.

"Wren! Wren!" a deep, familiar voice called as she was jolted awake.

She blinked, sitting upright in bed, with someone's hands firm on her arms. The haze of the dream bled away, revealing the inside of the tent.

Sorcha was kneeling, watching Wren with a worried look in her eyes. A thin bandage wrapped around her forehead.

Closing her eyes again, Wren took several deep breaths, letting herself calm down before she opened them again. Sorcha sat on the ground, looking at her with a concerned expression.

"Bad dream?"

"Something like that," murmured Wren. "Enough of me, though, how's your head? It looked like you took a nasty blow."

Sorcha touched her forehead, wincing. "It's better this morning. They wouldn't let me sleep until Madam Kara had checked me out. She gave me some tea and then I slept in her tent."

"And Lorca? Is he okay? Where is he?"

"He's just outside. He stayed in his dragon form, refusing to leave you. Terrified the other girls who sleep here when they woke up this morning."

Wren bit back a smile as relief flooded her. Lorca was okay, and so was Sorcha. The only problem was with her now. As her gaze dropped to her hands, there was no hum of magic like there had been before. Hells, she *almost* felt normal.

"What did he *do* to me?" whispered Wren.

When there was no immediate reply, she glanced up. Sorcha was biting her lip.

"Wren, I don't know how to say this, but you are different. When I first met you, I could feel *something* different about you, but I couldn't pin it down. You didn't feel like anyone I'd ever met before. I sense magic in you, but it's strange." Sorcha paused, silent for a moment, her gaze unfocused before she blinked and continued on, "There is spirit magic, which is a fire-based type, but there is also something else. It's quiet and I can't work out what it is right now."

Wren knew what she was talking about. That dark magic lingered just out of reach, whispering cruel and vengeful things into her mind.

While that was probably meant to sound helpful to Wren, it only left her more confused. She didn't enjoy feeling so out of depth and ignorant.

"Spirit magic? Isn't fire more like Dragonir magic?"

Sorcha tilted her head to the side, silent for a moment as she appeared to ponder this question. "There are three true sources of magic—primal, spirit, and demon. Primal is the rarest and the only folk I've known to wield it are the druids. They are long gone now and haven't lived in this land for centuries. I've also never seen anyone wield demon magic, only the monsters that attacked us in the forest. The most common type though is spirit magic, which is what the fae and dragons use."

Wren mulled this over as she looked back at her hands. *Spirit* magic was in her veins... had always been there? Was one of her ancestors a Dragonir? Given the proximity of the village to the mountains, perhaps some of the Dragonirs *had* settled in the village after the fall of their empire? And what of the darker magic? She wondered if it was demonic, which added only more questions to her mind.

"You know a lot about magic," remarked Wren, glancing up, thinking of the wall she'd seen within herself. It had been there the whole time, buried deep within her. Unease wormed its way through her gut. It seemed the further she ventured from the mountains, the more of her life was unraveling, revealing a stranger underneath.

A rumbling sound from Wren's stomach shattered the serious air in the room. The corner of her mouth twitched, mirroring the humor lighting up in Sorcha's eyes. "Hungry?"

"A little," replied Wren.

"Good. I'm starving. We'll go get some food and then Lorca wants to spend some time helping you learn how to use your magic. I know it's soon, but he's got a point. Your magic is prickly. Even now, I can sense how restless it is. You could hurt someone."

Wren swallowed hard, saying nothing. It terrified her, this magic stirring in her blood, but she knew from her years as a climber that the only way to conquer fear was to confront it. She just had to train and figure it out.

Somehow.

Lorca was still fast asleep when they slipped out. By the time they returned an hour later, having grabbed some food from the main tent, he was finally stirring. He lifted his head as she approached, those piercing green eyes focused solely on her.

Restless night?

She shrugged as she approached. "Something like that."

Sorcha glanced at her. "Chatting in your minds again?" Before Wren could reply, she spun around, as if hearing something from behind. "Nevermind, I have to go..."

Wren watched her hurry off, leaving her alone with Lorca. She turned to him as light flashed around him, dimming to reveal him in human form.

"Kara informed me they plan to rest here for today before they move on. If you're up to it, we'll head off to a clearing nearby and have a look at your magic."

She wasn't, not really, but there wasn't much good in delaying. With a curt nod, they set off to the horses. The stable hand, a young man of Wren's age, had already saddled them. He walked both out of the yard and stopped, holding the reins out.

Wren murmured her thanks and swung up into the saddle. A moment later Lorca followed suit, looking as awkward as ever on his horse. He kept silent, leading her out of the camp and along a well-worn but narrow dirt track.

They passed through the barrier guarding the caravan. The strange magic immediately kindled to life, stirring just beneath the surface. It was like a hum in her chest, growing louder the further they drew away.

"Lorca," she whispered. "I don't feel good."

He stopped and twisted in his saddle to face her. "That's just Kara's spell wearing off. She had to place it on you when you nearly lost control just before you passed out."

Ice slid into her heart, sending shivers rippling across her shoulders. "I don't remember any of that."

"I don't imagine you would. Let's keep going. The clearing isn't far from here."

With a nod, she gestured to him to lead on. They broke into a trot, riding briskly along the dirt track. In the mid-morning sun, the air was warm, almost strangely humid. A thin band of sweat gathered quickly on her brow.

The trees gathered in a little closer as the track veered slightly back toward the forest. Wren shifted uneasily on her saddle, her skin prickling.

"Do we have to be so close to the forest?" she asked uneasily.

"We won't enter," he replied as if that were sufficient. "It's safer to be closer to it. Less chance of anyone wandering close."

Less chance of you accidentally hurting someone. That's what he really meant.

They came into a small clearing where Lorca dismounted first. She slid off her saddle, taking the reins in hand to tie off next to Lorca at the edge. With the horses secure, she followed him to the middle of the clearing.

He turned to her. "Hold out your hands."

She did as he instructed, and the flames flickered to life in her hands. A thousand tiny birds beat their frantic wings against her ribs. It wanted freedom. The flames grew larger, twisting up along her wrists.

In a flash, Lorca closed the distance and took her hands in his. The fire retreated to her fingers, leaving her hands warm and humming with energy. Her gaze snapped up to his.

"How?"

"Your magic is linked to your emotions. If you let your fear control you, your emerging power will destroy you." He paused and stepped back, his hands falling back to his side. "I've seen it happen before."

"Where?"

"Dragonirs. Our magic appears around sixteen, though it was younger for Yelena and me. Sometimes, that magic can be too strong and they are unable to control it."

Wren didn't like the grim look in his eyes. "What happened to them?"

"They were given the choice of exile to the remote North... or death. I only saw one take the choice to go North. They found her body a month later. She'd cut her own throat. Her diary suggested she was slowly losing her mind and ended things before she went over the edge."

She digested the information with a heavy heart. At least he wasn't sugar-coating what might happen. With a deep sigh, she nodded uneasily.

"We're going to start with some basic exercises first," he began. "Sit down."

As he took a seat on the soft grass, she mirrored, watching him closely. For a moment, he remained silent, studying her.

"Okay, I'm ready," she declared.

He nodded. "I want you to hold out your hands, close your eyes and try to summon a small flame to your right hand. That's it."

As if that were the easiest thing in the world, she mused as she closed her eyes. She drew a deep breath in, held it, and then exhaled slowly and raised her hands. In her mind, a void of darkness encircled her, and a small, dancing flame before her. Instinctively, she reached for it, and the fire shrank away.

Again, she tried to touch the flame, but it moved further and further away. A hand fell lightly on hers, the warmth comforting, momentarily tempering the rising sense of frustration.

"You can't force it, Wren. Try again."

The hand left hers, and she turned her focus inwards again. The fire had returned to its original place, hovering just out of reach. She imagined herself holding out her hand and inviting it to approach without demanding it yield to her.

Come on, just a little closer to me, she begged.

If she could just take hold of it, then maybe she could summon it. She just had to figure out how to take the first step forward.

"You're hesitating," murmured Lorca.

Her eyes snapped open. "I—" She cut herself off, glancing down at her hands for a moment. Resolution steeled her spine, and she closed her eyes. "I know. Let's keep going."

Chapter 29

The past haunts us all. It clings to us and never lets us go and,
if we let it, it devours us whole.

—Excerpt from Lord Claudius Delmont's diary

IN THE HEART of the City of Slaves, Titania sprinted down the empty street. Night had fallen, descending the back streets of the Pleasure Quarter into near darkness. The moonless night had left the streets choked in thick shadows. Perfect for a hunt.

Clad in her leathers, a mask fastened firmly on her face, she was unseen—a wraith, silent death to the demons that prowled the streets.

The wolf-like creature had its nose to the ground, oblivious to her approach.

Her hand flew over her shoulder, grasping at the sword strapped to her back. A faint hiss cleaved the air as the blade came free. The demon's head snapped up.

Too late.

She swung the blade.

The demon made no sound as its head came free, rolling away. No blood was released as the creature turned to dust. Titania glanced up and down the street and let out a curse. Her magic prickled along her skin, lifting the hairs.

Somewhere unseen from the shadows, someone was watching her. She drew in a deep breath, trying to scent them. The stale air filled her lungs but did nothing to reveal the bastard who was just out of sight.

After a pause, their presence bled away.

Titania sheathed her sword, frowning. Whoever it was had stuck around for longer that time. Like they had been studying her. No doubt seeing if she could figure out where they were. Fury reddened her cheeks.

She set off into a jog. Down the street, she turned into a rabbit warren of twisting back alleys. If she were human, the thick darkness would have been impossible to navigate.

Then again, had she been human, she would've died years ago.

Smiling at that thought, she leaped silently down a series of steps down onto a narrow street. The soft footfalls of her boots were the only betrayal of her existence. The looming stone buildings flanked her, their windows shuttered and no light coming from within.

The witching hour had descended on the city.

Well, the demon hour, she thought ruefully as she rounded another corner. A chill brushed the back of her neck. The hairs lifted. Awareness coiled tightly in her belly. Slowing to a stop, she scanned her surroundings. Her hand rose slowly to her sword, not drawing it but ready. Exhaling softly, she inched forward.

The icy feeling sharpened on her neck, moving down her spine. She tasted the stench of ash and death in the air. The familiarity tugged at her.

Come out and play little demon, she entreated silently.

Up ahead, the street divided down two paths. The sensation dulled. Frowning, she turned around, glancing back up the way she'd come. She drew her sword slowly, a metallic hiss cleaving the air. Her heart thudded hard against her ribs.

A flash of movement darted in the corner of her eye. She spun, seeing another movement on the other side.

Two demons.

The corners of her mouth twitched before the shadow rushed past her again. She turned, swinging her sword, and heard a hiss as it cut through the air. As she stilled, a low snarl came from behind, then the soft pad of paws against the stone, scarcely above a whisper.

Patience held her for a breath.

The beast lunged at her. She darted to the side when a force slammed into her, knocking the breath from her chest. She hit the ground, the sword clattering across the stone. Cursing, she rolled over. One of them came at her again.

She threw her hands up, darkness exploding from her fingers, tearing a hole through the advancing demon. It crumpled to the ground, dead. Heart racing, she scrambled to her feet. This demon hadn't turned to smoke.

A rumbling growl wrenched her attention to a larger beast prowling closer. Its matted ears flattened back against its head, molten red eyes blazing.

Interest prickled along her skin. "My queen never had anything like you in her army..."

She raised her sword, swinging it with one hand. A wicked smile teased her lips.

The shadows swirled behind the beast. She exploded forward, cursing. A figure burst from the shadows, an arrow flying from their bow. It hissed through the air, slamming true into the demon.

As it hit the ground, it dissolved into smoke.

She sheathed her sword, frowning. "You're interrupting my fun, Claudius."

A tall, lean figure emerged from the shadows, cloaked in black. Blue eyes flickered to the demon behind her. "You found one of the real ones."

"I did. I might find more before the night is over," she replied. "Though going by the look on your face, the hunt is finished."

He dug into the folds of his cloak, fishing out something. He tossed a small stone and her hand snapped out, catching it in her palm. She unfurled her fingers and went white as she recognized what she held.

"That's—"

"It caught fire a week ago," he replied.

"*A week ago?*" she exploded. "Atlas sent out a call for help and you're only *now* telling me!?"

Claudius didn't even flinch at her seething tone. The calm bastard merely stared back, one brow lifted. "You were nowhere to be found when it happened. I left for the mountains as soon as I realized, but I was too late. The village had been reduced to ash," he snapped waspishly. "I rushed back but my portal skills aren't good with distance."

She reigned in the anger burning her cheeks, shame kindling in her chest. Had she not been running around the tunnels deep below the city, trying to find the source of the wolf-like demons, then maybe Claudius would've found her.

"Is he...?"

Claudius shook his head. "No. There were many dead, but he was not one of them. I'm sure."

"Then where was he taken?"

"Here."

Shock thrummed through her. Her breath hitched.

Surely that wasn't why Amara had sent her to the city?

But Titania couldn't be sure. The Keeper, with her dark abilities, had skills that were only privy to a select few—and even as Titania had stood as her queen's general, she had not been informed.

Nimue had viciously protected the secrets of her darling Keeper, Amara.

Titania strode toward him. "Then what the hell are we waiting for?"

Claudius rolled his eyes as she moved beside him. "Timing." He glanced at her. "I want to rush in as much as you, but we need to figure a few things out. Mainly why one of Nimue's generals was so easily taken by a bunch of humans. He was one of the strongest demons among us and yet he's now facing being enslaved. Something doesn't add up."

Unease knotted in her gut as they left the street. A single thought dominated her mind.

Atlas, surely you didn't do what I think you did...

Chapter 30

May the gods spare me for what I must do—and spare those whom I call my people, if only from the terrible wrath that will soon descend upon them.

—Excerpt from Litania's diary.

IT WAS DUSK when they left the clearing, and Wren hadn't even been able to summon a single flame on command. Let alone to the required hand. Which was maddening, because she could feel the magic within stirring restlessly. Yet no matter how much she tried to reach for it, the fire never appeared.

Mercifully, the other part of her, the dark magic, remained quiet. She still sensed it but it felt as though it were slumbering for the moment.

That at least left her with only the fire magic being tricky.

She rode in silence, mulling over ways to figure out a way to punch through the walls that blocked her. There had to be *something*. She'd never been one to give up so easily.

Streaks of burned orange stretched across the sky, yielding rapidly to twilight. Soon the cloudless sky was bursting full of glittering stars. With only the rustling of the trees and the crisp air, it was *almost* like she was back home.

She shook off the dark thoughts, and let one hand rest on her thigh, the other holding the reins gently. The horse knew the way back to the caravan, moving confidently through the forest.

"Do you think we'll head off tomorrow?" Wren was eager to be on the move again. "Or will we stay for a while longer? I guess if we do, then we can train more in the clearing."

Lorca rubbed the back of his neck thoughtfully. "Sorcha was up and about this morning, so I don't see why we won't move on soon. As for training, we'll just practice on the road."

"Who knows? Maybe I'll be able to summon a single flame to rescue my people," she mused. "I might need your help to look mildly intimidating."

Lorca's brow lifted, and he laughed. "I'd say you do that well enough without me."

The caravan was close by. A dozen tendrils of wispy smoke coiled high into the sky, heralding the evening fires burning. The night air carried the smell of hearty stews and spiced wine, making Wren's stomach grumble.

They'd only eaten some dried meat and bread, which had left her hungry for more. Lorca might be fine with eating rarely, but she wasn't. Her appetite was ravenous.

When they came to the pens, Wren dismounted first, her stomach grumbling.

"You'd think I starved you." Lorca chuckled softly.

She shrugged, glancing back at him as he dismounted. "Close enough." As she lifted the saddle off, she turned to him. "Can we work some more after we've eaten?"

His brow dipped. "You've been at it all day."

"And I've achieved nothing," she replied. "I don't like feeling afraid. Whatever the fae did, I don't want to let it control me."

A war seemed to play out in his eyes as if he was torn in wanting to train further or to insist that Wren got some rest. But she couldn't sit still. It had never been in her nature, and even less so with this power humming in her veins. Since waking up, as terrified as she'd been by the powers thrust upon her, she returned to her old habits. Train, train, and more training.

He sighed and nodded reluctantly. "Fine, but only for a few hours."

No sooner had they made it halfway through the camp than did Sorcha come bounding up to them. Wren forced a warm smile as Sorcha stopped in front of them.

"So, how was the training?" she asked curiously.

"It's going well," lied Wren. "We're going to practice more after we eat. This leads me to my next question. Is there any food left? I'm starving."

"Oh, this way. There's still some stew at our fire. I figured you'd both be hungry," declared Sorcha as she looped her arm around Wren, leading her away.

Lorca followed silently. When she glanced at him, he was staring ahead blankly, as if lost in his thoughts. The slight furrowing of his brow and tight mouth made him look troubled.

He's probably wondering why I couldn't summon a single flame today. She thought. *And whether I'll be able to help him with whatever it is he wants.*

Once more, she tried to figure out why he'd agreed to come along with her at all. What was he getting out of their deal? Her mind churned through the possibilities until Sorcha stopped her.

Wren turned her attention to the group of familiar faces seated around a low burning fire. A large metal pot hung over it, bubbling softly, with a little food still left inside. Her stomach growled again as she took in the wary faces of Lida, Jed, and two other women who huddled closely together.

"Hello," murmured Wren awkwardly.

A dark-haired, beautiful girl who had her hands intertwined with the smaller woman next to her stood up. She smiled warmly, holding out a hand to Wren. "I'm Eda."

"Oh, I remembered Sorcha asking about you back in Tarth. Said you'd stayed because you didn't want to upset Omi?" Wren blurted out, instantly cursing her choice of words. "Sorry, I—"

Eda laughed. "Don't worry. It all worked out in the end. I'm just sorry I didn't get to meet you sooner." She turned to the woman beside her, holding out a hand. "And this wonderful woman is Marceline, who Omi has finally permitted me to wed."

"She agreed? That's wonderful. When is the ceremony?" Sorcha inquired as she ladled some stew into a bowl and handed it to Wren.

"In two days. Marceline and I need time to finish the dresses," replied Eda, sitting back down. Her gaze slid to Wren as she and Lorca sat down. Curiosity flickered in her amber eyes. "I'm told you're from the mountains and that you," she paused, looking to Lorca, "are a Dragonir."

"Correct on both counts," murmured Wren.

"And you rescued my good friend here from that fiendish fae. That puts you in good stead with me," declared Eda.

Marceline leaned in, whispering something in her ear. Wren watched as the quiet woman stood, dipped her head, and quietly slipped away. When she left, Eda frowned, silent for a moment as she watched her leave.

"Is she okay?" asked Wren.

With a guarded expression, Eda looked at Wren. "She's tired. The trip through the Forest of Silence was trying on her nerves. I think we'd all hoped to take the capital road this year."

Sorcha stiffened on the log beside Wren. "We would have, but the threat of the Empress's men and how close we would've gotten to the Gray Army was too great. Madam Kara didn't want to put everyone in danger."

"And having demons attack us was not dangerous?" retorted Eda.

"We all made it through," said Sorcha. "I'm sorry Marceline's nerves were tested."

Wren shot Lorca an awkward glance, but he had a distant look in his eyes as he stared into the fire. Concern gnawed at her as she absently finished the food. Sorcha took the bowl and slipped away to wash up.

As the others chatted softly among each other, Wren turned to Lorca and gently touched his shoulder. He flinched, looking startled. She gestured for them to leave. As he rose, she faced the others.

"Thank you for the meal. We're turning in for the night," she said, then headed off with Lorca.

Once they were out of earshot, the question which had been bubbling away inside of her all day rose to her lips. "Lorca, why did you agree to help me?"

"You wish to know what I will ask for in return?" he replied and when she nodded, he continued, "I wish to find my own people."

"Why not tell me that before?" she pressed on. "I would have agreed."

"Agreed to abandon your friends and family the second you got them back to the mountains?" he countered, stopping as they neared the edge of the campsite and turned to her. "Would you have said yes?"

Heat flooded her cheeks as she stepped back. "You should have been at least honest with me." She glanced away. "I'll admit I'm not thrilled about the idea, but you've already done so much for me. If we're successful in finding my people, then I will go with you. Their safety is worth being parted from them for that bit longer. But there's something else I have to know. Why *do* you need me? Aren't I just dead weight?"

His mouth tightened into a thin line and he wouldn't meet her eyes. Clearly, she'd said something wrong. She opened her mouth to say more when he turned from her.

"You need to learn how to wield your sword," he declared.

She gaped at him. "What does that have to do with me helping you find your people? You haven't said how I could help you."

He looked at her from over his shoulder. "It's complicated, but I will explain it soon enough. Just not tonight."

"Lorca—"

In a flash, he spun to her. The hard edge in his eyes softened. "Drop it, *please*. Now, if you want to get some practice before bed, I'd advise that we focus on that as the priority."

She clamped her mouth shut, biting back a retort. Reluctantly, she nodded and followed him to a clearing just off the edge of the camp. Under the moonlit sky, there was no need for fires. She saw him perfectly. There was no missing the hard expression on his face and the firm set of his mouth.

When they sat down on the soft grass, she tried to shove all the gnawing questions back down. It was apparent Lorca wasn't in the mood for explaining himself that night. She closed her eyes and held out her hands.

"Now, let's try this again," murmured Lorca. "Trust yourself and turn your focus inwards. *Feel* the magic, listen to it and summon the fire to your right hand."

Chapter 31

It is only by the favor and protection of the Spirit of the Mountain that we all exist within these lands; with her, in all her infinite power, our future rests. So, this prophecy worries me—our end beckons with an outstretched hand, heralded by the arrival of Inakara and the crown of a dead queen. Does the Spirit abandon us? Do we commit some unforgivable sin against the dragons or, worse, the Spirit herself? I must stop writing now. Litania comes.

—Excerpt from Queen Evanya's diary.

AZIAH WAS DROWNING in a sea of memories. Down she sunk

into the chaotic whirl of scenes, each tangling together in a mirage of color and sound. Heavy rain erupted around her, cleaved by cracks of thunder. Dread coiled tight in her gut, a shiver of fear trickling down her spine. Instinctively, she tried to pull away, fighting the call of *that* memory. The one that haunted every dream and waking moment, that lingered with a cruel whisper at the fringe of her mind.

A coppery tang brushed her lips. The final herald as the chaotic memories snapped into focus. Darkness shrank into a palatial room filled with ornate furnishings, brushed with moonlight. The full moon did nothing to hide the blood splattered across the polished stone floor. Every droplet gleamed, still warm from the corpse of the woman that lay a few feet away. Her bruised body betrayed the fight, the last-ditch struggle to save her husband that lay dead on the bed, and the baby that was now pressed against Aziah's chest.

The Emperor and Empress were dead.

Aziah roared at her past self, cursing that fateful decision. She'd thought it was inevitable. The only way to ensure the princess survived. Someone else would have carried out the assassination, sealing Princess Sybilla's fate.

Hindsight was a cruel mistress. She cared naught for feelings or souls, only to drive home the agony of past mistakes.

Aziah screamed as her past self turned to the door, walking steadily from the scene of death as if it were simply another job. The people she'd butchered with her own hands had shown her more kindness than her own flesh and blood. They had trusted her with their lives only to look into her eyes and feel her cold hands as she dealt the killing blows.

How they must've cursed her soul in their final moments.

The door opened as she reached it. A cloaked woman stood there, shadowed by a soldier. Aziah passed the infant into the woman's arms as the girl's tiny fingers grabbed at her shirt. Those shining golden eyes found hers in the darkness, as wise and ancient as the spirits Aziah prayed to. A gaze that was full of power and destiny.

It was that look that let her gently pry the baby away and press her into the arms of the woman. She stepped back, shutting the door, sealing herself in the room of death. Their footsteps quickly faded until silence took hold.

"Why did you do it?" Kathrine's voice yanked Aziah around.

The Empress stood in the middle of the room, bloodied, her throat gaping open. Her moon-pale skin shimmered, stretched tight over her once beautiful face. Death had turned her cruel and cold, those eyes accusing obsidian pools.

Aziah stepped forward, abandoning her past self—that ghostly past self was moving to the other side of the room, carrying out the rest of the memory. Her gaze remained on Kathrine as she inched forward. "Your fate was sealed. I couldn't save you, but I could save your daughter."

Kathrine snorted mockingly. "Oh, you couldn't save us? Our great champion couldn't stop a little coup! We *trusted* you and you murdered us. You will never be free of this moment, of us. I will haunt you until your dying day for what you've done."

Aziah didn't stop moving as she yanked out a dagger from her hip and drove it into Kathrine's heart. The specter jolted, crying out as if the pain were real. No tears fell as the assassin leaned forward. "For the future of the Empire."

As she jolted awake, her skin was slick with sweat, her heart racing, the salt of tears on her lips. A knocking at the door echoed rudely through her room. She glanced at the offending source, scowling. Gods, could she not have just one *one* night without someone trying to bother her? Let her drown in the company of ghosts and her many terrible sins.

She threw the furs away and padded over to the door, yanking it open. A silver hooded man greeted her. Pale hands slid his cowl down, golden eyes staring back. Glancing up and down the hall, she pulled him inside and shut the door with a soft click.

"What's happened?" she asked softly.

"The retired soldier you had me keep track of? I kept my distance, watching for any threat. I received word that an assassin had been sent to deal with him."

The man hesitated as if he knew his next words would not be welcomed.

"Go on," said Aziah.

"I wanted to stop the assassin before he could reach the soldier, so I went into town," he blurted.

A knife twisted in Aziah's gut. "It was a trap?"

"A diversion."

Gods, no.

"The soldier, is he...?"

The man paused, then took a deep breath and went on, "I rushed back but I was too late. He was already dead... but there's more. It looked as though he had been tortured before they cut his throat."

Aziah was moving before he could say another word. Her hand flashed, pulling her dagger out. Before her heart made another beat, she drove it into his throat and twisted sharply. A gurgled cry sputtered from his lips as she withdrew her blade. The spy crumpled like a broken doll. She stared down at his body, his words replaying over in her mind.

Tortured...

She dropped the dagger, letting it clatter noisily to the ground as she turned away. Someone had found the last link to her crime. Was it the Empress? Or her spymaster who was biding his time for the moment? Or some other player she hadn't foreseen? Whoever it was, the net was closing in on Aziah.

The game had changed.

Chapter 32

"Litania has always been a different child; unable to take dragon form, yet exceptional with magic—far exceeding any other Dragonir. I've never been concerned with her powers until today when she woke up screaming. When I came into the room as my son was settling her, her eyes glazed over and that is when she spoke the prophecy."

—Excerpt from Queen Evanya's diary.

SORCHA JOLTED UP from her bed, her throat hoarse. Her heart fluttered like a frantic bird in a cage. It was desperate for escape. A restless urge swelled inside of her, clawing up her chest until she pushed herself to her feet. It carried her to her cloak that hung off the central post. She draped the thin cloak over her shoulders and slipped out, creeping barefoot through the slumbering camp.

Blood still roared in her ears as the vision kept replaying over in her mind.

The clear night sky glittered above, momentarily distracting her. Breathing in the cool air, she looked back down and continued her walk.

Only the soft snoring from several tents filled the air. In the corner of her gaze, she spied Lorca curled up in dragon form beside Wren's tent.

A sharp tug in Sorcha's chest, her magic pulling her attention away, drew her gaze from the sleeping Dragonir. It lured her focus beyond the edge of the camp.

She was being called by her magic. It had been that way since she was a child. If she let the visions come naturally, she might only glean information about her future once every few years. Given the state of events and what she was planning, that wasn't enough.

You're going to push yourself over a ledge to which there is no return if you continue to force the visions, Madam Kara continually warned her.

And Sorcha got the warning. She understood it, knowing full well the consequences if she pushed too hard. Hell, she suspected she'd already done irreparable damage.

Deep down, she knew she would not be on that throne until she was old. That wasn't why she was fighting.

With a sigh, she set off to the forest, her feet silent against the grass, softened by rain. At the last tent, she paused, glancing back, and froze. Omi stood behind her, one hand cocked on her hip, a brow lifted.

"*Another* midnight walk, little one?" Omi asked gently, a note of worry in her voice.

Sorcha glanced back to the forest, the whispers in her mind growing louder. *Accept who you truly are. Yield to your destiny. It is time.*

"I used to be afraid of my magic," she murmured. "Then the visions started, and I understood. I trained myself, but now I'm running out of time. What if I fail?"

Omi appeared beside her. "When I found you on the side of the road, clutched in the arms of a dead slave, I didn't think you were anything more than a bastard child. Clearly, I was wrong and I've never been prouder of being wrong." She paused for a moment, then turned to Sorcha again.

"You have to leave soon, don't you?"

Sorcha turned back to Omi, closing the distance, drawing into Omi's embrace. She buried her face into the crook of Omi's neck and released a shuddering breath.

"I'm so damn *afraid*—what if I fail?" The words came out harsh, desperate.

Hands seized her shoulder, moving her back so that Omi could look her square in the eyes.

"You are destined for greatness, my little one. You always have been. It is your *destiny* to reclaim everything that was taken from you and defeat the evil that has infected this land. So, you will step bravely into that future and I will be there, by your side as I swore that very day, I plucked you up from the side of the road. You are the future."

Chapter 33

Today, I saw a most curious sight. The Spirit of the Mountain kneeling by that favored red flower of hers, singing to it. Stranger still was that I recognized it as the same lullaby my mother used to sing to me.

—Excerpt from Princess Yelena's diary.

THE BLADE SLICED through the air inches from Wren's head as she ducked low and spun around, pivoting behind Lorca. She yanked her sword up just in time as Lorca slammed his sword down. Metal clanged, echoing through the clearing.

Staggering back, arms burning, she could barely hold her ground. With a defiant scowl, she met Lorca's gaze and heat rushed through her.

"Keep your focus, Wren. You have your natural strength but you're sloppy and for the sake of the gods, *watch your feet.*"

To prove his point, he moved quickly, hooking his foot around her ankle, and pivoted. As Wren lost her footing and fell back, his hand shot out, grabbing at her shirt to stop her fall.

Her breath caught in her throat as she hung there, completely at his mercy. The point of his sword pressed against her throat. "If you know you're the one at a skill disadvantage, try to keep your distance. Watch carefully and look for an opening, then strike. Fight smarter, not harder."

She swallowed hard, looking up the blade to his irritated face. Magic had been a failure this morning, so they'd turned to swords for another lesson. Right at that moment, this lesson was beginning to look a lot like the magic one.

He stepped back, pulling her up straight, and let go so he could put distance between them again.

With a deep breath, she raised her sword. A steady warmth had settled through her body, every muscle loose and ready to move. Breathing evenly, she focused on Lorca. The world fell away, the blazing sun forgotten, the sounds of the forest unheard.

Matching her focus, he raised his sword. "Again."

He shifted his feet, readying for her. So far, he hadn't shown an opening she could use.

I will just make my own then.

She exploded forward, swinging her blade. Lorca parried her attack, metal ringing out, and advanced. It took all she had to deflect each blow and retreat, keeping him just out of arm's reach.

On and on, they sparred and circled each other across the grass. Metal met metal, weaving with the sounds of her racing heart and harsh breaths. Sweat gathered on her brow as she studied him, hunting for an opening.

Lorca burst forward once more, swinging wide.

There!

She dropped low, rushed past him, and pivoted at the last second to swing her blade wide right across his back. A clean line sliced through his shirt.

The win was short-lived as he spun around and was on her in a flash, a blur of blade and blows. The shift in power caught her off, sending her staggering back. Her breath burned in her lungs, but she kept her mouth shut, her nostrils flaring with the effort to rein in her heart.

There *had* to be another opening, but where? She might be able to hold off his blows, keeping pace with his moves, but this was only defensive. She wasn't able to attack him. Wren watched him, saw how he studied her, with just as much intensity.

She swallowed hard, giving thought to what she could do... and then an idea blossomed in her mind.

With a teasing smile, she raised her sword to him. "Come on, is that *all* you have to offer?"

"Careful what you wish for."

In an instant, Lorca lunged at her, faster than she'd expected. She yanked up her blade just in time, steel colliding, sparks leaped, and the dance began anew.

The clearing gave way to the trees once more. Her back hit a trunk. She spun to the side, panting heavily.

"Tired?" he teased.

"Never. You?"

Sudden heat flared on his cheeks. His gaze as it dropped to her mouth.

Her heart fluttered. Sucking in a sharp breath, she forced a laugh and darted off, using the shadows and trees with thick trunks to stay out of view. Blood pounded through her, hot like liquid fire, singing through her soul. She wanted to win.

"You can't hide from me. I will find you. I will *always* find you. " His voice whispered through the woods, soft as a lover's caress.

She stopped against a tree, pressing herself against it, flattening her back. With a deep breath, she closed her eyes, looking within, searching. In the dark, she saw it, the tiny flicker of a flame right at her center. She reached for it, but it shrank from her like it always did.

Come on, just this one time!

"Got you."

Her eyes snapped open.

Lorca stood in front of her, his sword pressed against her neck, eyes molten. Only one hand held his sword, the other was on her shoulder.

"I have you," he said, his voice low.

She sucked in a sharp breath, heat kindling inside of her. An image flashed into her mind. Lorca was gone and she was standing in a small room, looking down at her chest where a sword protruded from it, slick with blood. Behind her, someone was saying those same words. *I have you.*

A single word exploded in her mind.

No!

Fire exploded from her hands.

Lorca flew through the air, slamming into a tree with a sickening crunch and crumpled to the ground. Her gaze dropped, hands trembling, flames dancing through her fingers. A sharp breath caught in her mouth. The echo of that distant voice ebbed away, abandoning to the silence that descended around her.

What have I done?

A soft groan ripped her gaze back up. Lorca pressed his palms into the earth as he attempted to push himself up, only for his arms to buckle. Wren shot forward as he fell back to the ground and dropped down beside him.

Heart racing, she grabbed his shoulder and rolled him over. Lorca opened his eyes and blinked slowly up at her.

"Where did *that* come from?"

She sat back, the vision of the sword coming out of her chest as crisp as any memory. The blistering sting of metal cleaving flesh, the metallic stench that wrapped around her. It had felt so *real*. Blinking, she looked at him, her stomach in knots. Bile burned her throat. She pressed the back of her palm to her mouth, swallowing, and as her hand finally fell away, she released a shuddering breath.

"I don't know. I just..."

The words evaded her. All she could do was stare at her hands, wondering what the hell had just happened.

It was dusk when they returned to the camp. The amber glow of sunset had retreated to softer blue tones to herald the approach of night. A cacophony of laughter and singing filled the air. Lanterns were lit at the front of each tent with a brighter glow originating in the middle of the camp.

Wren slid down from her horse and tied it off as she glanced at Lorca. "Did Kara say anything to you?"

His gaze was on the larger glow. "No. It sounds like, well, a wedding."

"A wedding?"

"Those are Dragonir songs..." His voice trailed off, his brow gathering into a frown.

She moved to his side. "Let's go see what happened while we were away."

He nodded idly, but there was a strange look in his eyes, as though at that moment he were back among his people. It reminded her of just how much he'd lost to the passage of time. He was just as much a stranger like her. She moved next to him, gently touching his shoulder.

Blinking sharply, he glanced at her. "Hm?"

"Where did you go?" Aware that she was still touching him, she let go.

His gaze shuttered as it drifted in the direction of the singing. "Doesn't matter. Let's go."

She flinched at his tone and set off ahead. Soon, the sound of his footfalls trailed behind her and he fell into step beside her. Normally, she liked the silence but, at that moment, she hated it. Everything inside of her was in turmoil, her thoughts a mess. What she'd done to Lorca still played over like a nightmare she couldn't escape.

The edge of the camp was quiet and thick with shadows. Cold fire pits heaped with piles of ash stirred faintly as a gentle breeze whispered through. Tiny flecks swept into the air and danced along with the wind, vanishing up into the starlit sky. A couple stumbled across the path ahead of them, paused to stare. Their arms were intertwined, a sheen of sweat glistening on their skin. She smiled at them, earning another giggled response before the pair vanished once more into the dark. Only the trailing retreat of their voices was left.

As they neared the center of the camp, the world seemed to change in a blink. A golden glow swept over them, thrown from dozens of lanterns hung from posts and wagons. Yards of shimmering ribbons were draped between tents, their bright colors lit by the lanterns. A heady warmth filled every breath, tangled with the aroma of spiced and honeyed wine, of cured meats and pastries. The sprawling space was brimming with people, laughing and dancing, singing and drinking. Flowing gowns in vivid bursts of color accompanied loose shirts and pants.

By the side of this dizzying display were tables, piled with platters of roasted meats and vegetables. Half-eaten plates lay strewn along the tables, forgotten by the revelers who were too busy drinking and dancing to care about eating.

"What is this?" she asked in wonder, the training session momentarily forgotten.

Lorca looked about, silent before he answered. "I think it's a wedding celebration."

Recalling their meeting with Eda and Marceline, she smiled. It made her think of the weddings they had in Fenware. Whilst not as opulent with food, there was music and brightly colored banners, and songs that filled the air until dawn. A pang of yearning squeezed at her chest. She told him absently who she thought the celebration was for, earning a distracted nod.

For a moment, they were lost to their past, caught unaware by memories. If she closed her eyes, she could almost picture herself back home. Her team would be around her, laughing and teasing. Flynn would be singing, the only one of them who could half-decently carry a tune.

The last wedding had been when Vaughn and she were still together. She had lounged in his arms, momentarily at peace. The restlessness that had haunted her mind her whole life was quiet. She remembered getting to her feet, dragging him towards the music. They danced barefoot, the firelight on their cheeks, smiling as if their world was just the two of them. That heady delight between them had felt unbreakable.

But that was how life went sometimes. Perfection until a single moment shatters it, reminding you how truly fragile something had been.

She blinked the memory away as Sorcha bounded over from the bonfire to them. Her cheeks were flushed and red, a smile from ear to ear, full of exuberance. There was life in those eyes, a youthfulness that, for some strange reason, made her feel weathered and aged.

"You were gone all day! I wanted to send word to you both, so you didn't miss anything but Madam Kara insisted that training was more important than all of this," said Sorcha. "I'm glad you're here now. I think you both deserve a night of fun as much as anyone, more so really."

"Is this for the wedding?"

"Yes, well, it's actually the celebration after it. The main ceremony was some hours ago," explained Sorcha. "But you must come and dance! There's plenty of food, so eat and have your fill of ale. I'm sure you're both ravenous!"

At the mention of food, Wren's stomach gave a loud rumble. She blushed, one hand falling to her stomach. "Sorry."

"Don't be. Let's get you some food first, then we dance!"

Sorcha looped her arm through Wren's, ferrying her off to the end of the closest table. They both grabbed a plate and quickly piled on food. Lorca followed behind but seemed less taken with the celebration. His brow furrowed deeply as he studied the affair.

It was as if he was upset or irritated by it all.

"This is for Eda and Marceline, isn't it?"

Sorcha nodded very rapidly that she wondered how much the girl had to drink, and if she could get her hands on some. "Yes, that's right. You met them briefly a few days ago."

Wren nodded. "I didn't know this was happening today. I would've..."

What, got them a gift? An inner voice sneered. *With what money? You're a stranger to them, nothing.*

Seemingly oblivious to her inner turmoil, Sorcha smiled. A little of her darkness eased, pushing the voice to the fringe, the whispers too faint to hear anymore. Tension bled from her shoulders, devoured by the revelry.

"Given how dangerous the world beyond our little caravan is becoming, there wasn't much of a desire to wait," said Sorcha, her voice dropping. The smile had vanished. "We need some joy right now."

She blinked at the intensity of Sorcha's words. She swore the girl was saying something else at that moment. The far-off look in those golden depths, lit like two burning flames, was unreadable. A shiver rippled across her shoulders and a question poised to her lips. Thinking better of it, she swallowed them away and turned her gaze to the revelry.

"I didn't know things were that bad," said Wren.

Sorcha's jaw tightened. "The north has it the hardest. Villages are being sacked, burned to the ground, labeled as traitors to the throne harboring rebels. The coast isn't much better. The closer we get the more you will see. It isn't...pretty. I hope you have a strong stomach."

She recalled the ruined village that Lorca and she had stumbled upon. The doll of a child who would never grow old. The rancid stench of ash and death, soon to be devoured by the coming snow. They had seen very few other villages since the forest, likely by Kara's voice. By what Sorcha suggested, their little illusion of safety would be over soon.

Death wasn't new to her. It had been a friend from her first climb as a child and shadowed her in the years that followed. In one form or another, it stayed by her side, reminding her of the fragility of life.

"How long has all this been happening?" She wanted to understand this strange land that she'd found herself in. Perhaps in its truths, she had a chance to discover a way to save her people. Returning them home was what mattered, no matter what parts of herself she had to sacrifice.

Sorcha stood. "Too long." A smile suddenly brightened her face and she thrust out a hand. "Dance with me?"

That slender hand was stretched out in the promise of festivity, of a night to surrender to music and wine. And she felt her own hand reach out when movement caught her eye. Lorca had risen from the table and was slipping away into the shadows. Reaching inwards, she felt their bond and flinched. Soul-cleaving grief met her, as vast as the night sky, and stopped her heart in her chest.

She was pulling away from Sorcha, who called out but soon whose voice was lost to the songs. The golden light yielded to shadows as she passed into the colder depths of the camp. Moonlight framed Lorca's retreating figure, cutting on the slope of his shoulders gathered in close, his head bent down.

"Lorca!" He didn't turn, forcing her to run after him.

The last of the tents fell away as she reached out, her fingers brushing his arm. He jerked to a stop and she ran straight into the back of him. Hard muscle met her face. She scrambled back, rubbing her cheek.

"What, Wren?"

She dug her heels in, refusing to flinch at his tone. He was hurting. "Talk to me, *please.*"

Jagged breaths rose and fell from his lips, his body shaking. His gaze lifted beyond her to the direction of the celebration. A new wave of grief howled down their bond, ripping the air from her lungs, and left her heart racing.

"The last celebration I attended was a wedding, back before...before it all..." His voice trailed off as that gaze returned to her, the faint shimmer of tears in his eyes. She ached to reach for him but held off, sensing he needed the space to talk, to *breathe*. He released a shaky breath and went on, "I was lost to the darkness for so long as a dragon. It allowed me to forget but since waking up from that, I can't stop the memories." He covered his face with his hands. "I can't *shut them out*."

She finally dared to wrap her arms around him, drawing him tentatively into her embrace. For a moment, he was frozen by her touch, then he eased into it and shattered into a thousand pieces. She felt him as he buried his head into her neck, the warmth of his breath brushing her skin. The grip on her tightened desperately, as if there were a fear she might vanish. The quiet tears turned to sobs that wracked his body, leaving her shirt damp but she didn't mind.

When he quieted in her arms, the shakiness lingered, and he spoke so softly she nearly missed it. "I miss them so damn much."

There were no words that she felt could truly ease the pain from his heart. All she was able to offer was her presence and touch, a reminder he wasn't alone. Even when he pulled away, she lifted a hand to his cheek, wiping the tears away. Ignoring the intensity of his stare, or the way his hand lingered on her hip, she then brushed his wild curls from his face.

"Do you miss them?" he asked.

Her breath hitched, the words failing her for a moment before she was able to summon them. "With every inch of my soul. I just wish..."

"Yes?"

"I wish I had been better to them before, that I spent more time with them. That I didn't seek to be alone so often." She couldn't bear the unreadable look in his eyes, the way it peeled back her defenses so damn easily. Shakily, she pulled away, wrapping her arms around her waist. "I wish I wasn't so broken."

She sensed him move to her but she stepped back. That small amount of space was the only thing from her breaking apart and she wanted to be strong for him. To be one person she wasn't failing. In the corner of her gaze, she glimpsed his hands drop to his side, curling into fists.

"Why do you think you're broken?" he asked.

"Because I was never what anyone wanted. Too cold, too different ...the fact that I *like* being alone. That's why I loved being a climber. I don't know why, but my whole life I preferred being on my own or watching from afar. When I tried—and by the spirits, I *tried*—I never belonged. Not even among my family!" She breathed raggedly. "Now they're gone, and I failed them. Which is why I'm here, trying to set things right. Prove that I can do right by them, be the daughter, friend, the team member that they deserve."

The world heaved in a breath of silence. She was as fragile as glass, the cracks already splintering across her, and that at the slightest touch, she would shatter. Even as Lorca inched towards her and she held still, there was no movement to gather her into his arms. She watched warily, stripped raw by her confession, as he tipped one palm to the sky. A tiny flame appeared.

"When I was...lost to my dragon side, I felt nothing and when I closed my eyes, all I saw was this fire. Two hundred years passed like that until, one day, the darkness lifted and I found myself flying through the ruins of the lower city." He paused to unfurl his other hand, a new flame flickering to life. She dared to look up as he spoke once more. "Do you know what I found?"

Her breath hitched. "That was the day we met but...how did I...?"

His hands dropped, the flames snuffed out, and she stilled as he drew closer, gently taking her into his arms. Her heart raced as his forehead rested against hers, their breaths tangling together in the cool night air. "Something has bound us together. I thought that it might be to lead me to my people and though I still yearn to see them again, I realize my destiny is taking a different path. You chased back my darkness and you do it even now. With every smile and touch and whisper. You aren't broken, Wren. You are exactly what you need to be and we will bring your people home."

Chapter 34

My marriage is wrought with secrets. I carry with me the truth of how the Empire of dragons fell—along with a child whose descendant will finish what I began. Though I wish to return to the mountains, there is nothing there now, nothing but ash and snow... and the dark secret that I shall carry with me until my death.

—Excerpt from Empress Litania's diary, the first queen of the newly established empire of Danomir.

THE CARAVAN HAD grown quiet in the night. Fires were extinguished and wreaths of smoke swirled through the camp, rising up lazily into the starlit sky. The lingering aromas of honeyed wine, sweet bread, and cured meats drifted on a whispering breeze, tangling with the hints of ash. And inside her tent, where the soft snores of the other girls, rose and fell steadily, Wren was stretched out restlessly in her bed, the blankets tossed aside.

Her heart had barely slowed since her talk with Lorca. Their confessions churned over in her mind. Though she felt comforted by his words, that small voice at the edge of her mind still reminded her of her failures. The faces of her people flashed in her mind's eye, the sound of her team's laughter and teasing jibes in her ear. Her chest squeezed tightly. What she'd give to be with them again, to go about their work as if their world wasn't ending.

Rolling onto her side, she closed her eyes and tried to will herself to sleep. Within seconds, though, her eyes flew open again and she sat up sharply. It was no use. Hoping that some air might help, she crept from the tent, barefoot and without her jacket. The night had cooled but she was used to the mountain's bitter winters, so she wandered unperturbed.

It was little wonder that she inevitably found herself at the edge of camp where Lorca slumbered. As she neared him, his head lifted, eyeing her closely.

Wren? The concern in his voice soothed the storm of emotions as she sat down on the ground next to him.

"I couldn't sleep," she murmured. "Sorry for waking you."

He gently nudged her arm with his muzzle. *Is this about before?*

"A little. Can I sleep here?" She wrapped her arms around her waist.

The second he nodded, she moved to his side and curled up on the ground. He draped one wing over her, as if to shield her from any weather. The warmth of his body was already chasing off the chill. Sleeping on the ground wasn't anything new for her. As part of training, and from a few instances once she was officially a climber, she had slept beneath the stars.

We will reach this city soon, said Lorca, pausing for a breath before he went on asking, *are you nervous?*

"I'd feel better if I had a handle on this magic right now. We're running out of time for me to figure this out," she grumbled. "I know I have to clear my mind and I've never had an issue with that on the cliffs. Yet every time I try to do it now, my mind refuses to. I see my family, my home burning, the fact I was born with magic, and the implications that come with it."

She closed her eyes and leaned against his side, his warmth soothing her. The steady beat of his heart hummed through her and finally sleep sank its talons into her.

Whatever the truth of your origin, I am with you, he urged, lifting one of his wings.

"I'm just afraid I'll fail them again," she confessed.

She felt him nuzzle her gently, his breath brushing her skin. *You will not fail them.*

In his presence, sleep came to her, dragging her swiftly into its warm and silent embrace. This time, the nightmares remained at bay.

The camp was packed up and on the road just after dawn. Wren rode beside Sybilla and Lorca, the rest of the wagons trundling along behind them. Hooves clattered softly against the pressed earth. Despite having got a few hours of sleep, she still felt strung out, her mind once again tangled into knots. A knot throbbed in her back and ached at every stride of her horse.

She was lost in her own mind when she heard Lorca's breath hitch.

"Is that...?"

Glancing up, she saw nothing but the scattering of trees that flanked them, and the sprawling fields across the rolling hills. Lorca lifted a hand and she followed his finger, her heart stopping dead in her chest.

Hanging from several of the trees at the roadside were bodies. Placards hung from their bent and purple necks. A few birds were perched on the rotting corpses, peeling strips of flesh off. The skin had already turned a sickly blue color, with sections torn away revealing bone. Her stomach rolled at the sight, bile pushing up her throat. This wasn't a climber having a lethal fall.

She glanced quickly at Sybilla, whose face had hardened to a dark look of fury. That usually smiling mouth was pressed into a scowl, her jaw twitching.

No one said a word until they passed the first of the bodies. She realized there was a symbol emblazoned on the placards. A golden hawk with a red circle and line through it.

"What does that mark mean?" she asked.

Sybilla glanced at her. "Rebels."

It was dusk by the time Inakara gestured for them to stop. Camp was made just off the main road, where the forest thickened around them. It had been an hour since they'd last glimpsed a body, the last of which had been fresh, barely a day old. A heavy silence hung over the caravan. Even the children didn't play or laugh; instead, most lingered close to who she assumed was their parents, clinging on tightly.

Sybilla's mood had only darkened and by the time the camp had started to set up, the girl dismounted and stalked off into the woods. Wren wondered why Sybilla's anger seemed different from the others. Whatever the case, it would have to wait.

Lorca helped her as they went about the camp, pitching tents, leading the horses to the makeshift pens, and doing whatever other jobs they could find. Night had fallen by the time they finished. Long shadows consumed the grounds, broken only by the intermittent glow of a fire. They ate a quick meal before heading off to get some training in before sleep.

She followed him into the woods. Bands of moonlight pierced through the canopy, lighting the leaf litter across the forest floor, and guiding their way. As she started to wonder just how far they were going to walk, he came to a stop.

"This will be far enough," announced Lorca as he turned to her. A gentle breeze rustled the leaves overhead. He drew closer into a patch of moonlight, the silvery hue brushing his skin. "When you used your magic before and threw me, what was going through your head?"

She looked down at her hands, recalling the time she'd lashed out at Lorca. The panic and fear had overwhelmed her senses. Her breathing became shallow and rapid. A strange sensation prickled along her arms, rushing right down to her fingertips. Heat built in her palms. She quickly pressed her hands into her sides.

The ache in her chest returned and if she closed her eyes, she could picture the sword protruding from her chest. "I heard a voice. It said the same words as you but it felt different. Colder, meaner. And then I had this vision of this sword being driven through my chest."

Lorca's gaze softened. "Why didn't you say anything before?"

"I was afraid. Not from what you'd say, but how that vision made me feel. It felt so real." She swallowed hard and realized a tear had slid down her cheek. She quickly brushed it away.

To her surprise, he closed the distance to her and held out his hand. "Take my hand."

"What?"

"Your hand, Wren. Please." The gentleness in his voice calmed her.

She slid her hand into his, a sense of warmth flooding through her. Flames flickered to life on his hands, dancing across his fingers and onto her own. He slowly slid his hand up her wrist, the fire trailing after him. At the sight of the fire playing out across their skin, dancing back and forth, there was no fear or unease.

"This fire burns inside you, too," he murmured. "It loves being out in the world, and connecting to the magic all around us. By releasing it, by forming that connection, and letting yourself be at ease with it, you will be able to wield it."

His hand slid back down to her fingers, lingering at the tips. She had the sudden urge to grab his hands, to hold on to that energy that flowed between them, but he let go before she could stop him.

She steadied herself and held out her hands. She wouldn't try to summon the fire, not yet. Closing her eyes, she turned her focus inwards to the flame flickering in the void inside her. She drew closer, reaching out, not in demand or even a request. Instead, in an exchange. In her mind's eye, she pictured the forest around her and opened herself up to the fire.

Exhaling, she opened her eyes. Her bare hands stared back mockingly. Refusing to be discouraged, she waited—

And then a spark. It crackled to life first on her right hand, then on her left, kindling quickly to a small flame that danced across her skin. She kept breathing slowly, letting the warmth flood through her limbs. A cold breath brushed against her, but she focused on her hand, willing the flames to move to the other.

On command, it leaped and sat on her palm. A rush of euphoria lifted the corners of her mouth, her gaze moving to Lorca. Her breath hitched. Only inches separated them now. She felt her attention slip to his mouth, wondering for a moment what he might taste like. Would he respond? Or would he push her away?

As her heart gave a traitorous leap, she leaned in. Then, just as his breath fanned her lips, an icy wave rushed over her. She jerked away, pivoting sharply to the direction of the caravan. Before she realized it, she was off sprinting, driving her feet into the ground. The wind hissed past. Blood pounded in her ears, drowning out Lorca as he called for her.

Up ahead, she spied the first of the tents through the trees and as she ran into the campsite, a scream pierced the air. Digging in harder, her limbs burning, she cut through the tents, being drawn by the dull ache in her chest.

As she burst through to a small clearing at the far end of the camp, people rushed past her. A huge, bear-like creature stood on the other side of the clearing. Its thick matted fur, twisted horns, and glowing red coals for eyes confirmed the instinct that had howled in her mind and brought her here.

Demon.

It dropped its head, snarling softly at her. All interest in anyone else vanished. That molten gaze found her. She took several deep breaths, calling on the flames to go to her fingers, but when she glanced down, there was nothing. Her gaze snapped up as a low growl filled the air.

Ah, hells, she thought, glancing around for a weapon. In the middle of the clearing, she spied a cold fire pit surrounded by several makeshift seats. A metal rod was propped up against one of them. *Perfect!*

She exploded forward, the demon surging straight at her. It was faster than her and leaped over the log before she could reach it. She dived to the left, rolling up onto her feet, and sprinted to the rod. As she jumped, she grabbed it and pivoted. A wall of fur and gnashing teeth filled her vision. She yanked up the rod, but a paw flew at her, slamming hard into her ribs.

Bone cracked, ripping the air from her chest as she staggered back with a cry. For a second, she couldn't breathe. Darkness nudged the edge of her vision. Her chest squeezed, pain splintering out across her chest, as she tried to gulp in air. Just as she felt herself start to sway, air rushed down her throat, expanding her lungs.

Jumping up, she took hold of the rod with both hands, tightening her grip. Then remembering her sparring session with Lorca, she spread her feet.

The demon came at her again. She dug her feet in, eyes focused, waiting for her moment. It slowed just before it hit her, drawing back its claws for a blow. *There!* She dived low, ducking under the swing of its paw, and turned, swinging the rod hard into the back of its head. The hook at the end sunk into flesh. She yanked the rod back, black blood spraying. A droplet hit her lips.

A burning heat rushed through her head. The world suddenly lurched and started to spin. Staggering as pain filled her limbs, something inside of her splintered. Part of her was being cleaved open from the inside. She threw her head back, screaming, as a familiar power surged through her.

Everything stilled, sharpening into focus. She blinked twice as the demon charged at her. Instinctively, she dropped the rod and threw her hands up. Darkness burst from her and slammed into the demon, hurling it into a tree. As it hit the ground with a deafening thud, she strode forward, ribbons of dark energy twisting up her arms.

Unlike the fire, this power came easily. Like breathing, it flowed naturally, and as the beast went to rise, she lifted her hands again. Another bolt of darkness shot out this time, sharpened to a point like a spear. It found its target and sank deep into the demons' chest.

It threw its head back with a shriek and then slumped down, black blood pooling around it. She shuddered as the magic retreated inside her.

"Wren!" Lorca called.

She turned shakily, swaying on her feet. Across the clearing, Lorca was running to her. Before she could speak, he pulled her into his arms, squeezing her tightly. The fight rushed from her, darkness nudging her vision. He drew back, searching her gaze with a strange expression.

"How the hell did you do that?" he whispered.

"Do what?"

"You wielded demon magic."

Before she could respond, she doubled over, emptying what little she'd eaten onto the grass. Lorca was at her side, holding back her hair as she wretched until her stomach twisted in knots.

"You're all right, Wren," soothed Lorca.

But his words fell on deaf ears. His words took hold of her mind as she stared down at her hands, clutching at the grass so she didn't fall on her face.

You wielded demon magic.

Chapter 35

The winds are changing. I must be ready for what comes now.

—Excerpt from Aziah's diary.

AZIAH EMERGED FROM the portal into the crisp night air. The blue hue of her witchlight illuminated the tree line that edged a small farm.

She peered out from beneath her hood, changed from her usual white to a mottled black and gray, paired with her darker uniform. Little sense in standing out. She inhaled deeply, savoring all the senses that washed over her; the woody scent of the forest, paired with the dewy tone of leaf litter and wildflowers. An acrid smell of smoke billowed up from a chimney at the cottage, with sage being burned too. She caught the presence of one person in the cottage. Someone familiar and earthy, like she was being called home.

It was dangerous.

With a deep breath, she closed the distance, and as she raised her hand to the door it opened, a man filling the doorway. There was no mistaking the similarities between them; the snow-white hair, the pale skin, the golden eyes, and the pointed ears.

"Aziah," he said coolly. "It's been a long time."

Eighteen years to be precise.

The barb died on her tongue. She needed him, loathe as she was to drag him back into the mess she started.

"I wouldn't come here if it wasn't dire."

His jaw tightened, holding his ground. The long silence ticked on between them. A battle of wills—one he would never win. Too much blood had been spilled for her to yield, even to him. But turning away? Walking from him? It had shredded her heart the last time.

Spirits above, it had nearly killed her.

To her surprise, his chin dipped once and moved aside, holding the door open for her.

She slipped inside, ignoring the brush of his woody scent that raked her soul with talons. Her soul ached, her fingers itching to reach out and draw him close. A cruel voice whispered that he'd forgive her if she only said the words. Which was entirely the problem.

Striding ahead, she moved across the sparsely furnished living area, basked in the buttery glow of a fire. Seeking the warmth of the hearth, she moved over and tugged off her gloves. Rubbing her hands together, she closed her eyes, grateful for the heat. The approach of winter left a lingering chill in the air, the kind that left her bones aching.

"You still bear our mark," he stated, watching her with dark eyes from across the room. "Thought you would've carved it off your skin by now."

Have you removed yours? She wanted to ask, but the words died on her lips as she glanced down. Their mating mark, as dark and clear as the day they came together beneath a sky full of stars. The night had been humid, the sea air prickling their skin as they moved as one on the softest grass. No one in the palace had known that the empress's assassin and the emperor's oldest friend had slipped out one night. But it had been glorious.

She blinked away the vision and the tears that nearly broke free and looked at the fire. "It's a reminder. It helps keep me focused."

He snorted bitterly. "Right."

She turned. Beneath the cold agony of those beautiful coal eyes, she saw his fury and his grief. In the chaos of their last meeting, there had been no chance to explain what was going to happen that night. By the time the dust settled after her cruel mission, he had gone. Along with all those suspected of ill-alliance to the new Empress.

Including her mate.

"What do you want?" he finally asked.

"Hellis powder. You always used to keep a supply," she said quietly.

A muscle in his jaw twitched. "What would you want with that?"

She took a deep breath in, then exhaled slowly. Eighteen years of secrets tangled in her chest, desperate to be released. "To find the princess I helped smuggle out of the palace after I murdered her parents."

The truth didn't free her.

Perhaps that had something to do with Gabriel's silence. The air grew still. The room hung heavy with the past. Her mate wasn't a fool. She knew she'd only have to confess in the simplest terms what she'd done. Then he'd know why she stayed by Empress Alexandria's side for eighteen years. Why she'd stayed far from him.

For Sybilla.

The baby they had hoped would herald a new age in the Mithra Archipelago. One they'd spoken about with such excitement in their bed, tangled together, whispering. A path *back* to the mainland after their people had been forced from their ancestral home in the mountains over eight hundred years ago.

So, she remained standing where she was until he moved. He vanished into what she guessed was a bedroom. Returning a moment later, he walked into the kitchen area. She watched him as he revealed a small pouch in his hand, setting it gently down on the bench. He tugged open the drawstring, then tapped some red powder into a mug and filled it with water from a pitcher.

For a moment, he stared at the mug, his gaze unfocused. He blinked, exhaling softly, and brought it to her.

She murmured a thank you and gingerly took the drink, downing it immediately. A rush of euphoria surged down her throat, bursting out through her chest. Aziah gasped, and the mug fell, clattering noisily to the ground as she staggered back. Gabriel's hand snapped out, catching her and guiding her to the chair. As she sat down, the whispers began, a vision calling out.

"Aziah?" Gabriel's voice was already fading, his face blurring.

"I-I'm okay. It's... working." Every word hurt as she forced it out.

Darkness crowded her, the room fading. Gabriel was holding her hand. Yet even the warmth he offered was fading. She was slipping away.

"Why didn't you tell me?" he asked, grief scraping his voice.

She laughed, a sound like broken glass. "B-because they would've killed had you stayed. I had to keep you safe, my love."

Then the vision finally hauled her under, and she felt no more.

Chapter 36

*I'd hoped the dreams would've stopped by now but... I suppose
some deeds cannot be erased.*

—Excerpt from Litania's diary.

THE COLD, SMOTHERING darkness surrounded Wren, drowning
her. Hands outstretched above, pawing at the water, she tried to swim
upwards. But further and further she sank into the cold abyss. Her
mouth opened, rancid water flooding in. Her chest fought to expel the
water filling it, to take in air instead.

Memories filled her. A palatial room, where a bone-weary woman lay
in bed, a wrapped bundle in her arms. The hollow look in her near-
black eyes. A man, his back to her, silent as death. The memory faded,

yielding to another. A castle crumbling, its stones falling like snow, fire raining down from tears in the sky. Screams in the air, people begging, their pleas ignored. An intense rage filled her, as endless as the void devouring her.

Burn it all.

Burn!

Burn them all!

The roaring flames in her mind spluttered out. Down she went, slipping further into oblivion. Desperately, her mouth opened and shut, trying to find air and relief from the pain raging in her chest.

She tried to reach up again but her arms fell limp, floating uselessly as continued to sink. Then a numbing cold reached her toes. It rushed up over her and then she was falling, icy wind nipping at her skin.

Before she could breathe, she hit the ground. Pain exploded through her as she instinctively hurled herself onto her knees, the contents of her stomach emptying. Fetid water pooled around her hands. She stared, blinking as she took in what was reflected back.

With a scream, she scrambled up. The sight of the featureless face sharp in her mind, void of eyes, mouth, of anything remotely human. Her hands flew up. Confusion bloomed. Beneath her fingers, a mouth parted in shock. Eyes wide open. The shape of a face as it shuddered, her body instinctively gulping down stale air.

Heart racing, she looked around. The ground was smooth, like glass, reflecting a starlit sky. And several feet away, a sword plunged a few inches into the ground. Its silver edge gleamed, calling out to her.

Before she realized what was happening, she began crawling toward it.

Within reach, she lifted her hand, brushing her fingers across its leathery hilt. A teasing warmth nudged her mind, tempting her to take the blade. Her hand curled around it, taking hold.

A new scene exploded around her. She stood in a cluttered room, tables with books piled high, boxes stacked against one wall. Sunlight streamed in through several windows, warm against her skin.

Without warning, agony burst in her chest. Her gaze dropped, shock numbing her instantly. A sword pierced her, dripping with blood. *Her blood.* Silence escaped her lips as they moved, a question roaring in her mind.

Why?

A presence leaned in close behind her, ice prickling her neck. An ancient power slid over her skin, cruel and savage, yet strangely familiar. Detached understanding dawned, the truth on the tip of her tongue, yet going no further.

Those silken words dripped with venom in her ear. *Consider my promise kept, my old friend.*

Wren woke with a scream lodged in her throat. Her hand grasped at her shirt, her heart slamming against her ribs. Sweat glistened on her skin, leaving her clothes clinging to her. She wiped her brow and pushed shakily to her feet.

A thin band of moonlit cut through a gap in the cloth, dimly illuminating the space. Shadows crowded the corners and gathered around the slumbering shapes of the girls. Fragrant oils from the girl's evening hair routine lingered in the air. It smelled of homely things, of safety, comfort. Nostalgia pulled at Wren's gut as she wiped her brow, peering about the tent.

None of the other girls stirred in their beds as she donned her cloak and headed for the opening. As her hand reached for the cloth, she paused. In the corner of her eye, she spied the sword resting against a post. Even in the tent's gloom, it called to her.

She strode over and grabbed it before stalking out.

Sleep wasn't to be hers that night. She felt it deep in her bones. The call of the sword and her magic summoned her out into the night. To practice or to burn, it was hard to say.

As she neared the edge of the camp, she paused, half considering getting Lorca. She shook her head. He needed sleep and to rest as much as he could in his dragon form.

One deep breath in and out, she pushed out of the camp and into the forest. The soft rustling of leaves, a faint breeze eddying through the trees, accompanied her walk. She had no actual destination in mind. Just far enough from the camp so she could work in peace.

To be alone with her thoughts and far away from people. To spare them the beast pacing in her chest, hungry to come out. The darkness nudged at her hands, ribbons slipping from her skin and twisting back up her arm. She didn't fight it—couldn't not when the nightmare nudged her mind once more.

The fetid water in her mouth.

The room.

And the *rage*.

With every day, she felt less like herself and more like a monster. It scared her down the core. What if she found her people? Would they even recognize her? It seemed increasingly unlikely and though she'd accepted that there would be a price to pay for their rescue, she was still afraid.

And if she wasn't drowning in waves of terror at the rising darkness, she felt that ancient anger swell up from the depths of her soul. A fury she couldn't explain away or define. Her chest tightened. That feeling burned like a sun in her chest. It spread through her limbs, like liquid fire, right down to the tips of her fingers and toes. She tried to shut it out, but a cry roared through her mind again.

It wouldn't be denied or ignored, no matter how much she tried to shove it back down.

Make them pay!

Without warning, her foot caught a rock. She tumbled forward, careening into the ground. The sword fell from her grasp, landing with a muted thud. Her hands grabbed the nearest tree. Heart racing, she tightened her grip on the trunk. Wood splintered against her palms. Looking sharply at the tree, she pulled back her hand, revealing a distinct handprint in the wood.

Ice prickled the back of her neck.

Black ribbons danced over the wood, then slid back onto her hand as she stepped back and retrieved the sword. As she straightened up, a warmth brushed against her mind.

"Why am I not surprised that I find you sneaking out?" drawled Lorca.

She turned slowly, the rage fading as she looked at him, bathed in a band of moonlight. Why had he followed her? He should rest, conserving his strength. She swallowed hard, holding her ground.

"I couldn't sleep," she explained. "I wanted to train."

"By yourself?" The teasing lilt in his voice should've made her smile but it didn't. She only felt cold and uncertain, a stranger in her own body.

"It seemed safer."

The declaration hung there, a poised blade. Lorca closed the distance between them until he stood only a foot away. His green eyes were near black in the gloom, studying her, as though he might gleam her darkest secret from a look.

Would he see the deep, unending darkness within her? The rage? The confusion twisting her into knots?

"Well, I consider myself a bit of a survivor," he said softly. "Might I join you?"

The offer for him to leave dangled temptingly. She knew if she asked, he would let her be. Perhaps he sensed that tonight at least, something was different within her.

She nodded and turned, setting off into the gloom. Lorca shadowed her, silent, his presence comforting. And for a moment, the rage was silent.

They trekked through the woods until they came upon a small bubbling stream. It wove defiantly through the ancient trees, the muddied water trickling over twigs and stones and half-rotten leaf litter in its journey downhill.

They crossed the stream and moved to the center of a clearing where moonlight turned the grass and surrounding trees into shades of gray. The sword remained warm in her hand, a steady presence, even as a sharp pain squeezed her heart.

"Take up your position, Wren," Lorca instructed softly as he moved in front of her.

"But you don't have a sword?" She eyed his bare hands.

He grinned wolfishly in the moonlight as he took up his position, holding up his open palms. "Who said I needed one?"

Magic crackled in response.

Squaring her shoulders, she lifted the sword and shifted her feet.

He beckoned her with a wicked grin. "Your move."

She lunged forward, swinging the sword. Just as the blade swept to his neck, he ducked, sweeping to the side. With a swipe of his hand, the fire surged along his skin and hurled a bolt at her.

Jumping back, the flames sailed past her face, narrowly missing. She scowled at him as he winked at her. He'd missed intentionally. A teasing warning.

In a blur, he shot forward. Hesitation seized her as she swung the blade again. But he was too fast, surging up inside her guide and slamming his shoulder into her wrist. The sword flew from her hand and his other hand hit her stomach, sending her staggering back.

Air rushed from her lungs.

The sword fell but, just as it almost hit the ground, he grabbed it and brought it up. Just like that, the tables had turned. She knew he wouldn't hurt her, but that didn't mean she wanted to lose to him.

Shifting her feet, she turned her focus inwards and called on the flames. Opening herself to the fire. Tiny orange flames flickered to life on her fingers. She sharpened her mind on them, willing them to grow larger.

He gave her no more time, rushing forward. The blade hissed through the air as he swung. She yelped, darting out of the way as the metal cleaved the air, cutting a stray strand of hair as she ducked. The brown strand floated down in front of her face, a second frozen in time before it shattered.

In a blur of steel and muscle, she did all she could to dodge every swing. But he was fast and relentless.

"Fight back, Wren."

She shot him a seething look, fire bursting up into her hands. It fed off her fury, perhaps on the lingering emotions of the nightmare. As he came at her again, she raised her hands and a column of fire shot out.

He yanked up the sword with both hands. The flames slammed into it and parted right down the middle. The fire sailed harmlessly past him until her hands dropped, the remnants still flickering on her fingers.

A grin lit his face. "Better." He stalked forward. "Again."

They trained until swaths of burned orange and red interweaved through the thin scattering of clouds that appeared across the sky. Wren still hadn't got her sword back, but she'd held her own—sort of. A few more shots of fire, and she had managed to keep the fight going.

He stopped and held the sword out to her, pride in his eyes. "You're getting better."

She eyed the blade, fearing he was going to come at her again, then cautiously took it. The weight on her near-dead limbs pulled her arm down.

Lorca snorted. "Tired?"

Though she wanted to keep going, her body had other ideas. Her legs wobbled. It was time to rest. "I feel like I could sleep for a week."

"Then let's head back."

The return to the camp was a silent one, but it was a peaceful silence. Companionable. Shadows still lingered in Lorca's eyes but he didn't seem as trapped by them. She hoped her words made a difference, that by sharing his pain, she'd eased it a little for him. After all, he'd done for her, it was the least she could do for him... and she hated that shame in his eyes. She wanted to whisk it away and bury it so deep so that he didn't feel it anymore.

Part of her felt like she hated Litania for hurting him. For all that she'd done to the people, she had called family.

At the edge of the camp, Lorca paused, touching her arm softly. "Wren?"

She glanced at him. "What's wrong?"

"We're only a few days from the City of Slaves now. You haven't said anything about it," he remarked quietly.

"I'm trying not to, at least to not let it dominate me. I have to focus on this magic... and while I'm *starting* to get it, there's still so much I don't know. So, I have to learn what I can control and be as ready as I can for when we arrive." She turned to look at the camp slowly awakening as people emerged from their tents. They would begin packing up soon. The task ahead of her loomed ominously in her mind, the weight of her people's survival resting heavily on her shoulders. "I have magic now and while it terrifies me, perhaps I can use it to save those I love. I'm too close to give up now."

Chapter 37

*No secret will be hidden forever—one way or another, it will
be dragged into life. I know this as I watch my child run to me,
bright-eyed and happy. I know that someday, they will know
what I have done and the love in their eyes will vanish. Then
they will see me for the monster that I am.*

—Excerpt from Litania's diary

THOUGH WREN COULDN'T see the sea, she could smell it in the
air and taste the salty tang on her tongue. It was as strange as she imagined, a far cry from the earthy tones of her home. Yet as she worked with
Lida in pegging down their tent, the sun hot on her back, she found herself savoring it.

She pressed the last peg into the soft earth and stood up, wiping the sweat from her brow. The physical exertion of helping to set up the camp calmed her mind, a steadiness she needed being so close to her goal.

Sorcha had told her the city was only a few hours away. Its presence bore down on her mind, the weight of her mission squeezing her heart.

"That should do it," said Lida from the other side of the tent. A moment later, she walked over and nodded at Wren. "So, you and Lorca are leaving."

Wren nodded, resisting the urge to shift restlessly on her feet. She didn't want anyone to see how nervous she was. "Yes, that's right."

Lida's expression grew cautious. "I hope you find your people."

"You and I both," confessed Wren, reluctant to say more.

Lida began to say something, but Lorca's arrival cut her off. She smiled at him. "Morning, Lorca. Sleep well?"

He glanced at Wren, then back to Lida. "I did. And yourself?"

Lida shrugged. "As much as to be expected. This festival we're hosting is important. We need it to feed us for the coming winter."

"Is it usually a fruitful affair?"

A shadow flitted across her face. Her shoulders drooped. "Usually but things are difficult lately. Folks aren't parting from their coin so easily and, well, it's just more restless out there...I'm sure we will be fine, though."

He nodded, then turned to Wren. His smile slipped slightly. "Madam Kara wishes to see us."

Wren nodded. They said a quick goodbye to Lida and set off toward Kara's tent. As they neared it, Jed strode out, scowling. He stopped dead when he saw her, his face hardening. She barely opened her mouth to say hello when he spun on his heel and stalked off, vanishing quickly from view.

"Well, he's in a good mood," mused Lorca with a smile.

Wren looked at him and saw no trace of the darkness in his eyes from their last talk.

She knew it was there, though. Buried deep and though they hadn't returned to that topic, she sometimes caught him staring into the fire. He appeared lost to his memories in those moments.

She forced a smile. "We better not keep her waiting."

"My mother always said it was unwise to keep an Avalon dragon waiting," he replied as he held open the cloth for her to enter. "It's considered poor manners."

She glanced at him, surprised he'd mentioned his mother. Lorca stood still, looking at someone inside the tent, his eyes narrowing. Wren stepped inside and followed his gaze. Kara stood by her table, holding up a letter as she read with a stony expression. Whatever was written didn't seem like good news.

As if sensing them drawing closer, Kara folded the letter and tucked it in the pocket of her flowing dress. She looked at them with a smile that didn't quite reach her eyes.

"You're both rested, I trust?" She gestured for them to sit.

Wren nodded. "As much as we can be."

Which wasn't true. She'd snuck from her tent last night and curled up with Lorca, the nightmares having assaulted her again. It wasn't something she was about to share with Kara, whose gaze was already far too perceptive.

"Good, good. A good friend of mine is on their way. When they arrive, I will have them escort you into the city. They will be your aid in the city," Kara explained. "The City of Slaves is a dangerous place, and I thought you would do well to have some help."

Wren was silent, but Lorca found the words.

"We thank you for your generosity. It's more than we could have expected from you, given the risk you have taken in allowing us to travel with you," replied Lorca smoothly, betraying no surprise at the kindness offered.

Wren glanced at him, wondering what he was thinking.

Kara continued. "Sorcha was quite persuasive in ensuring you had some help, especially after all that you have done for her. So, consider it the least I could do."

Instinct cautioned her that Kara was telling a lie wrapped in a hint of truth. Wren couldn't pick exactly what the lie was, only that she could feel it deep in her gut.

Lorca smiled, leaning forward, showing only gratefulness on his face. "I won't fight your kindness. I remember just how stubborn dragons can be."

Kara nodded, her gaze suddenly darting behind them. Wren turned in her seat as the cloth parted and Sorcha popped her head in. She greeted them with a smile.

"Helena has arrived. Shall I send her in?" inquired Sorcha.

Kara nodded. "Yes, and see that her horses are tended to and that her men are offered a meal and some water."

Sorcha nodded and slipped back out. Hushed conversation sounded outside, and a moment later, the cloth flew open. A striking blonde woman of around thirty strode in, clad in a high collared, sleeveless dress with a black sash tied off at her waist, an ornate dagger hanging off either side. She was carrying a small wooden box in her arms.

The woman stopped a few feet from the table, bowing her head to Kara first before her gaze slid to Wren and Lorca. Interest flickered in those dark blue depths before they returned to Kara.

"I brought what you asked for. Is this her?"

"Yes." There was a pause, and Wren glanced back to Kara. "This is Lady Helena Adara. She is one of my oldest friends and I trust her more than most. She is the one that will escort you."

Wren's gaze slid to the box, her chest tightening. Magic oozed from that box. The hairs on her arm prickled. Whatever was in it sung out to her, as if the contents sensed Wren's magic. She couldn't tear eyes away, like a rabbit caught in a snare.

"And what has she brought with her?" Lorca's voice was cool, breaking through her thoughts.

Helena set the box on the table and opened the lid. Her delicate hands, laden with glittering jewels, dipped in and lifted out a crown. Intricately made to resemble thorns and gleaming in gold, it hummed with ancient magic.

Wren itched to snatch it from Helena's hands. She kept silent as Helena walked around the table to her. It was impossible to look away from the crown. The blood roared in her ears. Everything else in the tent fell away as Helena stopped before her.

"Please, sit still," murmured Helena, her voice soft.

Wren's heart slammed painfully in her chest as Helena lifted the crown above her head and gently placed it on her head. The flood of magic was instant, rushing through her whole body. A gasp burst from her lips as a bright light suddenly erupted from above and the crown grew hot on her head.

The heat sharpened, and the dark beast that lurked inside snarled. Cold magic shot up from within. Whiteness flashed, blinding her, and pain erupted in her head without warning.

She reached up, trying to grab the crown, but her fingers collided with nothing. The pain dimmed as the light faded. As her eyes adjusted, wisps of gray dust fell in front of her face. She touched her head.

The crown was gone.

And everyone was staring at her. Kara particularly looked shocked, a look of horror on her face. Whatever had happened had not been expected. "Lorca, Helena, out."

The pair looked like they wanted to argue but eventually bowed and left the tent. Wren's mouth was dry with ash, her heart skittering nervously. Little wisps of ash dusted her shoulders and lap, the vague remnant of magic prickling her skin. She had no idea what to say or even how to apologize. Had she just ruined her chance of getting into the city? Her mind twisted itself into knots until a shadow fell over her.

After a pause, she looked up and froze.

Tears spilled down Kara's cheeks. "You're *alive*."

"What?" The question tumbled from her lips, scarcely above a whisper.

A warm had slid to her cheek. "My sister bore an egg shortly before the fall but when everything happened the egg still hadn't hatched. Vaska swore Queen Evanya to guard the egg but she must've been mortally injured, thus passing the oath to her son."

The words pounded in her like cracks of thunder. She jumped to her feet, mind whirling, heart racing. "I'm a *dragon*? But I...I've never transformed! I've been—"

A memory brushed her mind. Back in the mountains, during one of her first meetings with Lorca, she'd thrown up shards of bone. He said he'd caught her but what if she'd killed the wyvern that snatched her off the cliff? What if she'd *eaten* it? Ice wrapped around her heart. If that was the case, then he'd seen her as a dragon...and he *knew*.

And he'd said nothing.

"Child, look at me—"

"Did Lorca know what I was? Did he tell you? Was that why you tested me?" She wanted to be wrong, that he hadn't lied to her...that her heart hadn't been betrayed.

Kara's brow furrowed deeply. "He believed you to be the descendant of a Dragonir. It was I who believed you might be my niece."

Perhaps it was the quiet look of hope in Kara's eyes, that some connection to her past had been restored, but Wren felt a rush of panic. Her blood turned cold. The mission was still her people, even if her knowledge of what she was had changed.

"I'm still going to the city," she said quickly.

One brow lifted in response. "I was never going to ask you to stay. Your people need you. What I *was* going to ask is that you do seek out Idris and Vaska when you're ready. When you're ready, of course."

"Perhaps—"

"Kara!" Helena called from outside. "Is everything okay? I need to head off soon."

"We're done here." Kara glanced at her. "The city awaits. I hope that you find what you seek."

She managed a shaky nod and stumbled from the tent. Helena slipped past her into the tent.

In a flash, Lorca was in front of her, reaching out but she jerked back. Heat flared over her cheeks. He flinched, brow furrowing innocently, which only deepened the uncertainty that she floundered in. Doubts crowded her mind and flashes of their conversation

"Did you know I was a dragon?"

"What?" The raw shock in his voice made her hesitate.

"That's what the crown meant when it glowed. I'm an Avalon dragon...and I was the egg you guarded. Not sure on who took me, or bound my magic." She paused and gathered her words carefully. "Back in the mountains, you said you'd saved me from a wyvern attack off the cliff ...but I threw up bones and blood. I shifted, didn't I? Which means you would've seen color I was and known—"

"I didn't catch you. Truth is, I was out flying when I heard a dragon call. I got excited, thinking perhaps it was—" He stopped abruptly but the unsaid words ripped the anger from her.

He'd thought that the Dragonirs had come back when he'd heard the call, that his people had come back to him.

"What happened next?"

"I found a wyvern ripped apart and when I followed the trail of blood leading away...I found you. Only you were in human form. When you woke up, though, you seemed to have no idea who or what you were. So I *thought* you might have some Dragonir blood. Then later when you started using demonic magic as well... Well, I didn't know *what* to think." He rubbed the side of his jaw. "I'm sorry."

"Why didn't you just tell me?"

"You were only just coming to terms with magic. I didn't know how to tell you that you *might* be a Dragonir, not when I wasn't fully sure myself."

She opened her mouth to reply but Helena swept out. Before the curtain shut, Kara appeared, holding it open, and offered a small nod before retreating back into the tent. Helena stepped in front of her line of sight.

"It's time we go. Gather your things and meet me at the edge of the caravan near the horse pen. Don't take too long. I cannot be away from the city too long."

Helena swept away, vanishing amongst the caravan.

"Wren, I—"

"We should grab our things. The city awaits."

She didn't miss the way he flinched, or the guilt gnawing at her. He'd been honest. That she sensed through their bond. The truth was, the revelation had rocked her and she was floundering. What was she anymore? Dragon or monster? Whatever the case, her focus had to be on her people. One step forward at a time.

Just keep moving...

Two spare horses awaited them at the edge of the camp, whilst Helena and a couple of men sat astride their horses. Wren quickly tied down her bag, then swung up and glanced at Lorca as he did the same. They hadn't spoken since their talk but there would be time once they got to the city. Then she'd explain.

Just keep moving forward...

The ride from the camp was along a well-worn road. It skirted a thin forest and ran through wide fields, broken only by neat paddocks full of cattle. Every so often she spied a cottage, revealing hints of human life.

Trees eventually thickened on either side of them, the forest drawing inwards as the path began to wind and slope downward. Shadows closed in, chasing off the mid-afternoon sun that beat down. When they exited the forest once more, the sun returned in full force, tempered only by a rush of cool sea air.

The sloping road cut right down to a wider one that ran straight toward the ocean, and at the end was a sprawling stone city. It rose from the coast with imposing walls and spires in the middle, one rising polished and gleaming above the rest.

It dwarfed the city of Tarth, the first and only other city Wren had seen, which now seemed dull by comparison. From their vantage point, she spied the docks, which stretched out across the water like gnarled fingers. A dozen ships were moored, with at least half a dozen more anchored across the vast blue water.

As Wren took in the sheer size of the ocean, she felt smaller than she ever had in her life. Her gaze slid back to the city, her heart squeezing painfully.

Helena stopped next to her. "Welcome Wren, to the heart of the Empire, the City of Slaves."

Part 3

THE CITY

Chapter 38

I do not fear death—it is the ghosts I fear, the truths they know,
what they might do if given the chance.

—Excerpt from Queen Litania's diary, the fourth year of her reign.

SORCHA WAS CALM as she waited for Omi to return from her meeting with Madam Kara. Her bag was packed and propped up against a post inside her tent, her black cloak draped over it. The sheathed sword, too, was leaning against the post.

It felt like an eternity before Omi swept into the tent. The second she saw the bags, the sword readied for travel, understanding dawned on her face.

"Must you go today?" Omi asked quietly.

The pleading look nearly broke Sorcha. She swallowed hard and closed the distance between them, drawing Omi into her arms. For so long she'd felt protected, loved, and safe in those arms. But she was no longer the little girl that hid her magic and pretended she was like everyone else. That her parents hadn't been murdered and her throne stolen.

"It's time," murmured Sorcha, pulling away. "I wanted someone to see me in this form one last time. I'm glad it was you."

Omi nodded, tears glistening. "Madam Kara told me this day would come, but I prayed it wouldn't. That you would be my little girl forever. When did you grow up?"

Sorcha fought back the tears and smiled. "When you weren't looking. Otherwise, you wouldn't have let me."

Turning to the mirror hung from the post, she took one last look at her face, saying goodbye to the girl staring back.

She lifted her hands to her cheeks and closed her eyes, summoning the magic buried deep within. Heat rippled over her skin, but she welcomed it, embracing as bone and skin shifted, a mask falling away. When the heat dimmed, her hands fell, and she opened her eyes slowly, half afraid of what she might see.

Golden eyes. *My father's eyes.* They were brighter than the deeper honey color she'd become used to. Without the glamor, there was no mistaking her fae heritage.

Her shape was sharper and her ears pointed, though not as much as a full-blooded fae. Long hair, as dark as the night, hung down her back. She looked like her mother now, save for the eyes and ears.

The woman that had haunted her visions since she was young, whom she'd heard sing while she held a protective hand over her growing belly. One that had embraced her throne so young, so full of life and hope. Who had dared to enter a foreign marriage and found unexpected love. There had been fire and rage, kindness, and love, in those eyes, in that voice.

Sorcha's hand lingered on her cheek. As she turned, she found Omi kneeling before her.

"Omi?"

The woman that cared for her, fought for her, scolded her when she took too many sweet tarts, was on her knees and there was a look of pride shining in her eyes.

"You are ready, *Sibylla*."

Sorcha was no more.

Chapter 39

It is not armies that keep rulers on their throne. It is the spy-masters and their birds, the truths that gleam from the shadows and whispered conversations. Even those closest to me have no secrets for me. The trick is knowing when to wield it against them.

—Excerpt from Empress Alexandria's diary

A GENTLE HAND brushed Aziah's forehead as she emerged from the haze of the vision. Dappled morning light tumbled in through an open window, warming her cheeks. Blinking, she glanced up, taking in the familiar shape of Gabriel's hand. She stilled, savoring the moment. His earthy scent filled every breath, their old mate bond humming softly.

"You're awake," he whispered. "How do you feel?"

Her thoughts cleared. She bolted up, twisting to look at him. "I saw her!"

His hand stilled in the air between them, a shadow of worry knitting across his brow. "Sybilla?"

"Yes! Gods, she looks just like her parents. And Gabriel, her *power*." The weight of eighteen years finally shattered the walls around her heart. Tears welled in her eyes as she launched forward, throwing her arms around him. Together, they hit the floor. She straddled him, holding his face as she laughed through her tears. "She's already starting her rebellion as we speak!"

His eyes widened. "What!?"

Seeing him beneath her, the hope daring to glow in his eyes, the warmth of his touch on her hips. She kissed him.

He froze.

Aziah pulled back, moving to climb off him when his hands moved. Slowly, at first, from her hips, lingering at her waist. Through her shirt, the heat of his fingers, all while his molten gaze never wavered from hers. Her heart slammed against her ribs. Even after so long, his mere touch had her crumbling, aching for him, for the flames to devour them both.

"Gabriel—"

He flipped her, pinning her beneath him, crushing his mouth to hers.

Fire exploded between them. Her hands flew up, tangling her fingers in his silken hair, drawing him close. She felt the scrape of his hands as he tugged her shirt free. Their lips broke, just long enough for her to pull her shirt over her head. His mouth dropped to her breasts as they shed her pants, his hands slipping between her legs.

A gasp tore from her lips as his mouth pressed a fiery trail of kisses down her stomach, then lower still. "Gabe!"

He kept going until his mouth found her heat. She threw her head back, crying out as he devoured her, caressing and licking her with his tongue. It drove her to the brink, teasing her with oblivion. Higher and higher she rose, the world tumbling away into chaotic euphoria. Breathless cries filled the room, pleas ignored as she fell off the edge.

Lightning cracked through her, fire flooding through her limbs, all sense and thought scattering. For a moment, she couldn't find the words. She pressed the back of her hand to her sweat-slicked brow, closing her eyes for a moment.

"Gods, I forgot how good you are at that," she said, chuckling.

He kissed his way back up, taking hold of her mouth for a long, savoring moment. When he slowly drew back, he grinned. "I'm not done with you yet."

As she dressed, acutely aware of Gabriel watching her from the bed that they had eventually made it to, thoughts of the world outside returned. Worry kindled in her chest, squeezing it hard. Icy talons dug into her heart. What had she done? She had made a lapse of judgment in bedding him. How in the god's damned hell would she walk away from him now?

You stupid bloody fool.

"Stop," said Gabriel.

Blinking, she frowned at him. "Stop what?"

"I can tell what you're thinking. This wasn't a mistake. *We* are not a mistake."

She opened her mouth to argue. What they'd done *was* a mistake, even if their mating bond wasn't. There was a difference. For an assassin, the timing was everything. Yet, at that moment with him, she'd ignored her training. Sighing, she turned to him. "My cover might be blown. You could be in danger, Gabriel."

"Was that why you came?" he asked.

"I came for the powder," she replied but his arch look suggested he didn't believe her at all.

He sat up, swinging his legs over. The blanket shifted, slipping dangerously low. "You want me to run?"

"Yes."

"This is our home, Aziah or, well, it would've been, had you—"

"And it still can be, but not now," she snapped. "Gods, Gabriel, they tortured the soldier who smuggled out Sybilla. He was one of the few who knew about us."

Gabriel stilled. "You left him alive?"

She didn't miss the accusatory note in his voice, touched with surprise. Sparing a loose end wasn't normal for her. Closing her eyes, the memory of that fateful night surfaced. The blood on her hands, the scent of death in the air. "There was so much death that night... I couldn't do it. I swore to them that if they got Sybilla out of the palace, I'd help them be together. He'd fallen in love with that slave girl and just wanted to run away with her. How could I deny them that? They were going to raise the baby in secret. Unfortunately, they got separated and she must've gotten injured. I found her body outside the capital beside the road. He was crushed but I couldn't kill him, not even then."

Gabriel sighed, leaning forward resting his elbows on his knees, his hands massaging his brow. "Ok. I'll go but, on one condition."

A tentative hope flickered in her chest as she looked at him. "Yes?"

"You come with me."

"Gabe—"

He sat up, grabbing her hand, that fiery gaze holding hers. "I won't lose you. Not again."

Whether it was the words or the pleading look in his eyes, she nodded. Leaning in, she pressed her forehead to his. "But first, I have to clean up a few loose ends and get rid of some materials back in the palace. Then I'll come for you. I promise I won't be long."

"Very well. I'll be waiting."

Chapter 40

It has been nearly a year since the dragons left, followed soon after by the Dragonirs; an entire year since I have last taken human form. I know I should not keep so often in my dragon form. How I feel myself slipping with every day—I hold on, though, for I must guard Idris and Vaska's precious egg, which remains cradled by the castle's eternal flame. It should have hatched by now, and I am running out of options. I do not know what to do anymore...

—Excerpt from Prince Adrian's diary.

WREN STARED WIDE-EYED as the coastal entrance into the city

loomed like an open mouth, set to devour all who entered. Guards stood atop the gate and were positioned at regular intervals on the towering wall. They were so high up they appeared little more than ants. More men were stationed on the ground, checking the papers of everyone who trundled past.

Even with the cool sea breeze tempering the heat of the day with the approach of dusk, the whole process moved at a painful crawl. Wren shifted anxiously in her saddle, clutching onto the reins with an iron grip. The idea of entering another cramped city set her nerves on edge, like she was willingly walking into a trap.

When they arrived at the gate, the guards bowed their heads to Helena. "Welcome back, Lady Adara."

"Thank you, Ferris. Do pass on my good wishes to your wife. Is the little one born yet?"

The guard blushed. "Came into the world screaming two nights ago."

"I shall have a package sent over. New life should be celebrated." Her gaze passed over the rest of the soldiers as they inspected another group. "New men?"

"Recruits blessed to us by the esteemed Prince of the City," the guard drawled. "They're trained well enough."

Wren didn't miss the way Helena's grip tightened on her reins or the sharp breath that followed. Who was this prince and why did he make Helena react like that? Was he an enemy?

"That stuffy lord is no prince. You would do well to remind your men of that," said Helena tightly. "Good day."

Helena clicked her tongue and with a flick of her heel, her horse broke into a trot. Wren hurried after her, with the rest of the group soon in tow.

Hooves clattered along the cobblestone road. Single-story wooden buildings flanked either side, densely packed, reeking of fetid water and rotting food. It was the stench of too many people squeezed together.

The roads were busy with horse-drawn wagons, laden with goods and people shadowed by collared slaves, whose arms were clutching boxes of goods, dark eyes downcast. Loud chatter, the rumbling of wheels over stone, horses neighing uncomfortably; all blended in a cacophony of dizzying sound.

The stone road continued up, with the buildings remaining tightly packed until they hit another internal wall. Two guards at the gate went to stop them, but seeing Helena, they smiled and waved the group through. None appeared curious about the strangers.

Not for the first time, Wren wondered about the woman Kara trusted so implicitly.

Beyond this gate, the buildings were strikingly different. They were larger, with at least two levels and built of gleaming white and gray stone. Some wore beards of ivy, sprung up from ornate pots by grand front doors. Many of these homes were pressed together, yet it all seemed less oppressive than the wooden thatch dwellings in the previous area.

A few people glanced up at Helena, bowed their heads, some murmuring a quiet greeting. Helena returned only a curt nod and continued.

They came to a stop before the iron gates of an enormous home, three stories high with a cobbled stone courtyard before it. A guard hauled the gates open without question as everyone approached, then locked them shut with a resounding click.

Helena dismounted at the front door, which opened as her feet touched the ground and several people rushed out. In simple clothes, Wren assumed they were her staff. One collected the reins of her horse, leading it away, while the others moved to Helena. She murmured a few quiet instructions, and they all hurried off.

Wren had barely dismounted when a young man came over, gathered the reins of her horse, along with Lorca's too, and led the horses away. Wren went to follow, her bags still tied to the saddle, but Helena turned to them.

"Your belongings will be taken to your rooms. Come with me. There is much to discuss."

Then she was gone, vanishing into the mansion.

Following the group inside, Wren shed her cloak and draped it over her arm. When the doors shut behind them, one woman approached her, gesturing silently to the cloak. Nodding awkwardly, she handed it over, watching as the woman strode away with it in her arms.

"Kara has powerful friends," remarked Lorca, appearing beside her.

She followed his gaze to the vaulted ceiling and ornate wooden grand staircase that dominated the foyer. Polished stone statues of warrior women guarded the stairs, seeming to hold real swords in their hands. Wealth oozed from everything Wren cast her eye over, breathing the power Helena wielded into the air.

Yet, despite its beauty, it seemed pale compared to the Dragonir palace.

"I don't know how anyone gets used to all of this," she murmured. "It's all so... well, *this*."

Lorca leaned in close. "Well said."

She elbowed him, her mouth twitching. "Ass."

The tension inside of her from their chat and her own identity revelation eased a little.

Helena had stopped at an open door and turned to them; one brow lifted. "Are you both done gawking or shall we continue?"

Wren hurried forward, Lorca chuckling as he followed her.

Through the doorway, they entered a smaller room covered with an array of portraits on the wall and an enormous fireplace. Helena strode to one of the many plush couches heaped with brightly colored cushions. A side door swung open and a young woman hurried in. She greeted Helena with a bow, who returned a surprisingly affectionate smile back.

"Sarah, you may tell the others they can sleep once the bags are taken to the guests' rooms. I won't need you further tonight," said Helena softly. "Rest, for tomorrow shall be busy."

Sarah bowed and departed. The door clicked shut firmly behind her. Wren cast her gaze over the room, still absorbing its sheer opulence. Lorca appeared unaffected, leaning against the wall, his arms folded over his chest. His gaze met hers, then moved back to Helena, unreadable.

Wren glanced at Helena. "What did Kara tell you of us?"

"She explained your mission to me, but I was hoping you might clarify a few matters—half for my curiosity, half for the aim of determining where to begin my search tomorrow," she explained, curiosity flickering in those sea-blue depths. "What is special about your home? Foreign slavers attack the coast, not inland remote villages, which leads me to believe it was by the Empress's hand. It is her signature for those who have offended the Crown."

Heat flooded her veins. Her hands curled into fists and she had to stop herself from snarling back that her people hadn't done anything wrong. They kept to themselves and always went above and beyond to treat the merchant with respect. Her people were warm and kind.

She sucked in a deep breath, trying to quell her racing heart and hot cheeks. Exhaling slowly, she tried to sound calm. "*Offended* the Crown? My village barely communicated with anyone beyond their lands." She turned to the fire, looking at it as if it might offer her insight into why her village had been destroyed. "All we did was harvest a red flower that grows on the mountains. After that, we would take the flowers down, dry them and grind them into a red powder. A merchant would come every year and supply us with money, grains, and furs, or whatever we asked for, and then take the powder."

Helena appeared beside her, the firelight glowing in her eyes. "That red powder—we call it Hellis powder. It's rare, prized among the royal family. Did you know of its magical properties?"

Wren hesitated for a moment, but, for the sake of her village, she went on. "We would all take the tiniest amount each and no one ever fell ill over winter. We never used more than that."

Helena clasped her fingers against her chin, as if she was considering what she knew. "This flower cannot be grown in the lower lands, correct?"

"The flower favors the colder weather and the rich soil of the mountains." Wren sat down, the weight of Helena's words bearing down on her. "We *always* delivered on time but this year was to be a slightly smaller amount because of a poor harvest. We hadn't sent word of that, so they could not possibly know of the issue."

"Perhaps she no longer needed the powder," pondered Lorca. "Or she found a better alternative and sought to ensure that no one else could obtain it."

Had their dwindling haul really condemned her people? Her stomach clenched, bile rising up her throat. If she had found a way to improve their haul, would they have been left alone? She pressed her hand to her mouth, fighting the urge to throw up.

Helena pressed her lips together for a moment. "If she found an alternative source of magic, she would not want the powder falling into the hands of someone else. I would imagine if your merchant stopped coming you would seek another buyer. Whatever the case, your village could not be left alone. It had to be removed."

Oh, gods.

The bedroom seemed too small and filled with a deafening silence. Walls pressed in on Wren, taunting her—soft voices that slithered from the shadows. And as she tried to muster the will to move, she found herself frozen. Her feet remained bound to the floor, as though roots had embedded from her into the mansion itself.

A gentle knock shattered the silence, shards of her thoughts crumbling to the ground. She lifted her gaze to the door.

"Come in!"

It opened slowly at first, then widened fully as Lorca filled the doorway. His cheeks flushed, a faintly pained expression tightening his features.

"Can't sleep?" he inquired, stepping into the room.

"Haven't even tried. I just keep thinking about my people, how I might've failed them long before the attack." She wrapped her arms around her waist, shivering. Hindsight had become a cruel demon in her mind. "About before...I'm sorry. My mind was a mess and I immediately blamed you for—"

"I should've told you."

She didn't realize Lorca had moved deeper into the room until his arms wrapped around her, his hand rubbing small circles on her back. In his embrace, the demons of her mind retreated, and eased into his touch, pressing her cheek against his chest. The steady drum of his heartbeat filled her ears.

In such a short span of time, she'd come to lean on him so easily, to find comfort in his steadfast presence. He was a quiet soul, who steadied the raging storm within her and anchored her when she felt herself being swept away into darkness. But this scared her. Deeply. Never before had she felt so connected to someone or sensed her heart softening so quickly.

His grip tightened on her. "Don't let yourself think that way. It will only lead to madness."

She pulled away, releasing a shaky breath. "Perhaps you're right. Do you know what else scares me though?"

"What?"

"This magic inside of me, the dreams I'm having, the visions. It's like I'm losing myself. There's this...monster inside of me, full of rage and pain and it's growing stronger. Everything I knew about myself is being stripped away and I barely recognize the girl in the mirror anymore. So, how can I save my people? Do right by them if I lose myself?" She stared at her hands, trembling from the confession. "I'm being torn apart from within and I don't know how to stop it."

His hand cupped her cheek, the gentleness making her look up. The air rushed from her lungs as she met that burning gaze. Tension crackled in the air between them.

"If that happens, I will be there to help you put the pieces back together."

She smiled quietly. "I'll hold you to that." Realizing how close they were, she stepped back. "I'm glad you're here right now but something tells me that you didn't come here originally to listen to my confessions."

The corner of his mouth tipped up in a sheepish smile. "I couldn't sleep...and I had hoped to interest you in some sparring. However, there is no obligation. If you do not wish—"

"I'd love to."

Chapter 41

Today, I watched as the last of the dragons flew across the seas; I wonder if the Dragonirs are among them, too, or if that bond has been broken. I must be strong; bear the decisions I have made and step forward to the future.

—Excerpt from Princess Litania's diary, prior to her marriage and coronation.

WREN JERKED UPRIGHT from the syrupy darkness, gasping at the icy water she sat in. It was the same dream as before. The shallow water ran all the way to the horizon, mirroring the burnished orange sky. Her damp clothes clung to her body as she pushed to her feet, teetering awkwardly for a moment. A shiver rippled down her spine.

She took a step forward when something icy clamped around her wrists. Her gaze snapped down. Silver chains gleamed on her wrists, holding her to the ground. Those hadn't been there when she'd woken up...They were cold against her skin and as she tugged against them, the metal rattled but didn't break. She yanked harder but the chains only tightened against her skin, biting in hard.

Her heart started to race, and her mouth dried. She tried to fight the rising dread, even as icy tendrils coiled around her heart. This wasn't like the dream before. Something was wrong. Knots tightened in her gut. She gave another hard jerk and the chains suddenly went taut, sharply yanking her down to her knees. The chains pulled taut, a splintering pain lancing up her arms, forcing her hands wide at her side.

"Well, well, what do we have here?" inquired a vaguely familiar and bored voice.

A familiar figure loomed over her, more lively than her portrait in the Dragonir palace, with the same piercing gaze.

The Spirit of the Mountain, clad in her flowing white dress and the golden thorny crown atop her head. A sharp look of disappointment clouded her ethereal face, her mouth tightening to a thin line.

"You—" She was cut off as a golden-haired man materialized in front of her, cut from the same cloth of haunting beauty. His gaze hardened on her, disgust curling his lip.

At the sight of him, Wren was silent—not in awe, but with something else kindling deep in her gut. It festered, like a rotting corpse, and the taste rose in her throat like poison. Fire burned across her cheeks at the sight of him and she felt her hand curl into a fist. Uncertainty swept through, tempering the anger kindling in her chest, and she wondered why he'd conjured such an immediate reaction.

It was almost like they'd met before.

"*This* is her?" he mocked. "She's a shadow, a pathetic thing not worthy of us."

"I agree," chimed in a dark-skinned woman, taking shape beside him in a warrior's attire. Her piercing gaze locked on Wren. "She's enslaved by her fears, and it looks like those chains will not break anytime soon."

Wren had no idea who the rest of these people were.

A young, hooded girl suddenly emerged from behind the spirit and knelt before Wren. Luminous brown eyes peered out from beneath the hood, searching. Ancient power burned in that gaze that sent shivers across Wren's skin.

The girl reached out a slender hand, brushing a stray strand from Wren's face. "I don't know about that. The chains are damaged."

"Not because the girl did anything, Amara," chided the warrior-woman. "A fae did that."

A shadow fell over Wren, a hand settling on her shoulder. Ice slithered down her spine.

Amara shook her head. "You're wrong. She *was* the one who struck the first blow at the spellbinding her, even if the fae constructed the events. What do you think, Atlas?"

The strangers in front of her parted, admitting another man—yet this one she knew, for it was a face that had been there her whole life. Through the years had not touched this man's face, there was no mistaking who it was... and Wren's face paled.

"Father?"

He strode silently toward her... and her gaze dipped to his hand, to the sword she knew so well. Her eyes grew impossibly wide, a plea forming on her lips. The blood drained from her face. She tried to surge to her feet, to break free of the chains. It was useless. Her mouth opened for a scream that never came as he plunged the sword into her heart.

Chapter 42

The ties that connect both the Dragonir people and the drag-ons themselves run deeper than most believe. It is by a com-mon connection to the spirit magic that most know—yet few seem to realize the role of the Spirit of the Mountain. For her magic is not entirely what we believe.

—Excerpt from the Dragonir Chronicles, Vol 3.

TITANIA HUNKERED LOW on the rooftop as the trail of caravans trundled along the empty cobblestone street.

The street was cleared, and all access was cut off to ensure the transport was undisturbed. Only guards astride their stocky horses rode along with the wagons, while armored men sat at the front of each wagon. One hand holding the reins, one on their swords, they cut a threatening air.

She cast her gaze over the slaves shackled together in the wagons, hunting for the familiar face. Yet none that she saw cut the striking figure of her old friend. She closed her eyes and let the chains holding her power fall away. At once, little orbs of light appeared in the shadowy version of the street below. Each a human soul that blazed with a fiery red hue.

Her eyes flickered open. Confusion made her sit sharply up on the roof. A sharp breath caught in her throat. "What in the spirits?"

"What is it?" asked the young half-blood fae next to her.

"Nothing," she said, dropping down low before anyone saw her. Sitting back, she glanced at the three half-bloods that were with her. "The plan is the same. I need a big distraction. Keep the focus away from the second from the rear wagon."

"Consider it done," murmured the dark-haired boy who spoke before.

Gods, could Claudius not have selected one who didn't look barely more than a child?

Shaking the thought away, she turned back to the edge of the roof. "We attack now! Sound the signal!"

The boy pressed two fingers to his lips and blew. The ear-splitting whistle cut the air like a knife. Titania stood up and threw herself off the edge.

Roars erupted from the roofs as dozens of half-blades dropped into the street. Chaos descended as she hit the ground with a roll, surging quickly up to her feet. She turned on her heel, sprinting down the line. A guard galloped toward her; sword raised.

At the last second, she dropped low, sliding past the horse. His sword hissed through the air, missing her head by inches. As he wheeled around to face her, she spun, yanking a dagger from her hip. She hurled the dagger, not waiting for it to hit before she turned around, rushing off down the line.

A panicked neigh split the air behind her, followed by a heavy thud.

She honed in on the end of the procession, ignoring the cacophony of swords clashing and shouts. Four wagons away, Atlas's head lifted from the slaves in his wagon, meeting her gaze. His lips parted, shock etching his weathered face.

A face that was far too old for a demon.

In the corner of her eye, a guard lunged at her. She jumped back, the blade narrowly missing her throat. Off-balance, she staggered back, catching herself against one of the wagons. Digging her heels in, she pushed off and swung her blade.

Metal collided in a ringing clash. He grinned savagely. Snorting, she surged forward. The force sent him staggering, the shock of her strength wiping his smile. His sword dropped an inch. She surged in for the kill, sweeping her foot out underneath him, sending him falling back. He hit the ground hard.

Titania plunged the sword into his heart, then yanked it out. Blood sprayed across the stones.

She jumped off him, sprinting back toward Atlas. At the back of the wagon, she stopped and, with hand, grabbed hold of the lock. She tore it clean off, tossing the crumpled metal away.

"Titania!"

Frowning, she hauled herself up into the wagon. "Claudius sends his regards. It's time to go."

Atlas sat up stiffly, glancing about the confused and startled looks of the other people. His gaze darted back to her. "Can you free us all?"

"No. That wasn't the plan," she replied. "Look, this isn't the time to argue. We came to get you out."

"Save them—"

"We don't have time or the men to free everyone here," she snapped. "Now, come on!"

"No!" he snarled.

The lack of power in his voice made her pause.

His gaze narrowed, then he looked to a red-haired boy next to him who was holding a slender blonde girl. "If you can't save all of us, then get him out."

Titania's gaze flickered to the boy, then back to Atlas. "We don't have time."

"He's my son," he snapped. "Titania, he can't stay here."

Ice flooded her veins. *Son?* No, that was impossible. Demons couldn't sir or bear children. That had been tried before, to devastating results. She didn't want to consider what deals he'd struck to sire a child or the price he might've paid.

You stupid bloody fool...Why didn't you learn from Nimue's mistakes?

"You can't either!" she argued. "I won't leave you with these people."

He shook his head vehemently. "You must."

A series of shouts from her men rang out down the street. The fight was turning fast. Time was running out.

"You expect me to leave you here?" she hissed.

"I know what I'm doing. Look, Titania, things are not what they seem. You must seek Amara." He glanced at the men advancing, then back to her. Desperation burned in his eyes. "Get him out of here!"

Curses spilled from her lips as she spun to the boy and grabbed his chains, tearing them off his ankles and wrists. His hand shot out, grabbing hers.

"Her as well," he begged. "I won't leave her."

The pale girl shuddered in his arms. By the looks of it, she wasn't long for the world.

The shouts beyond the wagon grew closer.

Titania scowled and ripped the girl's chains free, then bent down and scooped her out of the boy's arms. The boy was quick on her heels as they hurried out. She turned to meet Atlas's steely gaze.

"It's still not too late—"

"My wife is another wagon. I won't leave her, or any of them," he insisted. "Now, go!"

With a final nod, she spun to the approach of her men. She quickly passed the girl into their arms, then turned to the boy. Outwardly, he appeared very plain; all lean, weary, and pale. How was *this* the son of a powerful demon?

She shook off the thought. "Right, let's go!"

But as she turned to lead the way out, a sharp pain exploded in her shoulder. The boy shouted in alarm, his gaze darting to her back.

"Gods! Your shoulder!" he shouted, reaching for her back. "There's—"

"An arrow? Yes, I know!" she snapped as her chest throbbed, flinching from his hand.

"Let me get it out," he argued, reaching again.

His fingers brushed the arrow, fire surging down her spine. Her head snapped back. A scream tore from her throat.

C.M. Quinn

"Go, get out of here!" she snarled, shoving him away, and she pushed her hands down, trying to stand.

Her legs buckled.

Oh, hells.

She looked up sharply at her men. "Get them out of here and back to Claudius. I'll buy you time!"

Not waiting to see them go, she forced herself to face the men approaching her. Darkness nudged her vision. The world blurred around her. The taste of ash filled her mouth.

A poisoned arrow.

She raised her trembling hands, howling into the void to summon her magic, and this time the monster that lurked within her roared back.

Darkness erupted.

272

Chapter 43

The court knew not how to react upon the return of the heir apparent from the dead—or his new bride, the lovely, and magical Dragonir enchantress, Litania. The nobles might not have seen it, but I saw demons in her gaze, inhuman shadows that followed her every step. She had the look of a girl who had struck a deal with a demon.

—*Excerpt of the Memoirs of Court Advisor, Edward Danomir*

WREN JOLTED AWAKE in the bed with a choked-off scream, clutching at her chest. Her gaze snagged on the sword resting on the table on the other side of the room. It mocked her from across the room, teasing a death that kept assailing her mind.

Scowling at the blade, she hauled herself out of bed, wincing as her feet hit the cold wooden floor. Halfway across the room, she glimpsed a dress draped over the back of a chair. Curious, she drew closer and lifted it. The material felt softer than anything she'd worn before.

She changed swiftly into the dress and slipped on a pair of shoes left for her. As she walked across the room, she caught sight of herself in a mirror and froze. In Fenware, she'd never worn dresses or anything feminine really. Whilst her sister draped herself in thick woolen dresses, Wren lived in her climbing furs and cloaks.

The transformation was unsettling, another reminder of how much she had changed.

Looking away, she headed out of the room, trailing back down toward the grand staircase. At the top of which she encountered a servant—or slave, Wren wasn't sure precisely as the girl had a brand but no collar.

"Excuse me," said Wren, awkwardly raising a hand to the girl. When she paused, Wren asked, "the dining room?"

The girl stared at her for a moment, then turned silently and gestured for Wren to follow. She followed the servant down the main staircase and off into a side hallway, where they eventually came to a tall dark door. The girl knocked, paused only to hear a muffled 'enter!' and opened the door for Wren to go in.

The room was dominated by a long ornate wooden table that was surrounded by chairs. Only three places were set up with plates and a few platters of bread, pots of jam, some cut fruit, and eggs.

Helena sat at one of them, raking her gaze up and down Wren. "The dress fits well. I'm glad."

"It's lovely, thank you," replied Wren, a little unsure of what proper protocol was. "Lady Adara—"

"Helena," she corrected. "And please, sit. No need for such formalities here."

Wren nodded awkwardly and slid down into the chair to Helena's right. "Where's Lorca?"

"He's sleeping in the ballroom. Poor thing seems exhausted."

They had sparred until after midnight and even after she'd trudged back to the room, sweaty and exhausted, she'd sensed his restlessness through the bond. He hadn't gone to sleep immediately, nor when she'd washed, changed, and crawled into bed.

"Best he rests, then. Where do we begin, though, for my people?"

"Your story has given me some ideas about whom I might meet with to determine where they are being kept," replied Helena. "So, our first call will be to a friend of mine at the docks. If anyone can pin down a specific group of slaves, it will be her."

The gates to the slave markets towered over Wren and Helena, casting a long shadow. Unlike any other of the other inner-city walls that Wren had seen, this one had spikes running along the top. The middle ones bore decaying heads, the fetid stench soured the air.

Charming.

She didn't miss the slave brands on their foreheads, either.

The guard standing by the gate strode out from his little booth and approached Helena. She lifted a medallion from her dress pocket. He studied it for a moment, then returned to his post.

"Open the gates!"

A series of heavy clattering noises resounded, followed by a long groan as the gates lifted. Once there was a loud clicking noise, the guard waved them through. Then lowered the gate back down behind them.

She kept silent as they headed down the main road that ended with an open yard, fenced in by a single-story wooden building—one long one on either side and one stretched out in front, forming a horseshoe shape of the yard. In the middle of each building, she spied a small arch gate, guarded by two guards.

Their dark green uniforms looked uncomfortable in the heat; their faces impassive. An eerie silence hung in the humid air.

Barely an hour out of the house, and she was becoming increasingly grateful for the light material of the dress. A thin sheen of sweat glistened on her skin. Strands of hair clung to the nape of her neck. How anyone actually liked the heat was beyond her. Give her the cold of the mountains any day.

She glanced at Helena, one brow lifted. "I thought this place would be busy."

"The official sales won't begin until this afternoon. Buyers and slavers flock in and fill the whole square, with slaves being sold for several hours until the allotted groups have been processed," said Helena.

She wheeled her horse off to the gate to the left, trotting over, with Wren hurrying after her.

"All this to sell people," murmured Wren, her stomach in knots, bile rising in her throat.

Wren fell in behind Helena and only then did Helena speak again. "Slaves are first brought into the markets to what we call the pre-sale yard. Once there, they are given a basic slave brand to denote their new status and a collar. Of course, later these will change to reflect their new owners. Slaves are then grouped under demand, appearance, orders for large numbers, and so forth. After that, it's simply a matter of determining which days to sell them, and then they are taken to the sale yards to wait. When they're sold, they are branded again and all the paperwork is completed."

Wren felt cold and hollow inside. "How organized of them."

"It wasn't always like this. Alexandria overhauled the entire system to ensure they turned a better profit," muttered Helena. "Then she turned her gaze outwards to neighboring lands to procure slaves there."

There was something unsaid in her words as if she was biting her tongue in the long silence that followed as they gradually descended toward the seafront. The cool salt breeze rushed up the narrow veins of the city, washing over her.

"Do you believe we will find my people?" Wren asked quietly.

"Yes," she replied immediately. She paused for a moment then, before saying. "I can't say where they are now, but since they passed through this city, there will be records, in one form or another. This city never forgets those who pass through its gates."

Silence hung between them again until they reached the docks, where rows of wharves jutted out into the bay like fingers. Several boats were tied up alongside, their sheer size overshadowing the other vessels nearby.

Crews moved on and off them busily carrying boxes and shouting orders. They took supplies on board some boats and carried goods off others, which were then loaded onto wagons. Once they were full, teams of sweat-soaked mules hauled the wagons away from the wharves.

As Helena set off down the road that ran the length of the docks, Wren nudged her horse after her. The sailors stared at her, several gazes lingering on the red sash around her waist. It made her uncomfortable, exposed, never wishing for her furs more than in that moment.

She trotted up beside Helena, falling in beside her, eyes trained ahead but barely able to focus. A hand fell on hers. She flinched, looked at Helena, who gestured for her to follow, and they came to a stop before a busy three-story house. It looked nicer than anything on the shore, with a balcony on the two floors above the ground, several scantily clad men and women were hanging around outside, their gaze scanning the men below with hawkish interest. A few cast considering looks over Helena and Wren, lingering on the latter for a fraction longer. Two pretty blonde women sauntered out from the front door and approached Helena.

"Madam expecting you?" one asked impatiently.

"No, but it is urgent," replied Helena. "Summon her for me. Tell her Lady Adara is here to see her."

Wren's eyes nearly bulged at the imperious tone in Helena's voice, though she kept silent. She slid down from the saddle as Helena did, following her to the entrance. The other woman took the reins of the horses, leading them down the side of the building.

The one who'd spoken nodded and gestured for them to follow. Wren followed Helena inside. She hoped she'd finally have some answers. Her heart had steadily raced faster as they walked. They were led into the house, down a hallway, and past two open living areas full of low couches with women draped over them. Clouds of smoke swirled above, wisps of cloth scarcely covering their skin. Their gazes lit on Wren, curious. Yet for their airs of ease and sensuality, they all wore collars and brands.

Up a flight of stairs, they continued down to the rear and stopped at a door as the girl knocked. The door cracked open, and she slipped inside, with the door shutting behind her. Hush chatter sounded beyond the door, then fell silent after a moment.

The door reopened, and the girl ushered them inside then she stepped back out into the hallway, closing the door behind Wren and Helena.

The room was choked with smoke and heavy perfume. On one side of the room was an enormous bed, draped with furs and vibrantly patterned blankets. By the large window, there were two couches, with a brightly clad woman stretched out on one of them.

She held a pipe, pinched between her slender fingers, wisps of smoke rising. The lady, with a striking face and long black curly hair which hung loose down her back. She held her upper arm, drumming her fingers into the skin.

"I have clients, Helena," she drawled. "Make it quick."

Helena fished out a scroll from her bag and closed the distance to the woman, handing it over. "I need information on a group sale that would have occurred within recent weeks. Details are there. If you please, Luce."

Luce plucked the scroll up, unfurling it. Her lips tightened as her gaze swept over the contents. When she finished reading, she set the scroll aside.

"There was a disease outbreak at the temple construction, so the head architect had purchased just about every slave available. Your people were probably sent there," remarked Luce, studying her fingers as if they were the most interesting thing in the room.

"I have to be sure," explained Helena. "This is a survivor from the attack."

Luce's attention flicked abruptly to Wren. "You're a climber. I heard about your kind." She drew the pipe to her lips and drew in a deep, steady draw of smoke, then exhaled, smoke swirling around her face. "You're not what I expected."

"Likewise. Helena keeps interesting company."

A ghost of a smile lifted Luce's mouth. "Indeed."

She rose from the couch and swept across the room to an ornate wooden desk. Leaning over, she slid open a drawer and plucked out a journal, opening it and leafing through several pages before she found what she was after. Pursing her lip, she ran a finger down the page, then stopped.

Her gaze flicked up as she set the journal down. "I was right. One week ago, Lord Robert Craven handled the sale of a particular batch of slaves from the far north. They were only to be sold for hard labor—no private sales or pleasure work."

Helena frowned, though Wren didn't know what to make of the look. "Was no one allowed to view them?"

Luce nodded. "Well, not officially. I heard Lauri bought a girl from the bunch, a pretty blonde—under the table, of course. One of the men involved bragged about it to one of my girls two nights ago."

"She dared to steal one after they'd branded?"

"Not just her. Do you remember that commotion in the markets with that batch of slaves? That attack is making a lot more sense now." Luce's gaze slid to Wren.

"Those are my *people* you're talking about," snarled Wren, striding forward. Fire surged up from the depth of her soul, spilling through her veins. Her palms prickled with heat, the flames pushing to be unleashed.

Helena touched Wren's shoulder, warningly. Her hardened gaze cautioned silence as she spoke. "What about the red powder your people sold? Kara mentioned your people were the only ones who produced it."

"We've been selling that as part of a long-standing deal. It's as old as our village is," said Wren. "The merchant always comes, but..."

"But?"

"He came early this year."

Helena's lips pinched into a thin line.

"Did you say red powder? Does it have healing properties?" interrupted Luce.

Wren nodded warily.

Luce's hand dropped to the desk, pulling out a leather pouch from one of the drawers. She carefully untied the string and tapped the bag. A tiny amount of red powder spilled into her palm.

"Is this it?" inquired Luce as she moved around the table and closed the distance.

Wren eyed the powder, then leaned in, pinching it between her two fingers. The familiar floral notes filled her, tugging at old memories. Tears pricked as she drew in a deep breath, the sweet aroma dancing over her lips.

Euphoria erupted without warning through her, sending her staggering back with a gasp. The world lurched, colors blurring, all sound bleeding away. Her legs buckled and Wren hit the ground, pain exploding in her head.

"What the hell did you do to her?" shouted Helena.

"Nothing! Gods, I know some fae can react badly but gods, I have no idea what's happening to her!"

Their voices grew distant as blood roared in her ears. The powder had never made her feel like this, like something was clawing up from deep inside her. She threw her head back, an inhuman sound tearing from her throat.

"Oh gods, is that *scales* on her skin?" someone shouted. "Get her out of here!"

Fire erupted deep in her chest, flooding through her. Pain tore along her bones like they were all breaking at once. She tried to scream, but only that terrible roar ripped from her lips.

And as she tried to beg for it to stop, a warmth brushed over her mind, dragging her into oblivion.

Chapter 44

The Harvest Ball is meant to be a celebration of a fruitful year. Yet as folk danced and drank and whittled away the hours into the night, unease lingered in the air. Normally, the dragons are in attendance, but even now they refuse to be anywhere near us. Even now, they distance themselves from us.

—Excerpt from Queen Evanya's diary.

WREN SURGED UP through the darkness, power roaring up, propelling her upwards. Light blazed, drawing her like a moth to a flame. And, just as her hands brushed the light, she jerked to a stop.

Looking down, the chains wrapped around her body, trying to drag her back down into the darkness. Desperation burned through her soul, howling to resist. She strained with all the strength that she had, viciously railing against the dark.

Something inside of her pulled taut.

The world around her shattered, splintering into a thousand shards. Colors and sounds erupted around her. Her eyes slammed shut, trying to block out the sensations that assaulted her.

Her eyes flew open.

She was back in the ballroom of Helena's mansion. Blinking slowly, she tried to remember how she'd gotten there. All that came to mind was the powder and then, darkness.

As she looked around, she froze. Lorca stood several feet away, wary and holding a mirror in his hands. The polished circle of metal gleamed in the morning light that spilled in from the row of windows.

She tried to speak but, rather than words, a strangled and inhuman cry choked out. The sound of a beast. Panic erupted as she stumbled forward, her body moving strangely.

Lorca rushed forward, holding up a hand as if to calm her. "It's okay, Wren. Calm down. I know you're a little disoriented, but trust me. I want you to look at this, okay?"

He raised a mirror.

Wren froze.

A golden dragon stared back at her. She blinked slowly, and the dragon blinked too.

It was *her*.

A long face with two distinct horns that curved over to her back, along with a ridge of spines that ran from the crown of her head and down her neck. She glanced behind, seeing the spines run all the way to her tail, too, where they fanned out. Slowly, she began to unfurl her wings when Helena emerged from the shadows of a pillar.

"Might I advise you to keep those tucked? I'd rather this room remain undamaged," Helena requested cautiously.

Wren tucked her wings back in place and looked at Lorca. In his dragon form, he'd spoken to her in her mind, so she wondered if she could do the same. She turned her focus to the bond that bound them together. It glowed gold in her mind's eye, humming with energy, and warmth filled her as she latched onto it, pushing her voice through.

Can you hear me?

Lorca winced. "Uh, yes, I hear you. Loudly."

She released her grip a little on the bond. *Sorry. Is that better?*

"Much. Now, how do you feel?" His gaze slid over her form, inspecting it closely before it returned to her face.

She brought her head down so that her gaze was level. *I'm okay but how do I turn back?*

"Picture your human form in your mind, drawing your magic deep within and exhaling," he said, reaching out and placing his hand against her cheek. "*Breathe.*"

Wren closed her eyes. In her mind, the fire burned all around her like a ring. She held out her hands and touched the flames, letting them rush across her arms and flood over her skin. She let it settle over her and then she pictured her human form materializing before her. With a gasp, she released the breath she was holding and drew her magic inwards.

Molten heat rushed along her body, a white-hot pain that ripped the air from her lungs. It dimmed rapidly, the heat cooling until she felt it no more. She opened her eyes slowly and looked down. Her hands stretched out before her.

Slowly, she lifted her gaze to Lorca. "I did it."

A shadow passed in his gaze. He turned to Helena. "What the hell happened?"

"Hellis powder, as I explained," returned Helena coolly. Her blues burned with caution as they fell on Wren. "You really don't know much about that dust, do you?"

"I'm starting to think there are some gaps in my knowledge," replied Wren cautiously. "It's certainly never made me transform before. So, what am I missing?"

"Hellis powder is one of the rarest magical items in the kingdom—expensive as all hell. So only the gods know how Luce got her hands on it. For us mere mortals, funny enough, it's not much more than a healing powder. For anyone with magic, it can amplify their power. The more you take, the bigger the effect. Yet I've seen Kara touch the stuff and have no reaction. You had the slightest sniff of it and you had a fit."

Wren frowned. "I've never reacted like that before."

But my magic was bound before...

"Something had bound your magic before," remarked Helena. "Which makes me infinitely more curious about your village. Luce was right. No one had dared to take slaves before, especially those that had just been processed. Now, Lauri stole one right out from underneath Robert Craven's nose, and then the attack—"

"About that—what did she mean exactly?"

Helena didn't answer at first. She glanced around the ballroom as if she sensed someone listening in. When that cautious gaze returned to Wren, she turned around, gesturing for them to follow.

"Come with me. This isn't a discussion to be had here."

As Helena lowered herself behind her desk, her face hardened. She pulled out a letter from the drawer and set it down, unfurling it with care. Wren tried to see what was written on it, but she was too far away.

"I don't have the details of exactly how many of your people were processed. Luce will have her little birds out getting that as we speak. All I know right now is that once they were loaded into the wagons and were moving out of the city, there was an incident. A group of armed men attacked, snatching two slaves in the process. I *believe* one of the attackers was caught, a woman, but none of my birds have found out where they're hiding her."

Wren's heart thudded hard in her chest. Questions burned her tongue but refused to come out. Fear of what Helena would say made her hesitate. Like a god's damned fool.

"What happened next?" growled Lorca. "They didn't go looking for them?"

"The guards were likely on a deadline. This little construction project for our esteemed Empress won't be delayed," mused Helena. "Still, that doesn't mean it's being ignored. I imagine it's being investigated quietly and I can't be sure if those two slaves are in the city."

"But they could be," whispered Wren. "There could be three of my people in this city right now?"

Helena opened her mouth to reply, but a knock at the door silenced her. "Enter!"

The door cracked open. A young woman stood at the entrance, dipping in a slight bow.

"I have a missive for you, my lady," she murmured.

Helena nodded, beckoning her over. The woman hurried inside, setting the letter on the desk before slipping out without another word. Wren watched as she opened the letter, her gaze darting down. At the bottom, her eyes narrowed, and she set it down with a disdainful expression. Her lip curled.

"I see this is how my day is going to be," she declared as she looked up.

"What is it?" asked Lorca.

"Nothing to concern you," replied Helena dismissively. "As for the location of the two that were taken, that may be tricky to determine. I have power in this city but current circumstances have made things clear that I'm not the only one at work here. It seems I have a competitor."

Lorca stepped up beside Wren, his jaw tight. "And pray tell, what are the current circumstances we have entered into?"

Helena rose from her chair. "Rebellion, my dear, and it's about to begin."

"*Rebellion?*"

Wren stilled. "We're not here to get involved in that."

"But here you are and I am not halting my part in this simply for you child," returned Helena frostily. "I agreed to provide entry into the city and shelter while *you* searched, as per my agreement with Kara. Beyond that, I was not required to do more."

"Then why the meeting with Luce? Why help us at all?"

Lorca glowered. "Because you want to strike a deal."

A Cheshire smile tugged at Helena's mouth, though it didn't quite touch her cerulean eyes. "Clever little Dragonir, aren't you?" retorted Helena. Her gaze darted to Wren. "So, what will it be?"

Wren stepped back, hesitating for a moment. "I don't—"

"Do you think you can arrange a meeting with her? Can you buy your friend with whatever meager funds Kara provided you? Because Lauri won't sell her cheaply and if you plan to steal the girl, that won't go well either. Lauri controls the Pleasure Quarter with an iron hand and she won't take kindly to theft."

Molten metal burned her veins, heating her cheeks. A venomous response burned her lips. She'd been cornered like a damn fool, trusting the woman simply because Kara had. The demonic magic stirred awake, hissing softly. Her hands curled into fists.

"And what do you want of us?"

Helena smiled. "You'll see soon enough, my dear, but let me make myself clear that if you run off on your own, thinking you can save your people without me, I won't aid you further. You can stay here but, beyond that, we are done." She walked around the table and held out her hand to Wren, ignoring the fury in Lorca's eyes. "Do we have a deal?"

Wren slid her hand into Helena's, squeezing hard. A flash of pain tightened in the woman's face.

"Yes, we have a deal."

Later that night, with sleep refusing to yield to her, Wren wandered the halls. Magic thrummed in her veins, fire and demonic, vying for dominion. Her body and mind had become a battlefield, two vicious monsters tearing her apart from within.

Then there was the deal with Helena. It made her feel like a cornered beast, manipulated into something she really didn't understand. The problem was how few choices she had. She tried to play it smart for the sake of her people but she was way in over her head.

She passed dozens of closed rooms, walking with no destination in mind. When she came to a door slightly ajar, she paused. Moonlight spilled through the gap and onto the floor. Frowning, she gently pushed the door open, freezing as a small library greeted her.

The room was two levels, with an open void stretching up the middle. A mezzanine circled it, revealing more shelving. Her gaze spied a familiar shadow standing on the second level, half-turned from her.

"Lorca?" she called out.

He didn't respond. She tried again, but he didn't even move. Frowning, she strode across the room to a spiral staircase. When she came to the second floor and found him, she reached out. As her fingers brushed his back, he jumped, spinning around.

"Wren?" he asked hoarsely. "Why aren't you asleep?"

"Why aren't you?" she retorted.

His gaze dropped back to the book in his hands. "I didn't like how little I understood of this land, so here I am."

As she looked down, tiny flames erupted to life on his fingers. The book caught fire. Lorca's grip tightened, squeezing until the fire turned blue in his hands. Her gaze snapped up, her heart squeezing painfully.

His gaze was unfocused. "I found Litania in these pages. The life she got to lead after she murdered the Spirit of the Mountain."

"What?" Wren's voice was scarcely above a whisper. In the stories, it had been assumed that Litania perished in the fall of her people.

"I tried to forget, to move on, but seeing this reminds me of the same damn question that has haunted me for three hundred years. Why did she do it?" The book crumbled to ash in his hands as the flames spluttered out. "Why, Wren?"

She reached out tentatively, taking hold of his hands and gently opening them. Smoothing out his palms, she wiped his hands clean with her robe.

"I wish I had the answers," she confessed. "I wish I could drag her soul from wherever it is now and ask Litania that question. Maybe, we will never know, but if that truth exists somewhere, then we'll find it."

When she looked up, his molten gaze bore into hers. "We?"

She couldn't tear her gaze from his as she squeezed his hands. "You're stuck with me, for better or for worse. This city won't know what hit it—the dragon and the Dragonir. No secrets will be safe from us."

Lorca leaned down, pressing his forehead against hers. "They don't stand a chance."

Chapter 45

I caught Litania creeping out from the catacombs this morning. She told me she was in the ancient library, seeking to better understand our history. Since her return, she has been filled with a desire to learn. Does she think I am so easily fooled?

—Excerpt from Princess Yelena's diary

THE LETTER SAT atop the wooden desk, gleaming in the candlelight. Wren stared at it from across the room, sorely tempted to burn it to ashes. Her gaze flicked to the dress hanging up on the wall. It had arrived only hours ago, accompanied by the letter with its simple command.

There will be a party tonight. Your presence is required.

Her fists tightened. Schooling her temper, she decided to bide her time. She would figure out a way to take advantage of Helena's knowledge and use that to save her people.

For the moment though, she had to be patient.

Her bedroom door opened again, admitting two young women carrying boxes. She watched them, silently, as they unpacked jewels and a pair of shoes. The women stepped back, letting Wren inspect the items with wary interest.

"What are your names?" asked Wren, looking up.

The dark-haired woman's blue eyes widened, quickly hidden behind a calm facade. "Eren and this is my younger sister, Ilanna."

Ilanna shifted on her feet, eyes downcast. Sensing Wren's gaze, her dark blue eyes darted up for only a moment before dropping.

"You're surprised I asked your names," noted Wren.

Eren smiled wryly. "A little. Sometimes the guests here see the brands and, well, we are little more than objects to be used by them."

"And Lady Adara permits that?"

The smile fell. "No! She abhors it. Spirits above, we're free here. Our work is easy, we are paid well, fed well. There is no discomfort here. If any guests misbehave, our good lady ensures they are dealt with."

Wren's brow lifted. "So, you'd call her a good person?"

Eren nodded. "As much as one can be in this city."

Ilanna swept over to the boxes while Eren led Wren to the dress hanging on the wall. She turned to Wren.

"Time to strip," ordered Eren.

"Oh, I..."

"Darling, it's nothing either of us hasn't seen before. Now, hurry!"

Wren awkwardly peeled off her nightgown and stood there naked. Ilanna appeared at her sister's side, the forest green gown in hand. Eren nodded, taking it from her.

"Fetch the rest," she instructed, then turned back to Wren. "Hands up."

The dress slipped down and settled loosely around her body. Its silky material felt heavenly against her skin until Eren yanked on some strings at the back, sucking the bodice flat against her stomach. Air rushed from her lungs.

Blinking, Ilanna was kneeling in front of her, lifting the skirt and pushing shoes on her feet. Wren stepped into the heeled shoes and teetered awkwardly for a moment before she steadied, squaring her shoulders.

The gown was a far cry from the day-gowns she'd been wearing. Jewel-blue with an intricate swirling silver pattern on the bodice, it had a plunging neckline and high slit in the skirt. When she moved, her bare leg peeked out.

"Now we just need to attend to your face and hair, then we'll be finished." Eren ushered her over to a seat.

The women worked in a dizzying fashion as they set about her. Ilanna vanished behind, attacking the wild nest of hair with a series of combs, pins, and fragrant oils. Every so often she'd tug hard, making Wren wince, and Ilanna would whisper an apology. Wren tried to assure her it was fine, but Eren had already descended on her face. Forced to shut her eyes, she could only be silent and still as the women worked.

It took an eternity of prodding and painting before it finally stopped. She didn't dare to open her eyes, afraid of what she might find—of what they'd turned her into.

"You can look now," murmured Eren.

Wren inhaled deeply and opened her eyes. Eren held up a polished mirror in front of her, a stranger staring back. Gold paint on her eyelids and red on her lips erased all echoes of the climber. Someone different stared back at her.

Ilanna appeared beside Eren, eyes wide. "You look like a queen."

As the grand staircase appeared up ahead, Wren slowed. A lone figure stood at the top of the stairs. He faced away from her, hands clasped behind his back, and his fingers twitched restlessly. Framed by a buttery golden light, his black tunic cut sharply against his lean body. His bare arms flexed with every shift of his hands.

She swallowed hard as she approached, taking a moment to calm her racing heart.

He stilled. As if sensing her, he turned slowly, watching her with those dark eyes, like the depths of an ancient forest. Heart racing, she paused at the threshold of the hall, her gaze drifting to the crowd of people gathered in the foyer below. It felt like a world apart from the one she knew. They acted as if there weren't people being dragged from their homes and enslaved...

Do they even know or care?

"Wren?" Lorca's low voice tugged her focus back.

Heat flooded her as she took in the molten look in his gaze as it surveyed her dress. When it returned to her face, her cheeks were on fire. He held out a hand.

She released the breath she'd been holding and closed the distance. Smiling softly, she slid her hand into his.

"You look—"

"Terrified?"

His eyes widened. "Gods, no. Beautiful. I was going to say beautiful." He laughed softly and rubbed the back of his neck, heat creeping into his cheeks. "I'm not good at this."

Her mood darkened once more, straying inevitably to her people. What was she doing? Dressed up for a spirits damned party, dancing to the whim of a woman she didn't understand. Her breath sharpened to jagged breaths. Her stomach twisted. She was going to be sick. How the hell could she pretend to smile and be okay whilst her people suffered?

"I can't do this," she whispered.

"Wren—"

"My people are *enslaved* and I'm attending a damn party. How does this bloody help them?" Her hands closed into fists at her side.

His hand gently lifted her chin. "We may not trust Helena right now, so let us use this party to learn. These are likely some of the most powerful people in the city. Why not use this to our advantage?"

The anger cooled in her veins. He was right. This might not be the situation she imagined when trying to rescue her people. However, it could be turned to their advantage. Her shoulders dropped as she mulled this over. "You're right. We should make use of this."

The corner of his mouth twitched. "Now, shoulders back, chin up.

You look like you want to set fire to this place—a sentiment I share—but we have to play the part of guests now."

Arm in arm, they descended the stairs. A few faces looked up, then more followed, until the entire room seemed to watch them. Wren tightened her grip on Lorca's arm.

"How are you so calm right now?" Wren whispered.

Lorca offered a reassuring smile. "I'm a prince. This isn't the first party I've had to pretend I'm enjoying myself."

They reached the bottom of the stairs. Lorca's hand came over hers, squeezing gently. The smell of perfumes and wine filled the air and grew stronger as they passed through the side doorway and into the ballroom.

At the last door, they joined a line, moving slowly before they entered a large room packed full of people. Musicians played at the far end of the room, scarcely loud enough to pierce the laughter and chatter that rose and fell across the sea of heads.

Lives were being destroyed outside the mansion but looking at the glowing procession it would be easy to forget. Perhaps that's how those people did it. They kept the ugliness out of sight, out of mind.

She looked around for Helena, who might help them make sense of all the people, but didn't see her at all.

"Can you sense Helena?" she asked, glancing up at Lorca.

He shook his head. "Nothing."

Together they stepped into the tightly packed crowd, passing groups of men and women dressed in finery and decked in jewels that glittered under the hundreds of brightly burning lamps. Wren had seen nothing like it before. It was blinding, every person shining, every surface of the room gleaming. And it was so damn *loud*. As it rose to consume her, she was jostled.

Her hand slipped free of Lorca's and as she turned to grab him, she was ferried off into the chaos. She tried to push back, find her way to him, but as she called out, her voice was drowned out in the cacophony of noise.

Stumbling back, she struck someone. Wren straightened up and turned around to apologize.

The air was sucked from her lungs as eyes like polished obsidian met hers. Shock lit that piercing gaze. He bowed, raven curls falling over his brow for a moment, and she had a vision of him asleep in bed beside her and brushing those wild curls from his face.

A man she'd dreamed about before. During the dream where she'd met the Spirit of the Mountain, she'd encountered her father and strangers she didn't recognize. One of which she hadn't expected to meet in a ballroom.

"Have we met?" The question fell from her lips before she was able to claw it back.

He opened his mouth, then shut it again, as if at a loss for words. "I don't think I would have forgotten a beautiful woman such as yourself. Now I must, what is your name?"

She curtsied awkwardly. "Wren Dumare. I'm sorry for bumping into you."

"Think little of it." He bowed deeply, rising slowly as his gaze locked onto her. "Lord Claudius Delmont, Prince of City."

The hairs on the back of her neck lifted. She bit back a shiver. "Fancy title."

A smile lit his face, but it didn't quite reach his eyes. "One not self-given, I assure you."

"Oh?"

"More of a joke. I wasn't born to all this wealth, made it myself from nothing," he explained. "And once I'd accrued a degree of power within the city, it was a jab at my blood. But I decided I liked the sound of it."

She couldn't stop staring at him; not for his looks, though to be fair he was handsome. Rather, it stemmed from a sense of familiarity and the strange sadness she felt in his presence.

"Have we met before?" she asked. "You just seem familiar..."

He shook his head. "Afraid not. I would not forget someone like you. Perhaps I remind you of someone you know—a lover, perhaps?"

She snorted. "You're bold."

"You didn't correct me," he remarked. "So, is he present tonight?"

A smile lifted her mouth, dampened quickly with a frown. "He is, but we were separated."

He held out a hand. "So, for this moment, you are unaccompanied. Might I then tempt you to dance?"

She hesitated. Something warned her against taking his hand. Despite her reaction to him, a little voice whispered from the fringes of her mind, *don't take his hand.* "I—"

"Lady Adara has been harassing me for months to attend one of these parties. If she finds out I've attended and not danced, then I fear I should be in trouble with her. The woman is terrifying when crossed." Claudius smiled sheepishly.

"The good prince fears her?"

"No, and one could argue my power in this city rivals hers. However, one should not create unnecessary enemies. It's bad for business."

An idea sparked in Wren. "You would consider yourself a man of business? So, you would say that you know a great deal about this city?"

"I have my connections," he replied conspiratorially. "In the market for a business partner?"

His tone dripped with wicked promise.

Heart pounding, she slid her hand into his. "Perhaps, but we should dance first. We wouldn't want to disappoint Lady Adara."

The darkness inside of her stirred, hissing softly, stretching out its talons into her mind.

Don't trust him! The voice bellowed.

Unaware of her internal war, he pulled her closer. "Indeed. Such a thing would be truly dangerous."

Blood howled in her ears, drowning out the dizzying music and laughter until the world shrank to just the two of them. Her dark magic raged against the moment, snarling and snapping, repeating the same warning over and over again. But for her people, she had to at least see if there was anything she could use. Was he someone she might be able to manipulate? To steal from? Or was the darkness wrong and he was someone she could trust?

"Wren?"

Blinking rapidly, she pushed the questions away and smiled sheepishly. "Would this be a good time to confess I don't know how to dance?"

He held up a finger, snapping his fingers. Ribbons of light danced through his fingers. "No matter. Do you trust me?"

"Do you want an honest answer?" she replied.

"Probably not, but you have my word. I will only aid in the dance—you can ask anyone in this room, my word is worth its weight."

She didn't miss the way people looked at him or the presence he had. This was a man with power and as he spoke, she had a sense he wasn't lying to her. Whatever strangeness she sensed about him, she trusted her gut when he spoke.

That, and she was hardly defenseless.

Around the crowd thinned and several pairs lined up on either side of them, taking their place, hands on hips, shoulders, hands intertwined. With a tremulous breath, the ribbons slide from his fingers and onto her skin. They vanished beneath the surface, and a strange sensation pooled in her feet.

Like they wanted to move on their own.

"I'm going to make you look silly," she whispered nervously.

He leaned in, grinning. "They'd be fools to laugh."

The music changed again, transitioning into a new song.

Before she knew it, they were moving slowly, nearly chest to chest, in perfect harmony. He spun them off as the group of pairs moved into a circle, gliding across the floor, every step matched by the delicate music.

Wren could've closed her eyes and swore she was flying.

A smile tugged at her mouth, returned on Claudius's face, lighting up his face. "Enjoying yourself?"

She couldn't reply as they swept through movements with every shift in step and flick of her hand feeling like she'd done it before. Hells, she swore it wasn't his magic moving her but her own body. Like it was aware of what to do, just as it did when she was on the cliffs.

Without warning, he drew her out from the formation and into the middle of it, taking several steps back from her. Her breath caught in her throat and her knees trembled, threatening to give out.

Oh, gods.

He was still smiling at her, then bowed suddenly, deeply at the waist, and then rose slowly. The smile had fallen away, staring at her, as though that very gaze bore right down into the depths of her soul. He straightened up and took a step toward her.

The music shifted suddenly as his foot hit the ground.

It was a slower song, deeper, and as he drew to her, he stepped suddenly to the side, hands shooting out—and hers moved out as if they knew. The second they touched she drew forward.

They spun together, drawing closer, then pushing away. A dance between them, a kind of story, unfurled across that glimmering floor. In every breath, he seemed to reach for her, only for her to slip out of his grasp and spin away. He drew to her again. His hands slipped to her waist and suddenly she was up, lifted by him, and her back arched. She looked to the ceiling with its shining gold and glittering chandelier, sparkling dizzyingly before her.

The music grew faster, and he pulled her back down the tips of her shoes barely touching the ground. Their faces were only inches apart. Her heart was racing. She put her hands to his face, as though her body moved without her, commanded by something else. Her feet touched the ground as he let go.

Another change came, and the music became sadder, mournful even as she spun further and further from him. She reached up to the ceiling, twirling on her own. As she slowed, her hands fell back down to her side, and she stopped. He was in front of her again, grasping one of her hands as she dropped back, arching down as his other hand slid to the small of her back. He caught her... as she *knew* he would.

Her gaze was on his, so focused she barely noticed the music bleeding into silence until applause suddenly erupted around them. Blinking, she carefully rose and stepped away from him, her cheeks on fire.

They stood side by side, bowing to the crowd.

As the applause faded away, he held out his arm. But she shook her head. The magic of the dance had fled her and her mind roared with a thousand different thoughts, her heart still racing. She turned to him.

"Do you think that would satisfy her now?" she asked breathlessly. "Because I should go find Lorca now."

The smile remained on his lips but it no longer touched his eyes, and there was a slightly cooler note to his voice as he spoke. "Lorca? That is the name of your lover?"

Heat blossomed on her cheeks, burning the tips of her ears. "He's... I need to find him."

"A shame. I was enjoying your company," he drawled, grinning wolfishly. "I would like to seek your time again."

"For a business arrangement, perhaps?" she replied.

His brow lifted. "You danced with me to get something, didn't you?"

She shrugged. "Does it matter?"

"No, I suppose not. Well, I should let you go find your lover. Until we meet again, Miss Dumare," he said, bowing deeply.

He turned and melted away into the crowd. A sense of sadness squeezed her heart.

Steeling herself, she turned and plunged into the crowd. She kept going until she made it to the side of the room. There she took a reprieve to clear her head, and she pressed her back against the wall.

Her gaze closed for another breath, then opened. Claudius's face was still clear in her mind, his words playing over.

Who the hell is Claudius Delmont?

"Wren?"

The sound of Lorca's voice broke through the tangle of her thoughts. She blinked, dissolving the image of Claudius.

Lorca squeezed through the crowd and stepped out to her. As he drew closer, all thoughts of the prince fell away. She pushed off the wall, moving toward him.

"Have you found Helena?"

He nodded. "She said she would seek us out soon, that she had to speak to some people now."

"Did she say why she wanted us here?" she asked.

"No, but I imagine she'll reveal her intentions tonight," he replied. "Don't suppose you're still interested in setting fire to this place?"

"Don't tempt me," she retorted. "Though I may have found an alternative to Helena."

"That man you were dancing with?" he replied, an edge to his voice.

She glanced at him, seeing the tightness in his shoulders. It was a look that she'd seen in Vaughn before when she'd become friends with Flynn—which had proved unfounded.

"You're jealous," she remarked.

"I'm not jealous. I just don't like the look of him," he replied gruffly. "And I don't like the way he looks at you."

With a smile, she leaned in close. "That's exactly what jealousy sounds like. Don't worry, though. He may be pretty, but that dance was a means to an end. Nothing more." Her stomach rumbled. She stepped back, grinning. "Don't suppose you happened to see where some food was? I haven't eaten since breakfast and I'm starving."

He snorted, breaking the tension, his mouth twitching. "I saw a table. Come, we'll get you some food—can't have a hungry dragon. That's just a disaster waiting to happen."

She looped her arm through his. "The night is young."

Chapter 46

I saw her again, sitting atop an outcrop, her legs dangling over the edge. She looked so young sitting there, so mortal, that it might've been possible to mistake her for one of us. I followed that gaze of hers and found it, watching Adrian as he soared overhead. I wonder if he has ever noticed that the Spirit of the Mountain watches him.

—Excerpt from Litania's diary

WREN HAD NOT set the ballroom on fire—yet.

She stood side by side with Lorca, her feet itching to move forward and join the dance that was playing out across the glittering floor. The music swelled, rising with euphoria, no one faltering. It tugged at her chest, a voice whispering to her to join in. The same that, only moments before, had snarled at her to stay away from Claudius.

The shadowy magic stirred, responding to the chords that quivered through her chest. As though it was being summoned and she, the vessel of this darkness, weakening to the desire. To enter the dance, even though she did not know how to move like that.

All she could do for the moment was watch the dances one after another. She memorized their steps, listening intently to the music. To her surprise, much seemed to follow a similar pattern of steps and spins.

A kindle of daring hope flickered in her heart.

When the music slowed, tapering off into silence, the couples ceased their movements. The dance had ended, but a sense of excitement and agitation still burned through her.

Across the room, the orchestra launched into a new song. Wren grabbed Lorca's hand instinctively, hauling him with her to the line of couples gathering. She spun around, moving one of his hands to her hips.

"Wren?"

"Dance with me," she asked restlessly.

He stared at her, startled. "I didn't know you knew this dance."

"They played this song before. The women take the lead in this one, so follow me," she replied. "All you have to do is trust me."

His hand tightened on her hip as he stepped closer, his earthy scent filling her lungs, calming her racing heart. "Then lead away."

The strings sang out, and the dancers began to move. Wren stepped back, Lorca following. She spun, drawing him with her, and as she let go of his hand, and moved her own to his face. They circled, eyes locked, his hand hovering over her cheek. Fire danced beneath her skin as they stepped back. The women moved to the right, circling each other before Wren was back in front of him.

His hand slid over her hip, luring her back. Every touch burned as they glided across the floor. The ballroom melted away. Only the music filled her ears, guiding every step and shift of her hand.

They drew apart again, the music fading with a breath.

The strings rose again, faster, twining together in a heady rush. Wren surged forward. Lorca's hands took hold of her hip and lifted her. She threw her hands up as the line of women around her did. Her hands fell as Lorca lowered her down, moving to his face, hovering just above his cheeks.

His burning gaze sucked the air right from her lungs. The world spun a little as the melody tapered off. The darkness in her chest purred, as though it hungered and enjoyed the close contact with him. To the heat that raged between them.

"Wren..." His breathless voice, low and thick, stole through her chest, squeezing at her heart.

"Not bad, prince," she teased.

He leaned in close, his breath fanning her lips. "I am no prince, not anymore, little dragon."

"*Little* dragon?" she blurted out, grinning. "Pretty sure when I changed in this room, I was bigger than your form."

His mouth twitched. "But right now, you are smaller than me."

"I can still kick your ass!"

"Oh, I have no doubt," he replied, his eyes glittering with delight. "I am only a mere Dragonir, while *you* are a true dragon. As for your golden form, it is stunning."

She couldn't wipe the smile from her lips or stop herself from leaning in. Nor did she miss the way he leaned in, their lips near touching. Gods, the need to yank him close and crush her lips to his burned through her. Her grip tightened on his tunic, his fingers digging into her hips.

Suddenly, his eyes widened, dropping to her hands. "Wren!"

A feeling like ice rushed down her spine. Her gaze dropped. An icy wave dumped over her. Ribbons of shadowy magic danced through her fingers. Lorca yanked her close, wrapping his arms around her. His lips dropped to the shell of her ear.

"Deep breath, Wren. Try to summon it back in," he instructed.

She sucked in a long gulp of air, focusing on her hands pressed up against his chest. Exhaling, she called the magic in, shoving it back down. A clearness settled in her mind.

"I think I'm good," she whispered.

Nodding, he drew back and followed her gaze, falling to her bare hands. Relief flooded through her. She lifted her gaze, meeting his.

"I need some air."

He slipped his hand to the small of her back and guided her from the middle of the dance floor. Curious eyes tracked their exit, whispers stirring in her wake.

Had anyone seen her hands? Or worse, had she shown her magic during the dance without realizing it?

She was silent as Lorca pushed open the glass doors and led her onto the terrace. Turning to him, her thoughts tangled again.

"What the hell is happening to me?" she whispered, wrapping her arms around her waist. "Gods, how can I save my people when I have no control over these damned abilities?"

"You will master them," replied Lorca.

She scowled. "How the hells do you know that? This darkness inside of me isn't dragon magic! It's... it's something else and I don't know why it's so much easier for me than fire. You can't know that I'll figure it out, that everything will be okay."

His gaze narrowed. "That's where you're wrong."

"Oh?" she challenged. "Pray, tell me how you know everything will be fine. Because I am terrified right now."

He stepped up to her, lifting her chin to meet his gaze. "Because I have watched my world burn and all I know turn to ash. In that darkness, I surrendered to the beast within. Yet even in those moments, I kept the words of my sister with me. The dark will always yield to the light—it may take days, months, years but the darkness will not last. You shattered mine the day you came running to save a dragon you didn't know with a sword and a look of fury in your eyes."

"My people don't have the luxury of years for me to figure this all out," she replied hoarsely.

His thumb circled her cheeks. "True, but you're not alone, and if I must tear this world apart to find you a teacher, then I will do it. The darkness will not conquer you."

As the last of the guests trickled away, the music faded off into absolute silence. Wren watched the exodus from the safety of the garden, her restlessness bleeding away with each one that left. When only a handful remained in the ballroom, clustered around Helena, she turned to Lorca.

He was fast asleep, sitting on a stone bench, his back resting against a tree trunk. There was a peacefulness in his face that she envied. It wasn't the look of a man suffering nightmares—not at that moment, anyway. She didn't want to wake him, but she also didn't want him sleeping outside.

The darkening sky was enough to whisper the approach of rain.

She gently shook his shoulders. His eyes snapped open, momentarily confused.

Blinking several times, he glanced up at her. "Are you okay?"

"The party appears to be over, and it looks like it might rain soon. Figured you might want to sleep inside at least," she murmured and, after a beat, she asked, "how are you? Do you need to change?"

He pushed up from the bench and rolled his shoulders, the muscles in his arms flexing. "I can hold it for another hour or two. It's not uncomfortable right now."

The sound of the lie falling from his lips made her frown. She reached up, cupping his face as she looked into his eyes. Sparks flickered in his eyes.

"You shouldn't force yourself to stay in human form if it's hurting you," she scolded. "I can handle Helena."

His gaze darted behind her, narrowing immediately. Her chest squeezed, sadness brushing her mind. She dropped her hand and turned, not surprised to find the source of the unexpected emotion standing there. Claudius's dark eyes flickered between Lorca and her, his lips a thin line.

"Lady Helena requires your presence," he said stiffly before he stalked back inside.

Once he was out of earshot, Lorca moved to her side, his arms folded across his chest. "I don't know why you wanted to dance with him."

She snorted, gently digging her elbow into his side. "I saw an opportunity. Now, come on, let's go see what the good lady finally wants with us."

They headed inside where Helena awaited them. Claudius stood beside her with his hands clasped behind his back. That stony gaze darted to Wren, lingering there.

Behind him, a man and woman stood with their arms interlocked. They cut a striking pair, with handsome features and shimmering clothes. The man stood a head taller, his lean frame defined by his blue tunic. His snowy hair and alabaster complexion cut a deep contrast to his wife, with her much darker skin and elaborately braided raven-black hair. The pair of them studied Wren and Lorca with curiosity in their eyes.

Helena clasped her hands together. "Right, now that everyone is here, we should continue the conversation in my office."

It was a silent walk to Helena's office. Only once the door closed behind Wren and the others sat down, did Helena speak once more.

"I'm glad you decided to join us tonight, Claudius. I thought you might be too busy once more," she declared.

Claudius stood by the cold fireplace, his arms across his chest. A wicked grin twisted his lips. "Busy, yes, but not enough to keep me away tonight. I found myself filled with a sudden desire to attend."

The other woman snorted. "So, you're not covering your own ass?"

"And what would I be covering my ass from, Amelia?" returned Claudius, his brow lifting.

Amelia leaned forward on her chair, disapproval in her obsidian gaze. "From the attack on the slave caravan exiting the city. I heard from my little birds that it was men hired by you to snatch some slaves."

Wren froze. The very attack that Luce had mentioned. Her gaze snapped to Claudius, whose stony expression didn't even so much as crack.

"And do you share your wife's opinion of me, Othello?" inquired Claudius.

The pale man frowned. "You're not denying it."

"I wouldn't be so foolish as to *steal* slaves—gods above, I'm wealthy enough to buy," said Claudius dismissively, irritation flickering across his face as he turned to Helena. "I'd hate to think you invited me here to be interrogated."

Helena rested a slender hand on her desk. "Oh, I know it wasn't you. An idiot did that attack and that is one of the few things you are not. As for why you are present tonight, why we are all here, is to discuss something important. Well, more of a confession from myself."

"That you're madly in love with me?" teased Claudius.

She rolled her eyes. "I'm not *that* desperate. No, this is about someone I have been in communication with for two years now. Whose goal aligns with all of ours." Pausing, she pulled a drawer open and lifted out an amulet.

At once, the other guests grew still. Othello let out a low whistle; Amelia's eyes widened, her hand reaching instinctively for her husband. Claudius froze, his hands falling to his side.

Wren frowned, glancing at Lorca, but he appeared just as baffled as she was. Shrugging at her, he looked to Helena.

"Could you explain for those of us in the room who don't get the significance of the pendant?" inquired Lorca.

Claudius sneered. "Where are you from to not know *that* jewel?"

"The mountains," Lorca said without missing a beat. "Where people are a little less concerned over material things."

"That material thing is the Danomir Jewel, which went missing eighteen years ago. Rumors persisted that it was smuggled out with the princess, who some believed survived the massacre of her family," explained Claudius before turning to Helena. "So, is the girl alive?"

Helena's gaze flickered about the room. "Yes."

"Is she in the city?" asked Claudius.

Helena inclined her head. "Her current whereabouts are not known to me. You understand the need for a sensitive response. If the Empress were to even catch a hint that her niece was here, we would have an army breathing down our necks. I for one, have little interest in trying to defend the city against the Gray Army—for now."

It wasn't the first time that Wren had heard the Gray Army mentioned. From the uneasy expressions mirrored on Amelia and Othello's faces and the way Claudius stiffened, it was a threat not to be underestimated.

As Helena spoke, Wren glanced at Lorca. Her stomach twisted into knots. She was beginning to see the role they expected her to play. Shadows darkened Lorca's gaze. His hands curled into fists. She reached out, setting her hand over his. Green eyes flickered to her.

When she turned her attention back to Helena, drawing her hand away, she saw Claudius looking at her. His dark gaze met hers, narrowing before darting away.

Suspicion brushed against her mind.

"And that's where we come in, isn't it?"

Helena studied both of them before she deigned to reply, her expression unreadable. "In one respect, yes but this won't be unfair to you. After all, I have received a drawing of Lauri's new purchase. It would only be right to confirm if this girl is one of your people."

Wren's heart raced. Silence bound her tongue as Helena rose, fishing out a folded piece of paper from her desk. Then, with a stony expression, she crossed the room and handed it to Wren. She snatched the drawing from Helena and opened it.

Ellie.

Chapter 47

The Spirit of the Mountain was at her usual spot again, kneeling before the edge of the cliff, where a single red flower grows, somehow defiant against the raging storms that batter the area. I think by now she knows I watch her, though she does not seem to care... I cannot help but wonder, though, why this flower? Why does she visit on the same day every year without fail—and how has this flower survived, untouched?

—Excerpt from Princess Yelena's diary.

NO ONE IN the mansion was aware of Sybilla's arrival. She swept down the shadowy halls like a ghost, silent and unseen. Passing into the east wing where Helena's office dwelled, she slowed. Voices resounded from within, muffled by the door. Magic prickled along her skin.

Even without seeing inside, she could sense Wren and Lorca with Helena. She frowned, wondering who else was in there.

The voices fell silent. A moment later, the door clicked and swung open. Sybilla stepped back through an open door, hiding just out of view.

One by one, the occupants exited. First, a couple with their arms linked, their heads bent together as they whispered. Behind them, a familiar figure strode out, leaving her confused. Lord Delmont had refused every invitation that Helena had sent at Sybilla's insistence—so why had he come tonight? As her frown deepened, watching the strangers go, Lorca headed out. Wren was quick behind him, clutching at a piece of paper in her hands.

"You think it's really her?" she heard Wren ask Lorca.

Lorca's muffled reply was lost as they rounded the corner. The hall fell into silence, Sybilla's thoughts twisting over in her mind. Shaking her head, she slipped out of the room she'd been hiding in and cautiously approached the open door. Warily, she peered inside and saw only Helena sitting there.

Sybilla stepped into the room, closing the door behind her. Helena's gaze snapped up, eyes widening.

"You're here..." Helena's gaze took in Sybilla's new appearance. "You're not wearing the glamor."

"I don't need it anymore," replied Sybilla as she sat down in front of the desk. "How are things progressing?"

"Exactly, according to your instructions," said Helena, sinking into her chair. "I must admit though, Lauri wasn't exactly happy about this plan of yours. Complained the whole time that it was a big risk for her to snatch a slave like that."

"But the girl is in her possession?" clarified Sybilla, leaning back in her chair. "Safe and sound?"

A shadow passed in Helena's gaze. "I can only assume but Lauri's definition of 'safe and sound' is quite different. She will probably put the girl to work—"

Sybilla rubbed her jaw, uneasy. While she'd never met Lauri, the most influential madam of the Pleasure Quarter, Helena had told her how petty the woman could be. Hells, it had been a risk to pick Lauri but the other options hadn't been any better.

"If the situation deteriorates, have the girl killed. At the very least, I will take a vengeful dragon. That can still be a weapon I can use," said Sybilla.

"Are you sure that's wise? What if the dragon girl and the Dragonir realize our hand in all of this?" A note of worry tightened Helena's voice.

It was well beyond the point of turning back. The bed had been made, for better or for worse. She'd simply have to accept the consequences once the ash settled.

"It is under control," said Sybilla. "Any other issues I should be aware of?"

Luckily, Helena didn't seem to need any encouragement to change the topic.

"An attack took place in the city recently. Wren's people were the target, and they snatched two of the slaves. The situation was quickly brought under control and they took the rest of the slaves out of the city. They should be at the temple construction now."

Sybilla straightened up in her chair. She hadn't seen that attack. Schooling her features, she tapped her fingers on the arm of the chair. Such a bold attack in the heart of the city set her nerves on edge.

"Who was behind it?"

"There are a number of families in the city with the power and money. Though, as to why anyone would do it now, I can't say. From what I've got from my spies, the chains were cut on just two slaves and the rest were left. It might've been a matter of time but I doubt it." Helena frowned. "Just who the hell were these people? You said they were just a bunch of peasants who harvested a rare flower."

Sybilla's brow lifted. "I do not know why the attack happened. See if your birds can find out if he was responsible; if he was, this may complicate matters." She glanced out the window at the lightening sky. Sighing, she got up out of the chair and fished out a letter from her pocket. "Here is the last set of instructions. The next time we meet will be when the bells ring out across the city."

Helena plucked the letter from Sybilla's hand, unfurling it quickly.

Her gaze slid down the letter, taking in the list. When she finished, she stood and bowed.

"Consider it done," she intoned.

Sybilla nodded and headed to the door. As she opened it, she half-turned back. "Thank you for your faith in me."

"Of course," murmured Helena. "Long live the true heir."

Chapter 48

Today, I spoke with my brother, but I fear my pleas have gone unheard. He doesn't see the darkness following Litania. He sees only his beloved; a woman whose heart already belongs to a mortal prince she's hiding in a cave close by. I must speak to our mother today before it is too late... Brother, forgive me.

—Excerpt from Princess Yelena's diary.

THE PICTURE OF Ellie stared back at Wren as she braided her hair the next morning. The artist had captured her sister's soft features and wavy blonde hair. If only he hadn't shown how sad she looked, the lost expression tearing at Wren's chest.

Her hand fell, eyes closing shut. *I will get you back, I swear it.*

As her eyes opened, a fiery resolve burst in her chest. Whoever hurt her sister, she'd make them pay. She'd make them all pay.

Standing up, she turned around and took a step—

A vision burst into her mind once more. She stood back in that stone room, cluttered with books. A bloodied sword protruded from her chest, dripping with blood. The metallic stench hung heavily in the air.

Gasping, she staggered forward, shattering the image. Her legs wobbled, then buckled, sending her to her knees. Ragged breaths passed sharply over her lips, blood roaring in her ears. Her heart pounded. Wren shut her eyes, trying to force everything away.

Breathe, Wren. It's not real, she chanted to herself until the stabbing pain receded. *You are stronger than this.*

She pressed her palms into the floor and pushed herself up, biting her tongue as a wave of nausea washed over her. Reaching out, she grabbed hold of the back of a chair and steadied herself.

Forcing even breaths through her mouth, the world cleared. She hurried out, making her way straight to the ballroom. It was the largest room in the house and with its roaring fireplace, was the best place for Lorca to sleep at night.

She pushed open the doors, her heart fluttering in her chest. She swallowed hard as she headed for his sleeping form by the fireplace. Her footsteps tread softly, echoing faintly.

Hearing her, one of his lids lifted; then, seeing her, the other opened, and he raised his head.

Did you get any sleep?

"I was in bed," she replied with a yawn. "That's about as close to sleep as I got. You?"

Yawning, he stretched his long neck, ebony scales glinting in the firelight. *I had my eyes closed. It counts.*

"Of course it counts."

As much as you being in a bed, he returned.

"Think about me a lot in bed, do you?" she ventured, heat flooding her cheeks.

Oh, gods, why did I have to say that?

He snorted and slowly pushed himself up. White light flashed, dimming quickly as he walked to her. Those green pools darkened, his mouth quirking into a faint smile.

"A gentleman never tells."

Her fingers twitched, itching to reach for him. Pressing her hands to her legs, she forced a calm mask on her face. Gods, he must know she liked him well enough and how close she'd gotten to kissing him. Not to mention their dance.

"Shame."

Hells, no, that's not what I wanted to say!

Scowling, she spun around. "I just came to grab you for breakfast if you were feeling hungry!"

Chuckling, he followed her out.

The dining room was set up when they arrived. Platters of food, along with pitchers of juice and water, were laid out on the table. Sunlight streamed in warm and buttery from the tall window at the end of the room. Sitting on one of the chairs was Helena. She gestured for them to join her.

"Good to see you're both up," she remarked. "Dare I ask how you both slept?"

"As much as could be expected," said Wren as she slid into her chair.

Lorca sat down beside her, his thigh brushing hers. She swallowed hard, forcing her attention on Helena. In the corner of her eye, he leaned forward and began heaping food on her plate, then moving to his. All the while, a ghost of a smile remained on his mouth, like he enjoyed the effect he was having on her.

Smug bastard.

She hadn't realized Helena had been talking until she heard her sister's name.

"Ellie will be difficult to procure. Lauri won't be easy to convince. She went through a great deal of effort to buy your sister, so she will be reluctant to sell." Helena paused as she took a sip from her glass before continuing. "I am awaiting some information from a friend of mine today. If needed, we will have some leverage that will aid in convincing her."

"Forgive my ignorance here, but you mentioned an attack in which two of my people were taken? Why can this mysterious party take them and we can't just grab my sister? What am I missing?"

She wasn't being told everything. That much was clear. It felt like she was being backed into a corner, all routes to her sister dwindling. She told herself that so long as she saved Ellie, the personal price was no matter.

Helena's face betrayed only a calmness that Wren envied. "The city was sealed after they moved out your people. Then they undertook raids to find the escaped slaves. We had to move quickly to ensure certain parties kept their mouths *shut* about the incident, lest it got back to the Empress and we had an army breathing down our neck."

Lorca leaned forward. "The theft of *two* slaves would do that?"

"Given the unusual interest the Empress has shown in the enslavement and sale of Wren's people, the theft of two slaves might be enough for her to look more closely at the city—and if she has her reasons why she wanted them all kept together, then she may seek to locate the two slaves," replied Helena tightly. "And the *last* thing we need is the Empress paying too much attention to this city before we're ready."

"Especially given you're about to start a rebellion," stated Wren.

Helena nodded. "Timing is everything. If we play our cards wrong, we will have an army at our gates before we are in a position to respond."

A distraction was in order.

Helena had left, advising she had meetings to attend to and would return later once she had information for them. Rather than wait around, twiddling her fingers, she wanted to burn off some energy. Divert her mind to something she had control over.

Which was working as Wren entered the ballroom ready to spar and found Lorca warming up. Shirtless. She stopped dead.

Gods.

His back was to her as he idly spun his sword, shifting through movements. For the moment, he didn't seem to know she was there, watching him in silent appreciation. Sunlight glinted over his muscles, catching the rivulets of sweat that ran down his back. A faint flush reddened his face, where curls clung to his brow and cheeks. Barefoot, he glided across the polished floor, effortless in every transition.

Slowly, he turned, one arm out wide, arcing the sword as he moved. His gaze focused firmly on the sword, flickered to her. Caught by her gaze, he stilled, heat flickering in that dark expression. There was no surprise, like he knew she'd been watching him. The corner of his mouth tipped up smugly, a glint on his eye.

She drew her sword from her back, his gaze devouring every movement she made. Matching his stare, she stepped forward, idly swinging it. Desire wound tightly within her, ready to be unleashed. Heat pricked down her arms, to her fingertips, hairs lifting as she stepped to the side and went into a training set. The whole time, she kept her focus on him, flicking her head back as she spun, all the time drawing closer. Inch by inch, the air heating up, thickening with hunger.

At the last movement, she spun sharply, arcing the blade, stopping the point inches from his neck. Harsh breaths fell steadily from her lips, filling the space between them. The only sound that either of them dared to make for a moment. A steady heat burned in her arms, right down to her grip on the sword, but she held firm, still as a predator. He was trapped by her gaze, right where she wanted him. Within reach.

"You should stop looking at me like that," he said, his voice hoarse.

She stepped back, suddenly swung her sword idly with one hand, a smile lifting, tugging at her mouth, her gaze sparking coyly. "Like what?"

His gaze darkened. "You're playing a dangerous game."

"I don't know what you're talking about. I just came to spar, to burn off some energy," she replied innocently.

He drew in a deep breath, nostrils flaring. The expanse of his chest sent shivers down her spine. Equally entranced, she tracked every movement he made. From the way that his fingers tightened on his sword, to the draw of his breath and the slight shift in his stance.

"Well, how could I refuse that?"

He burst forward, a momentary blur before he was on her, his sword flashing down. Laughing, she dug her heels in and surged back, parrying off his blows coyly. He stepped sharply to the side, swinging wide. With one hand she brought her sword up, deflecting the blow as she stepped back. The force sent her staggering back, teetering awkwardly.

There was no reprieve as he came at her again, ruthless in his attacks, frustratingly light on his feet. She barely had time to brush off his blows as she searched for an opening. Her chest tightened, like a string being pulled in her heart.

"Surrender," he growled.

Surrender. Taunted another voice at the edge of her mind. *You are nothing. I own you.*

The string snapped. A strange calm flooded her body, rushing down to her hand.

Lorca swung his sword.

She parried the blow, using the momentum to spin behind, and she drove her foot forward into his back. Black energy exploded from her foot.

Lorca went flying. He hit the ground, hard. Cursing, he forced himself up, and she was on him in a flash. His sword met hers as she swung. The clash of metal rang out across the ballroom.

"Cheat," he muttered teasingly.

She winked. "Never said I couldn't use magic."

"Fair point. Try to use your fire now to beat me."

Fire exploded from his hands, rushing up his blade. The heat licked against her cheeks.

She called on her fire, opening herself to the magic burning in her chest, only instead of the flames rushing up, the darkness erupted from her soul. Ribbons of energy flowed from her fingers, surging up her arms. The smoky black magic was hers to command.

Lorca flinched, his grip slackening for a second.

Wren surged forward, leaping for the opening, and hooked her foot around his ankle, yanking back. He fell back. She dropped, ready to pin him when he rolled to the side and swept his foot out. Too slow. She jumped back clearly, tossing her sword to the side.

It clattered away, forgotten as it slid from view.

Lorca pushed up to his feet, frowning before he threw his sword away as well. Flames danced through his fingers, a contrast to the shadows that threaded through hers. A frown dipped his brow.

"Those aren't the flames, Wren."

She tilted her head, a sense of excitement skittering through her mind. "No, but these feel so much better."

"Then let us see whose magic is stronger," he taunted, and burst forward, hurling his fist forward.

Fire flew from his hand. She darted out of the way, throwing a bolt of her own. At the last second, he yanked up his hands, an orb of fire exploding within his hands. The fire caught the orb, the darkness devoured by the flames.

She burst forward, the darkness on her arms rushing to her hands, closing them like a glove. The distance closed; she hurled her energy forward. He dodged, then rushed at her in a flurry of fiery fists.

They danced in a flurry of punches and dodges, neither landing a solid fist. Every step was instinctive as he came at her like someone else was controlling her, making her move in just the right way.

Fire flashed against her own darkness when she threw bolts. Seconds later, fire rushed past her head, narrowly missed.

Behind him, she saw her chance to get him pinned.

She moved quickly, guiding him with her blows and steps. Unaware, he stepped back, every attempt to evade blocked. In a flash, his back hit a pillar. It caught him by surprise and she dove in, pressing up close. A blade forged of her darkness pressed at his throat.

He stilled, his gaze burning on hers. His hands dropped to his side. Ragged breaths drew over his lips. "It seems you've won, though where you learned to move like that, I have no idea."

Truth be told, she did not know either. Only that it had been pure instinct, mere muscle memory from a skill she never remembered learning. It had felt as natural as climbing.

She opened her mouth to speak, but the words failed to come. Unease consumed the calm that had steadied her in the fight only moments before. The darkness retreated into her hands. She stepped back and turned around.

"I... "

His hand shot out, grabbing her wrist gently. "Wren."

She spun around. "Gods, what the hell is wrong with me? First the magic, the visions of the sword impaling me, now *this*?" Her heart thudded loudly. "What *am* I?"

"You're a dragon," he replied, but she didn't miss the note of uncertainty in his voice.

He didn't know what she was.

"Let go of me," she growled.

"You can't run from this, Wren," he replied sharply.

"I'm not running from—"

"Yes, you are."

"I'm just tired!" she exploded. "I hate having so many goddamn questions in my head. So how the hell are you so calm about it!"

His gaze darkened. "You don't think I have questions?"

"We haven't exactly talked about the fact that I remained in my egg for three hundred years before I hatched. Don't you think that's awfully odd? I mean, perhaps there's something wrong with me and that is why I have these powers. Why they are so goddamn easy to use compared to using fire, like a real dragon!"

A shadow of anger flickered in his eyes. Like she'd pushed him too far.

"You *are* a real dragon," he argued, letting go of her wrist. "Now your parents may have dabbled in some dark magic to produce you, given they could not have any eggs before you. I don't know. Maybe it's something else. What I know is that you are a dragon and I'm right here, with you, always. Wren, I—"

The ballroom doors swung open. Whatever Lorca had been about to say died, his gaze shuttering, revealing nothing to her.

Helena strode in, stopping a few feet away with an unreadable expression as she studied the pair of them. Wren could feel that curious gaze inspect everything about her, from the fury in her eyes to how close she and Lorca stood.

"Am I interrupting anything?" she asked.

"No," said Wren, turning to Helena. She needed space from Lorca before she said anything else to him. "I didn't expect you back this early."

Surprise lifted Helena's brow. "Early? I've been gone for hours." She glanced between Wren and Lorca again. "What happened?"

Lorca strode to Wren's side. "Nothing. What did you find?"

Helena didn't answer immediately, like his response bothered her. Her mouth tightened fractionally. After a pause, she blinked, that unnerving calm mask sliding on, and closed the distance to Wren, handing over a letter.

"Two things, the bill of sale for your people, which states how many were sold... and a way to get your sister back. Some friends of mine have agreed to help us," announced Helena.

Heart racing, Wren snatched the bill from Helena and read the contents. Her gaze locked on the number noted at the bottom before she looked up sharply.

"So few?"

"From what I learned, they killed any they deemed not worth selling. I'm sorry, Wren. One hundred and seventy are all that's left."

Wren's knees buckled, and she hit the floor.

Chapter 49

Today the Spirit of the Mountain was alone once more as she stood before the red flower... and for the first time, tears flowed freely. Her knees buckled, and she sank down, throwing her head into her hands as she screamed... and as that terrible sound tore from her lips, the sky boomed with thunder.

—Excerpt from Princess Yelena's diary.

THE PALACE WAS far too quiet for Aziah's liking as she hurried to her chambers. Guards stood silent at their posts, their eyes steady, hands resting on the hilts of their swords. Shadows crowded every nook and crevice, offering little to dispel her darkening thoughts. Normally, she liked the dark and silence, but at that moment, it chafed at her nerves. Her jaw was clenched, teeth aching, as she tried to keep her thoughts from Gabriel.

She'd been exposed. She knew that. Somehow, somewhere, she'd been found out. Why hadn't she been dragged before the empress yet? What was Alexandria waiting for? She considered that the spymaster maybe hadn't told the empress yet. It suited his style. He was planning something big, his moment to throw her to the fire and watch her burn.

That showy shit was his style.

A few glanced at her as she swept past, watching her until she was out of view. Slaves hurried about, looking down. Everywhere she looked, everyone was tense, the air crackling.

By the time she made it back to her door, she froze. It was slightly ajar. A thin band of moonlight spilled through and across the hall, whilst a murmuring breeze brushed her cheek. She'd left her window ajar, preferring the humid sea air at night. It usually calmed her but, at that moment, it chilled her to the bone. Ice trickled down her spine as she crept forward, gingerly pushing it open enough to slip in.

A hand shot out, yanking her in. A glint of silver flashed in the corner of her vision. Her hand snapped up, grabbing the attacker's collar; spinning, she flipped them over her shoulder and drove them to the ground. She yanked out her dagger and pressed it to their throat.

The man stilled, staring up at her, breathing hard.

"Who sent you?" she snarled.

He spat in her face. "Traitor!"

Dammit.

She snapped her wrist, cleaving the dagger across his throat to a bloody smile. Hot blood sprayed, the coppery drops splashing her lips. The man went limp, his lifeless eyes staring up, a lock of shock frozen on his face.

The fool gave her all the information she needed in a single word.

Scowling, she pushed up to her feet, looking about the mess that was in her room, and wiped her face with the back of her hand. Scattered papers across the floor, chests tipped over. Clothes and what little items she'd collected from missions over the years were spread over the floor. It didn't take an idiot to realize what had happened.

They were looking for something but what? What in this room had damned her?

Her heart froze. For a second, she couldn't move or think.

Gabriel.

She was across the room, dropping down by her bed, and stopped dead. Her bed had been shoved back, a stone lifted from the floor, revealing a hidden space. Empty.

No.

No.

Spirits, no, not him, please not him.

Her heart raced hard in her chest, the blood pounding. Dread sunk into her gut like a knife. It ripped every rational thought and destroyed years of training in a single breath. Ancient pleas bubbled up her throat, spilling from her lips. To gods and spirits alike, she prayed, and jumped up, spinning away from the bed.

Please tell me Gabriel that you didn't wait for me.

Aziah threw her hand out, summoning a portal. The bright sphere flashed.

Without looking back, she sprinted through, latching onto her mate bond. Her soul cleaved in two. She couldn't lose him, not after she'd just got him back and he'd forgiven her. They had plans, hopes, time to heal what she'd destroyed. Gods, why had she been so damn foolish?

Please, let me not be too late, she prayed as the portal spirited her away.

The meadow around Gabriel's cottage materialized around her. Aziah stopped dead. A wave of thick smoke and heat slammed into her. Her knees buckled. She hit the ground, a broken scream tearing free. All thoughts and focus on the mate bond fell away.

The cottage was burning.

Aziah didn't stop screaming as her magic exploded from her and the world flashed white.

Chapter 50

The true depth of the Spirit's rage is terrifying. I fear the day it descends upon us all.

—Excerpt from Queen Evanya's diary.

BE READY TO *go by sunset.*

Wren eyed the letter, with its neatly written message, as she slipped on the red dress that had accompanied it. As the silken material settled around her body, she turned and strode to the bedroom door. Halfway across the room, passing by the mirror hung on the wall, she glimpsed a woman's blood-splattered face staring back at her.

Startled, she spun around. This time, her reflection stared back.

That had been... surely not... she thought, shaking her head. *Focus. My priority is Ellie.*

And with that thought, she hurried out of the room.

Downstairs in the foyer, Lorca and Helena were talking, oblivious to her arrival until she was halfway down the stairs.

"Helena—" Lorca broke off suddenly and looked up.

She grabbed hold of the railing, feeling his gaze as he drank her in, the heat coiling low in her gut. When he met her eyes, she forced herself to keep moving down until she stood before them both. A beat of silence followed. Words bubbled up, tangling at her lips. There was...gods, she had so much to tell him.

Because at that moment, she knew. This was the man who had followed her far from all he knew, across a land neither of them knew, faced dangers without question, trusted her with ease. This man she...

No. There would be time later for the words.

She headed to him, stifling the traitorous thump of her heart.

"Everything ready?" she asked, glancing at Helena.

"My friends are outside waiting for us," announced Helena. "Are you ready?"

Wren nodded. For her sister, she had to be. "Let's go."

As she trailed behind Helena on her horse, shadowed by two men and a woman at the rear of the group, her stomach was in knots. The dark magic stirred restlessly the deeper they moved into the city. Like it was hungry, demanding to be fed.

Tightening her grip, she stared ahead down the darkening street. Hooves clattered quietly along the cobblestone. The fading light left shadows thickening along the narrow and empty streets. With only time on her hand, her mind wondered. Once she had Ellie, she had to get away from Helena.

Find an alternative to get her people free rather than become entangled in a fight she didn't fully understand. Helena spun a fine enough story of rebellion, of removing an evil leader. It would've been easy enough to believe, were it not for the blatant manipulation to use Wren and Lorca in the fight.

Of course, that she'd been candid about using them had struck Wren as odd. She was missing a piece of the puzzle. One that would make the situation become clearer.

After tonight, she wanted to see Claudius again, to figure out if he was a viable alternative.

In the corner of her eye, Lorca rode on silently. His fingers curled tightly around his reins, an air of tension about him. She doubted he'd be interested in dealing with Claudius, but their options were few at the moment. Unless they found another way to free her village and get them back to the mountains, they had to play it cautiously for the moment.

His nostrils flared. "We're getting close."

She smelled it; the touch of perfume and ale in the air, of pleasure, and an undertone of something rotting. Her blood heated. This was not where her sister belonged. If any harm had come to Ellie... Her nails dug into her palms, blood prickling. The metallic note nudged her nose.

Releasing her hands, she wiped her palms clean on the saddle.

Guided by a thin sliver of moonlight, they arrived at one of the internal gates. A painted black flower encircled by a collar marked a panel.

Four guards stood vigil as they approached, dipping their heads to Helena as she rode past. She returned with a slight bow, then trotted on. Wren wondered if these men were also part of her rebellion or if they'd been paid off? Just how much of this city did Helena control?

No sooner had they entered the quarter than had Helena edged her horse down a side street. The narrow squeeze forced them to fall into a single line.

Helena suddenly stopped and dismounted. The men swung down, taking up position behind Helena. Their hands rested on the pommels of their swords. The woman followed suit, falling in behind Helena, though she bore no sword. Instead, her pale hands remained clasped behind her back.

As Wren got down, her hand fell instinctively to a belt that cinched around her waist, holding the two daggers given to her. With simple silk-wrapped sheaths, matching the tone of the dress, they looked almost ornamental. She felt naked without her sword, but Helena had been firm on leaving it behind.

She glanced at Lorca as he swung down. Abandoning his horse, he moved to her side, eyeing the three strangers who had said nothing on the ride. Wren knew their role in the plan, but that offered little comfort. These folks were strangers to her.

Helena turned to them. "Is everyone happy with their roles and understands what they must do?"

What little plan we talked of during the ride, yes. Wren wanted to ask more questions but was shut down every time. Have faith. *Trust her,* Helena had said.

When a murmuring of 'yes' chimed through the small group, she nodded curtly, spinning around. One by one, everyone trailed after her, with Wren at the rear with Lorca behind her.

They descended through a series of narrow winding streets, void of people and thick with shadows. Eventually, the first hint of life reached them. Shrieking laughter, singing, raucous chatter seemed to promise something fairly innocent.

Every so often, a sob or panicked scream pierced the veil of levity, only to be rapidly swallowed up. Wren tried not to think about what the silence meant for whoever had cried out.

The fetid stench of sour beer drifted on the soft breeze that snaked through the streets, mingling with notes of perfume and stale water. The smell of the Pleasure Quarter, Wren realized, as they stepped onto a busy street. It was as though they stepped into a whole new world, the transition bright and jarring.

It was nothing like what she had seen during the day.

The brothels and taverns ran the length of the widened street, brightly lit with a myriad of torches hung from wooden posts and off buildings. Several brothels had a small decking out the front, where patrons sat with collared slaves draped over them. In each of them, the front doors opened and shut, in rapid succession. Slaves rushed in and out, their arms laden with drinks and platters of food.

The dark energy inside of her stirred at the sight of it all, growling softly.

"I don't like this," muttered the man just behind Helena, as the small group waded through the busy street.

Helena's hawkish gaze surveyed the crowd. "Don't balk now. Tonight is important, so keep your head."

There was a strange weight to those words, a warning tone that unsettled Wren.

The man opened his mouth to argue, but a look from his friend silenced it. A warning expression on his face.

After passing numerous brothels, they slowed and stopped. This one stood out from the others. The painted walls seemed fresh, the wood free of rot and cracks. Windows cleaned to a shine hinted at the warmth and pleasure offered within. Every so often, the flash of movement as a girl swept past caught Wren's eyes. One she swore had blonde hair.

Ellie?

The girl stopped by the window; the side of her face revealed. Her heart slammed sharply against her ribs. It wasn't her sister.

"Right, everyone, take your positions. Wren, Fox, you're with me," declared Helena. "The rest of you, wait for my signal." She glanced at Lorca. "You're ready? Everything will move quickly once we see the signal."

Lorca appeared unfazed by the way Helena's companions watched him and gave a steely nod. "Consider it done."

With sufficient assurances made, the group split in two. Helena and the fae woman, Fox, moved toward the entrance of the brothel. Wren went to follow when Lorca grabbed her hand, spinning her around back to him.

In the brightly lit street, he held her for a moment. A thousand unsaid things raged between them, at her lips, and by his stormy expression, his too. She tightened her grip on him, trying to muster the courage. Even as she told herself that she'd tell him how she felt later, worry crowded her mind. Her breath hitched. Spirits, she couldn't get the damn words out. Why was it so hard?

"Be safe," he growled, his gaze burning.

There was so much she wanted to say, but her tongue remained in knots. All she could manage was a nod, even as her mind screamed for her to tell him. Kiss him. Make sure he knew.

Reluctantly, he let go and stepped back.

The loss hollowed out her chest.

She watched as he melted away into the crowd with the two men.

Only the faint hint of his earthly smell lingered... and even that soon faded away. They'd be reunited soon enough.

"Wren, come on," urged Helena. "We shouldn't waste time."

A sense of worry tightened in her chest. She reminded herself everything would be okay. Lorca would be fine, upholding his end of the mission and she would whisk Ellie away from this shit hole.

As she ascended the steps of the brothel, shadowing Helena and Fox, a sharp stab of pain lanced through her heart. Her magic flared down her hands. Slamming her eyes shut, she willed the magic back down, refusing to expose herself just yet.

Slowly, she released a shaky breath and opened her eyes.

They stopped in the brothel's foyer. Directly in front, a narrow staircase spiraled up to the floor above.

On either side of the large open doorway were sprawling front rooms, full of collared men and women lounging on cushions, drinking. A haze of fragrant smoke swirled above them. Lanterns hung from the ceiling, both in the rooms and right above Wren with a crisp white glow. It wasn't fire.

It was magic. The hum of it brushed against her skin, lifting the hairs on her arms.

A wave of warmth washed over her, and the pain dimmed a little more. The darkness paced inside of her, leaving her skin clammy and her hands twitching.

Something isn't right.

From the stairs, a striking dark-haired woman, clad in a silk robe. Her naked arms were etched with a strange swirling black pattern. She stopped before Helena, one manicured brow lifting faintly. A feline smile lifted from her rouged mouth.

"I never thought I'd see the day you'd grace my establishment," mused the woman. "The high and mighty Helena, who once declared this kind of pleasure was beneath you."

Lauri, concluded Wren, *the powerful madam of the Pleasure Quarter.*

Helena stiffened. "I came to discuss a business proposition—one I would like to do in private."

Deigning to acknowledge that Helena wasn't alone, Lauri's gaze slid curiously over Fox and Wren, then back to Helena. "Will your friends be joining us?"

"Of course. Now, about somewhere private for us to discuss?"

Lauri gave a curt nod and spun around, gliding to the stairs. "Follow me."

They followed her up the narrow stairs for three floors before they stepped out into the long hallway. The many doors on either side had a lantern hanging above each one, and large locks keeping them shut.

They weren't there to keep people out.

She wrenched her gaze away and hurried after the others. At the end of the hall, they came to an open door. Lauri stood just inside, waiting until everyone was in before she shut it behind Wren.

The room itself was spacious, with a large fireplace to one side and a window just off that. They were high enough up that Wren could see over the roofs of several buildings, glowing silver in the moonlight. She drew her attention back to the room, to the luxurious furnishings. Paintings of naked men and women, lounging in vibrant parties, adorned the wall.

A curious sweet smell hung in the air, like a kind of fruit Wren swore she'd smelled before. It stirred a strange, almost nostalgic yearning through her. She blinked, realizing the others were taking seats in the plush chairs by the fire.

A lantern kindled to life in the middle of the ceiling, chasing the shadows from the room.

"Now, what's this proposition?" Lauri inquired, reclining back in her chair, her gaze flickering between the three of them. "I'm a busy woman."

Helena leaned forward. "Actually, this isn't for me. I said that for the sake of any prying eyes. My friend here is from the northern city of Caldor. She's been—"

"I can speak for myself," cut in Wren. "My name is Lady Nimue Castamere, of house Castamere. I'm here on business, purchasing slaves for members of my family. I have fulfilled all the needs aside from one, which is why I am here."

The title meant nothing to Wren, but Helena had informed her it was one that bore weight. The Castamere family was powerful but reclusive in the northwest. As for the name, it was one Wren picked. It was the name of a girl from a story her father used to tell her.

Back when he bothered to tell stories at all.

As Lauri leaned back, considering the speech carefully, she studied Wren through narrowed eyes. "And what exactly are you after?"

"My brother has *very* specific tastes. A lover scorned him, and now takes great delight in toying with slaves that look like her. Unfortunately, he gets in quite a disdainful mood when he doesn't have a toy. The last girl only lasted a few weeks before she threw herself off a tower. Tragic, really." Wren sighed dramatically as she reached into the folds of her cloak.

From it, she took out the sketch of Ellie. They had changed enough that it looked only a little like her sister. Hopefully, it was what Lauri would need to bring Ellie out. Pausing for a moment to admire it, she then slowly handed it over.

Lauri snatched the picture, eyeing it for a moment before rising sharply. She strode out of the room, shutting the door behind her.

Wren's heart thumped rapidly in her chest, a beast desperate to escape. Her stomach contracted into a tiny ball. Soon, she'd see her sister, and that was the only thing that kept her from doing anything rash.

Much to her dismay, Helena stared at the crackling fire, her face impassive, guarded in the amber glow. If she was even remotely nervous she gave no sign. Even Fox, who rose from her seat and moved to the window, showed only an air of calmness.

The silence in the room was maddening, making the seconds tick by in agonizing slowness. She wrapped her arms around her waist, digging her fingers in to stop them from twitching.

Finally, the door opened again. Lauri swept in and returned to her seat.

"I might have something. She's new, though, and has only been working for a week now. If you're after someone a bit more *experienced*, then I can make some inquiries at my other establishments."

Wren snorted. "Honestly, I don't much care if she's been with a thousand men or none. I just need a girl that looks close enough."

Lauri raised a hand and snapped a finger. The door opened again, and a girl staggered in. She was pale and thin, wearing a revealing white silk dress. Long blonde hair hung in loose curls down her back.

There was no mistaking who it was.

Ellie.

Blood roared in Wren's ears, her heart slamming against her ribs, as she stared as her sister approached the fire.

It took all she had not to run to Ellie, drag her sister in her arms. Her mouth felt like it was full of ash as she tried to maintain a look of critical interest as if inspecting a horse or a piece of equipment.

Ellie kept her eyes to the floor, so she didn't register her sister's presence. She looked broken, devoid of emotion. The fire had been extinguished from Ellie's eyes.

I'll save you, Ellie, and I'll make them pay. I'm going to make them all pay.

"So, does this interest you?"

Lauri's voice dragged Wren's attention from her sister. The words lodged in her throat. A scream threatened. Her hands burned, the darkness burning to come out.

"I—"

Helena burst forward out of her seat. There was a flash of silver in her hand. Lauri threw her hands up, but it was no use as Helena drove a knife into her throat. Ellie blinked as if finally returning to the mortal world.

That's when she screamed.

Wren jumped to her feet, anger exploding through her control. "What the hell Helena? That wasn't part of the plan!"

Helena spun around, drenched in blood, still holding the knife. A chilling calm on her face. "It was part of mine."

Chapter 5 1

The dragons grow ever restless. They haven't spoken to us in weeks now and hunt further afield, refusing the company of any Dragonir. I hear the whispers at court. Our end is approaching, but I will not yield to this darkness. I will find a way.

—Excerpt from Princess Yelena's diary

"WHAT IN THE seven hells do you mean *your* plan?" hissed Wren, stalking forward. "Since when was killing her part of the plan?"

Before she could get her hands around Helena's neck, Fox stepped in front, ready to defend her mistress. A warning flashed in Fox's golden eyes, daring her to get past her. Helena lifted a brow, looking amused by

Wren's fury. It made her want to tear the woman's throat out all the more.

"We can discuss the details later, but right now I advise we leave," replied Helena. "You should deal with your sister."

Wren's gaze snapped to her sister, who now stood silently in the corner. Her blue eyes pooled with unshed tears. As Wren rushed to her, Ellie scrambled back into the corner, dropping to the floor. She curled away, trying to make herself as small as possible.

Stopping dead, dread coiled tight within Wren's gut. "Ellie?"

"You're not real!" whispered Ellie.

"I'm real, Ellie! I'm here!" she kneeled, holding a hand out. Tentatively, she inched closer.

Ellie couldn't move any further away, breaking Wren's heart with every flinch. As her hand brushed Ellie's trembling one, the shuddering finally stopped.

The silence in the room was deafening as Ellie's head turned slightly. "Wren?"

Tears burned her eyes. All she could do was nod and squeeze her sister's hand in silent reassurance. Ellie slowly uncurled herself, turning cautiously to Wren.

Finally, the words moved to Wren's lips. "I'm sorry I'm late."

Ellie's mouth opened, then shut, silent as she looked Wren up and down. "You're here... you're really here."

Wren took her chance and surged forward, wrapping her arms around her sister. Ellie stiffened, and through their embrace, Wren could feel the rapid thump of her panicked heartbeat, while fury kindled within her own. A raging inferno roared in her chest, heat spilling out across her limbs. Even the darkness answered the call of her anger. Both halves were in agreement, for the moment at least.

Lauri was damn lucky she was already dead.

"Let's get you out of here," Wren whispered to her sister's ear.

Ellie nodded shakily and didn't fight as Wren pulled her up. One arm snaked around that slender waist, refusing to let go of her sister. Only hell would tear them apart again.

Helena turned to Fox. "Send the signal. It's time."

Wren felt the blood drain away. Lorca. In the original plan, he'd been the Fox nodded, spinning to the window, and, without hesitating, drove her fist through it. Glass shattered as she leaned out and raised her hand. White light exploded from her hands, bursting up into the sky.

"Time to go," declared Helena, turning to the door.

As she reached for it, someone knocked at the door.

Ellie stiffened but didn't fight as Wren moved in front.

"Wren?" whispered Ellie, terrified.

Ignoring her sister, she focused on the door and held up her hands. The fury stoked the darkness within, summoning it effortlessly to her fingers. Tonight, was for the beast pacing within, hungry for revenge. A new thought rose to her mind, cold as death.

I will kill them all.

Another knock came again, harder, each blow sharp against the wood.

"Lauri? Is everything alright?" A man's muffled voice came through the door.

Helena held out a hand to Fox, gesturing for her to take a position on the other side of the door. Then she drew her two daggers out.

The door finally cracked open, and a figure stepped into the room. He never stood a chance. Energy exploded, slamming into him, sending him flying back through the doorway. A resounding crash followed as he hit the wall.

Shouts erupted in the hallway with footsteps rushing off. Fox rushed out, light flashing. Helena strode to the door when a man barged through, slamming into her. The daggers went flying, clattering to the ground.

They came together in a tangle of blows. Wren dived forward, reaching for the dagger. Scooping it up, she lunged at the man. He turned at the last second, helpless, as she drove the blade deep into his heart. He staggered back, falling to the ground. She yanked the blade out, driving it in again and again.

Hot blood sprayed. But she didn't stop until he finally stopped moving and a hand settled on her shoulder. Finally looking up, she met Helena's gaze.

"He's dead."

Looking down, she saw his chest shredded to ribbons. She stared, breathing hard. The viciousness of his death made something inside of her howl in delight. Blood glistened on her hands, warm and sticky, but she didn't give a damn.

With monstrous delight, she only managed a single word as she pushed up to her feet. "Good."

He lay on the ground with blood pooling around him.

"Wren?" whispered Ellie, horror choking her voice.

The terrified look in those blue eyes sent ice rushing down Wren's spine. Suddenly, the bloodlust fled, leaving only a shaky uneasiness churning her insides. She'd just murdered a man...and she hadn't even flinched, or even felt guilty. It had been terrifyingly instinctive and easy, almost like her first time climbing.

"I will do whatever I must to keep you safe. I won't lose you again," said Wren, holding out her bloodied hand, praying her sister wouldn't reject her. "But know that I will never harm you. You know that, right?"

Ellie hesitated, biting her lip. Finally, to Wren's surprise, she reached out and took the offered hand. Even as she trembled, she didn't let go. Perhaps in a city of monsters, Wren was still the least frightening thing. The lesser of two evils.

I'm going to destroy every person who hurt my sister.

A second later, Fox came in, her dress splattered with blood. She shook her head grimly.

"One got away, and I heard another run off before. We should head off."

Helena nodded, hurrying out first, shadowed quickly by Fox. Wren behind them, holding onto Ellie as if her life depended on it.

Wren kept close to Helena as they left the office, hurrying back down the stairs to the ground floor. Fox broke off, moving to the front door, and set her palms against it. The wood glowed beneath her touch.

In the front room just off the foyer, all the slaves that she had spied on entry, huddled together. Their wide, cautious eyes fixed on Helena.

"Now what?" asked Wren, leaving her sister to sit on the stairs.

Turning to her, Helena opened her mouth to speak when an explosion thundered in the air. There was a flash of blinding light against the door, the force making the earth tremble beneath her feet.

Wren staggered back, catching herself quickly against the wall, and straightened herself up. Her gaze snapped to Helena. The woman held herself against the wall, eyeing the front door. Tracking her gaze, Wren realized what Fox had done. She'd created a barrier, keeping the outside forces away for the moment.

"Helena," growled Wren. "I thought the purpose of the plan was to ensure we didn't create a mess in this city and wreck your..."

Wren stopped as she realized the truth of what was happening. Helena stared back at her, unflinching. Gods, it was like she didn't give a damn that Wren knew she'd played her for a goddamned fool.

"This rebellion is more important than your people. It's unfair, I know, but it's true," Helena replied. "I will get your sister to safety and I will uphold my promise."

"We'll see," said Wren.

As Ellie let out a soft moan, Wren's anger dimmed for the moment. If she killed Helena out of spite, then she risked endangering her sister's escape. Despite knowing she was simply being used, she had to follow along.

For the moment.

"Helena?" A woman from behind Wren called out tentatively.

Spinning around, she saw a young slave woman standing before her, holding up a key. Her pale eyes went straight past Wren to Helena.

"We're good to go?" asked Helena, appearing at Wren's side.

Oh, I really want to put my dagger in your neck right now.

"Yes, come with me," said the girl, gesturing for them to follow.

Reluctantly, Wren grabbed her sister and followed Helena from the room and down a narrow hall. Fox followed, making Wren feel uneasy.

They stopped at a door at the end of the hallway. The slave girl used her key and jammed it into the lock, looking nervously around. Then after some frantic twisting, she shoved it open with her shoulder and stepped through. Holding the door open for them, to reveal a narrow staircase that led into darkness.

The second Helena descended, a lantern flickered to life above her, and as the group continued down, more lit to guide their way. The girl didn't join them, instead she headed back through the door. Before she shut it, she met Wren's gaze through the gap.

The girl gave a steely nod, pulling the door to and locking it with a resounding click.

Wren turned away, holding firm to her sister.

At the bottom of the staircase was a tunnel that ran off into the darkness in two directions. Helena didn't hesitate and headed off to the left.

Wren bit her tongue, trying to hold back the questions rising in her. This underground wasn't part of the plan.

They moved swiftly along the tunnel, with the lanterns remaining lit only enough for them to pass before sputtering out in their wake. The stale air, stinking of something foul and festering from an unseen source, filled Wren's lungs. The taste was sour on her tongue, and yet it carried a strangely familiar tone.

It was *soothing*.

When they rounded a corner, the tunnel widened and a series of cells with black metal bars flanked them. Each had a single torch suspended outside. As they passed the first, Wren stopped, an icy sensation rushing down her spine.

The dark energy inside of her flared like an explosion. Her breath hitched sharply as, one by one, the demons crept forward and stared at her from behind the bars. Far larger than wolves, their eyes glowed like burning coals and they displayed rows of sharp teeth in drooling mouths. They oozed with demon essence, their low growls slicing straight into her soul.

She wasn't afraid of them, but she could feel their presence nudging her magic. They watched her closely as she passed.

"What are they?" whispered Ellie, clutching at Wren's arm.

"Monsters."

"Demons," corrected Wren, as if there was a difference. She wasn't sure why she needed to make the distinction as if there was one at all.

Fox whispered something under her breath but didn't speak again.

"They won't harm us," said Wren.

Ellie's grip tightened. "How can you be sure?"

How indeed.

The crooning voice in her mind, the one that spoke from the demonic magic within her, whispered that the demons weren't her enemy. She wasn't afraid of them, not like she'd been with the demon wolf back in the mountains.

She squeezed Ellie's hand. "I promise I'll keep you safe."

The sounds of approaching footsteps grabbed her attention. At least half a dozen of them, she guessed. Fox might be able to take down some, and Wren would fight with all she had. But the tunnel was narrow and the chance of her sister getting hurt was high.

Helena spun around, her confidence momentarily fracturing, drawing Wren's focus. "They broke through the enchantment. How did they do that so fast?"

Fox cursed. "You know what that means."

Wren stepped forward. "What? Who is coming?"

"Alexandria must've sent her squad of assassins," explained Helena. "Their dark magic is powerful. It's only the way those wards could've been broken."

"They might've broken the enchantment but they'll try and avoid coming down here. My guess is they sent soldiers first," said Fox. "This tunnel is going to make fighting hard."

Wren glanced down at her sister's trembling form. She hadn't come so far just to see her sister killed in a fight she had no business in.

For her sister, she would surrender to the monster within. For her sister, she would kill them all.

She turned to Helena. "Take my sister and get her to safety."

Helena frowned. "What will you do?"

"I'll buy you some time and meet you back at the mansion after this is all done. Keep your promise and save my sister," urged Wren. "If your word means anything, *keep your damn promise.*"

After a beat, Helena nodded, reaching out to take hold of Ellie. Her sister shrank back, lifting her frightened gaze to Wren.

"You're leaving me again?"

Wren pulled her sister into her arms, savoring the moment. "I am keeping you safe. We won't be parted for long, Ellie. I will find you. I will *always* find you."

She drew back and stepped out of reach. Fox moved in and took hold of Ellie's arms, and together with Helena, they dragged her off. Ellie struggled, fighting to break free, but didn't have the strength.

Tears threatened Wren as she forced herself to turn her back on her sister. She stared into the dimly lit passage, listening as the footsteps drew closer. Closing her eyes, she reached for the darkness inside of her.

For my sister.

Chapter 52

My brother is off flying again. I ask him where he ventures off to, but he is evasive. There is something out there in the mountains calling to him. I know it. I only wish he would reveal to me what has him so twisted up.

—Excerpt from Princess Yelena's diary

HE'S MY SON.

The words of Wren's father boomed like cracks of thunder in Flynn's mind. As he paced the opulent room that they had placed Mira in to recover, he dissected the conversation between Alaric and Titania. *No*, not Alaric—*Atlas*. That's what she'd called him, her eyes burning with familiarity and desperation. She'd come for him, not for Flynn or anyone in the village.

Spirits, the only reason Mira was alive was because Atlas had insisted that she take him. There was no way he'd leave Mira behind. It would've been a death sentence. She was like a sister to him. They'd been attached at the hip as small kids, then close friends at the climbing school. As they got older, he suspected she'd developed feelings for him. It lasted only a few months, then her mood changed, and he wondered if she'd found out that he preferred something different in bed.

If she knew, she never treated him any different.

So, he'd been so happy when Wren had picked her for the team.

Pausing in the middle of the room, he glanced at her sleeping in the bed. Healers had come in hours before, giving her some medicine before slipping back out. Since then, her breathing had grown steadier, her skin no longer flushed.

A flicker of hope eased his rattled nerves.

As he moved toward the bed, the door cracked open. A chill flooded the room. Turning sharply, he dashed in front of Mira, standing in the way of an attacker. A man stood in the doorway, clad in a fine green tunic. His dark eyes studied Flynn, his expression unreadable.

For a moment, the man said nothing, then he stepped into the room and shut the door behind him. He looked again at Flynn with a dark, piercing gaze. "My men informed me that Atlas insisted Titania take you both. They didn't hear her reasoning."

The unspoken question cleaved the air like a knife. *Why had she saved the pair of you?*

Flynn shifted uneasily. This was a man who radiated power. The kind you didn't mess with. Problem was, he didn't really understand why being 'Atlas's' son meant he was saved when the others were left behind.

He swallowed a lump in his throat. "I'll tell you what I heard but first, who are you? And where are we?"

The man's face pinched in frustration, his jaw twitching. "You humans really are a strange bunch. You're always so hung up on names, but if you are so desperate, my name is Claudius Delmont. This is my mansion. The woman who led the mission to collect a mutual friend is Titania."

Flynn didn't miss that the man didn't ask after his friend. Either he knew where she had ended up or he didn't give a damn.

"I always knew him as Alaric but you call him Atlas. Is that his real name?"

Claudius nodded, straightening up. His hands clasped behind his back. "Why was he so insistent on your rescue?"

He's my son. The words caught in Flynn's mouth. He tried to work them to his lips, but he couldn't. It made no sense. Alaric had never shown any paternal interest in Flynn. Hells, their interactions had been casual but not common. Then there was the very obvious fact that they bore no physical resemblance.

"He said... "

"Yes? He said what?" Claudius bit out. "What makes you so damn special? Or is it the girl?"

The second Claudius started to move, Flynn intercepted. "He said I was his son."

Claudius froze, the color rushing from his face. The steely resolve crumbled, betraying a startled man. He became a statue. Then, without warning, he closed the distance to Flynn. Mere inches separated them. Those dark eyes bore down into his. A hand shot out, grabbing Flynn by the throat.

"What did you say?" he snarled, leaning in close.

Flynn's hands shot up, trying to tear himself free. It was useless against the iron grip, choking off the air. "He—"

"*Choose your next words carefully human,*" sneered Claudius, lifting him as if he weighed nothing at all.

Human? Just what the hell was this guy? He held Flynn as if weighed nothing and wasn't even breaking a sweat. As he dangled there, staring into the empty abyss of that cold fury, fear rushed down his spine.

"He said I was his son."

The man let go. Flynn hit the ground, pain bursting in his knees. He rubbed his throat, trying to work the air back into his lungs. All the while Claudius watched him with barely contained disdain.

"*You?* That's impossible. We can't have children," he said vehemently.

Flynn looked up. "I don't know anything about being his son. He didn't raise me but he sure as hell had two daughters—Ellie and Wren."

C.M. Quinn

Silence arrested Claudius, a violent battle of emotions playing out in his eyes. As his hands opened and shut into tight fists, he remained silent. Minutes passed before he turned to the door.

"Come with me," he commanded.

"I'm not leaving Mira," replied Flynn, pushing himself up.

Claudius stopped at the door, holding the frame with white knuckles. "Your friend will be fine. She'll sleep for several hours. Which means you can come with me."

He made no move to follow. "And go where?"

Finally, Claudius turned around. "I want to see if there is demon blood in your veins."

The row of weapons on the wall gleamed with the promise of death. From swords, daggers, even a couple of whips, every single item looked lethal. He eyed them all, wondering which one Claudius would use to kill him. If he proved not to be Atlas's son, would he die?

Forcing himself to look away, he took in his surroundings and Claudius, who stood in the middle of the room. He held a silver orb in one hand, gleaming in the burnished light. Its smooth surface polished to a mirror surface, showed Flynn's distorted, uneasy expression staring back at him. He wondered what the orb was, how it would determine whether he had demon blood.

His heart thudded at the thought. All his life he'd thought himself normal, perfectly average, aside from his preferred interest of men, rather than women. That had been the only mark of difference about him. He'd been good enough as a climber to earn a spot on the squad. Which had been just as well. He'd proved useless at horses, blacksmith work, and poor at writing.

So how was he meant to be part demon?

"Come," ordered Claudius.

He swallowed hard, doing as he was told. Every step was exhausting to make as if he was walking to his death. Coming to a stop, he held his breath, eyeing the orb once more. Claudius thrust it toward him, forcing him to take it in his hands.

As the cold metal settled in his palms, a rush of energy shot up his arms. He jumped back with a start, dropping the orb. It clattered to the ground, rolling away.

"What the hell was that?"

Claudius ignored him, striding forward to grab his hand. Before Flynn could get free, his grip tightened. Black flooded his eyes, devouring the whites. His harsh features sharpened, taking on an inhuman edge. An icy hand squeezed Flynn's heart, splintering outwards, rushing down his limbs until his whole body was frozen from within. He tried to move, but his body refused to obey.

It was an agonizing wait before Claudius stepped back, releasing Flynn. His nostrils flared. The whites returned, and that same handsome face looked back at him. Nothing in his expression betrayed what he was thinking. Flynn fought down a sense of frustration as he waited for the man to talk.

"It seems my old friend is full of tricks," said Claudius disdainfully.

Flynn swallowed deeply. "I'm a demon?"

"Gods, no," snorted Claudius. "Your body is as human as they come, but your soul is another matter. It's a strange one, demon magic courses through it but I can sense something else there, just beneath the surface. I just can't make sense of it... Enough of that for now, you mentioned he had two daughters?"

"Ellie and Wren, but they took Ellie from the warehouse days ago," murmured Flynn. "And Wren..."

"What of her?"

"She wasn't in the village when it was attacked. I don't know what happened to her," he confessed. "She... she'd left that morning. Vaughn said she was raving on about a Dragonir, that she was looking for a place to hide our people."

Claudius's gaze shuttered. "I see." He turned and collected the orb. As he stood, he held it out again. "Take this, but try not to drop it this time. We're going to use it to assess that bind on you, and find out what we're working with."

Reluctantly, Flynn took it in hand, fighting the urge to let go as the energy jolted again up his arms. It moved down his chest, squeezing before it splintered out through the rest of his limbs. After a few seconds, a soft humming followed. He swallowed hard, wondering what had just happened.

There would be no answers going by the guarded look in Claudius's dark eyes. Not even as they swept him over from head to toe, dissecting every tiny movement that he made.

"Interesting," he hummed, circling Flynn like a carrion bird.

He didn't elaborate further, and Flynn kept his mouth shut. The hard look silenced questions for the moment. When Claudius removed the orb, he had Flynn hold a series of weapons; swords, daggers, even a spear. He watched him closely for any reaction. Some made Flynn hurt, others gave him no reaction at all.

They moved into a small side room, where a long table had a series of assorted objects laid out in a neat line. An amulet, a polished red stone, a plate with red powder on it, and an arrowhead. Flynn approached cautiously, running his hand along with the table. Acutely aware he was being watched, and that Mira's care likely depended on Flynn going along with whatever Claudius wanted.

As his hand passed by the powder, he paused. He pressed his thumb and forefinger in, then lifted it to his nose. It had the same faintly floral notes he expected.

"How did you get this?"

His shuttered gaze flickered. "It's a prized commodity in these parts. Do you feel anything when you touch it?"

"No, should I?"

Claudius shook his head. "No. Not in your current condition. The orb is an ancient Druid relic, the kind used to hunt for demons."

He didn't explain the weapons, however as he neared Flynn and picked up the plate, a strange expression darkened his face. Flynn swore it looked like sadness, but it was buried quickly under a stone mask. And then he stepped back.

There was something in the powder that made Flynn step forward. "And the powder? It means something to you?"

Claudius set the plate back down with surprising gentleness. "No."

The lie rang clear in his voice.

Three days passed before Mira's fever finally broke. Flynn remained close by as she drifted in and out, murmuring incoherently enough to keep him within earshot. Each time he hoped she'd wake, only to watch as she'd slip back into a deep sleep. It left him with long stretches in silence. Claudius had left him alone, keeping away since the last session.

All that he ever saw of the strange man was from the window, watching as Claudius would leave on horseback. Sometimes he heard shouts bellowed down the halls. Once, when Flynn was wandering the house, trying to distract himself, he passed by a shut door. On the other side, he'd heard Claudius talking, but had no idea who was in there with him. Flynn had hurried back to his room, not wanting to be caught eavesdropping.

That had been early this morning, hours before dawn. Now, as he stood by the window once more, watching as the sun began its descent, a restlessness seized him. His people were still out there, enslaved, likely terrified and in pain, and he was as idle as he'd been when they'd first arrived.

All that centered him was Mira's recovery. Then, together, they'd plan their next move.

"F-Flynn?" Mira's hoarse voice snapped him from his reverie.

He spun around, heart pounding. A relieved smile split his cheeks as he strode over to the bed. "Good to see you awake."

She glanced around blearily, confusion furrowing her brow. "Where are we?"

"Bit of a story. How much do you remember?" he asked, thinking back to when they were rescued. Had Mira heard what Atlas had claimed?

She sat up slowly, rubbing the back of her neck. As her hand fell away, she looked at him. "It's all pretty hazy since the warehouse. Ellie... I remember her getting away. Did she escape?"

Flynn hesitated. "I don't know."

"Oh spirits, that attack on the wagons...Why did they save us?" she asked, her gaze falling to her hands.

"Does it matter? They saved you," he insisted, reluctant to confess what he knew.

Her brow lifted. "So, you know something."

"Maybe."

"Flynn," she said, pinning him with a warning look. "What did they say?"

He pulled away from the bed and drifted to the window. Even with his back turned, he felt her gaze on him, questioning. Several deep breaths and he turned to her again, though he remained where he was.

And in the darkness of that little room, he told her everything. He covered the last few days, detailing the session with Claudius. Mira didn't interrupt him, watching only with an unreadable expression. When he finished, she didn't speak. Her gaze dropped to her hands, which were twisting the sheets.

"Do you believe them?" she asked.

He folded his arms across his chest. "I don't know. Maybe. It doesn't matter though because my mind keeps circling back to the why. Even if it's all some lie, why me? And if I am what they say I am, then why did he raise Ellie and Wren? Are they not like me?"

The questions carved an abyss between them, filling the room with silence. Mira bit her lip, pondering the questions that he gave. An eternity passed before she opened her mouth to speak—when a burst of red lit up the room.

Flynn spun to the window, eyes widening. Flames shot up into the sky from across the city. A few seconds later the fire fell away, leaving a reddish hue lighting the darkening storm clouds.

"What in the spirits was *that?*"

Chapter 53

Today, I visited the red flower that the Spirit of the Mountain guards so vehemently. I believe I know why she protects it so fiercely and for the same reason, shall not write what I suspect. However, I will inform Lorca. For I will not bear this secret alone.

—Excerpt from Princess Yelena's diary.

THE DARKNESS WITHIN her roared to life, spilling out along her limbs, shadowy ribbons wrapping around her hands. Blood pounded in her ears, devouring all other sounds, leaving her mind to focus on the demons and the guards. And on the hunger that howled in her chest, the beast within, snapping to be released.

The demons in their cells paced back and forth, hissing softly, as though responding to her. Anger rolled off them in thick, smothering waves, adding to her own kindled fury. Like called to like.

The footsteps thumped closer, and rounding the corner, the guards finally appeared. Five of them, swords drawn, geared up in fighting leathers. The glowing witchlights that ran along the tunnel ceiling caught their scowling faces, the fury burning in their eyes.

"Step aside little girl, and you may yet live to see the dawn," ordered the closest one, his leathery face pinched into a scowl.

Her lips thinned as she considered her options. A savage bloodlust burned in her chest. She wanted to tear them apart, slowly, limb from limb. Have their screams fill the air, the pleas like sweet honey. Oh yes. She'd like that very much. Make these men *bleed* for the pain her sister suffered.

By the spirits, she'd become death incarnate.

The men drew closer. Wren held up her hands, revealing the ribbons coiling tight around her fingers, like a glove. Tendrils writhed along her forearms. Awareness sharpened to a knife's point, the hairs lifting along her skin, every sense focused. She felt like a predator closing in for the kill.

Caution flashed in their eyes, and they paused their advance. She scented their fear, acrid, deliciously sour. They tried to hide it behind reserved masks, failing. Their bodies betrayed them.

Good.

She just had to buy enough time for her sister's escape...and maybe just have a little fun with these men. It was a damn shame she couldn't take dragon form and devour them whole. Oh well, she'd just have to tear them apart by hand.

The climber in her had retreated. Something else had taken hold; older, crueler, a beast unchained. She smiled savagely.

"You're not getting through me," Wren said defiantly. "I didn't journey across an entire kingdom to let my sister be torn from me again."

The man who spoke considered her warily. "You really believe you can beat us?"

"Oh, I rather think I can and I'm going to enjoy making you scream."

As she spoke, the demons were inches from the bars, watching her.

They had grown quiet.

She had an idea.

With a smile, she lowered her hands. Confusion flickered on the man's face, though he held firm, unsure what she was doing.

"Changed your mind?" he asked, wary of her shifted stance.

She smiled. "More like a change in plans."

Wren threw her arms wide, the power surging from her hands. It slammed into the bars, shattering them. The men staggered back, startled. Shouts erupted, but she paid them no heed. Their panic fed the beast within her, fueling the energy spilling out in thundering waves.

Then silence fell. A beat of it followed. Her hands fell to the sides, her body humming with energy. The men looked toward the open cells and backed slowly away.

A snarling rumbled from within the cages. One by one, the demons prowled forward. Their eyes glowed like molten coals. Ancient energy akin to the kind humming within her soul radiated off their matted raven fur.

She sensed their hunger and their rage. Images flashed through her mind. Their violent birth into a world that was not their own, dragged screaming from a crack in the human realm. To their enslavement, chained and forced to fight in pits for the entertainment of nobles. Their fury burned like fire in her veins, becoming hers, kindling a murderous rage from deep within.

These demons weren't her enemy.

All they hungered for was their revenge—and their freedom.

They called to her, pulling at something ancient buried deep at the core of her soul.

She pointed at the guards. "Kill them."

The leader opened his mouth to scream, but he never had a chance.

A demon lunged, knocking him to the ground, latching onto his throat. With a brutal twist, the demon ripped his throat out, blood spraying. As his sword clattered away, the other men stumbled back. Their panicked screams erupted as they began to turn and tried to run, two never making it as demons launched, pinning them to the ground. Their heads were torn clean off before they could cry out. The others ran but the demons shot after them, howling with wicked delight.

One stopped dead, just shy of the shadows, turning back to her. It dropped its head, shutting its eyes for a moment. Appreciation brushed her mind.

It's good to see you again. Thank you for freeing us.

Her mouth parted. The demon *talked?*

It lifted its head, then spun around and burst forward, vanishing into the dark with a whooping cry.

Wren spun around, taking off in a sprint, the sound of agonized screams chasing her. She held out her hands, energy surging from her hands, destroying each cell she passed.

Demons, freed from their prisons, flooded the tunnel.

Let them have their revenge.

When she came to a crossroads, she stopped.

The tunnel was silent, broken only by her breathing and the roar of blood in her ears. Her heart continued its rapid thump on her chest, like a bird desperate to escape. She shifted restlessly on her feet, considering her options.

Which way?

She saw footsteps pressed into the dirt down both paths. Neither particularly stood out to her at first; then a quiet tug at her gut, like a thread pulling out from her, stretching down one of the tunnels.

She took off again into a run when the screaming behind her stopped. The silence, broken only by her sharp breaths, thumping heart, and boots on the ground, was eerie.

The path sloped downwards. She slowed, uneasy, half considering heading back when it evened out again. Cautiously, she jogged forward until she came to a narrow passageway descending a little further. Flickering witchlights lit the way, their blue hue duller as if they were drained.

A sharp pain stabbed through her chest without warning, splintering along her arms. The shock sent her staggering forward, catching on the wall. An image flashed in her mind. A sparring yard set beneath a deep red sky, stars glittering like polished gems. The smell of ash, rich oil, and the fragrant touch of the red flowers she remembered so well filled her lungs.

A woman stalked across the sands, her black skin and thick curly hair, was unlike anyone she knew...and those eyes. Fierce, lit with wicked delight. She wore golden armor, flecked with scratches and signs of battle, and held a golden staff, the tip a sharpened blade.

"Are you giving up now?"

She swung the staff suddenly and the image dispelled.

Wren blinked, confusion burning in her mind, and she pushed herself off the wall, the pain faded as quickly as it had come. A strange ache tugged at her, and she lifted her gaze down the narrow tunnel to the iron door at its end.

Her feet were moving her toward it before she realized it. By the time she registered the steps, she was within reach of the door. Something was pulling her towards it, a command rising from a source buried deep within her soul, refusing to be denied. Instinctively, she reached for the handle, testing it. A hard rattle ricocheted off the walls.

Locked.

Rationally, she knew she had to run, but her feet refused to move.

Open the door, came another voice from within, a woman, duskier but familiar.

This time, she summoned magic to her hands and closed her eyes, focusing everything she had on the door. Then she yanked back with all she had.

Metal screeched, and the door gave, sending her staggering back. Her eyes flickered open, heart racing. The door was shattered, and the remains clung to the wall by a single hinge. Heart racing, she stepped closer and peered inside. The light from the lantern illuminated a tiny cell.

Within it, a figure slumped over in a chair.

Curious, Wren drew closer. It was a woman.

The same one she'd just had a vision of. There only a few differences were the tattoos stretched along her arms, twisting up to her neck, and vanishing beneath her hairline. She wore a tattered tunic, ripped in several spots and stained with blood on her shoulder. Bruises mottled her skin.

Wren thought the woman was dead until she moved, slowly lifting her head, frowning.

"You're not who I was calling for." She laughed harshly. "Demons below, I must have lost more blood than I thought."

"What?" asked Wren, drawing forward.

The woman stared, silent for a moment, that penetrating gaze cutting like a knife right down to Wren's soul. As though it were peering into every crack and crevice, hunting. "Nothing. I was just...well, I thought I'd sensed someone I once knew, which is absurd because..."

Her voice trailed off, grief touching her eyes.

Wren eyed the gleaming chains holding the woman down. "Why are you here? What happened to you?"

Those dark eyes flickered with power. "I was rescuing someone. The situation changed, and I had to buy them time to get away. Obviously, things didn't go how I planned. Then they dragged me down here looking for answers."

"They?"

"The Empress's spies. Contrary to what Lady Adara thinks, this city is full of them," replied the woman, her mouth quirking to a dry smile. "But I'm not so easily broken, and they hit like children. It was pathetic."

The defiance in her voice left Wren fighting to hold back a smile. "You're with the rebels?"

"More or less," she replied cryptically. "Are you going to free me?" There was a look of interest on her face as she cocked her head to the side.

Even before she said the words, Wren knew she wasn't leaving the woman down there. Something had drawn her to this cell. There was a sense of familiarity about her as if they'd met before. Had she seen this woman in the dream with her father, the Spirit of the Mountain and Claudius? She tried to summon the memory but it was slipping through her fingers like sand. If she had to guess, however, it was that the woman had been there.

Was it her demon magic that called to the woman? She didn't know and time wasn't on her side to ponder it further.

She dropped to her knees, summoning the shadows to her hands. They came easily, surging out from her fingertips to the chains as she took hold. With a jerk of her hand, they broke apart, clattering noisily to the ground.

"Aren't you full of surprises?"

"I don't know why I'm doing this," Wren muttered. "But all I've got right now is my gut, and it's telling me to help you."

As she stepped back, giving the woman room to stand, Wren shifted restlessly. The curiosity burning in the other's eyes was too prying as if it was peeling back every defense she had. This woman saw her, all the darkness and fire, the vengeance and fury.

"What's your name?" she asked, rubbing her bruised wrists with a wince.

"Wren."

She said and held out her hand. "Titania."

Cautiously, Wren took her hand, and a jolt of energy shot up her arm. She gave a squeeze in return and slowly drew back her hand, refusing to let her shock show. Something buried within her recognized Titania, and Wren hadn't the faintest clue why.

"We should go," said Wren. "I mean, I'm on my way out, if you want to come with me?"

Titania's brow lifted. "As opposed to staying here?"

Nodding, Wren hurried out of the cell, Titania close behind her. Out in the dimly lit passage, she broke into a jog up the incline and back to the larger tunnel.

After a steep incline, they came to another crossroads. Titania moved without hesitation down the left passage, Wren following. They stayed silent as they wove through the labyrinth and until they came to a set of stone steps leading up to a door.

Titania pressed her ear against the door before opening it. She held it open for Wren until she passed through, then shut it. With a whisper, she waved her hand over the lock and a blackish ink spilled from her fingers, melting over the handle and lock, fusing it.

Wren released a low whistle. "Aren't you full of tricks?"

"What can I say? I have a lovely assortment of them but the same can be said of you," retorted Titania. "First time I've met someone with demon and spirit magic."

She froze. "What?"

Titania drew her hand back from the door, turning to Wren. "You shouldn't be alive right with those opposing magic in your blood, which intrigues me, but that's a chat for another time. One I hope to have."

I shouldn't be alive? Dread pooled in her gut, doubts brushing her mind once more. She dashed them away.

"Another time," she agreed because, whilst her instinct cautioned her from Claudius, there was no such warning with Titania. In fact, with that woman, there was only warmth.

Apparently satisfied with that answer, Titania led the way out of the small stone room, which opened onto a cemetery. Neat rows of weathered and gleaming new gravestones stretched out beneath a moonlit sky. The cold night air bit into her skin and right through her tattered dress, shivers rippling down her body and lifting the hairs along her skin.

The woman stood unaffected, as though she were some ethereal being and the weaknesses of mortals didn't apply to her. She flexed her fingers out in front, the joints cracking audibly. "Claudius is going to be pissed. Oh well, that can't be helped."

Claudius? Surely, she doesn't mean...?

"Do you mean Lord De—"

Titania turned to her, opening her mouth to speak when a thunderous bang ripped through the air. A flash of fire burst into the sky, the darkening storm clouds turning red. Heat flared through her, pulling at the bond she had with Lorca. Pain and fear bled through, interwoven by flashes of a fight he was and fires raging all around.

Lorca.

"Is that what I think it is?" asked Titania, glancing back at her.

Wren was moving forward already. "I have to go. Will you be okay from here?"

"Yes, go. You promised me a chat soon, so try not to die tonight, okay?"

Wren bit back the urge to ask for Titania's help when the strange woman darted off into the shadows, vanishing into the night.

Well, then, guess I am doing this alone.

As she sprinted off toward the column of fire, Wren prayed she wasn't too late.

Her feet hit the ground as she tore off down the street. She sprinted desperately along the stone road, her boots' rapid thumps echoing steadily into the air. As she navigated the rabbit warren of streets, her limbs burned, but she pushed on desperate to get to Lorca. The bond pulled her along, like an invisible thread, leading her to him.

Another roar tore through the air.

She rounded a corner, where the street widened with empty stalls on either side. Up ahead, the area narrowed again. A faint amber glow reflected on a row of buildings, the sound of shouts and the clang of metal growing closer.

The air thickened with magic, washing over Wren. Her palms burned in response, the darkness inside of her stirring once more. She didn't let herself slow until she hurled around another corner, coming into a street of brothels.

Two of the brothels were ablaze, throwing off waves of suffocating heat and blinding flames. The street was strewn with bodies, soldiers burned black. Wagons were upturned, their goods spilled across the blood-stained cobblestone. A thin layer of ash was already falling steadily, dusting everything in wisps of gray.

Dozens of men surrounded Lorca in dragon form, a metal net thrown over him, struggling to hold him down. Fire spluttered from his mouth as he struggled to escape. Blood dripped from several deep gashes across his body and his wings were shredded, hanging limp.

Their bond began to weaken.

No, no, no!

Just behind the row of wrestling men, another stood apart, clad in black with his palms raised to Lorca. Dark magic radiated off him. He stared at Lorca, arms folded across his chest.

Lorca threw his head back, howling in agony.

She dashed forward, darkness erupting from her skin and dropped low, snatching a sword up from the ground. Magic rushed down the blade, infusing it. It felt light in her hands, all hesitation about her skill falling away. Confidence filled her, calming her.

Kill them, the darkness crooned in her mind. *Kill them all.*

She stopped and snapped her fingers, summoning an orb and hurled it at the lone figure. It hissed through the air, splitting the haze like a knife. The man spun, shouting in alarm as he jumped out of the way. The orb shot past him, crashing into the wall. Stone cracked and fell, clattering to the ground.

Wren snarled and threw another orb, then two more. The man went to dodge again but she'd already predicted it. The last one landed true, sending him flying and hitting the ground, sprawling across the stones.

She advanced forward, wreaths of demonic magic swirling around her. "I'm going to make you regret hurting him!"

Lorca unleashed a thundering cry, surging up against the net. Men shouted desperately, trying to hold on but it was a losing battle as Lorca swung his tail. It collided into two men with an audible crunch before they were sent flying, crashing into a nearby wall. The others scrambled forward to grab the net once more.

Her gaze flew to him, their eyes meeting across the carnage and fire. Relief thrummed both ways through the bond.

A couple more soldiers rushed in, grabbing at the net. She burst forward as Lorca twisted to try and rip the next away. His wings were quickly entangled. Her breath hitched as he tripped, falling back to the ground. Men rushed in, grabbing the ropes, hauling it tight, and driving him back down. A pained cry tore out as he struggled to stand once more.

Wren! His voice thundered in his mind, full of alarm. *Run!*

She met his gaze across the chaos. *Like hell, I am leaving you!*

In the corner of her gaze, the man she'd attacked was pushing himself to his feet. Turning to him, she snapped her fingers, summoning another orb of shadows. He looked up, dark eyes finding hers. Interest sparked as he appeared to take her in.

Let him see me. I'm going to kill him anyway.

Several others behind him, seeing Wren, advanced to her, swords drawn. The sorcerer threw a hand out, stopping their advance, and dusted himself off.

He was a striking man, lean and dark, glowing gold in the firelight. A savage gleam lit his eyes as he stalked forward, eyeing the dark energy rippling up Wren's arms. His hand snapped up, stopping the advance of his men, who shrank back with a flick of his wrist.

"Well, what a curious power you have," he said, amused.

It took all her effort to not want to run to Lorca, to help free him. If she took her focus off the sorcerer, he might just stab her in the back. She spat at the man, her eyes narrowed, blazing with fury.

"You're going to regret hurting him," she snarled, venom dripping from her voice.

He laughed mockingly. "*You're* going to stop me? Well, come on girl, *beat me.*"

Wren threw her hands up, the darkness spreading up her arm, rippling across her body. Rage burned hotter through her than anything else before.

With a scream, she hurled herself forward, the darkness howling with delight and savage fury.

Time for you to die.

Chapter 54

I told my brother my concerns about the Spirit of the Mountain. It is by our decision that we choose silence.

—Excerpt from Princess Yelena's diary

AZIAH WATCHED AS the sky turned red with fire and the screams of people spread out across the city. Fear rose from the merchants as they spilled out of their homes, clustering in the streets. Husbands held their wives and children.

Her soul ached as she tried *not* to think of Gabriel as she watched the chaos unfold. The mate bond was still there, even if it felt weak enough that it would vanish at any second. That kept her going, for the moment. Later, once this was settled, she'd find him.

Don't make the last eighteen years be for nothing, she told herself, even as her soul begged to find Gabriel.

She needed to keep moving, one step at a time. She blinked away the tears. All she had left now was Sybilla. She had to find the girl.

Somewhere, in all the chaos, the baby she had risked everything for had grown up and was running this mess.

She hung back in the shadowy street, out of view, as the flames finally fell away, leaving a lingering glow. Then turned and slipped down a quiet street. The chaos faded away behind her as she picked her way through the winding streets, her hood drawn down around her face. The few people she passed paid her no mind, dismissing her shadowy advance, their mind on the gathering crowds a few streets away.

Navigating her way toward the docks was an easy enough task. She moved swiftly, darting down the streets she knew like the back of her hand. Though they'd changed since her time as a small child, when she scrambled about hunting for her next meal, the layout was much the same.

By the time the first glimpse of the dark water came into view at the end of a narrow street, she slowed. She drew in deep breaths of the salty air. It helped to keep her senses tuned. Energy hummed in the air, the city holding its breath.

By the end of the night, that breath would be released. Only time would tell what the city looked like after.

She paused at the threshold of the docks, lingering in the shadows. Taking the moment, she dug out a letter, holding it to a snatch of moonlight that cut through a gap in the cloud. Her gaze darted over the message, blood from the messenger whose throat she'd slit only hours before staining the edges.

When flames light the sky, take your position. We take the city at dawn.

Heart pounding, she tucked the letter away. Gods, she just had to make it in time.

Setting off again, she picked her way along the warehouse fronts. The wharves stretched out across the calm water like gnarled fingers. Several boats were berthed, the shadowy outline of men standing guard on their decks. No doubt a few watched her hurry alone, though none raised any alarm.

Their concerns weren't for her.

By the time she reached the interior wall that divided the merchant and the slave docks, she stopped at the warehouse pressed up against the wall. She eyed the large wooden doors, then set off down the narrow alley that ran down its side. The shadows thickened there, obscuring nearly all light. Halfway along, she turned toward the wall of the warehouse, pressing her palm against the wood. Closing her eyes, she reached out, hunting for the girl's magic.

In her mind's eye, she glimpsed a single glowing light. Spirit magic. Retreating, she opened her eyes. She raised her hand, about to summon a portal when doubt seized her. All the worries and fears that had haunted her for the past eighteen years gnawed at her. She'd gambled so much, burned more bridges than she cared to admit, and knew exactly where her path would lead. She told herself it'd be worth it, that it had to be.

But what if the girl she'd pinned so much on fell short? By what she'd gleaned, the girl had her father's prophetic ability. Unfortunately, she was using it far too much and the price would need to be paid. Aziah only hoped that the recklessness at which Sybilla wielded her power would not be a sign of what was to come.

For such a trait could easily herald someone far worse than Alexandria...

With a deep breath, she snapped her fingers, materializing a portal beside her. Then she walked into it, the world blurring away.

Inside the warehouse, a makeshift fire pit warmed the air in the middle of the main space. She sat on one of the beams holding up the ceiling, peering down into the cluster below. Several men and women sat by the fire, nursing mugs of steaming tea in their hands. They spoke in indistinct murmurs, tension hanging between them. A copy of the letter she'd stolen lay unfurled on a crate behind them.

Her gaze moved to the stack of boxes at the end, untouched by the glow of the fire. A lone woman sat there, watching the fire with amber eyes. Even in her youth, she was a spitting image of her mother, different only in her father's eyes and the hard set of her mouth.

The resemblance was startling.

Then that piercing gaze darted up. It locked immediately on Aziah, yet no surprise flickered there. It was as if she'd known Aziah had been there the entire time.

Aziah stood and then dropped down into the warehouse below. Shouts erupted behind her, but she paid them no mind as she stood before the princess.

Sybilla pushed off the boxes, a smile softening the harsh edges of her face. She raised a hand, gesturing her men to stand down, and as it fell, the smile widened. It was full of warmth, tears filling her eyes.

"It's okay everyone. This is an old friend—well, I suppose you're more than that. This is the woman who saved my life the day my family was murdered," she said, her voice soft, humming with power. She held out a delicate hand, the kind one didn't expect to hold so much power with a single touch, and beckoned Aziah closer. The second she was within reach, Sybilla drew her into her arms. "It's good to finally meet you, Aziah."

And in the quiet glow of that warehouse, as the war was about to erupt outside, the weight of nearly two decades crashed down around Aziah. She didn't know where Gabriel was, if he was captured or hiding somewhere safe. But he was alive and it gave her hope.

She leaned into Sybilla's embrace and closed her eyes, letting that spark grow.

I am coming for you, Gabriel.

Chapter 55

My wife's body was discovered at the base of the castle wall. No one knows why she jumped, but I do. She carried to her grave a secret, one she refused to impart to even myself. I only hope that the past is finally settled. Now, my people prepare for war.

—Excerpt from Emperor Alderan, husband to Empress Litania, final entry.

THE MAN VANISHED in a plume of black smoke, Wren's bolt sailing harmlessly through it. A shadow flashed beside her. She spun, drawing up her hands, firing another bolt. It missed again.

Dark laughter rang out behind her.

He's toying with me.

Scowling, she saw him appear in front of her, several feet away, smirking. Fury curled hot and viciously through her gut, a blazing inferno that wanted to burn her from the inside out. Her hands curled into fists, nails biting into flesh, drawing rivulets of blood down her palm. That dark power howled in response, flooding through her limbs, rushing to her hands. It raged against her control, demanding to destroy the man, to make him kneel before her.

"I've never met anyone quite like you before," he remarked tauntingly. "It's quite—"

Her hand snapped up, energy exploding out. It slammed into him, sending him staggering back. The smile fell, cold fury showing on his face. Dark energy rolled off him, as though something truly evil had been unleashed from within.

Harsh breaths fell from her lips.

This was a fight for survival.

And she'd be damned if she'd let him win.

Shifting her stance, one foot slightly back, lifting her hands again, just as Lorca had taught her. Tendrils of energy wrapped around her arms, creating gauntlets forged from her dark magic. Hauling in a deep breath, she considered her options.

A chill rushed over her body, goosebumps rippling down her back. She pivoted one hand up, blindly throwing a bolt of energy. It pierced a plume, exploding on impact against an overturned cart. She scanned the burning street, straining for any brush against her senses.

Then she heard it. The scrape of a boot on the stone. A flash of movement to her right. She dropped low, sweeping her leg, knocking his feet from beneath him. He careened to the side, staggering. Wren was fast, surging forward, driving her shoulder into his chest and slamming her other fist under his ribs.

Air rushed from his lungs as he hit the ground, desperately trying to breathe again. In a blink, she straddled him, plunging her fist down. He rolled, and her fist hit the stone. Pain shot up her arm and she was thrown sideways, cursing as she hit the ground.

Scrambling to her feet, he was on her, this time coming at her with a dagger. She jumped back, the tip of the blade slicing the front of her shirt, missing skin. As he lunged again, she slammed both hands down, connecting with the top of his hand, surging magic out. She let go, shoving her palm into his chest, hurling a bolt forward.

The force sent him flying back. Staggering, he threw the dagger her way. She leaped to the side, the glint of silver flashing before her eyes. Blinking, she barely had time to react when another dagger flew at her.

She dodged to the side, darting left and right as more came. Two came at once, then one more. She dived to the side, catching the far-right dagger as she fell. Hitting the ground, she rolled up and threw it at him with one hand.

It sailed harmlessly past his head.

He grinned and spread his arms wide, snapping his fingers. One by one, daggers materialized above him, all aimed at her. The blood drained from her face as realization hit her.

I haven't been holding my own against him at all.

She could dodge a few of those daggers, but not all of them. Her eyes turned to Lorca, wrestling to claw the rest of the net off him when more soldiers emerged from behind him. They were throwing more lines across him, dragging him back down to the ground. Wrenching her gaze away, she glared at the man, her heart slamming against her ribs.

As she raised her hands, summoning her magic, nothing happened. Her heart stuttered in her chest, a chill stealing through her soul. A sharp breath hitched in her throat. *Oh, gods, this can't be the end—I refuse to die here dammit!*

The man snapped his fingers. The daggers shot forward. Wren kept her eyes open. If she was to meet death, she'd do it head-on.

It never came.

Time slowed. A soft roar was all she sensed before a wall of fire exploded toward her from behind the man, devouring them all. A rush of heat swallowed her. For one blinding moment, fire consumed her.

It was over in seconds.

The fire bled away. A savage dragon cry ripped through the air. Lorca slumped to the ground. The net dragged over the rest of him, pinning him fully down.

Run, Wren!

She blinked, looked back at the man. He stood unharmed, smoke swirling around his body. Lorca had given her time to run. She couldn't. If she did that, he'd be dead. She wasn't losing him, not anyone else, not anymore.

With a snarl, she shoved herself up to her feet when a shadow fell over her, a force slamming into her from behind. White flashed over her vision as her head was slammed into the stone. Her teeth bit into her cheek, hot blood filling her mouth. The world around her spun dizzyingly as she tried to push herself up. Something was pressing on her upper back, keeping her pinned. She strained, fighting with a rush of adrenalin.

Darkness was fighting to devour her vision. The unconscious world was clawing at her mind, trying to drag her under. She fought viciously, screaming until something suddenly yanked her up to her knees. Ice flooded through her veins.

Something was stopping her from moving. She was a prisoner to her body, frozen. The man she'd been fighting approached. His jaw tightened as he looked beyond her. His lip curled back in a soundless snarl, fury glinting in his eyes.

"I had this under control," he sneered. "Let her go. I can do this without you."

A hand curled around her shoulder, tightening his grip. Nails bit into her flesh through her clothing. He squeezed again. Bone shattered. Wren screamed, tears burning her eyes. Fiery pain erupted, heating viciously as his grip tightened. Nails cut flesh, leaving sticky blood trickling down her arm.

"We have new orders," snapped the man holding her. "We need to finish up here *now*."

Defiance warred on her attacker's face but nodded reluctantly. His gaze fell to Wren with an expression of cruel delight. He bent down, grabbing her chin. Forcing her to meet his gaze, to smell the sour stench of his breath, he eyed her.

"How disappointing you turned out," he said dismissively.

She spat her blood at him, right on his face. "Same to you. Needed your friend here to beat me."

She felt the sting of his blow on her cheek before she registered the punch. Stars burst across her vision. Cursing, she swallowed hard, refusing to show this man any more pain or weakness. He hauled her up again, eyeing her furiously.

"I'll make you regret that," he spat, throwing her back into the man that held as he spun away.

Understanding dawned as she saw him stalk right toward Lorca. He snapped fingers, a long spear appearing in his hand, the metal glinting in the firelight.

Oh gods, no.

"Lorca, move!" she screamed, straining against Rohan's magic. "*Move, you stupid dragon!*"

She strained desperately, tears burning her vision. A savage, pleading scream tore from her as she fought to break free, even as her shoulder was shredded to ribbons. Desperation cleaved her soul two. She tried to summon her magic but an icy silence responded instead.

No, please no!

Again and again, she screamed into the abyss of magic raging within her, begging it to answer her call. Once more, it danced out of reach. Tears spilled down her cheeks, like liquid fire that burned her skin.

"*Lorca, please, just move!*"

Hearing her, his head snapped up, inches off the ground, his gaze locking on the man that advanced towards him. An agonized roar filled the air as he tried to stand, fire glowing in his mouth. For a split second, those green eyes found hers.

Wren... He spoke her name like a desperate plea, laden with a thousand words, and she felt his emotions crash against her. All that he couldn't say and all that he felt.

The man threw the spear.

"NO!"

The blade slammed into Lorca's chest, sinking deep. A choked cry ripped from his throat as swaying, he crumpled to the ground.

Wren's heart was ripped from her chest, screaming in unleashed fury, tears streaming down her face.

In a blink, the man vanished, materializing at Lorca's side, yanking out the spear. Blood sprayed. A pained groan rippled from Lorca as he stopped struggling, the dark blood pooling around him.

Tears streamed down Wren's cheeks as she screamed, her heart shattering.

"Lorca, get up!" she begged frantically. *"Move!"*

His mind faintly brushed hers. *Wren...*

Silence devoured her whole.

Deep inside, she felt the depth of her dark magic and realized she'd been only drawing on droplets of it. That wall binding her powers she'd damaged when she was captured by the fae was cleaved by a widening crack. A primal rage roared up inside her as she drew on the last scraps of power she had left, hurling it at the wall.

It shattered.

She threw her arms wide, tearing free of Rohan's control as she unleashed her magic. It exploded outwards, a wave of dark energy.

Wren had become destruction and chaos incarnate.

She surrendered, letting it devour her whole.

Chapter 56

I am fighting a losing war with my mind. I cannot last much longer. Day by day, I feel myself weakening. If I surrender, I fear the terrible fate that will descend upon the people who embraced me. I must find a way—not for myself but for my daughter, for my husband, for my people.

—Excerpt from Empress Litania's diary.

MADNESS DESCENDED AT DAWN.

Soldiers loyal to Sybilla spilled from homes, warehouses, barracks, and stores. They fanned out across the labyrinth of streets, swift, like carrions of death. Those who resisted were captured and dragged away to the catacombs deep beneath the city to be imprisoned.

The few that fought stained the cobblestone streets with their blood.

As for the nobles who refused to yield, they barricaded themselves in their homes, waiting for a rescue that wasn't coming. The walls had already been shut, the orders given at dawn. The city would be hers soon enough, the first phase of her plan complete.

Patience.

As she sat on her horse, eyeing the looming metal fence that guarded the Craven family home, Sybilla wondered if they knew that.

Her horse shifted restlessly, snorting. Leaning down, she rubbed small circles on his neck. "I know, boy, but this will all be over soon."

The soldiers beside her cast curious looks, wondering what she'd do. Rumors had swirled in the amber light of that warehouse. They'd thought she'd been asleep, missing their twilight musings. But she'd heard everything.

And those words nipped at her mind as she straightened up in the saddle. She slid down from the saddle and stepped up to the gate, tugging her gloves off, finger by finger. Tucking the gloves into her belt, she pressed her palms against the iron.

She closed her eyes, calling on the spirit magic that burned through her veins. Warmth pooled in her chest, then fanned out down along her limbs, gathering in her hands. Opening her eyes, she drew her hand back and slammed it back into the gate. White light exploded from her fingers, splintering up like bolts of lightning, and as it struck the top, the metal shattered. The fragments tumbled down around her, clattering noisily. As the last piece fell, she strode forward, her men hurrying after her.

A wave of nausea rushed up her throat, threatening to remove what little she'd eaten that morning. Swallowing it back with an internal curse, she pushed on, refusing to let the men see how much that trick cost her. A lack of proper magical teaching was already paining her.

If the men required any more proof of her power, she was afraid she'd fail that—or worse, lose control. Madness ran in her bloodline, and it was a fate she was determined to avoid for as long as she could.

At the front door, one of her soldiers rushed forward to the door, testing it. The locked door rattled defiantly. No sooner had they stepped back than the metallic slide of a lock on the other side clicked. The soldiers formed rank around her, swords drawn.

The door opened.

A tall, middle-aged man with graying hair and a worn face stood before her. Dressed in an ornate green suit, the Craven insignia—a golden hawk—emblazoned on his chest told her who he was. She took in the hard set of his mouth, the stubborn glint in his eye, the way his hand rested on the pommel of his sword.

"So, you're her," he said, scowling. "How the hell did you survive?"

"I was smuggled out during the attack and raised away from the court, preparing for my return," she replied, squaring her shoulders.

He glanced over at her men, then at the city behind her, likely taking in the pillars of smoke that were billowing up across the quarters. A frown darkened his face, those green eyes falling to her, his disapproval clear. "So, you chose *this* city? Why now?"

"Now, now, you haven't sworn fealty to me. It'd be awfully stupid of me to disclose my plans," she teased. "But I didn't come here for your loyalty. I know you owe too much to my aunt."

Caution flickered in his eyes. "Then why did you come here?"

"Because I wanted you to hear this order to come directly from me." She set a hand on one soldier, gesturing for him to step aside. Reluctantly, he signaled his men, and they moved to her side, poised to strike. "Your slaves are to be freed by day's end. Failure to do so will mean your imprisonment. You will be confined to your house. Should you wish to swear fealty, you can send word, and then we can discuss your role in the future of this kingdom."

His frown deepened. "You would spare us?"

"Your death would not serve my interest." She glimpsed a woman descending the stairs behind him, holding a small child in her arms. "For the sake of your family, I would advise you to act wisely. There is one thing I share with my aunt. I do not tolerate betrayal. Consider this your first and *only* warning."

As she turned from him, the men closing in behind her, she headed back to her horse. Once she was back up in the saddle, one of them drew closer.

"What benefit could there be in letting him live? He will send word to the capital the first chance he has," said the man softly.

Sybilla looked at him. He was a captain of the city guard, one of those long loyal to Helena. This was someone who had fought before, who didn't shy away from violence. He was not dazzled by her use of magic. His features were a little sharper, his build firm and lean, and there were flecks of gold in his brown eyes. She wondered if he had any fae blood in him.

She replied, "What's your name?"

"Oren."

She nodded. "The reason I spared him is simple. I know he will send out a message. It's what I'm counting on."

He opened his mouth to reply but a shout cut him off. A rider galloped toward them, slowing only at the last second. A woman, clad in city guard uniform, her face flushed, flecked with blood. Her storm-blue eyes settled on Sybilla.

"Trouble in the Pleasure Quarter," she announced. "We thought we'd secured it by chasing those Gray Guards out, but a bunch of soldiers has hunkered down in one brothel. There are at least fifty girls trapped with them."

Helena had reported that a small group from the Gray Army had appeared in the city, an elite team. It had been discovered too late and now Sybilla cursed that she hadn't seen them in her visions.

Dammit.

Sybilla's grip tightened on her reins. "Where are the Gray Guards now?"

"They vanished through some portals before we could grab them," she replied. "What would you like done with those we've trapped?"

The men looked to her, silent, poised to follow her word. The weight of that bore heavily on her shoulders. The first hint of what was to come. She'd hoped it wouldn't feel so... *suffocating.* But dreams were for children, and Sybilla had long since abandoned childish ambitions. Her own goals were much larger.

She glanced at Oren. "Return to the mansion and inform Helena of the issue. Tell her to send what she can and that I will be there."

His jaw tightened. "You would be in danger. I will send my men to resolve the situation."

"You have your orders, Oren," she replied crisply. "Ride swift and safe. This city isn't ours yet."

His chin dipped, the irritation glinting in his eyes. As he wheeled his horse and took off down the road, Sybilla turned back to the woman.

"He's right. If you die—"

"This city isn't secure yet, so my life is in as much danger as anyone else's. Now, let's ride!" She didn't wait for them to reply as she dug her heels in and her horse shot forward into the night.

Chapter 57

Today I questioned Litania about her comings of late. No sooner had I asked her than she spun around, pinning me against the wall with one hand. Her eyes were black and dark power rolled off her, smothering me. It was over as quickly as it had begun and she fled. That is when I understood what had happened to my friend. I wait for my mother to return from her meeting with the nobles. She must know. Litania is possessed.

—Excerpt from Princess Yelena's diary

IT WAS THE night after they saw the fire in the sky when Claudius finally reappeared. He strode into the room, his face splattered with blood and ash. Close behind him, Titania followed, looking just as rough.

Flynn stood by the window, Mira by his side, watching them warily. A thousand questions burned his lips. He'd heard the sounds of fighting and screaming outside, leaving him wondering what the hell was happening.

Claudius eyed Flynn. "We're getting you out of the city. The both of you."

"What?" The word tumbled out of his mouth. After a beat, he glanced at Mira, then back at Claudius. "Where are you taking us?"

Titania stepped forward. "We're not going anywhere. We're needed here, but it's not safe for you. Ideally, we'd find a way to break the spell on you safely, but we don't have that option. And you need a proper teacher. So, we're sending you to an old friend of mine. She knows how to break the spell and she'll train you how to use your magic."

He'd barely thought about the supposed magic in his veins. All his focus had been with Mira, on ensuring she got better. Yet at that moment, he realized it could help him in freeing everyone he cared about. And he'd be better able to protect Mira.

"Do you know how I'd be able to find my people after I do that?" he finally asked.

Titania and Claudius shared a look before the former looked back, clearing her throat. "You will send us a message through our friend when you're ready. We can help you."

His heart jolted hard in his chest. It was more than he'd expected from, well, *strangers*. Yet she'd said it calmly, without hesitation. He sensed no lie from her.

Mira touched his arm, stepping forward slightly. "You'd help us?"

Claudius's jaw tightened. "For better or worse, he's family."

The hard edge to his voice made Flynn think Claudius didn't exactly like the familial connection. Yet, just like he said, they were blood, and that clearly meant an obligation of aid. Flynn wasn't about to dismiss the offer. He just hoped it would hold true.

"When do we leave?" he asked.

"Tomorrow," said Titania. "Be ready to move when we give the order."

Flynn woke screaming, his face slick with sweat hours later. As he sat there, surrounded by the shadows of his room, moonlight spilling in from a tall window, he took several deep breaths, trying to calm his racing heart. It seemed like a useless exercise, with every thump of his heart a knife against his ribs. Keeping his eyes closed, he forced longer breaths in and out, trying to still his pounding heart. After what passed for an eternity, his pulse slowed, and he opened his eyes.

No one had come rushing in, though he was sure from how hoarse his throat had been that he'd been loud. Maybe the sound of someone screaming in terror was the norm in this mansion?

Realizing sleep would not return, he crept from the bed and slipped outside. The halls were silent, broken only by the soft tread of his feet against the rugs. Every so often, a squeak echoed off the walls. He passed by Mira's room. Peering inside, he discovered her sleeping soundly. He withdrew and continued on his walk.

He made his way downstairs, wandering until he reached the foyer. The grand doors loomed in front of him, intricately carved, painted with a strikingly beautiful woman and Claudius. The woman, with flowing brown hair and dark, haunting eyes, stared back at him. She wore a golden thorny crown and a flowing white dress.

As he studied the hard lines of her face, and the strange sense of sadness about her, the sound of boots on the ground beyond the door broke the silence. He jumped when the door opened with a crash and a group of armed men surged through.

He opened his mouth to raise the alarm when one of them rushed at him, sword drawn. Panicking, he ducked, the blade hissing through the air inches above his head. As he started to rise, a fist collided into his chest, knocking the air out. With a gasp, he fell back, frantically trying to gulp the air back in.

The back of his head struck the ground. A flash of stars leaped across his vision as a burst of pain splintered through his skull, throbbing hard. For a second, he couldn't move, his body limp on the ground.

"Flynn?" Mira's frightened voice cut the air like a blade.

A man cursed.

Flynn's heart flipped and willed his body to move again, gritting his teeth. The world lurched violently as he rolled over and lifted his head. Mira stood halfway down the stairs, clutching the banister, her wide eyes frozen with fear. A man was stalking past him to her, a dagger gleaming in his hand.

No!

He pushed himself up, shakily and hurled himself onto the back of the man. They collided into the ground with a heavy thud. The man grunted, rolling over, throwing Flynn aside. He scrambled up, driving his fist into the man's face. As he pulled his hand back to hit again hands grabbed him from behind, yanking him away.

"Run, Mira! Get help!"

She spun around, but as she went running a man sprinted up the stairs, grabbing her by the back of her neck. Crying out, she tried to tear herself free, but he tossed her down the stairs as if she weighed nothing. Mira landed on the ground with a sickening thud and didn't move. Flynn roared, trying to wrench away, but something slammed against the back of his head. Darkness surrounded him, nearly dragging him under as he hit the ground.

Groaning, he rolled onto his back, his vision clearing just as he saw a man straddling him, a dagger in hand. A vicious smile curled the man's thin lips as he drove the blade down.

No!

His life flashed before him, the sum of his failures an eruption of memories.

The blade never landed.

A force crashed into the man, sending him flying back. The blade clattered across the ground. Shouts rang out around him...and someone laughed. A woman.

Groaning, he rolled over, blinking as he looked up, trying to clear the fog from his mind.

Titania appeared, spear in hand, leaping from the stairs and landing with a roll. She surged to her feet and moved swiftly, effortlessly, carving her way through the men. Flynn couldn't pull his eyes away as several men rushed her. A chilling calmness settled about her as she surged forward, dodging the first few blows without attacking.

The men closed in around her. A ghost of a smile fluttered across her mouth.

She was toying with them.

Winking at him, she shot forward at the closest man. They swung their blades, trying to cut her down. None got close as she ducked and weaved around them, her feet barely touching the ground. Every blow she parried, barely breaking a sweat.

As their faces grew red, sweat glistening on their brows, the expression on her face shifted. She lunged forward at the closest man, ducking at the last moment as he swung, and drove her spear into his chest. As he fell, she yanked it out and spun around, rushing at the rest.

The revelation that she'd been holding back came too late for them.

One by one, she cut them down, parrying every blow and dodging with ease. The last man tried to turn and run, but she dropped low, slashing her blade across the back of his knees. He fell to the ground, screaming, blood pooling around his legs.

She bent down, ripping the sword from his hand and throwing it away. As he screamed, she rolled him over and poised her sword at his throat.

"That's enough, Titania," shouted Claudius, striding down the stairs.

Flynn struggled to his feet, wincing as pain lanced through his chest, and scrambled to where Mira lay still on the stairs. As he scooped her into his arms, he touched her neck, feeling the faint but steady pulse of her heart. He breathed a sigh of relief and looked up at Titania and Claudius. "Spirits above, who are they?"

Claudius stalked to the man writhing on the ground and drove his foot into the man's chest. Shadows rolled off him, the fury burning in his eyes. "You dare attack my home?"

"The false heir cannot take the city," said the man, his face twisted with pain. "We could not have you interfere!"

"Oh, you poor little fool, you have no idea who you've just threatened," chuckled Titania. "Do you want to finish him? Or can I have a go at making this human scream?"

Claudius shook his head. "He's *mine*."

Titania snorted, her gaze quickly flickering to Flynn. She strode over, cupping his jaw as she inspected him. "I'll summon Heather."

"He's hurt?" asked Claudius, glancing over and after a beat, looked at Mira, his gaze lingering. "And the girl?"

"They'll live, but we need Heather to patch them up, especially if we expect them to travel tomorrow," she replied. "I'd say this proves our point that they can't stay here, not while his power is bound."

Nodding, Claudius's gaze returned to the man, the shadows darkening around him. "You and I are going to have a little chat."

"I won't tell you anything!" the man hissed.

A cold and brittle laugh tumbled from Claudius, like glass shattering on stone. Flynn watched his eyes bleed to solid black, his mouth curving to reveal fangs. The inhuman smile sent chills down his spine.

"Oh, my dear man, I'm going to make you beg for death by the time I'm done with you," he crooned.

The man paled. "W-what *are* you?"

Claudius winked. "You entered a lair of demons and I am their prince."

Chapter 58

I have returned from my meeting with Idris and Vaska. They fear their egg won't hatch soon and that, if trouble happens, they will have to abandon their egg. I know what they will ask but now I am faced with a terrible choice... what fate do I doom each of my children to?

—Excerpt from Queen Evanya's diary

SYBILLA RACED ON horseback through the city, shadowed closely by her men. All around her, chaos raged in the streets. Slaves were escorted from their owner's homes if they wished to leave, their collars destroyed. Any owners that refused were dragged kicking and screaming from their homes while their wives cried and children wailed. People looked up as she galloped past, some cheering, others stonily silent in their judgment.

She kept her gaze focused ahead, and crouched low, flicking the reins of her horse to go faster. Hooves clattered noisily along the cobblestone, the haggard breaths of her horse mingling with her own. Blood roared in her ears, devouring the sounds of screams that had chased her.

Focus, you fool.

But it was hard, even as she barreled through the open gate into the Pleasure Quarter. The carnage that was strewn along the street was all that was left of Wren's battle with the Empress's men.

And Wren is nowhere to be found...

She stopped by a group of armed men, leaping down from her horse. Helena stood among the blood-splattered, leather-faced men, pristine in her blue gown. She turned as Sybilla strode over, dipping into a courtesy.

"You're here," said Helena. "These are your commanders, scraped together from the best in this city. They are war-hardened men and will fight to the death for you."

Sybilla cast her gaze over the men, dipping her head in greeting. Her gaze slid to the brothel with the second makeshift barricade out front, along with more of her men positioned behind it. "Do you have a plan?"

One of the men, tall and built like a bear, appeared beside her. "We have attempted to infiltrate from the roof, along with cutting through adjacent buildings. Problem is that the place is heavily warded. They're hunkering down."

"Why?" she wondered. "We've all but secured this city. There is no escape for them. Have they made any demands?"

He shook his head. "No, they have remained silent since they locked themselves in."

The mystery confounded her. She contemplated trying to summon a vision, but she'd called on her powers too much in the past few days. It had left her with a thumping headache and an almost endless nosebleed. The fact it wasn't pouring blood at that moment was a small reprieve.

Eyeing the brothel, she considered her options. She had no experience in war, let alone dealing with issues like this. Helena had been her advisor in a lot of the delicate matters, while her visions ensured she didn't err too badly. None of which aided her in the conundrum like the one before her.

She had no men with fae blood in her forces, so she was alone in her magic. From what she'd gleaned from Helena, the Prince of the City, Claudius *might* have someone, but he was holed up in his mansion, oddly silent. Shaking off the thought, she wondered if she could break the wards herself.

Magic twitched in her fingers, ribbons of light trickling out, dancing along her skin.

"Cover me," she instructed the men as she strode around the first barricade, then moved on to the next.

One of the men argued heatedly with Helena, whose cutting voice silenced them. Their voices faded away as she stood in front of the brothel. In the corner of her eye, she saw every man with a bow aim at the building, covering her.

She knew it wouldn't do shit if these idiots inside used magic but if she couldn't take them down, then what kind of ruler was she? They had to secure the city quickly.

Wishing that Wren hadn't been kidnapped after her fight, that she was with her at that moment, Sybilla steadied her nerves. She raised her hands, calling on the light within.

At first, nothing happened. The power remained quiet at the depths of her soul, indifferent to her call. She called again, snarling into the void. This would not be the day that she choked.

She had not spent years scheming and manipulating to balk now.

Like hells. Work dammit!

Light exploded from her palms. She slammed her fists together, then yanked them apart, summoning a wall of light. Sweat beaded her brow, the power fighting to retreat.

No, you don't.

She dragged more power to her palms, forcing it out to the wall, expanding it until it shot up, standing as tall as the brothel. Gritting her teeth, she threw the wall forward. Just before it collided with the brothel, it struck a shield. Light flared up, the shimmering ward defying her blast.

Before it faded away again, she slammed her hands together, summoning another wall of light. This time she kept it small and thrust it forward, driving into a crack that splintered in the middle of the ward.

The crack widened.

She snapped her fingers, summoning an orb of light to one hand, and hurled it right through the crack. It smashed into the front door, shattering it into wooden shards. Screams resounded from within.

Her hands dropped and the ward shattered in a burst of light. Heavy breaths fell from her lips as the world lurched, nearly sending her crumpling to the floor. It took what little strength she had left to stay standing and raise one fist.

"Surrender now!" she bellowed. "Your ward is broken! Surrender the slaves within and we will spare your lives!"

Silence roared down the street.

No one dared to speak.

Even the city itself seemed to hold its breath, the air still thrumming silently with the after-effect of her magic.

Then a man appeared in the doorway. "So, you're the one. Nice power you have there."

She squared her shoulders, straightening up, refusing to look weak as the man stepped to the edge of the porch. "Why did you even bother to try this? You were never going to succeed."

He smiled. "I didn't have to."

Ice slithered down her spine. "What do you mean?"

"You will not keep this city," he taunted. "And you will not free these slaves."

She didn't have a chance to respond as his body began to glow. Seconds later, his skin blistered.

Oh shit!

She threw up her hands, a wall of light erupting from her hands as the man exploded. The force slammed into her, sending her flying back, right into the barricade. Pain sliced through her like a sword and splintered out across her limbs. Stars flashed over her vision. She let out a cry as she dropped to the ground, her knees striking the stone first.

Shouts roared, all the men speaking at once. In a blink, someone was at her side, but their form doubled in her eyes. The world spun as she fought to stay conscious, her head thumping. Trying desperately to focus, she blinked, but nausea surged up her throat. Before she could resist, she threw up onto the ground.

Even in her unfocused gaze, she spied the blood splattered on the stones.

Someone called her name and she was lifted but by who, she didn't know or care.

Darkness was already dragging her under.

The smell of a burning fire tickled her nose as she rose from the haze holding her down. Her whole body throbbed with pain, making her wince as she forced her eyes open.

"Don't push yourself, Sybilla," warned Helena.

As she blinked, she realized she was in a plush bed, Helena standing at her side, arms folded across her chest. Sybilla ground her teeth as she forced herself to sit up. "What the hell happened?"

"The bastard killed himself. Tried to get you too, but your shield took most of the blast. Think that the barricade did more damage than the blast," said Helena tightly.

Sybilla studied the expression on the woman's face and frowned. "What's going on?"

Helena blinked, the look retreating behind a frown. "I had it under control but you need to know, he betrayed me. I never asked him to try to kill you."

A chill settled in Sybilla. "You orchestrated it?"

"Of course. Why else do you think I let you go there?" she replied, arching a brow.

"Did Torin know?"

She shook her head. "No, I told him to trust you, that you could handle yourself. That he just needed to have his men cover you."

"And he believed that?" said Sybilla, irritated that Helena had planned the event... and didn't even tell her. It left her feeling cold and uneasy inside.

Helena nodded. "Of course." She was silent for a moment before she spoke again. "Kara wrote to me. We'd been discussing how to ensure this little rebellion began right. She said that the best legends were born from small moments, as well as big ones."

Sybilla fell silent, staring at her hands. Her thoughts twisted into knots over Helena's actions when they circled back to the slaves. Looking up, she searched that unreadable face for answers when, finally, she mustered the question. "What of the slaves? Did you ensure—"

"He killed them," she cut in. "Not part of the plan, I assure you. His loyalty to the Empress ran deeper than I realized. A mistake I am not intending to repeat."

The loss hit Sybilla hard. Part of her mission in taking the city had been to free all the slaves within it. Logically, she knew she'd lose some, but those within the brothel she'd believed she was going to save. The failure filled her mouth with poison.

Sybilla stared at Helena. "You will not conspire to create such events without my knowledge. Not again."

Helena was silent for a moment. She nodded, her jaw twitching. "As you command."

Sybilla threw back the sheets, hauling herself out of the bed. Pain screamed through her limbs as she forced herself to stand. Helena moved to her, but she threw up a hand, brushing the woman aside. Frankly, she didn't trust herself not to strangle the woman for the brothel incident.

Those slaves were dead because of her.

"You should rest," said Helena.

Ignoring her, Sybilla shed the shift that they'd put on her and grabbed the fresh set of clothes on her dresser. She dressed quickly and headed to the door, her body fighting with every step. At the door, she paused, half turning her head. "Have my men secured the walls?"

"Yes. There are only a few pockets of resistance left within the city," said Helena. "Oh, one of my men received a missive for you just before we shut the gates. It's from Madam Kara."

Sybilla turned. "What does it say?"

"She's moving the caravan back north. That some things have happened which she couldn't write about and that has left them needing to head off. She said to send messages via Tarth, as they'd be camped close to the city."

Sybilla's heart grew cold, icy tendrils stealing through her body. Winters were brutal in the north and the caravan was already running low on supplies when she left them. What had happened that Kara didn't feel safe enough to include in a message? And why to Tarth? Once the city was secure, Sybilla would send out a messenger. Something was amiss, and she didn't like it one bit.

Nodding, she turned back to the door and pulled it open. "Good. Then sound the bells. It's time the real work begins. There's much to do before my aunt sends her army."

Chapter 59

*Litania has been in the underground library for weeks now.
She appears frantic and dark shadows linger under her eyes.
I ask her what she is seeking, if I may help, but she refuses.
Once, I heard her talking to someone but when I entered, she
was alone.*

—Excerpt from Princess Yelena's diary

WREN TUMBLED DOWN a well of darkness. Wind roared in her
ears. There was no end in sight, no sense of when the fall had begun
either. Down she spiraled into the void, her stomach hollowed out. Ash
choked her throat as if she'd been screaming. If she had, she couldn't
recall... She tried to call out and stretch out her hands so she might take

hold of something and stop.

No sound escaped her lips as she continued to fall, helpless. Closing her eyes, a sense of grief welled up from within. Talons tore their way up her throat, ripping her mouth open. Eyes snapped open.

Color exploded around her, blinding, smeared together with no chaos. Her gaze snapped down.

The ground rushed to meet her. A panicked scream surged out as she slammed into the earth. Pain exploded through her, devouring all other senses for an eternity. Crying out, she rolled over, her body fighting every action. When she finally forced herself onto her knees, she wrenched her gaze up and froze.

A sprawling, blackened field stretched out before her.... and an army was racing towards her. Thousands of men, clad in black, their collection roar thundering through the air. She scrambled to her feet, terror seizing her.

The ranks split in two and a wave of darkness surged through, revealing hundreds of wolves. Their glowing red eyes locked on her.

She spun and burst into a sprint, pounding her feet.

The cacophony of snarls and war cries chased her, growing closer. A long shadow swept over her, ice flooding down her spine. She stopped, turning—

The army collided with her.

Her hands flew up, bracing for impact.

It never came. Her heart slammed against her ribs, a bird frantic to escape. Blood howled in her ears, fading off as her hands fell. She froze.

The blackened earth was littered with bodies, torn apart, saturated in blood. The very army that had been rushing at her lay dead at her feet. Beasts encircled her, cut into ribbons. Their red eyes, glassy with death, stared up at the blood-red sky.

Wren turned slowly, absorbing the surrounding carnage when she discovered she wasn't alone.

Only a few feet away stood the Spirit of the Mountain, clad in bloodied leathers, clutching two short swords. Blood painted her face, broken only by the slight part of her lips as she breathed hard and by her dark eyes, burning with intensity.

It was a far cry from the maidenly guardian depicted in the stories

Wren knew so well.

"Spirit—"

In a flash, a hand snapped around Wren's throat, yanking her in. Inches separated them, that burning look tinged with disdain. "That is *not* my name. It is Nimue."

"What?" Wren wheezed, grasping at Nimue's hand, clawing.

Darkness nudged her vision, talons threatening to claw her into oblivion. Every breath burned like liquid fire. She tried to summon the question again, the name even, but the words were choked out. Oblivion whispered to her in a silken voice.

Panic burst up through her limbs, a rush of icy water through her veins. One final fight, a strangled sound stumbling from her lips.

Nimue sneered and spun, throwing Wren as if she were nothing but a broken doll.

Wind hissed as she flew, then hit the ground, colliding into a pile of bodies. Pain erupted along her side, a cry finally broke through. She cursed, scrambling to her feet, swaying as she snapped her fingers. Fire burst from her hands and wrapped itself around her arms.

"What the hell—"

Nimue sprinted at her, shadows wreathed in her hands, surging out and sharpening to a spear. She stopped, twisting as she flicked her wrist, hurling the spear straight at Wren.

The hiss and glint of silver flashed past as she narrowly dodged. Nimue bore down with dizzying speed.

Wren's hands snapped up and the flames sputtered out.

Shit!

She dropped low as Nimue swung both blades in, cutting only hair as she dodged. Strands fell around her face as she shot forward, driving her shoulder into Nimue's stomach. Together they tumbled to the ground, a tangle of savage blows. Wrestling over the blood-soaked earth, Wren tried to fight her way free, to get some distance.

Lorca's words stole through her mind. *Look for an opening!*

But in a flash, Nimue loomed over her, scowling. "How can you expect to save your people if you can't even beat me?"

"What?"

"You can't even wield that fire magic properly or turn into a dragon at will. You are *weak*." Venom dripped from every word.

Anger burned her cheeks. Heat prickled on her fingers as she called on her fire again, howling into the void, willing it out. She wasn't weak. She had power roaring in her veins. It flowed through her.

Wren threw her head back as fire exploded from her, slamming into Nimue. The spirit went flying.

Breathing hard, she forced herself up, fighting back the waves of pain that threatened to tear her down. She lifted trembling hands, fire blazing on her fingers.

Nimue twisted mid-air, landing as she sank her hand into the ground, sliding back several feet. She rose and extended her arms, shadows wreathing her hands once more. She stalked forward, the bodies of the fallen dissolving to ash around her. "Not bad, but you cannot beat me. Do you know why?"

Every breath burned, but Wren forced the question to her lips. "Why?"

"Because you won't do what it takes to save your people. You say that you will do anything, but those are empty words," sneered Nimue. "You have power, but you are too damn scared to embrace it. Hell, Lorca had to *die* for one moment's surrender, and yet now you still want to hold back."

"You're wrong!"

Nimue stopped, one brow lifted. "Oh? Prove it!" She burst forward, hurling the shadow daggers.

Wren ducked and flung herself forward, hurling the flames. Surprise flashed in Nimue's eyes as Wren sprinted forward. No hesitation filled her as she bore down on the spirit, throwing everything she had. Nimue smirked, slamming her palms together, then yanked them apart. Darkness shot out a wall of black right as the flames slammed into it and were devoured.

The shield shattered. Nimue burst through, a blur of movement. Wren threw her hands up, barely deflecting the blow. The force sent her staggering back, nearly tripping. Yanking up her hands, she pressed forward, hunting for an opening. Each one closed quickly, Nimue was too quick, too strong.

She had to think. Victory was in Nimue's words. She was holding back. She hadn't fully embraced her magic, because a part of her was still terrified of that monster. The one that rose up and took control so easily, the one that hungered for blood and death. She had to accept both parts of her, the darkness and the fire.

For her people, she had to let go of her fear of herself and embrace the power.

Awareness had bloomed within her. From the moment her magic had awoken, she had been fighting to maintain who she was, *what* she was. Clinging to the past, to the girl who lived in Fenware, to a life that had turned to ash and snow the moment she left the village.

She hadn't just let go because Lorca died. She had let go because he was all she had left of the mountains, of her old life. Exhaling, she let go, surrendering to it all.

I am a monster and that is okay.

She knew what she had to do.

Wren's gaze sharpened as Nimue shifted, a dagger glinting in her hand.

Her opening.

And she stilled as Nimue drove the dagger into Wren's all-to-mortal heart. The pain burned in her chest, her strength slipping away. She sagged forward, gasping. Her hand dropped to Nimue's waist, grabbing the blade there—and with a bloodied grin, she drove it into Nimue's side.

Her heart slowed as she slumped into Nimue's chest, dark laughter bubbling out, like glass shattering on stone. "I will die for my people."

And the darkness rushed to greet her.

Death was cold oblivion, a void of darkness in which Wren stood alone. The pain of the wound was no more, her heart steady and even, as if it had never felt the killing blow. She reached up, probing the un-blemished skin where the dagger had sunk in deeply. Frowning, her hand fell away.

"You said you would die for your people," murmured Nimue behind her.

Wren turned.

Two doors stood behind Nimue, one blood-red and charred at the edges, the other black, veined with silver. The Spirit was clad in a flowing white gown, the same from the paintings at the Dragonir's palace, the golden thorny crown atop her head. Only that same dark gaze remained of the bloodied warrior from before.

"What is this?" asked Wren, eyeing the doors.

"Two possibilities," said Nimue. "Through one, you will return to the real world but the spell binding you will be restored, rendering you powerless. As such, you will live but your people will not."

"That is the opposite of what I want," argued Wren. "Why would I choose that? What is behind the other door?"

Nimue smiled sadly. "Your death. You see, I am not a spirit, Wren. I never was. Had I been so, Litania's blow would've killed me and my story would have ended. But I am not so easily killed. I am a demon and to survive, I possessed a dragon's egg. There, I rested for three hundred years until I hatched, where I quickly found my memories and powers bound before I could resist."

The terrible truth of Wren's powers roared through her. There was no lie in Nimue's words. Wren's gaze dropped to her hands. How she sensed demons, the way she wielded the shadow magic easier than the fire, why it called to her so temptingly when she lay awake in the night... and why it scared her so much. Because it was the truth buried in the darkest pit of her soul, the one that her unconscious mind had fought so viciously to bury.

The body she'd held for eighteen years was taken in a moment of desperation. Memories stirred, trickling through. She lifted her gaze. "Did you kill the hatchling?"

Nimue didn't answer immediately. A shadow of regret lingered in her eyes. She shook her head. "The young dragon was dying. I simply showed it mercy and ended its suffering. The body could house only one soul– our soul."

Spirits above...

Wren swallowed the lump in her throat. "So, if I choose the black door, I die and you take over. What will that mean for my people?"

Nimue didn't even hesitate in her reply. "If you choose that door, I will honor your mission. I will bring *our* people home." She stepped aside, gesturing to the doors. "It's time to choose, Wren. Life or death."

But Wren knew even as she looked back to the doors what one she would choose. She drew in a deep breath and strode forward.

The door cracked open.

Wren stepped through, and she was no more. A final proclamation to her soul. A promise to herself howled into it the void that welcomed her.

Save them.

Chapter 60

We had believed for so long that we could bear no children, for demons are forged from The Pit, crawling out of it every five years in our realm. All our heartbreaking experiences cemented that fact—yet, now for the first time, two half-bloods walk the land. Atlas, what have you done? Why would you give them your power?

—Source redacted

THEY GALLOPED AT full speed through the chaotic city streets. Gathering crowds were marshaled away by soldiers into narrow streets or back to their homes. Claudius led a brutal pace ahead of Flynn, clearing a path through the chaos. Smoke choked the air. Dozens of plumes billowed high into the sky, gathering in a darkening cloud over the city, blocking out what weak sunlight squeezed through. The bitter taste dried his lips and hurt every breath he hauled in.

Claudius charged ahead of him, nearly barreling down several unsuspecting folks who were fleeing the distant fires or trying to evade the marching soldiers. The latter jumped out of the way but didn't pursue, or even try. Like they knew who he was.

Up ahead the street narrowed, coming to an interior gate. Men guarded the entrance, swords drawn, faces flushed from the heat that beat down without mercy. Flynn slowed his horse, Mira shifting on the saddle behind him, peering over his shoulder.

Claudius jerked to a stop, digging out a golden amulet from his necklace. As Flynn drew closer, he spied the same insignia that was emblazoned on the fresh uniforms of the soldiers. His own men, perhaps? Or was that the insignia of whoever was running this battle?

A soldier nodded and turned around, shouting up at the men on top of the gate. "Let them through!"

The soldiers stepped aside as the gate opened. Claudius dug his heels in, shooting forward. Then he flicked his heel and the horse shot forward. Titania fell in beside him, her gray mare keeping pace easily. Flynn flicked his heel and his horse shot forward, racing after them. Mira let out a squawk of alarm and squeezed his waist, burying her face into his back.

Flynn focused on the road ahead, keeping low, holding firm on the reins. Sweat beaded along his brow, the strain of the ride burning in his muscles. He was unaccustomed to such riding, let alone having to focus so he could navigate the twisting streets.

The looming warehouses that pinched in around them, with their tiled roofs and windowless walls, made it impossible to know where they were going. All the buildings looked so similar that Flynn was envious of Claudius knowing where he was going.

They wove through a series of sloping streets before they rounded a corner, and a morning sea breeze surged toward them from the sprawling blue ocean. The sky had cleared over the ocean, exposing a glittering expanse that stole the breath from his lungs. He'd seen glimpses of it from some of the higher rooms at Claudius's home, but it had never been so close. It was daunting, as though it might reach out, swallow him whole. How anyone found it *inviting* he didn't know. Perhaps madness helped.

His fingers itched to plunge into that icy water, to feel the saltwater on his skin. He couldn't swim worth a damn, but that didn't make it any less enticing for him.

"Keep up!" snarled Claudius.

Blinking sharply, Flynn saw that he'd fallen behind. Wheeling his horse sharply, he trotted after them, following Claudius along the foreshore. More warehouses cast imposing shadows on his left, while the docks stretched out across the water like broken fingers. It was eerily empty, save for one vessel which remained docked.

Claudius turned onto the wharf with the ship, slowing to a walk, giving Flynn time to catch up. Titania trotted ahead, dismounting first. By the time Flynn reached the ship she was already striding onboard, her cloak billowing behind her.

He stopped, letting Mira dismount first before he slid off, looking with unease at the vessel that would ferry them. Once they were out on that ocean, he'd be leaving the only land he'd ever known and be even further from whatever was left of his village. Only the knowledge he'd return to free his people moved him from the horse to the ship.

At the gangway, Claudius held out a hand, stopping him. Shadows danced in those unreadable eyes. "Inside the pack, you'll find you all that you'll need to reach your destination. Once you reach the town of Faranelle, you will be greeted by an escort who will take you to the temple of Hava."

Flynn nodded. "I read over everything twice. We'll send word once we're settled."

Claudius shook his head. "No, wait for us to send word first. This city is going to be a very dangerous place, so we will find a way to communicate safely."

"How?"

A shadow of a smile tugged at Claudius's mouth. "We demons have our ways."

We...

Flynn's mouth opened. But Titania was striding back down the gangway, looking at Claudius who turned to her.

"Time to go," she said.

As she turned to Flynn, she stepped forward, hugging him. It took him a moment to respond, and then he hugged her back. Smiling, she stepped aside. "Goes without saying, kid, you're family now and you're going to learn what that means. If anything happens, Mathias will get word to us and I'll be there."

He looked to Claudius, who only offered a curt nod, and gestured for them to get on the boat.

Drawing in a deep breath, he held out his arm to Mira, and, as she took it, they stepped onto the ship.

One of the crew ushered them up to the rear and told them to stand by the stony-faced captain. Flynn kept close to Mira as they watched the crew hurry about, hauling the gangway back onboard and readying the lines. He spied Titania and Claudius mount up and head off down the wharf without a backward glance.

As shouts carried over the deck and men scrambled up the masts, Mira let out a gasp, pointing back to the city. "Look, Flynn! Up there!"

He followed her hand, his gaze rising beyond the docks to one of the tallest spires at the heart of the city. The air fled his chest as he stared, wide-eyed, as a golden dragon soared over the city.

"A dragon... Wren was right," he whispered. "They're real."

Mira shivered. "I wish she could've seen it."

A pang of sadness struck Flynn as he watched the dragon turn back toward the tower, aiming for the top. He'd given anything for Wren to be with him at that moment. "When we see her again, we'll tell her about it."

As they sailed from the city, thoughts of the dragon fell away. Flynn turned his gaze to the horizon far across the ocean. The salt wind blew fiercely, filling the unfurled sails, ferrying them further and further from everything and everyone they'd ever known.

Chapter 61

My daughter sleeps soundly in my husband's arms, giving me time to write in this diary. I am hopeful for the first time since my coronation; the prospect of finally abolishing slavery looms ever closer; my sister is no longer cold to me. As the sun rises across the sea, it looks to be a beautiful day.

—Excerpt from Empress Kathrine's diary

HER NAME WAS Nimue.

As her eyes fluttered open, taking the wooden paneling of the ceiling, she knew she wasn't trapped in another memory. Wren and Nimue had become one, a divided soul no more. Relief hummed through her. She slowly took stock of her situation. Shackles pinned her down to a long wooden table, dulling her magic. But it was there at least and she was confident that if she pushed, she could break free.

Not yet, though. First, she wanted to use this to her advantage.

They believed she was their prisoner but they were wrong.

The fools thought they'd done enough to silence her magic, she thought, bemused, as she eyed the small room around her.

On one wall hung an array of gleaming torture tools. Nimue remembered she had a wall like that once, though her tools were much more impressive.

The rest of the room remained bare. Even the plain wooden door offered very little in interest. She was staring at it when it opened. Lorca's murderer swept in, clad in a fresh black tunic, ignoring her gaze for the moment.

If he noticed the change in her, he gave no sign. Irritation flared through her, indignation burning in her mouth like poison. Once, men like him groveled on their knees or begged for their lives. Men that kneeled before her, teary-eyed, pathetic.

Demons below! How long has it been since someone pleaded to her for their life?

He moved to the window first, peering outside. From the angle, she couldn't see his face, but he stiffened slightly. His hands remained flat against his thighs, almost like he was forcing himself to remain calm.

With his back to her, she gently tugged on the shackles. They yielded faintly, so she dropped her wrists back down. Her gaze shifted to the ceiling as she sighed loudly, drawing his focus back to her.

"Something the matter?"

"Just considering how I'm going to kill you," she mused. "You killed Lorca, so I am in a mind to make you die screaming. What do you think?"

When he didn't answer at first, she glanced at him. Confusion flashed in his eyes, dimming as he smiled and laughed softly. He closed the distance to the table and leaned over to caress her face. His touch sent ice lancing through her skin. No one touched her without her consent and got away with it. He would be no exception.

I'm going to rip that hand off first, she decided.

"Don't worry. This metal is repressing your dragon and demon sides, so you're not escaping." He tapped her chains with a wink.

She snorted. "I mean, you're mostly correct but, back to my question. What do you think of how I'm going to kill you? I used to be told I shouldn't make a game of killing people. It's unseemly."

"What does a child know of killing?" he inquired indulgently. "What makes you an expert?"

The fool has no idea what he has within reach.

"Oh, I'm not an expert—I haven't perfected all the methods of death," she said. "Out of curiosity, how would you like to die? The glory of battle? In the arms of a lover or perhaps *by* your lover?"

"You're talking confidently for one about to be tortured," he remarked coolly. "What did you think you were here for when you woke up?"

She smiled sweetly up at him. "I figured the torture bit out when I saw your pathetic arrangement of toys."

He moved to his wall of instruments, running his hand along the curved edge of a gleaming blade, his back to hers. "You're going to be the one begging for death when we're done, little girl."

Laughter bubbled up inside her as she stood, shattering the chains pinning her to the table. Startled, he spun around, eyes widening. He remained still as she dusted the shards of metal off her skin, then swung her legs over the side.

"I'm not a child," she replied, sobering.

Blinking, his shock gone, he took a step forward. He flicked his wrist, hurling a summoned dagger straight at her.

Her hand snapped up, catching the blade between two fingers, inches from her face, and spun, flinging it back into his chest. The force sent him slamming back into the wall, tools clattering loudly to the ground.

She hurried forward and grabbed his hand, yanking it up in her iron grip. Before he could fight back, she surged fire through her hands and into his. He threw his head back, screaming, trying to break free. But she was the stronger one now. She stepped back, releasing his hand, crumbling to ash, exposing a cauterized forearm.

Cursing, he clutched at his arm, staring up at her with burning eyes. To his credit, he didn't move or cry. He knew the woman before him wasn't the same one he'd fought. The power had shifted. Right now, he was probably hunting for a weakness.

"As I said, *not* a child. I should thank you, though. The fight? Killing

399

Lorca? I'd lost so much by that point. Well, that destroyed me. You broke the shell that had been hiding my true self for eighteen years. So, I'm free now, with all my memories and power."

"What the hell are you? Those chains should've repressed—"

"Yes, yes, you said," she cut in, "but that kind of metal works on *beast-level* demons, the lowest of my kind. Shall I tell you what it doesn't work on?"

His eyes narrowed in scorn, his jaw twitching. "What?"

"*A demon queen.*"

His face drained of color. "That can't be..."

It was...because only a demon ruler had the ability to possess a body. And when her true form had a sword driven through it, she'd taken the first shell available. A dragon's egg.

She opened her mouth to reply when a wave of sadness struck her mind, a voice whispering at the edge of her consciousness. One that stopped her dead.

Wren, I'm sorry.

Lorca.

Fire exploded to life in her hands as rage took over. She focused her gaze on the man. "Lorca isn't dead. He survived." She stepped forward, fury burning through her like an inferno. "How is he alive?"

He grinned smugly. "Doesn't matter. He changed back, barely alive, so they dragged him here and tortured him. Even then, he never talked. So now I expect they'll be executing him."

I don't know if you can hear me, but I hope you can. I just want you to know I love you. His voice was soft, scarcely a whisper in her mind.

The peace in his voice, the damn acceptance, tore her heart from her chest.

She glared down at the man, letting the darkness flow from her body. It wrapped around her, turning her fire black, engulfing her. She ignored the sharp burning in the middle of her chest and held her hand over him.

Defiantly, he lifted his chin, as if he was refusing to be afraid of dying. Frankly, she didn't care. His bravado meant nothing, just like his life.

"You shouldn't have made an enemy of me," she said coldly. "I've burned empires to the ground. Do not think I am a child. I'm one of the four rulers of the demon race. I am Nimue, bringer of death and pain. And you are nothing."

The black fire leaped from her, rushing over him. He threw his head back as he screamed. The sound silenced as his body turned to ash and crumbled before her eyes.

She spun away and raised her hand to the wall by the window. Fire erupted from her hands, destroying the wall, stone flying outwards. Plumes of dust sprung up before her.

The opening revealed the slave markets below, the docks, and the glittering ocean beyond it. The wind howled against her, and she was Wren again, if only for a moment. She stepped away from the edge, closing her eyes, trying to connect her thoughts to Lorca. With a long exhale, she opened her eyes.

You swore an oath to me, Lorca. Do you plan on breaking it now by giving up?

Surprise shot through their bond. *Wren? You're okay? Where are you?*

She sprinted forward, hurling herself off the edge and diving to the city below. She surrendered to the dragon form. Light exploded around her as her body grew larger, bones shattering, reforming in a single moment.

I'm coming for you.

The second her wings snapped open the change was complete.

The city blurred beneath her as she shot forward above the rooftops, letting out a thundering roar that ripped through the air. She flapped her wings hard, angling upwards, and she swung back around to the tower she'd jumped from.

As she hurled herself toward the tower, she shifted her wings and shot up along the long face of it. She burst over the top of it and grabbed hold, sinking her talons into stone. With a roar, her wings flared wide.

Lowering her head back down, she eyed the guards standing around the execution block; the executioner with his blade held in the air... and Lorca, chained and kneeling with his head over the wooden block.

He stared at her.

Wren.

Her name was like a prayer in her mind, his voice thick with emotion.

She lifted her gaze from his, eyeing the executioner. Flames trickled through her teeth as she snarled at the man. Slowly, he stepped back, lowering the blade to the ground.

One guard shouted without warning, the four of them taking a step toward her.

With a roar, she snapped open her mouth and hurled all the fire she had forward—a wave of fire exploded across the roof. Men became ash, their swords pools of metal, and as the fire died away, only Lorca remained.

He rose unsteadily, dusting the ash off himself as he kept his gaze on her, a look of awe on his face

"You're here," he whispered hoarsely.

With a nod, she closed her eyes and called on her human form. A bright light devoured her for a moment, warmth flooding through her body as she felt herself become smaller. The light dimmed, and her eyes opened. Before she knew it, her feet were carrying her forward. She burst into a run, as did Lorca, meeting her halfway.

His hands took hold of her face, crushing his mouth to hers. The heat of the kiss consumed her as she grabbed him, yanking him close, meeting his kiss with her own fire.

His hands slid down to her waist, leaving no space between them. He held her like he was afraid she'd vanish, kissing her like she was the air he needed to live. When she slowly drew back, her heart slamming against her ribs, blood roaring in her ears, she was smiling.

"So *that's* what I was missing," she mused.

One hand rose, cupping her cheek, one thumb stroking her skin. "I—"

"I love you too," she broke in, leaning into his hand, closing her eyes. "You're not allowed to die on me again. Do you hear me?"

"I promise, Wren."

Her eyes flickered open, meeting his. "That's not my real name. Nor is the Spirit of the Mountain my name."

Confusion clouded his face as he frowned at her. "How can that be? The Spirit died..."

"It's a long story, but one we've lived together. You kept your promise to your mother and to me. You stayed by my side," she explained softly.

His lips parted, shock clear on his face as he reached up, tentatively touching her cheek. "You continue to surprise me."

"Nimue. My real name is Nimue."

Nimue, Queen of Azradan, the fourth kingdom of the demon realm, she finished to herself. *The Queen of Death.*

But the story of how a demon queen came to the mortal realm, who masqueraded as a spirit and died, only to steal a dragon's body? That was a story she was almost ready to share.

"Nimue," he corrected. "It's a—"

The tolling of bells cut him off, dozens of them ringing out across the city. Nimue stepped out of Lorca's embrace and strode to the edge of the roof, shadowed closely by her prince.

Plumes of smoke rose from dozens of spots across the sprawling City of Slaves. The bells continued to toll ominously. Nimue cursed her idiocy, realizing at that moment she'd been played. The alternate mission to save her sister, Nimue's capture... it all felt sickeningly orchestrated.

Someone had played her for a damned fool.

"What's going on?" asked Lorca.

Her hands curled into fists, rage kindling to life inside of her. "War."

Chapter 62

There is a darkness to the Spirit of the Mountain. All the times I've seen her seal those demon cracks, I cannot help but wonder who or what she is protecting us from.

—Excerpt from Princess Yelena's diary

DEEP IN THE catacombs of the palace, Empress Alexandria walked alone. The steady click of her heels echoed in her wake, echoing. It was madness that drove her to descend to hell at the summon of a monster. It had to be. Unless, in the long years since her coronation, she had finally become what they whispered her to be.

From the darkness, the souls of her trapped ancestors watched on through the vacant eyes of their stone statues. Forever trapped to guard over bodies long reduced to dust and bone. Like her, they were prisoners, bound to this hellish place.

She passed beyond the last tomb and stopped before the black stone doors barring her way. A lantern hung on either side, the flames flickering a chilling blue. It cast swaths of sapphire across the four ghoulish figures engraved on the doors, two on each. Three men and a woman, each wearing flowing robes and a crown.

Their dark eyes stared back at Alexandria, daring her to enter.

Her heart thudded hard in her chest. She swallowed back the unease that chilled her spine and raised her hand to the door.

The doors swung inwards.

An icy wind blew against her, whipping up her hair for a moment. As the gust ceased, the chill remained, and from the darkness before her, a presence reached out.

One that had been her constant companion since the moment she was born.

You've finally returned to me, my little bird, whispered the soft, silken voice of a woman, dripping with wicked delight.

Alexandria stepped into the darkness. The doors slammed shut with a deafening bang, snuffing out the light. She drew in several deep, steadying breaths, barring the panic that threatened. It was dangerous, showing fear to the creature that lurked in the shadows.

More than one of her ancestors had fallen short and paid the ultimate price for their weakness.

I trust you have an update for me. The voice echoed softly through the threat like a lover's caress.

"The temple is nearing completion and should be finished by the end of summer," announced Alexandria. "It's right on schedule, as I promised."

But? Did you come to tell me all is going according to my plan? The teasing lilt chafed on her nerves, but she refused to show it.

Swallowing her irritation, she summoned the question that had kept her awake for weeks now. One that none of her useless spies seemed able to answer.

"Is my niece alive?"

There, I said it.

For an agonizing moment, the creature remained quiet.

Fire erupted, flashing hot and blinding. Alexandria threw up her hand, shielding her eyes. A moment later, the inferno dimmed to a small floating flame.

A ghostly woman stood beneath it, clad in a flowing silver gown that faded away, revealing the absence of feet. She looked *almost* human, were it not for her black eyes absent of any white... and the collar around her neck.

It was the only thing solid about the creature, connected to a chain that trailed off into the dark.

Perhaps. The woman's lips didn't move her but her chilling voice slithered through the air. *That is not your only concern, however.*

"What now?" Alexandria snapped waspishly, her temper slipping.

The edges of the woman's mouth lifted, revealing a row of pointed teeth, gleaming white. *It seems that your ancestor, Litania, failed the task I set for her.*

The blood drained from Alexandria's face. "What?"

The Spirit of the Mountain lives.

The Girl of Ash And Snow

Special thanks

THIS HAS BEEN a journey years in the making and by no means a solo mission. From its beginning on Penana, its brief time on both Wattpad and Tapas, to this form, it has gone through so many changes.

I've been blessed with a team behind me and it's because of them that we've reached this point. There are so many people who had a hand in bringing this to life, so I will do my best to cover them all.

Thank you to my Discord community. Ancient Doom, Heather, Sib, Wolfie, Housie, Marjorie, Lena, Aowna, Occa, Tanya, and to everyone else that I have missed. You guys have been a constant source of support, sharp eyes, information, and friendship. Some of you fulfilled several roles in this journey and have remained steadfast to the end.

Thank you to Kerry Murphy, my editor. You saw potential in the rough script I gave you and transformed it into something truly wonderful. Your kind words, faithful support, in-depth assistance, made this whole process so much easier.

A special mention to Aowna. You created such a plethora of amazing artwork for the merchandise of this story. Time and time again, you nailed the brief and delivered perfection. I look forward to working with you again in the future.

For the book cover, a special thanks must go to Miblart. A company of professionalism and creativity. They've also created book 2's cover and I look forward to working with them on future projects.

I would also like to express my deepest thanks to Breakout Designs for formatting this story. You helped turn this from a word document to a novel.

To all my beta readers, you have been a wonderful blessing, and I hope to see you on the remaining books for this series.

I cannot forget my friends and family, whose unending support and love have pushed me to pursue my dreams. Your kind words and faith helped me through all the ups and downs. To my girlfriend, whose creative hand produced the map in this story, and for all your steadfast love and support.

Finally, thank you to my readers, words cannot sufficiently express my appreciation and adoration to you all.

C.M Quinn

The story continues in 'The Queen of Blood and Fury' 2022

C.M. Quinn

About the author

C.M. QUINN IS an author from Sydney, Australia, who has been writing since her early teens. She began writing on numerous online platforms, including Wattpad, before making the transition into self-publishing in 2021. With a deep love of fantasy and paranormal stories, she's often lost in the worlds she creates or buried under a pile of notes, though never too far from a pot of tea.

The Girl of Ash and Snow is her debut novel.

C.M. Quinn

www.ingramcontent.com/pod-product-compliance
Lightning Source LLC
Chambersburg PA
CBHW070158120726
47909CB00001B/160